# FINDING KAIT

## Suzanne Cass

S C

STORM CLOUD
PRESS

Finding Kait

Storm Cloud Press, Perth Australia

Copyright © 2024 by Suzanne Cass

Edits by Evermore Editing

Cover by Vikncharlie

All rights reserved.

*To Thelma and Louise.*
*And all the other beautiful, strong, like-minded*
*women out there.*

# CHAPTER ONE

The wreath of flowers was as light as a feather in her hands. Insubstantial. Kait De Luca laid it gently on the water, watching as it floated, rising up and down beside her knees on the swell. Dusky-coral bottlebrush and hot-pink everlastings wrapped in a gauzy green ribbon—Susan's favorite colors—picked fresh from her garden this morning. Susan had loved her garden. What would happen to it now? Would Mike keep tending it? Her husband had been good at keeping the garden looking nice so Susan could sit in it until the very end.

A small wave lapped at her knees, and Kait absently picked the hem of her skirt out of the water, her eyes never leaving the wreath that was now gaily heading out to sea. Away on a new adventure. It joined a raft of other wreaths and flowers bobbing on the waves.

A final farewell.

The sun rested gently on the horizon, turning the sky to crimson and orange. Such a gorgeous evening. Kait turned her head with a smile to ask Susan if she'd ever seen anything more beautiful than a West Australian sunset.

And then she remembered.

Susan would never sigh at another sunset again. Her best

friend in the entire world was gone.

"Kait."

She ignored Dario, continuing to stare out to sea, her back facing him and the beach.

"Kait, are you coming?" The irritation was palpable in his voice, and her neck itched with the need to do as he requested. She almost turned and walked out of the water, but she fought the urge, needing a few more minutes of peace. Couldn't he leave her alone for one second?

Others around her were turning to wade back to shore. The ceremony was over; it was time to leave. Time to go back to their normal lives, to move on as if nothing had happened. But she wasn't ready. Couldn't move on.

The water was cool on her calves, the sand gritty beneath her toes, a balmy summer breeze blowing her hair back from her face. A perfect night. They couldn't have picked a better day. Susan would've loved it. That's what people would say now as they gathered on the beach.

They could all go to hell.

Because they were wrong on one very important point. Susan would've hated the fact that she was dead.

\* \* \*

Morning sunlight streamed in through the large, floor-to-ceiling windows as Dario flung the curtains open. Kait buried her head beneath the blankets, not wanting to face the day. Not wanting to face her husband. He'd been surprisingly conciliatory last night after the funeral. Even leading her by the hand up the enormous marble staircase to their bedroom, helping her to undress, and tucking her beneath the sheets. Strange. But she hadn't had the energy to overthink his actions.

Kait had expected the pain to hit her at the funeral. Wracking grief so raw that it ripped her heart right out of her chest. That's what everyone warned her. She'd finally be able to grieve; there would be closure. But even this morning, she felt…anesthetized. There was nothing. Merely a deep, all-encompassing numbness that turned everything she saw, or smelled, or felt, to a soft, dull gray.

Including her husband. He was a fuzzy silhouette against the harshness of the sun flooding in around him.

It was hot under the blankets, the heat of a Perth summer day already building, warm air wheezing in through the windows Dario had now opened. The white Italian tiles in the bathroom would be cool. If only she could rest her head on those for a few moments, perhaps she'd be able to think properly.

"Come on, my love, time to get up. It's after nine. Don't you think you've sulked enough now?"

Sulked? He thought she was sulking? In his twisted mind, perhaps she was.

She felt Dario's hand on her thigh, squeezing through the bedclothes. She froze. Stopped breathing. And willed him away. *Please leave me alone. Just this once.*

"I brought you coffee. Made it exactly the way you like it." His voice took on a slightly wheedling tone.

Dario had no idea how she liked her coffee. He thought she enjoyed a cappuccino first thing in the morning because that was what he drank. She much preferred her coffee dark and bitter, a single shot of caffeine—or a double if she could get it.

His fingers walked up her body, snaking their way toward her neck where he found the edge of the blankets and tugged them down to reveal her bra and then panties.

She tried to assemble her features into a smile because that was what he was expecting. But she couldn't seem to work her facial muscles; they were frozen into a rictus of weary resignation.

Here it came again. The same thing almost every other morning. At least she'd been allowed a few hours' peace to sleep in. Normally, he was at her before she was even fully awake. Their *morning devotional*, he'd dubbed it.

Calling on depths of emotion she wasn't even sure she possessed, she finally marshaled her face into something appropriating a smile. But it was too late, he wasn't fooled.

"Don't give me that look." His dark eyes flashed, a spark of anger in their depths.

Uh, oh. She steeled herself, forcing her body not to shrink away from his. It was always worse if she showed fear, or God forbid, revulsion.

The blankets were completely stripped away, leaving her lying on the silk sheets in her plain cotton underwear. Normally she wore those slinky negligees he loved so much, but last night…she'd been too soul weary to care.

"Hmm, that's a change." He frowned, his large, caterpillar eyebrows almost meeting in the middle. "But I'm okay with it. Change is as good as a holiday, hey?"

As he stared down at her, he unbuttoned his trousers. He was already dressed for work. Which might be a blessing in disguise, because it meant he would be quick. He probably wouldn't even remove his shirt, saving her from the sight of his hirsute chest. "All Italian men had hairy chests," he'd tell her proudly, slapping his pecs with gusto. Dario kept himself in fairly good shape; his personal trainer came to the house at least three mornings a week. Pity this morning wasn't one of those days; maybe she would've been spared otherwise.

Dario grabbed her by the feet and pulled her toward the edge of the bed. She didn't resist. His pants now down around his ankles, he yanked at her panties, and they ripped free. Dragging her buttocks closer to the edge, he positioned himself between her legs.

Their bed was extra large and extra tall, a bespoke bed frame made in Italy and shipped over at great expense. But then again, nothing was expensive when your husband was a multi-millionaire.

Then he was inside her, pumping away with vigor.

He never looked at her face when he was fucking her. Even if he kissed her, he did so with his eyes shut.

Normally she made small, encouraging noises, pretended to enjoy it. If she did a good job, made sure he was satisfied, he might not even bother her for the rest of the day.

Today, she couldn't raise the required energy. Instead, she lay there and watched a tiny spider crawl across the ceiling, wondering at its temerity as it staked a claim to one of the corners and began building a home. Maria would have it down with her busy duster before the day was out. Which was a shame really, because Kait liked the idea of an insect breaking though the barriers of this pristine house. This spider was a rebel. With a will to live. She just wished she had half its pluck. But she was... Who knew what she was? A coward. Weak. Dario's chattel. Contemptible.

Sooner than expected, Dario was done. He withdrew and disappeared into the bathroom to clean himself.

She slithered off the bed and landed on the floor, her legs folding beneath her. Lucky the bed provided support for her back, or she may well have fallen over completely.

Dario returned, smirking through his beard. He thought it made him look rakish, like a pirate of old. She thought it made him look even more like a bad portrayal of Lucifer.

"You really need to get yourself to a hairdresser, my love. I can see your gray hairs showing. Not a good look." He tutted to himself.

*Why shouldn't I let my gray hairs sprout?*, she wondered, surprisingly defiant? At forty-four years of age, perhaps it was time to show she no longer cared what other people thought. She was a natural redhead, something her hairdresser was ecstatic about. "You're so lucky," Fernando would coo at her. "So beautiful and rich, like a good wine. If it weren't for the gray, I'd hardly need to add color at all."

Instead of telling Dario any of this, she said robotically, "Yes, dear." He hadn't seemed to notice she was still sitting on the plush carpet, head draped back against the bed.

"What are your plans today?"

Apart from mourning her dead friend, she didn't know what she was supposed to do.

As if taking pity on her, Dario leaned down and offered her a hand. "Come on, let me help you." She took his hand, more out of instinct than anything else. Why was he being so nice to her?

"Today is Tuesday. Isn't that when you normally play golf with the ladies from the club, or something like that?"

No, because she'd stopped all her other commitments months ago, so she could spend time with her dying friend. Every morning, she would pop over to Susan's house with a bunch of brightly colored flowers and sit with her on the front porch, admiring her beautiful garden and talking. But Dario wouldn't know that, because he hadn't asked, and she hadn't told him.

What was she supposed to do now? Now there was no more Susan?

"Yes, I'd better get dressed," she lied, standing on wobbly legs.

"That would be best. If you get back into doing the things you normally do as soon as possible, you'll feel much better."

Kait made her way toward the bathroom, not caring if he stared at her bare ass as she walked away.

"I'll see you tonight," he yelled after her. "I'll be late. I've got a dinner meeting at the casino."

Small mercies. She had the whole day to herself.

# CHAPTER TWO

Kait sat on the carpet, running her fingers through the thick pile, her gaze drifting between the doorway to the balcony and then back to the oil painting on the wall. Dressed in athletic shorts and a tank top, she cared little about how she looked. She hadn't even bothered to wash her hair. Dario had left two hours ago, taking his two hulking bodyguards with him. Kait had sent Maria, the housemaid and cook, home until the afternoon, and texted Lupo and told him not to bother coming to tend the gardens today.

She needed to be alone.

This house felt oppressive. Who would've thought this gorgeous mansion, set high on a cliff face with a view that was the envy of every single person who visited, could ever feel oppressive? But it did. Kait laid a hand on her chest. It was like she couldn't breathe. Like the air was tainted. Why did she feel this way? She was ungrateful. Unworthy. Didn't appreciate what she had. Everything Dario always said she was.

Using her arms, she slowly pushed herself off the carpet and walked slowly, as if in a dream, over to the door. Her shorts threatened to slide down her hips as she walked. It was the first time Kait really took note of how much weight she'd lost. Stress could do that to you she supposed. The frailer Susan had become, the more Kait's appetite had seemed to desert her.

She and Dario lived in a mansion on the edge of the Swan River. Sometimes called Millionaire's Row, Jutland Parade in Dalkeith contained the best of the best. Venetian Villa could easily be at home on the Italian Rivera. Dario liked to tell everyone he got it for a steal: a mere fourteen million dollars.

Kait couldn't believe any house cost that much.

The sun beat down mercilessly outside. Kait shaded her eyes and wandered out onto the balcony. Dario's office was on the third floor, its balcony overlooking the river. She could look straight down from here to the rocks at the bottom of the cliff, thirty meters below. Not a jot of wind stirred the air. It was as if the whole of Perth was holding its breath. The temperature would soar into the forties today, for sure.

Kait leaned over the railing and stared at the rocks. Small wavelets lapped against the limestone, shifting a fluff of foam back and forth, back and forth.

A certain kind of peace waited down there.

Of its own accord, her left leg lifted, and within seconds, she had one foot over the railing. The other leg followed, until she was suspended above the cliff by a small lip beneath her toes, her hands wrapped around the metal balustrade.

On the wrong side of the railing.

Her body draped out in the open, nothing below her but air. It would be simple to just let go. Perhaps she could learn to fly. Fly out of this life.

Suddenly, Susan's voice was in her head, *What the fuck do you think you're doing?* Kait was so shocked to hear her dead friend's voice that for a second she couldn't remember where she was. Then, in a flash of comprehension, she gasped and clutched the railing tightly to her chest.

Gingerly, she eased one leg and then the other back over to

safety.

What had she been thinking?

She didn't want to die.

Susan hadn't wanted to die. But she want't given a choice. Kait did have a choice.

But she also didn't want this life anymore.

When she'd first met Dario, he'd swept her off her feet. He'd dazzled her with his easy Italian charm. And his money. Let's not forget the money. It was part of the attraction, Kait freely admitted it. But the luster had well and truly vanished on that front. Now she'd give up all that money for a life of freedom.

Her gaze drifted to the oil painting on the wall again.

Susan was her only friend left from Kait's life before she met Dario. Her best friend from school. The only one who'd stuck by her after she started to change, becoming the wife Dario expected her to be. To become the woman he said her status dictated she should be. She drifted around in elite society, pretending she fit in. Some of the projects she took on were actually of interest, and even gave her a sense of satisfaction, as if she could make a change in the world. Like the Indigenous Literacy Charity Foundation, which helped improve Aboriginal literacy; reading and writing and even staying on at school. She'd persuaded Dario to donate some of his obscene amounts of money toward the group, but her true joy was in the smaller things she did for the charity, such as volunteer to shake donation tins at local events or organizing high tea fund-raising drives and speaking earnestly to her rich friends about the difference the charity was making.

But the rest of it merely drained what little energy she had left. Like the-Ladies-Who-Golfed. They were supposed to meet every Tuesday morning at the exclusive Lake Karrinyup Country Club, to improve their golf swing. But invariably it ended in a gossip session about whose husband was shagging whose secretary.

Kait no longer cared.

She walked over to the painting and lifted the edge of the frame.

Behind the picture was a wall-mounted safe. It was about half a meter square, with an electronic keypad in the middle of the heavy door.

Dario didn't know she knew about the safe.

He also didn't know she knew the code to open it.

Her guilty gaze slid toward the door. No one was in the house, but still, she should be careful. If Dario came home now…

Gently lifting the picture off the wall, she placed it on the floor next to her husband's large, wooden desk. Her fingers punched in the code and the door made a buzzing noise, then slowly slid open.

Stacks of one-hundred-dollar bills filled most of the lower shelf of the safe. The top shelf contained documents and files.

Could she do this?

*Yes, you can*, Susan whispered in her head.

Susan had always been the daring one.

The money *was* technically hers. What was hers was his, and his was hers, wasn't that how the saying went?

If she took the money, Dario would surely come after her. But she needed that money to survive. If she wanted to hurt him, one sure way to do it was through his wallet. She reached out to touch the cash but withdrew her hand quickly. It was dirty money. Kait didn't know exactly how Dario did it, but she was sure he was into illegal dealings. There was no way he made this much money purely from business. He'd started off in insurance, helping the company make the most of their funds using complicated computer algorithms, but then quickly moved on and set up his own hedge fund, talking other businessmen into investing in his new advanced software, trading huge sums on Wall Street. Kait never asked, and Dario never told her the specifics.

He would tell her he was meeting clients. Like his dinner at the casino tonight. But she knew they weren't your normal clients. Tonight, it might be some bigwig Chinese businessman who needed help to dodge his extra-large tax bill. Or it could even be a trio of tattooed men with shaved heads and unfaltering gazes, who needed to shift a large sum of money quickly. Dario would never ask where the money came from. That wasn't his business.

Kait had decided quite a few years ago that Dario was into money laundering. She told no one about her epiphany, not even Susan. But she was pretty sure that's what he was doing.

Without touching it, she mentally calculated how much money might be stashed in the safe. The stacks would be in bundles of one hundred bills. One hundred bills times one hundred dollars would make each stack worth ten thousand dollars each.

It was too hard to see all the way to the rear of the safe, she'd have to pull the money out to figure out how much was in there. Gaze raking the office, she finally saw what she needed. A black backpack sitting on the floor beneath the armchair in the corner. A pair of sweaty socks and some black sport shorts sat at the bottom, along with a couple of squash balls. Dario sometimes played squash with one of his mates and had probably dropped the bag here last week and forgotten about it.

She began stuffing bundles of money into the bag. Ten bundles. That made one hundred thousand dollars. Holy Mary. Ten more bundles and then ten more after that. The bag wasn't even a third full.

Kait stopped when she reached a total of one million

dollars. There was more money stashed in the safe, but she'd removed over half of it. She hefted the bag in one hand. It was heavy. She sat it on the carpet and walked around it. Did it look like there was one million dollars in this bag? Nope, not really. The backpack looked perfectly innocent. Like it was stuffed with clothes, not money.

A noise outside the balcony door made her look up sharply. It was only a flock of pink-and-gray galahs winging their way to find a late breakfast.

Shit, she needed to get going. Without looking at exactly what she took, Kait grabbed the handful of documents on the top shelf and shoved them into the bag's front zipper pocket.

Her movements hurried now, she shut the safe and rehung the painting, then closed the doors to the balcony with a clang. Collecting the dirty socks and shorts from where she'd dropped them on the floor, she glanced around Dario's office to make sure nothing else was amiss. If she was really going to do this, the longer Dario took to discover the money was missing, the better.

A note. She could leave her husband a note. He wouldn't like it, the fact that she'd taken any decision into her own hands, but if she used a good excuse, she might get away with it for a few days. Before he started hunting her.

Her hand shook as she picked up a pen, sat down at the desk, and tore a sheet of paper from a lined pad. If she got this wrong, the implications could be disastrous. Dario's punishment would be swift and unforgiving. But if she didn't do this, her life was essentially ended anyway.

*Dear Dario,*

*I've gone to visit my sister. I need a little time to process Susan's death.*

*I'm asking you to give me a few days to grieve. Please.*

*I'll be in touch soon.*

*Your Loving Wife.*

Would it be enough to keep him at bay for a few days? It was simple and to the point. A heartfelt plea to her husband for understanding. Anyone else reading it would see it as that, and nothing more. Only Dario would perceive a possible underlying meaning.

Her sister, Monika, lived in Sydney. They hadn't seen each other in over four years, mainly because Dario had a simmering hatred for Monika ever since she'd called him out as an overbearing, ignorant, misogynistic, racist pig. It was true; Dario was a misogynistic pig, and she was proud of Monika for standing up to him, especially when she couldn't —or wouldn't—but it meant that Monika was banished from Kait's life.

Dario wouldn't like the fact she was visiting her outlawed sister, but he also wouldn't like to cause a scene. He'd grin and bear it, for a few days at least, before the desire to control her became too much.

And Kait had no one else to turn to. Both her parents were gone now. Her mother had been taken by breast cancer when Kait was barely eighteen, and her father in a horrific accident where he been knocked of his bicycle by a drunk driver a few years later. So it wouldn't seem too odd that Kait would turn to her sister in her time of grief.

Monika needed to be warned. She'd never normally answer a call from Dario, but if he continued to hound her, she might give in, in the end. Shit. Would she be putting Monika's life in danger by implicating her in this dangerous deed? Surely not. Surely, Dario wouldn't touch Monika?

No, she'd be safe. She just needed to be on the lookout and know what to say if Dario happened to get hold of her.

Her sister didn't know about Dario's...controlling side. Kait told no one. Monika might've guessed some of it though;

she hated the way Kait was always so deferential to her husband. Kait explained it away by saying he was Italian, brought up by an Italian momma, and there were certain things he expected from his wife. To be at his beck and call was one of them. They had certain roles to play; he was the man who brought in the money and she was the homemaker who looked after home and family.

Kait winced as she thought of family. She and Dario had never been able to conceive. It was a problem with Dario, she was sure of it, because after numerous tests over numerous years, she kept coming back with a clean bill of health. But he'd never admit to it, so it became Kait's fault they couldn't have children.

There was a loud bang from downstairs, and Kait nearly jumped out of her skin. Oh, God, was Dario home?

She stood, clutching the bag to her chest, straining to hear any more. After many moments frozen in time, Kait took a breath. There were no more noises.

Quick. She needed to pack a bag and get out of here. The bedrooms were all on the second floor, and she hurried down the curved, marble staircase. Just as she reached the second-floor landing, a fluffy, black streak flew past her.

"Casper," she yelled after the cat impatiently. Maybe the cat had knocked something over downstairs.

It only took her a few minutes to pack. She knew exactly what to take; she'd been planning this escape for far too long. Emerging from the bedroom wearing white capris and an aqua silk shirt with leather sandals on her feet, she paused to look back, just once. Back at the bedroom she shared with Dario for the past eighteen years. At the bed she'd shared with her husband. She was determined she would never spend another night with him. This was the beginning of her new life.

On swift feet, she hurried down the steps, a small

overnight bag in one hand and the black backpack in the other. Grabbing her handbag and keys from the kitchen counter, she descended the small internal steps leading to the multi-car garage. Her little Mercedes SLR sat waiting for her up the front of the pack. Dario had around five or six cars he liked to drive, with others he kept only for show, but she loved her compact little sports car. It was easy to park and zipped around the streets like it was on rails.

But her Mercedes wasn't the perfect car for what she was planning. In fact, it was possibly the worst. It'd be easily recognizable. Shit, she hadn't thought this out properly.

Then she looked at the bag full of money and had her answer.

# CHAPTER THREE

Kait pushed on the gas pedal, tentatively at first. But when not a lot happened, she pushed harder. Damn, this brute of a car was nothing like her sweet little Mercedes to drive. But she was going to have to get used to it.

Her Merc was sitting in the long-term parking lot at the airport. Hopefully, Dario would be fooled into thinking she'd actually got onto that plane and flown to Sydney. She'd even purchased a ticket, using her credit card, so he would see the charge.

She turned to grin at Susan. Weren't they having a blast?

The heavy blanket of grief that'd lifted for a second, descended again. Now she was finally on the road, she remembered what'd driven her to do this in the first place.

The traffic lights ahead turned red, and Kait clumsily changed down a gear and came to a grinding halt. Why on earth had she thought she could drive a stick shift? Her new vehicle was a Toyota Hilux dual cab. The saleslady at the secondhand car lot had assured her they were one of the most common cars on the road. Which was exactly what Kait wanted: to blend in. Besides that, it was the only four-wheel drive available in the tiny used-car lot. Kait had given the lady a fake name and address, telling her she'd left her driver's license at home. At first the saleslady had balked at her lack of identification, but when Kait produced the full price of the vehicle, eleven thousand, nine hundred and ninety-nine dollars in cash, then added an extra two thousand to the pile, the lady's misgivings had miraculously disappeared.

Oh shit, the lights were green. She eased the clutch out, hoping like hell she didn't stall the car. The engine rattled and complained, but the vehicle slowly crawled off the mark. The other thing the saleslady had told her was that diesel vehicles were more forgiving than gas cars, had a lower torque to something ratio, whatever that meant.

It was early afternoon, the rush for the school-pickup was approaching. But Kait planned on getting out of town before the true rush hour started. She had no idea where she was going. All she knew was she was heading north. Western Australia was a big state. She could easily get lost up there. At least, that's what she was hoping.

There was so much potential on the road. Things to see, lessons to learn, people to meet. Perhaps she could become a whole new person. No one would ever have to know the old Kait.

\* \* \*

Kait smothered a yawn, looked at the clock on the dash and then rubbed her eyes. She'd only been on the road for three and a half hours and she was already exhausted. Time for a break and a strong coffee. The sun was getting low on the horizon, and while she wasn't driving directly into it, it was vaguely annoying.

Kait had no idea where she was, but at the next town or service station, she was definitely going to pull over. As if someone upstairs had heard her, a sign suddenly appeared ahead. Dongara five kilometers. Kait had never heard of Dongara and was at a loss as to what kind of town it might be. But, big or small, as long as it had a device station and a café, she'd be happy.

Five minutes later, she was rewarded by a large green-and-yellow sign proclaiming a service station chain she knew well, right on the outskirts of town.

She pulled in, careful not to bang her wing mirror on the gas pump as she maneuvered her car into position so she could refuel. This vehicle would take some getting used to, it was so damned big.

Grabbing her handbag from the front seat, she jumped down and went around to open the gas cap. As she did so, the words *diesel fuel only* stared back at her. Crap, she'd forgotten this car took diesel. A quick perusal of the pump told her this wasn't the right one.

Kait sighed.

It looked like the pump at the other end of the line was the one for diesel. She hopped back in and moved to the correct pump.

Once the vehicle was full, she moved it to one of the parking spaces out the front of the shop and carefully locked the car. The backpack with all the money was stashed in a little compartment behind the rear seats in the back of the dual cab. It wasn't ideal, but then carrying that much money on her was never going to be ideal. Perhaps she'd stop somewhere soon and open a bank account. But you needed ID for that, didn't you? Kait pursed her lips and went inside to pay. Cash, of course.

"Is there a café somewhere in town I could buy a coffee?" she asked, picking up a map of Western Australia and handing over a hundred dollars to the guy behind the counter. The Google Maps app was no use to her at the moment. She'd turned her phone off just in case Dario could track her that way. It was probably some urban myth, spread by all those bad TV shows she watched, but nevertheless, she was taking no chances.

The man checked the bill by holding it up to the light before he answered. "It's after five thirty, all the cafés will all be closed, luv."

"Oh, silly me." Of course they would. She was in the country now. Things didn't run on quite the same schedule as they did in the big cities. At least the man had mentioned cafés, which was a good sign. It meant the town was semicivilized, if it had more than one.

"We do a good coffee and sausage roll next door. Or a meat pie, if that takes your fancy." The man waved a helpful hand in the direction of where she'd just come from. "We're open till nine."

"Oh. Thank you." Kait retraced her steps out to her vehicle —she had to remind herself that the large, white four-wheel drive parked in the lot was actually her car now—and sure enough, when she turned her head to where the man had pointed, there was a small sign leaning against the wall proclaiming food and hot beverages.

Inside, there were four or five tables, all covered with bright-red plastic cloths and four plastic chairs set up around each one. A couple of them were occupied. Two men, dressed in bright-yellow Hi-Vis clothing, were wolfing down a meat pie each at one table. Locals, or perhaps truck drivers passing through. An older couple—the man wearing a Hawaiian shirt, and the woman in a bright floral-print dress—were poking at a wilted salad each. They might belong to the four-wheel drive and caravan parked out front. Gray nomads. She was kind of proud she knew that term. The saleswoman at the used-car lot had told her to watch out for all the gray nomads on the road, and she'd imagined small, gnome-like men walking along the dusty edges of the bitumen. It'd taken Kait a good two hours, passing many slow-moving caravans on the way, to figure it out.

Kait ordered a coffee at the counter, and on a spur-of-the-moment decision, opted to try the sausage roll. She knew she'd probably regret it. At the last moment, she added a handful of candy bars to the countertop. Not ideal, but they'd keep her going for a while, until she could find something fresh and tasty.

The woman at the counter told her she'd bring her meal out in a *mo*.

Kait snorted. Meal! This wasn't a meal. This was a greasy, calorific snack.

Maria was probably creating her delicious version of a meal right now, not even suspecting her mistress wouldn't come down the stairs to eat it. Maria knew Kait's tastes in exquisite detail, and she was likely cooking some freshly caught fish and a tasty Thai green salad topped with a zesty salsa. Kait's mouth watered at the thought. But there would be no more of Maria's cooking she reminded herself. She'd have to learn to cook properly now she was on her own.

Susan laughed long and hard at the idea of Kait preparing a healthy, delicious meal and Kait frowned.

The table in the corner near the window was free, and she sat down, unfolding her map across it. She looked over the strange names on the map. She'd been born and bred in Perth, how was it that she hardly knew any of the towns? Apart from Broome, because, well, everyone knew where Broome was. Never the adventurous type, Kait had hardly traveled in her own state. When she was younger, if her family ever went on holiday, they headed south, where the air was cooler in summer and the land lusher. But this whole northern part of the state, Kait had never really cared to learn anything about before now. All she knew was there were big deserts and lots of mining up north.

She needed a place where Dario was least likely to come looking for her.

*Where to next, Susan?*

Susan didn't answer. Which didn't surprise Kait.

But a few moments later, there was a tap on her shoulder. "Need a hand with directions, lady?"

"Oh, um…" Kait swiveled in her seat to see a pretty, young woman standing behind her. She must've been so engrossed in her map she hadn't noticed her come in. This woman was also wearing Hi-Vis clothing, like the two men at the other table. They were now staring licentiously at her, as if she was some kind of new snack who'd just dropped into their laps.

The girl ignored the men.

"I know the area pretty well. I can help, if you're lost."

"Oh, thank you. I'm not lost. Not really." Well, that was both correct and incorrect. She wasn't lost because she didn't know where she was going.

The men were still staring at the girl like she was a piece of meat. Kait took pity on her. "Actually, I would like some advice. I'm traveling north. And I need some ideas about where to go. I want to see some of this great, brown land for myself."

"So, you're a tourist?" One look at the girl's face showed how dubious that sounded. But Kait had started down this lie, and she needed to make it sound plausible.

"Yes, I am. I'm ashamed to admit that I've lived in Perth all my life, but never visited this beautiful state of ours, and I need to rectify that. You could say this is a bit of a spontaneous holiday." Kait waved her hand gaily in the air, hoping to sound like an avid sightseer. Actually, it wasn't a bad cover story. Better than, *I'm running away from my abusive husband, with a million dollars in stolen money.*

The girl stared at her, enormous blue eyes surprisingly analytical. What was wrong? Didn't she look like a tourist? Kait glanced down at her apparel. Smart capris from her favorite designer, Arnsdorf, and a lovely, cool, Carla Zampatti silk shirt. A complete, casual outfit that Kait would've been happy to wear out to a late brunch with friends or shopping in the afternoon.

She took a quick look around the other people in the kiosk and that's when the girl's quizzical glance began to make sense. Perhaps Kait's version of casual and theirs were slightly different. And perhaps, if she was hoping to blend in better, she might need a new, toned-down wardrobe. Possibly even bought from Target. Or Kmart. She suppressed a shudder. Once upon a time, before she'd met Dario, those types of shops had been the only ones she could afford. She could do this. No more labels for her. A tiny voice inside her head screamed that she could never truly live without her Chanel slingbacks and her Dolce and Gabbana jersey knit dress, but she ignored it by gritting her teeth and smiling.

"Where are you headed tonight, then?"

"Oh, I don't really know."

The girl cast her another long, appraising look. "My name's Deanna, by the way." She held out a hand, catching Kait by surprise.

Kait took it on instinct and was surprised to feel callouses on the girl's palms. The Hi-Vis workwear wasn't merely for show, then.

"Hi, Deanna, I'm Kait." The name was out of her mouth before she could stop it, and Kait withdrew her hand hurriedly. Shit, she probably should've thought of a fake name to use while she was traveling. Too late now. She'd been caught on the hop, and her lack of planning was showing.

The girl's eyes were already on the map, however, as if she hadn't noticed Kait's reaction. "How about Geraldton? It's around forty-five minutes up the road. Fairly big town, there are plenty of hotels and stuff there, like."

Kait waited for Deanna to continue. *Like what?*, she

wondered? But Deanna was looking at her expectantly, as if waiting for an answer. That's when it struck Kait. It was a form of speech.

"Yes, yes, Geraldton sounds lovely. You say I can get a hotel up there?"

"Yep. I was born in Geraldton. But my parents died when I was young and my granny passed away a few years ago, so I haven't got family there anymore."

"Oh, I see. That's no good." Kait was a little lost for words. She hadn't asked for any personal details, but the girl was oversharing, anyway.

"I can go with you. Show you the way, like."

Kait sat back in her chair. "Oh, are you heading to Geraldton?"

"You could say that. I'm hitching my way up the state. The farther north I can get, the better." Deanna speared her with those bright-blue eyes again, almost as if daring Kait to refuse. For the second time that afternoon, Kait wondered what a gorgeous girl was doing here in Hi-Vis, with hands as rough as a man's. Had she just been conned?

But Kait couldn't come up with a reason not to give Deanna a lift. Apart from the fact she didn't want the young woman tagging along. She was on the run from a dangerous husband who'd stop at nothing when he discovered that missing money. Then again... Perhaps having someone else in the car with her might throw anyone Dario sent to follow her off the scent. They'd be looking for a woman traveling alone.

What would Susan make of the whole situation? But Susan was, again, uncharacteristically quiet on this one.

"All right then. Just to Geraldton, though, no farther."

"Fair enough," Deanna replied.

The woman from behind the counter approached the table and plonked down a chipped plate with Kait's sausage roll in front of her, right on top of the map, and then placed the coffee—served in a takeaway cup—beside it.

"Bon appétit."

"Oh, ah, thank you," Kait said, unsure if she was actually grateful or not.

"Yours will be out in a minute, luv," the woman said to Deanna, her large, rolling hips brushing unapologetically past Kait's chair as she turned around to retreat to the counter.

"The snagger rolls are really good here," Deanna said, tilting her chin toward Kait's plate. "You're in for a treat, like."

Watching a small dribble of fat ooze out of one end of the meat pastry, Kait was beginning to doubt that.

# CHAPTER FOUR

Deanna Jones sat in the passenger seat, watching the road unfurl within the small sphere of the car headlights. This woman was a hoot. Completely certifiable. Probably belonged in the looney bin, but that was okay by Deanna. Because, really, who didn't go a little crazy at some stage in their life?

Deanna gave Kait a quick sideways glance. Who the hell did she think she was kidding with that sad story back at the gas station? A spontaneous tourist, this lady was definitely not. Who in their right mind set off on a trip up north with no idea where they were going, and no supplies in their car? Wearing that get-up? She looked ready for a luncheon with the ladies at the local Ritz Hotel, not a driving holiday in the desert.

But Deanna was going along with Kait's story, for now. She needed a lift north. And this lady was the best of a bad bunch, as far as Deanna could tell. She could've asked one of those truckies who'd been eyeballing her in the café. But Deanna knew you got nothing in this life for free. And she'd rather avoid giving out sexual favors if she didn't have to.

Kait was driving with one hand on the wheel, her eyes glazing over a little as she stared at the dark bitumen ahead.

It seemed she wasn't paying as much attention to the road as she perhaps should.

"You wanna make sure you watch out for those bloody roos," Deanna said, nonchalantly picking at a ragged nail.

"I beg your pardon?"

"The roos. The kangaroos," Deanna elaborated when the woman continued to stare at her as if she had no understanding of the word. Was this woman even an Aussie, or what?

"Kangaroos come out at night. To feed on the grass at the edge of the road, like."

"So?" Kait's puzzled frown made Deanna sigh.

"So, you're gonna hit one if you don't slow down and pay more attention."

"Oh. Really?" Kait backed off the accelerator a tad and sat up straighter in her seat.

A roo chose that very second to jump out onto the road in front of them. But by the time Kait had reacted, the roo sailed on past the front bumper and kept going. Kait hit the brakes, and the vehicle fish-tailed to a stop.

"Holy fuck!" Kait yelled.

The words *I told you so*, were on the tip of Deanna's tongue, but she noticed that Kait's hands were shaking, so she refrained, surprising herself a little. She wasn't usually this magnanimous.

Luckily, there were no cars coming the other way and once Kait had the vehicle going along the road again, Deanna said, "If that happens again, it's better if you don't slam on the brakes. Just hit the fucker. He'll do less damage to your car than a rollover. Or a tree, for that matter."

She'd learned that lesson the hard way. It was the way her parents had died. Deanna had been strapped into her child seat in the rear, which was what'd saved her, or so the coppers said.

"Right. Okay. You mean that? Just hit it head on?" Kait didn't seem to want to believe Deanna.

"Yep." Deanna went back to chewing on her nail.

"Well, maybe you'd better talk to me, to keep me awake."

"Sure thing. What do you want to know, like?"

Kait made a face. Was it something she'd said? But after a few seconds, Kait asked, "Tell me why you're hitching a ride with a stranger? It seems like a strange thing to do for a pretty, young girl, like yourself."

Deanna winced at the reference to a pretty, young girl, but the rest of the question was an easy one. "I was working at the pit in Kalgoorlie. Then, Tamika my—"

"Sorry, you were working in a pit? What's that?" The derisive curl of Kait's lip made Deanna wonder if she thought the pit might be some kind of brothel or titty bar. Not that there was anything wrong with working in a topless bar, but Deanna wasn't really into the men who frequented those types of bars, with their big hands and bad breath.

"The Super Pit. Australia's biggest open-cut gold mine. You know, in Kalgoorlie." Well, it had been the largest until a few years ago, when another mine in WA took the honor, but who was counting?

"You're a miner?" Kait's eyes went round with surprise. The woman had rather nice brown eyes; they reminded her of the Labrador puppy her best friend had owned. And her red hair was fabulous. In another time and place, she might've considered chatting her up. But not when her ride north depended on staying on the good side of this clueless female. And she didn't think Kait would appreciate being chatted up by a *pretty, young girl*, as she'd put it.

"Not really, I drove the trucks. They like women drivers, we're kinder to the trucks and have less accidents, like."

Kait winced again, and Deanna wondered what the woman's problem was?

"It was a good job, great pay, like. But then my girlfriend dumped me. Started going out with someone else. And we worked together, so I had to see her every day. It was dragging me down, you know? So, I just up and left, like."

That'd been nearly a week ago. Deanna had packed a bag and left without even handing in her resignation. Hitched a ride straight to Perth, just so she didn't have to look at Tamika's face anymore. They'd had a good thing going, had been seeing each other for eight months. She might possibly have even been in love. But not anymore—the lying, cheating bitch.

Deanna had spent a few days in Perth, sleeping on a friend's couch. She didn't really need another job; the inheritance from her parents made sure she never needed to work again. But she hated to be idle. Idle hands were the devil's work, her granny used to say. And her hands tingled every time she thought of Tamika, wanting to return to Kalgoorlie and beg her to take her back. She knew she needed to move on, to stop wallowing in her own self-pity.

"Oh. Your girlfriend dumped you. That's terrible." But the way Kait stressed the word *girlfriend* had Deanna's antenna twinging.

"Yeah, I can't really decide if I like girls or boys better." She twisted a lock of blonde hair around her finger and gave Kait a flirtatious wink. She couldn't help it, she loved to shock. Clearly from the swanky side of town, this woman wouldn't know a person from the LGBTIQ+ community if they came up and bit her on the bum. Deanna giggled at the thought.

"So, I'm going north. Might try and find another job, maybe up at Newman, or even at Port Headland."

"That sounds nice." The way Kait said it, Deanna knew she had no clue where either of those places were.

"So, what about you? Where's your tourist inner-self yearning going to take you?" Deanna asked. Time to poke the bear, see if she could get a rise out of her.

"Do you mean after Geraldton?"

"Yeah, Geraldton ain't really a tourist town. I mean, there's stuff to do and see, I suppose. But the good stuff is farther north."

"I don't really know. Do you have any suggestions?"

A sudden idea occurred to Deanna. If she played her cards right, she might be able to get this woman to take her more of the way north. It might be fun, riding along with her for a while. Deanna could certainly teach her a thing or two.

"Have you heard of Kalbarri?"

Kait merely shook her head.

"Well, you have to go. All the tourists go there. They have these amazing rocky gorges you can walk down. And a pink lake right nearby. It's actually pink, I've seen it. The town is right on the coast. Do you like beaches?"

"Yes, of course I like beaches. But there are plenty of beaches in Perth."

The lady had her on that one. Deanna paused to think. How else could she persuade Kait to go to Kalbarri?

"But the gorges sound interesting. I've flown over the Grand Canyon, that was amazing. But I've never seen an Australian gorge."

"I think it's time you did."

A sign flashed toward them. Geraldton was ten kilometers away. Deanna needed to think fast if she was going to stick to Kait for the next few days. Being able to afford to pay for a hotel for the night clearly wasn't a problem for Kait. But what if Deanna could offer her something better than a boring old hotel room?

Going on a hunch that Kait might be looking for something other than an expensive and very public hotel, Deanna said as casually as she could, "I have a place to stay in Geraldton. I mean, if you want to, like. It's an old beach shack that belonged to my parents. There's not many of them left now. It's right at the back of the dunes. You can even walk to the beach."

The sharp gaze Kait flung her way before quickly returning her focus to the road, told Deanna many things. It told her that Kait didn't trust her. And why would she? They were strangers who'd only met an hour ago. It also told Deanna that Kait might be interested in her proposal. Which meant perhaps Deanna was more right about Kait and her *holiday* up north than she'd first thought.

"Why didn't you mention that before?" Kait's guard was up now, but Deanna wasn't worried. She could sweet-talk most people around.

"I don't live there. I keep it, just in case. I should probably sell it, really." How many times had her granny tried to talk her into selling *that old shanty?* as she called it? Deanna couldn't bear to live in it, because it reminded her too much of her parents, even though she'd barely known them before they passed. But then, she also couldn't sell it, for the very same reason. She'd make a pretty penny if she ever sold it, that was for sure. Perhaps if her parents' money ever ran out, then she'd put it on the market. But Deanna lived a frugal life right now; she didn't need a lot of money to keep happy.

"It'll be fine to stay in," she added hurriedly. "A cleaner goes in every week to make sure it's all good. You don't have to, if you don't want to, it was just a silly idea." Deanna added the barest hint of a sulky touch to her voice. She knew better than to overdo it with this woman.

"Well, I wouldn't say it's a *silly* idea," Kait replied. "I was merely wondering why you didn't say anything about this house beforehand. But maybe…it might be a good idea. Save me some money," she added hurriedly. "As long as you're sure there's enough room. And it's right on the beach, you say?"

"Yeah. There's plenty of room. We could pick up some fish and chips on the way and eat them on the front veranda. Listen to the ocean. It'll be nice." Deanna kept the excitement out of her voice. She'd been meaning to go and see her parents' house—bugger, she needed to remember it was her house now—for a while. When was the last time she'd been inside? Was it around the time Granny died? Had it really been that long? She didn't think she'd been actively avoiding the place; but having someone around when she went back inside would make it less…intense.

"Hmm." Kait pretended to be considering the idea, but Deanna knew that little fishy was already hooked. "As long as you're sure you want to let a stranger into your house."

"I'd really like the company," Deanna said. That bit at least was the truth.

# CHAPTER FIVE

"This place is beautiful," Kait gushed. She'd been prepared to lie, just to save Deanna's feelings, because when she mentioned a beach shack, Kait had been expecting a lot less.

But the house was gorgeous.

"Yeah, my dad built most of it by hand. They were both artists, me mum and dad."

Once Deanna had flicked on the porch light, Kait could see it in all its glory.

The front door was solid wood, except for the round, stained glass window—a picture of a fish underwater in bright blues and greens. Kait was so mesmerized Deanna had to prompt her to step though the doorway.

"Mum did the stained glass," Deanna offered.

"It's lovely."

The inside was even better than the outside. The front foyer widened into a massive, open-plan room. There was a modern kitchen to the back, two comfy couches on a brightly patterned rug in the middle. One wall was made of glass bottles, stacked on top of each other, with clay between them, allowing a soft light from the outdoor porch to filter in through the tiny portholes. Another wall had gorgeous patterns worked into the structure, different hues of mud that creating swirls and geometric patterns. The wall was a piece of art in its own right. So much time and patience had been spent creating this home. Kait could feel how much love had soaked into the walls.

"Most of it is made of cob," Deanna explained, heading toward the kitchen to put the parcel of fish and chips on the countertop. "That's a mixture of mud and straw, essentially. That's what me granny told me. Dad could mold that into about any shape he wanted."

Deanna then opened two enormous French doors, leading out to a veranda and the beach. Warm, fresh air flowed in, as if the house had taken a huge, deep breath. It brought the smell of the ocean and the swish of the waves.

"Wow," Kait breathed. She couldn't help herself, she had to go and run her hand lightly over the cob wall, feel the texture of the patterns beneath her fingers. This was nothing like the opulent mansion she lived in. The complete opposite, in fact. It just went to show, money couldn't always buy beauty. Or happiness. She could definitely live here. Be happy here. What a shame that Deanna felt she couldn't. Too many ghosts, Kait surmised.

At least Deanna had something tangible she could remember her parents by. Even though Deanna had only been a baby when they died—hopefully if she could ever banish the ghosts—the house might bring her a kind of understanding of the type of people her parents had been. How much they must've loved her, to build her such a house of beauty to call home.

Thinking of Deanna's life growing up without her parents had thoughts of her own mother and father suddenly circling in her mind. Kait had nothing left to remind her of her parents. Now she thought about it, that was quite sad really. Neither of them had lived to see her marry Dario. And once they were married, he'd talked her into selling the old family house because she no longer needed it. Which had seemed logical and right at the time.

"Come on, before the chips get cold." Deanna waved her forward, plonking the fish and chips, still in their butcher paper wrapping, on the wooden table on the veranda. Kait took her seat but was too mesmerized by the vista in front of her. A half-moon was rising in the sky behind them, casting its light over a calm ocean. After the searing temperatures earlier today, this warm air was like a balm to Kait's soul.

If only Susan could see this.

If only she could stay here forever. Become a hermit and hide away from Dario and his sidekicks. But it wasn't to be. This was too close to Perth; it'd only be a matter of time before he found her here. She really needed to come up with some sort of concrete plan. Change her name, a completely new identity. But she had no idea where to even start.

Deanna had ripped off a piece of paper and piled her makeshift plate high with salty chips and a piece of battered fish. Now she was devouring it as if she might never see food again, with more gusto than Kait had seen anyone eat in quite a while. She even chewed with her mouth open.

Kait popped a chip into her mouth. Oh, God, it was delicious. Salty and oily and so hot it burnt her mouth. Why had she ever stopped eating fish and chips? She knew why. Because this was paupers' food according to Dario. The day she married Dario was the day she'd stopped eating takeaway. It was almost as if by eating cheap takeaway food, he might inexplicably be transported back to the days when he'd lived in the small house in Balcatta crammed in with the rest of his extended family.

It was time she started to remember the small pleasures she used to find in life.

"Will you point me toward a shopping mall tomorrow, before I leave?" Kait asked.

"Sure. What are you after, like?" Deanna answered through a mouthful of battered fish.

"I need some new clothes. I left in a bit of a hurry, you see. And I didn't bring a lot of…holiday apparel with me. Could you show me where you buy your clothes?"

"You mean you want some Hi-Vis? Sure, I can take you to —"

"No." Kait held up a hand. The Hi-Vis might be a great disguise, but Kait didn't think she was that desperate. Not yet, at least. "Just shorts and T-shirts, maybe a few dresses."

"And some thongs," Deanna added. "All tourists wear thongs."

"Oh, God, really?" Deanna shuddered. As a child, she'd lived in the rubber flip-flops that everyone in Perth seemed to think were normal footwear. People even wore them out to dinner, and to the football, and the cinema. It'd been a long time indeed since a pair of thongs had graced her feet.

*There's nothing wrong with thongs,* Susan's voice echoed in the corridors of her mind. Susan had said there was a time and place for everything. The beach was a definite yes. Even down to the local supermarket, if she needed a quick pint of milk.

"All right, and some thongs," Kait agreed with a grimace.

"Cool. I'll take you to Target first thing in the morning." The girl continued to chew thoughtfully for a second. "And then I guess you want to head to Kalbarri?"

"What? Oh, yes, Kalbarri." Kait had forgotten that was the next town she was supposed to visit.

"I could come with you."

"Why would you want to do that? You have this amazing house right here."

"I dunno." Deanna gave a hesitant shrug. "I already told you, I don't live here. And like I said, I'm looking for a job."

Kait had never considered taking the other woman any

farther than the agreed Geraldton. She couldn't decide if it'd be a good idea or not. There was the possibility that she might be leading Deanna into danger. Although, if Dario ever caught up with her, it'd be Kait in the firing line. He wouldn't dare hurt anyone else; they'd be of no importance to him. Thinking of Dario also brought the money to the front of her mind. Later, she'd go out and retrieve the backpack from its hiding spot. It might not be safe to leave it in the car. She really needed to do something better with all that money.

Deanna was still staring at her. That girl had the bluest eyes Kait had ever seen. That's when it struck her. Deanna was lonely. Why else would a beautiful young woman want to tag along with an old absconder like herself?

"How old are you?" Kait asked, suddenly curious.

"I'm twenty-two. Why?"

Exactly half her age. Young enough to be her daughter—if Kait had thought about having kids early, before she met Dario. "No reason." Kait smiled indulgently.

"Well, how old are you, then?"

Dodging the question, Kait said, "Okay, you can come to Kalbarri."

Deanna's face brightened.

Kait held up a hand. "But there's one condition." God, she sounded like her own mother. Kait cringed internally at the thought.

"What's that?" Deanna's face closed over, her blue eyes growing wary.

"Can you please stop using the word *like* at the end of every sentence?" Kait knew she was being petty and supercilious, but if she had to listen to this young girl talk that way for much longer, she was going to throttle her. Which sounded much too violent and not at all like the image of the woman Kait liked to project.

"Is that all?"

"Yes, that's all. But you need to stick to your promise. It might be harder than you think." Kait had a feeling the habit was so ingrained into Deanna's language she was going to struggle to banish it.

"Easy, peasy." Deanna waved a dismissive chip in the air.

\* \* \*

Kait stood at the edge of the beach, where the waves met the sand. Digging her toes deep, she let the wavelets lap around her ankles, the water cool against her heated skin. She looked down at the object in her palm, the half-moon casting enough light to glint off the metal edges of the phone. A burner phone. Wasn't that what they called it in all those TV dramas? A quick pit stop in Geraldton, where Deanna had directed her to the only Telstra shop in town right on the dot of nine pm— it was Thursday night, late-night trading—and she'd rushed in just as the sales assistant was closing the door, pleading with him. All she needed was the cheapest phone they had and a prepaid SIM card. Please, her phone had died, and she was desperate to call her sick grandmother.

Four hundred dollars later—burner phones weren't as cheap as they made them out to be in the movies—she walked to her car with her brand-new phone. It was simple to set up, the assistant assured her. Her old phone was still in her handbag, still turned off. She dare not risk even turning it on to check for messages, in case that was enough to bring him right to her door. Deanna never mentioned her sudden need for a new phone, as if she'd accepted Kait's story about her phone dying. But the way the young woman tilted her head thoughtfully on the side as she watched Kait fumble with the settings on her new phone made Kait think that perhaps she didn't believe her after all.

Would Monika even answer if she didn't recognize the number? Only one way to find out. It was late in Sydney now, well past midnight, but Kait hoped her sister was still awake.

Monika was the proverbial night owl. Or perhaps she was just a plain insomniac. Watching TV until the wee hours of the morning.

She punched in the number she'd memorized earlier before turning her own phone off. Wasn't it silly how nowadays, nobody remembered phone numbers because technology did it all for them? Back when she'd been a teenager, she could've easily rattled off ten or fifteen of her friend's phone numbers off the top of her head. Back when they'd used landlines and had to agree to phone each other at a certain time to talk about boys, or school, or the tyranny of the rules their mother and father had imposed.

The phone rang, three, four…six…eight times, until Kait was about to give up. Then, by some miracle, her sister's voice came down the line.

"Who the hell is phoning me at this time of night? I'm warning you, if you're a telemarketer I'm going to scream until your eardrum bursts."

"It's Kait," she replied hurriedly, knowing how deafening Monika's scream could be. "Not a telemarketer, please don't hang up on me."

There was silence for three whole seconds and Kait was just about to ask if her sister was still there, when Monika said, "I'm trying to come up with a single reason why you would call me so late."

It was true; Kait was the opposite of a night owl. And thinking about it, she couldn't remember a single time she'd called her sister this late at night. Certainly not once she was out of the teenage years, and even then it'd only been once, when she'd been so drunk at a party that one of her friends had phoned Monika to come and pick her up. Kait had never drunk that much ever again. It wasn't a nice feeling, losing control, having to rely on someone else to look after your safety.

Kait opened her mouth to reply, when Monika added, "And for the life of me, the only thing I can come up with, is that Dario is dead. Please tell me Dario is dead."

Kait couldn't help her gasp of shock. How ironic.

"Well, is he?" Monika demanded.

"No. But I've left him," Kait replied, testing the words out on her tongue. They sounded strange. This was probably the next best thing to Dario's death in Monika's book.

"Good on you," Monika crowed delightedly. "That's the best news I've heard all year."

Kait had to smile. At least with Monika you knew where you stood. She either liked you, or she didn't; there were no gray areas with her. And she'd made it abundantly clear she hated Dario.

"Are you sure he's not dead? Because that would be the icing on the cake."

"No, he was alive when he left for work this morning." She shuddered at the image of Dario doing up his belt buckle, that satisfied grin turning up the edges of his beard. Had it only been this morning? It felt like eons ago that she'd walked out of her house. "But, Mon, I need you to be careful. I need you to not answer his calls. And be vigilant about who you let into your house, and where you go for the next few weeks."

Again, there was silence. "Why?" she eventually asked. "Are you in some sort of trouble?"

Kait took a deep breath and tilted her head back to stare at the moon, hoping it would lend her some of its serene strength. This was it, the terrible truth. What would Monika think when she told her the facts about Dario, the reality about her own weakness? Monika already suspected there was something going on, but it was one thing to suspect something, and another to have your fears confirmed.

"You could say that," Kait replied. "But as long as you do

what I say, you shouldn't be in any danger."

"Why the fuck do you think I'd be worried about myself? Let that arsehole come over here, I'll tell him where he can fuck off to. If he tries to touch me, I'll take his balls and shove them so far up his arsehole, he'll be tasting testicles for a month."

Kait couldn't suppress a giggle. Monika had always been the fearless one, and the image of her sister with Dario's testicles in her hands was strangely hilarious. And a little delightful. If only Kait had the strength to do something like that.

"It's you I'm worried about. Tell me everything. I need to know what sort of trouble you're in."

So Kait told her. It was a sweet relief to unburden herself to her sister. No one else knew her story. Monika was the only one who came close to guessing. Apart from Susan. And Susan wasn't around to talk to anymore. It was an unwritten rule; they never discussed Kait's love life, or the way Dario treated her like a slave. Kait had lived so long with this secret. It felt like she was betraying Dario in a strange way by telling the truth about him, about their marriage, and about her suspicions regarding his business. Which was just plain stupid.

Kait spilled her guts to Monika, telling her about the money and the documents she'd stolen. She'd need more time to study those documents, but she already felt glad she'd taken them. And then she tried to explain why Monika needed to be careful. Why Dario might take it out on her if he couldn't find Kait.

They talked it over, came up with a fledgling plan. If Dario called in the next few days, Monika would confirm Kait was staying with her, but was too distraught to speak. After that, she'd have to try and convince him that Kait was still staying with her, even though it would become increasingly hard to do. Dario wouldn't stand not hearing from Kait for more than a few days. He'd see through their ruse soon enough. Kait just hoped Dario didn't decide to send some of his thugs to Sydney to check on her whereabouts.

It was nearly midnight according to her phone—which would make it two am with Monika—when they finally ended the call. Kait promised to keep her sister updated. And asked her to delete this number from her phone after they finished speaking. If Dario did pay her visit, she should have nothing incriminating on her that'd allow Dario to track Kait down.

"Take care," Monika had called down the phone. "You're so brave doing this. I love you."

Kait brushed the tears from her cheeks as she'd hung up. She wished she could be with Monika right now, basking in the warmth of her sisterly love. But as things stood, it may be a very long time before she ever saw Monika again.

# CHATPER SIX

Deanna dumped the shopping bags into the back seat. Wow, this lady sure knew how to shop. She'd bought the whole store. She'd even got a pair of shorts that Deanna said looked good on her in three different colors. Anyone would think she was buying a whole new wardrobe, or something. Maybe she was.

Deanna glanced across to the other side of the car where Kait was placing the last of her bags into the rear seat. She'd elected to wear one of the many dresses she'd purchased. It was as ugly as hell. A big floating caftan thing. Deanna decided Kait's old dress sense was much better than this new Kait. But then, maybe that was the point. A whole new wardrobe, a whole new Kait. As if she was running away from something. Or someone. Kait wouldn't be the first woman to be doing that, so Deanna wasn't going to judge.

"There's one more thing I need," Kait said, tapping a finger to her lips. "I meant to get some sunnies. Do you mind waiting with the car? I won't be a mo."

"No probs." Deanna hoisted herself into the passenger seat and watched as Kait wove through the cars in the parking lot back toward the shopping mall. She could still hardly believe her luck that Kait had agreed to take her. It felt like she was off on an adventure. One sure way to rid Tamika from her system once and for all.

The day was already warm. Definitely another scorcher, high thirties at least. But it was something you had to get used to, living out here on the fringes of the desert. She was wearing her Hi-Vis workwear again today. It felt comfortable, gave her a certain sense of anonymity. And it meant she didn't have to decide on whether she was going to be all girly and feminine in a dress, just the way Tamika had liked, or Deanna, plain and unadorned in shorts and a tee.

Her duffel bag in the rear tray of the dual cab contained a smattering of clothes that weren't Hi-Vis. She kept some clothes at her parents' old house, just in case. So this morning, she'd thrown in a few sets of denim shorts, skirts, a pair of bathers, and a couple of half-decent T-shirts. She could always buy clothes on the way if she needed them. It was better to travel light. Belongings merely weighed you down.

Deanna shifted in her seat and fanned her face. The vehicle was sitting in the blazing sun and it was becoming like an oven in here. She opened the door to let in some air, then let her gaze roam over the interior of the cabin.

Time for a little snooping session.

Firstly, Deanna flicked open the little glove compartment right in front of her. To her surprise, there was nothing in there besides some registration papers. Most people usually had all sorts of shit stuffed in their glove compartments. Like boxes of tissues, random pens, half a packet of chewy. It was odd that Kait had none of these things.

Deanna lifted out the registration papers and took a quick look. The date on the top was yesterday. Had Kait bought this truck only yesterday? That was damn odd. But it might explain why she was constantly grinding the gears. Deanna had pegged her as a really bad driver, but perhaps it was because she wasn't used to a stick shift. Also, the name didn't match. This truck was registered to a Sally Smith. Had Kait stolen the vehicle? Deanna couldn't see Kait as the sort to jack a car. Weirder and weirder.

Deanna found much the same when she opened the lid on the little compartment between the two front seats. Nothing. No spare coins, no half-eaten candy. The space was almost sterile. And if Kait had bought—or should she say appropriated—the car yesterday, then it made sense.

A sudden idea sprang into Deanna's mind. One of her mates back in Kalgoorlie had owned a dual cab, much like this one. In Mal's car, the rear seats had a small space behind them. A kind of storage space. It wasn't very big, and if you didn't own one of these cars, you might not know about it. You had to click the little button on the top of the rear seat, and the backrest would magically fall forward.

Deanna hopped out of the passenger seat and opened the rear door. She found the little button and pushed it. The rear backrest sprang open, but only a little, all the bags they'd stuffed in the back hampering its movement. Deanna stood on her tiptoes and peered into the small alcove.

Nothing.

Perhaps Kait hadn't discovered the little peculiarity of this car yet.

But Deanna wasn't finished. She closed that door and went around to the rear of the driver's side, popping that back seat open as well.

And voilà. A black backpack stared up at her from the dim recess. Now, that was more like it. A surge of guilty pleasure went through her veins. Almost like a hit of cocaine.

Deanna turned around and craned her neck, checking to make sure Kait wasn't already on her way back. She'd better leave the bag where it was, just in case. Reaching in, Deanna undid first one snap and then the other, and opened the flap.

Holy moly.

It was full of money. So much cash. Deanna had never seen that much cash in her life before. What the fuck…?

Deanna gave a secretive smile. Now, this was a mystery she could really sink her teeth into. What was Kait planning on doing with all that money? And where had it come from? She knew there was something hinky about this woman. But there must be hundreds of thousands of dollars in there.

A noise behind Deanna had her nearly jumping out of her skin. She swung her head around but it was only some old guy getting into the car next to her.

Shit. Hurriedly, she refastened the clasps on the backpack and slammed the backrest into place.

She was halfway around to the passenger side when Kait's voice drifted to her over the shimmering row of car roofs. "I got some." She waved a pair of sunglasses in the air above her head. "And I bought a packet of gummy bears in case we need a sugar hit." Kait beamed, as if she'd just solved the problem of world hunger.

"Great." Deanna slipped into her seat, ducking her head. "It's bloody hot out here, shall we get going?"

Kait started the car and turned on the welcome cool hit of air-conditioning. The trip should take them less than two hours. They'd be there around lunchtime. Deanna decided she'd better earn her keep and find some things for them to do once they reached the coastal town. As long as Kait kept up her charade of tourist-in-the-north, then Deanna was happy to go along with it.

"How about I find us a place to stay?" Deanna said, thumbing through her phone, as Kait popped a few gummy bears into her mouth. Deanna grabbed a handful as well. Gummy bears were irresistible.

Five minutes later, after directing Kait onto the main highway, Deanna had narrowed it down to two hotels. "Would you rather be near the river, or next to the beach? I'm assuming you don't want to go to the backpackers?"

"Oh, God, no, definitely not." Kait actually shuddered and Deanna snickered.

"There's the Kalbarri Beach Resort, or the Kalbarri River Retreat. They both look pretty cool. Or we could stay at the caravan park, they have basic cabins for rent."

"No," Kait replied slowly. "I'm on holiday, I want to stay somewhere nice."

Deanna slanted her a look but held in a smug smile. Of course Kait wanted to go somewhere nice. It was what she was used to, if all that money was anything to go by.

"The River Retreat looks good. A few little self-contained cabins, with their own porch and a view out over the river. Kind of rustic looking."

"Yes, let's do that," Kait said with determination.

Deanna glanced over at Kait. The figure-hiding caftan added to the oversized sunglasses made Kait appear like some kind of apparition out of a National Lampoon's holiday movie.

"I'll ring them and make a booking. I'll pay half the accommodation." They'd never discussed how the monetary thing would actually work. Deanna could well afford to pay for anything and everything on this trip, but Kait didn't know about her large inheritance. She preferred it that way. People looked at her differently when they found out she was rich. But it seemed Kait was also in the money. Which made them more or less equals.

Kait shot her an unreadable look. "No, I'll get this one. Tell them I'll pay cash when we arrive."

Deanna had to stop the words *I bet you will* from leaving her lips. She allowed herself a quiet smirk instead. "Thanks for paying, that's nice of you, li—" She shut her lips with a snap.

Now it was Kait's turn to smirk. Deanna noticed the curl of

her lip as she pretended to concentrate on the road. Deanna was determined to kick the *like* habit. Wasn't it strange, how she'd never even noticed she was saying it until Kait pointed it out? This might even turn out to be harder than kicking the ciggie habit, but she would do it.

Two hours later, just before they hit the Kalbarri city limits, Deanna directed Kait to turn the car onto a dirt road next to a small sign announcing the river retreat ahead. The Murchison River glinted in the distance.

"This looks…lovely," said Kait, parking the vehicle beside a building that said *office* and looking around. The country was dry, covered with a fuzz of sparse, spiky looking plants, dotted with a few large eucalyptus trees scantily spaced.

On Kait's suggestion, Deanna had booked two units, one for each of them. It'd be nice to have a whole room to herself. Back at the mine, she'd had a tiny donger, which was hardly big enough to swing a cat. But it hadn't bothered Deanna, because she hardly spent any time in her room. These rooms, however, were large and luxurious, with a little private veranda where you could sit and watch the sun set over the river.

The lady who checked them in was bubbly and red-faced, looking like she spent too much time in the scorching sun. Perhaps that same sun had gone to her head, because the woman wouldn't stop talking, going on in excited tones about how lovely it was to have them staying at her establishment, and how the river was only a short stroll away, and would they like pamphlets on the various activities here in Kalbarri, or would they like her to recommend somewhere nice to eat in town?

Kait was calm and serene in the face of the mini-cyclone of helpfulness the other woman projected, as if she were used to people sucking up to her. She probably was.

"I'm going to take a shower, and then a nap," Kait

announced after the owner had finally left them alone to investigate their rooms.

"Cool." Deanna was fine with that. "See you in a couple of hours. We can go and check out the town later, lik—" Deanna pursed her lips. Damnit. "See you later." She waved a hand and went inside her room and closed the door. The king-sized bed was set right in the middle of the room, with a kitchenette on one side and big, floor-to-ceiling windows opened to the malnourished country outside. Red dirt as far as the eye could see. It had a certain kind of beauty, which Deanna had learned to appreciate, especially working out in Kalgoorlie, where the flat land stretched on to the end of the earth and farther.

She fell backward into the soft embrace of the bed, arms out wide like she was falling into a cloud.

Now she had time to think. To let all those thoughts rolling around in her head percolate and perhaps come up with a plan.

First of all, she needed to decide whether she would reveal to Kait that she'd found her stash of money. A lot was riding on that single decision.

# CHAPTER SEVEN

Kait stared in wonder at the beautiful rock formations. Why had she never taken the time to come to Kalbarri before? A deep gorge dropped away in front of her, carved out by the Murchison River over millions of years. The riotous colors, red and white bands of rock, were so bright they almost hurt her eyes.

Kait waved away the hoard of flies all vying for a spot to land on her face. They were like little, black stealth bombers, intent on getting to her pink skin no matter how hard she waved.

"It looks like someone has piled a whole heap of orange pancakes one on top of the other," Deanna said gaily, her voice loud and excited. Some of Deanna's youthful enthusiasm was rubbing off on Kait, because she felt light on her feet this morning. More attuned to nature, or some such blather. Wanting to soak in this whole experience and hold it close in her heart.

She and Deanna had spent the whole day yesterday wandering around Kalbarri. It was so nice to pretend she was someone she wasn't. Just a normal person, doing normal, everyday things. She hardly let Dario intrude on her thoughts at all. She still wanted to turn around and tell Susan about everything she did and saw, however, and then the sorrow of her loss would push down on her until she could hardly breathe. Perhaps that mantle of grief would never leave her.

She'd embraced the tourist life like never before. After just chilling in their cabins on the first night they arrived, yesterday had been filled to the brim with touristy stuff. First cab off the rank had been feeding the pelicans on the foreshore in the morning. At first, the birds' long, clacky beaks had scared her. That and the fact they were nearly as tall as her. But they'd been surprisingly gentle and looked at her with wise, alien eyes and she'd become fascinated by the beasts. Pink Lake, or Hutt Lagoon as was its true name, had been amazing. It was nearly an hour away, south along the coast, and Kait has almost said she wasn't in the mood to drive. But when she'd seen the color of the water, it'd reminded her of flamingos or cotton candy and she'd been totally riveted. Could've sat there for hours on a nearby bench and stared at the water. Then they'd visited the craft stores and gift shops in the one lane Main Street, and Kait had found a gorgeous watercolor painting of the nearby coastline by a local painter that she just had to buy. The painter had captured the wild, vibrant colors of the red rocks and the azure water perfectly. Where she thought she was going to put it was anybody's guess, because she didn't have a wall she could call her own anymore.

The lady at the information bureau told them they should take their time to explore the gorges, and so they'd left it until today, setting off after a lovely breakfast of yoghurt and homemade granola, topped off with blueberry pancakes, Wilma, who ran the accommodation, was a great cook. She would miss the Kalbarri River Retreat, but she'd decided they should keep moving. They'd spend the whole morning here, perhaps do a short walk into the gorge and get on the road by lunchtime. It was too hot to stay long out in the midday sun anyway. They had no solid plan yet of where they were going to spend tonight, but Kait was starting to embrace the air of spontaneity Deanna exuded.

"Come and look." Deanna beckoned. "You can see the river through the opening. Exactly like it's framing a picture. Now I see why it's called Nature's Window."

Kait wandered over to where Deanna was pointing through the hole in the rock.

Deanna read from the information plaque attached to a metal pole. "This iconic attraction is a wind-eroded opening in the layered sandstone that frames a view of the river. Views of the gorge are available from the sealed path and lookouts before the final, rocky section. Please be careful near edges and avoid climbing on the fragile rock in or above the window." Deanna rolled her eyes. "Well, duh. You won't find me going anywhere near that edge."

Interestingly, the girl was still wearing her mining clothes. She obviously felt comfortable in them. Perhaps they offered a certain sort of anonymity. Deanna would be a stunning girl, if she dressed half decently. And therein might lay the problem. Deanna didn't want to attract attention. A form of camouflage. Her clothes must be terribly hot, however. Deanna had the long sleeves rolled up to her elbows, but that still left the long pants and heavy boots.

Kait was loving her new attire. These caftans were so light and breezy. Dizzying in their freedom. A ridiculous, floppy hat and garish sunglasses completed her disguise. Dario would most likely walk right on by her if he passed her in the street. It was so unlike what she was used to wearing. And who cared what she looked like? She certainly didn't.

They'd walked up from the parking lot along a dry, dusty path. The woman at the information bureau said it was often busy up here, but it was midweek and the middle of summer, so tourist numbers were down. They were the only two people around this morning. Which was great for a photo opportunity.

"Come and stand close," she said to Deanna as she positioned herself directly in the middle of the arch of rock. "Let's take a selfie." She giggled at the term. Look at her, taking selfies in Kalbarri, of all places.

Deanna leaned in and they made stupid faces while she clicked the button on her new burner phone. It wasn't nearly as good as her state-of-the-art iPhone, but it'd have to do.

"I want to take some too," Deanna complained, when Kait tried to move away. "Take your hat off, I can't even see you under there," Deanna said with a laugh.

Kait did as she was told, but then had a sudden thought. "Wait. You're not going to post it on your Instagram, or Facebook, are you?"

"What? Nah, I don't do them."

"What about that Snappy thing? And the clock one?"

"You mean SnapChat and TikTok?" Deanna laughed so hard, she doubled over. "No, I don't do them, either. This is just for me."

"Okay, as long as you promise," Kait said warily.

"Why, are you afraid someone's going to recognize you in that getup? I don't think there's much hope of that."

The young woman had a point. Kait leaned in and smiled for the camera. After Deanna had taken what felt like a hundred photos, Kait wandered over to the side of the pile of rocks constituting Nature's Window so she could stare down into the gorge.

She'd read somewhere that the gorges were over four hundred feet deep. A long way down indeed.

"You're a hard woman to track down, Kait De Luca."

She froze.

She didn't recognize the voice, but she knew it heralded her demise.

She wanted to turn and face her tormentor, but her feet were frozen to the red rock below.

"You led me on a merry chase, you did."

The voice was deep and gravelly, the menacing overtone turning her insides to water.

"Who the fuck are you?" Deanna said from behind Kait, belligerence oozing through her voice.

"None of your fucking business," the man growled in return.

Uh, oh. Deanna had nothing to do with this. She needed to warn her to stay out of it. If Kait was caught, she could at least save Deanna. She needed a distraction.

"Yes, it is my fucking business. You can't talk to her like that," Deanna said, and Kait turned in time to see her young friend striding up to a bulky, tattooed man—who was twice her size and looked as if he belonged in a biker gang—and getting right up in his face, snarling at him like a Doberman.

Kait had never seen this man before in her life, but she had no time to guess who he was. He knew her name and that was enough. Dario must have sent out his hounds to hunt her down after all. Her little note hadn't kept him at bay as long as she'd hoped.

In a frightening show of speed the man had Deanna by the neck. "Don't mess with me, little girl." Deanna froze for a second—shock could do that to you—but then started kicking out at the biker's shins.

"Stop that, you little shit." He squeezed tighter and Deanna stopped kicking, both her hands going to her throat as he cut off all her air.

"Don't hurt her," Kait begged.

The biker glanced her way and dragged Deanna over to where Kait stood, still frozen to the spot near the edge of the canyon. "Tell me where the money is, and I'll let her go," he said. The guy was a complete psycho. Kait didn't know from what dark gutter Dario had dug him up, but he was well suited to his job. Tall and broad-shouldered, bald as a badger, with tattoos on his head, he was intimidating, to say the least. But it was his cold, dead eyes that scared Kait the most. And he knew about the money as well. But she guessed that was Dario's main aim—recover the money first. She would just be an add-on to the man who caught up with her.

Deanna was making small noises, like a tortured animal. It was that sound that finally brought Kait to her senses. "Stop. Stop, I'll tell you where it is, just stop, will you?"

"That's more like it." The man released his tight grip on Deanna's neck, enough for her to suck in great gulps of air, but he didn't let go completely, keeping Kait at arm's length while his hand was still wrapped around Deanna's throat.

"It's in the back of the dual cab. I'll get it for you," Kait said dully.

"Good." He nodded approvingly. "And of course, Dario would like you to come back and explain why you thought you needed to steal from him."

Kait's mind went numb. She'd been hoping that just giving the money back would be enough. That he would let her free after that. But a small part of her knew Dario would never allow it. Would he kill her for her sins? That might be better than the alternative. Better than spending the rest of her life slowly dying from the small tortures he'd take great delight in inflicting upon her. Dario would never let her escape again. She'd blown her one and only chance.

Kait stared at the biker and shook her head.

But he merely grinned and said, "Oh, yes. You're coming back to Perth with me."

The numbness spread from Kait's brain, along her limbs, and down her chest. She felt heavy with the burden of the thug's words.

"Along with little miss feisty here."

"No." Kait wasn't having that. "You need to leave her out of it. She's an innocent bystander in all of this. You have to let her go."

Biker Man turned and seemed to consider Deanna for a second. "Hmm, you're a tasty morsel, ain't you? I bet you got a killer body hidden beneath all that clothing." His gaze raked over the young woman, and Kait's blood ran cold. "You and I can have some fun once I get this one back to her rightful owner." Keeping his hand on her throat, he turned her to look at him.

Deanna glared, then raised a hand and slapped him across the face with such force it snapped his head backward.

His reaction was swift and deadly. Releasing her, he slapped Deanna back so hard her hair flew around her face, and she cried out with pain. Then he threw her onto the ground, where her head hit the rocks with a sickening thud. Deanna groaned and writhed on the ground. Then the brute kicked her in the stomach. Once. Twice.

"Stop it!" Kait screamed. She charged at the man who was attacking her friend, pushing him with all her might, using her arms as battering rams. His leg was raised in the air, ready to aim another kick at Deanna's vulnerable stomach, and Kait had caught him off balance. He lurched, tried to step over Deanna's prone body, and lurched again.

A hand came up and grasped his ankle, tipping him sideways. He had no way to regain his footing in time. He stumbled forward in a headlong rush. One step. Two steps. Then he was gone.

Kait bent down when Deanna tried to sit up. She helped her to her feet, then arm in arm, they both leaned as far as they dared to peer over the edge.

"Oh, fuck," Deanna exclaimed.

Yep. Oh, fuck just about summed it up.

*Run*, shouted Susan emphatically in her head.

\* \* \*

"Do you think he's dead?" Deanna asked for the twentieth time. She was shaking, but she wasn't sure why.

"He didn't look very healthy," Kait replied, not taking her eyes off the road. Her hands were shaking as well, and she was driving way too fast, but Deanna said nothing.

"Should we call an ambulance?" Deanna wasn't sure why she asked this, but it felt like the right thing to do. They hadn't meant to kill the guy. Perhaps he was still alive, bleeding out at the bottom of the gorge. The idea made her sick to her stomach and she almost dry retched.

They'd sprinted back to the parking lot and jumped straight into the dual cab. The only other car in the lot was a dusty, black SUV with tinted windows. Kait drove out of there so fast the tires kicked up dust and gravel in a long stream behind them. Like a criminal fleeing a crime in a Dirty Harry movie. It was kind of exciting. If only she could stop her hands from shaking.

Deanna touched her throat. It hurt. She dropped the visor down and studied herself in the small mirror. Dark bruises were already forming around her windpipe and across the side of her face where he'd hit her. They were impressive.

At least Deanna now had an inkling of what Kait was running from.

"I'm so sorry," Kait said. "I didn't mean for you to get involved in any of this. I should never have picked you up in the first place." Kait hit the steering wheel with her hand. "Stupid. So stupid." It sounded like Kait might've been talking to herself, so Deanna didn't respond.

"Who's Dario?" Deanna asked, still staring at herself in the mirror.

Kait stopped muttering to herself and glanced at Deanna with a sheepish tilt to her mouth. "I guess you have a right to know. One of his thugs for hire nearly killed you."

"And threatened to drag me back to Perth to be some sort of sex slave," Deanna added helpfully. To be honest, that part had scared her more.

"Dario is my husband...was my husband. We're separated... I left him."

In a hurry by the looks of it. Deanna couldn't really say that she knew Kait well. They'd only been acquainted for less than three full days. But one thing she'd decided about Kait was that she was a woman with high morals. A woman of decency who wouldn't take the vows of marriage lightly. And so, Deanna decided that whatever reasons Kait had for leaving her husband, they must be good ones.

"He must miss you *a lot*," Deanna suggested. Anyone who sent a biker gorilla-man to get his wife back must either love her completely and utterly and couldn't bear to live without her. Or else...

Kait merely snorted. "That money is mine," she said.

It kinda sounded like the money was stolen, but Deanna didn't want to mention that, because Kait sounded so adamant.

"I'm entitled to that money. What's mine is his and what's his is mine. Right?"

Deanna screwed up her face in thought. Technically, that might be true. But try telling that to the ugly brute who'd had her by the throat. He didn't seem to think so.

She'd been looking for the right time to fess up to the fact that she knew about the money. Perhaps now, she didn't need to.

"How much money are were talking about?"

Kait turned away from the road to peer at her, an indecipherable look flashing across her face. Obviously, she was trying to decide if she could trust her. Deanna held her breath.

"A million dollars," Kait said.

Deanna drew out a long, low whistle. She was absurdly pleased that Kait had chosen to confide in her. It was more money than even she had guessed was in that bag.

"What are you going to do with it?"

"That money is going to save me," Kait stated.

Now, all the new clothes, and the car in a different name, and all the unconventional personalities were finally starting to make sense. "I can dig that," she said.

"You don't want to know why I left Dario?" Kait asked, a subtle edge to her voice that Deanna couldn't decipher.

"I'm sure you'll tell me when you're ready," she volunteered. It was true, most people told you their deepest, darkest secrets eventually, even when you didn't want to hear them. All it took was patience, and Deanna had always had plenty of that.

"Really?" Kait's eyes suddenly shone with unshed tears. What had she said to make the older woman cry?

"What?" she asked.

"Oh, nothing." Kait shook her head. "It's just that I lost a really dear friend recently. And she would've said the same thing. She never pushed to know things I wasn't prepared to tell. It's one of the reasons I loved her so much."

"I'm really sorry," Deanna said, then reached over and touched Kait's leg. She knew what it felt like to lose your best friend. She'd thought Tamika was her best friend. It'd broken her heart when she found out she'd been duped all along. Gullible, that's what Tamika had called her. Deanna didn't think she was gullible. She saw it as perhaps caring too deeply.

Kait shook her head as if to clear away those sad memories. "Anyway, the one thing I am going to tell you, is that Dario is a very dangerous man. And you should get as far away from me as you possibly can."

Deanna thought about the feel of Ugly Brute's hands

around her neck for a second. That part hadn't been fun. But he'd received his ultimate comeuppance. He was dead. Or really, really fucked up at the very least.

"I want to stick around. I'd like to help you, if you'll let me. Two heads are always better than one," Deanna said hopefully.

Kait shook her head but didn't reply; instead biting her lip and glaring at the windscreen.

After a few moments, Deanna decided that Kait's lack of a negative reply meant she wasn't going to say no. Besides, Kait needed to decide what to do with all that money. She couldn't keep carting it around in a black bag for the rest of her life. She needed Deanna's help. At least to get through the next few days. Deanna had knowledge about traveling in this area that might be the difference between Kait escaping her husband, or not. She knew how to deal with people, was way more worldly wise than the older woman would ever be. Kait seemed to have lived a highly sheltered life. But Deanna had lived the exact opposite. Even though her granny had done her best to raise Deanna right, her teenage years had been full of rebellion; where she'd joined a gang of sorts, and she'd even spent a few months living on the streets. Deanna knew she could be tough when it counted. Kait was soft and vulnerable. And for some strange reason, she felt protective of Kait.

As if the matter had already been decided, Deanna said, "We need to get off the road. Get rid of this car. They may have a description of it, which is possibly how they tracked you."

"What? Oh, yeah, I'd already thought about that. But how are we going to get around if we ditch my car?"

Deanna's mind was racing ahead. "There's a roadhouse at the turnoff to Monkey Mia."

"Monkey what?"

"Monkey Mia. Surely, you've heard of it?"

Kait rolled her eyes and shook her head. Wow, this woman really had led a secluded life. Everybody who lived in WA knew about Monkey Mia, didn't they?

"Are there monkeys there?"

"What? No." Kait was getting off track now. "I think, like, the place might've been named after a boat or something. It's not because there are monkeys there, that's for sure. The spot is renowned for its wild dolphins, like."

Shit, she was reverting back to her old manner of speech. It must be the stress.

Kait was looking more and more confused, so Deanna took a deep breath and dropped the subject. "Anyway, the Overlander Roadhouse is big. Lots of trucks and tourists stop there for fuel and food. We should go there. It's the only hint of civilization ahead, so we really have no choice."

"Okay. How far, do you think?"

"Two hours up the road," Deanna confirmed. Now that was settled, other questions crowded her mind. "Do you think the police might be on the lookout for us?" she wondered aloud. "You know, after we..." She made a chopping movement with her hand.

After a moment's hesitation, Kait said, "I don't think my husband will involve the police. Not unless he absolutely has to. He wants to get me back as quickly as possible and keep it all quiet, as if I never left. He won't want to reveal that missing money to anyone he doesn't have to."

Deanna wondered if that was true. The man sounded like he was one of those rich, arrogant types, who thought their shit didn't stink. A bit of a control freak as well. Deanna had met men like him. There were plenty of those fat bastards in Kalgoorlie. Men who were pompous and entitled because they'd made a lot of money getting rich on the back of the mining industry. All you had to do was stroke their egos and you could have them eating out of your hand. You didn't want to get on the wrong side of them, however. If he was one of those egotistical maniacs who thought they had a God-given right to control the women in their life, then perhaps Kait was correct about him.

"What about the dead man we left at the bottom of the gorge?" Deanna asked. "Won't the police be after us for him?"

Deanna glanced at Kait. She still had those ridiculous sunglasses on, but her face was terribly pale beneath the oversized accessory. She was scared. Scared of what they'd just done. Scared of being dragged back to that overbearing husband of hers.

"They might not be able to link us to him," Kait mused. "People fall to their death from up there all the time. Well, okay…not all the time, but you know what I mean. They might even think it's a suicide."

Deanna wasn't convinced, only time would tell. They'd have to keep an eye on the TV and radio news channels to make sure their names didn't come up.

"Right, so, we'll get rid of the car at the Overlander. Then what? What are you going to do with all that money?" Deanna asked pragmatically.

# CHAPTER EIGHT

The oncoming car headlights flared so brightly they nearly blinded him. Fucking tourists. No idea of the correct etiquette on the road. Jack Wolfe flicked his high beam on and then off, giving his truck horn a blast for good measure. He hoped he scared the fucking bejesus out of them as the white sedan roared past. They never turned their high beam down, however. Fucking tourists.

Only ten more clicks to the Overlander. He scrubbed a hand through his hair, tugging on the greasy, shoulder-length locks. He needed a shower. Bad. And a feed. Then perhaps a few hours' kip before he hit the road again.

He'd left Perth later than expected. The forklift driver at the warehouse had gone home sick an hour before Jack showed up to load his truck, and he had to wait nearly two hours for them to track down another one. Then he'd hit a traffic jam, a four-car pileup on the freeway; he'd been stuck for over an hour in that. Now he was going to have to drive through the night to get this load to Exmouth on time. At least he had one small consolation. He was his own boss, so he got to decide when he drove, and where. He'd taken this load as a favor to a friend. He was headed home anyway. And the money was good. This would be his last trip for a while.

He ached for the serenity of his house tucked away in the serenity of Cloudwater Bay. The place where his soul had finally found some peace. Two more days, and he'd be home. Three tops.

A roo flashed across the road in front of him. Lucky bugger. It missed the front bull bar by millimeters. It was a hazard of the job out here. He'd lost count of how many roos had died on his bull bar over the years. Driving a B-Double meant he had no room for error and definitely no room to swerve. It wasn't his fault if they were determined to throw themselves in front of his truck. He'd hardened his heart to those stupid, furry creatures. He didn't care if they lived or died; there were millions of them in the outback, anyway.

*Yeah, right, pull the other one. Keep telling yourself that and one day it might be true.*

Jack actually hated to see their poor, mangled bodies lying beside the road. He'd tried everything to stop them from jumping in front of him. His truck was lit up like a Christmas tree, with lights all around the outside of his cab and festooned across his bumper. He had *three* kangaroo repelling whistle thingamabobs affixed to the front. But none of it worked.

Ten minutes later, the lights of the Overlander Roadhouse loomed out of the darkness. Three trucks were parked in the truck bays and a fourth was filling up with diesel. He'd park and grab a burger and fries first. Then fill up his truck, pay for a nice, hot shower and snuggle down to sleep for a couple of hours. Exmouth was another seven hours from here. If he left before dawn, he'd have plenty of time to get the load to the warehouse by the midday deadline. It was cooler sleeping during the night. Trying to sleep in his bunk behind the seat during the day would be like sleeping in an oven.

"Hiya, Martha." He gave the woman behind the counter in

the restaurant his customary greeting.

"Hi, Jack." She batted her false eyelashes at him. "Hey, I've got a good one for you tonight."

"Go on, then," he said good naturedly.

"Why does Santa Claus have such a big sack?"

"I don't know."

"Because he only comes once a year." Martha laughed so hard she had to bend over to catch her breath, giving Jack an eyeful of her very plump bosom.

Jack laughed along with her. That was pretty good.

Martha had been making eyes at him for as long as he could remember. They kept up a friendly banter, and he went along with her bawdy jokes. But who was she kidding? She must be twenty years older than him. He was merely entertainment for her, a way to while away the boring hours behind the till.

"Same as usual?" she asked through her laughter.

He was still watching her heaving bosom. It did have a lovely bounce to it. "Yeah, thanks." Sliding his credit card over the reader, he waited for the beep before peeling off to find a table. The diner was full tonight. Rather unusual for this time of the year. Only two tables were free, and he made a beeline for the small one tucked away in the corner. Slouching down in the seat, his stomach rumbled. He hadn't realized he was hungry until right now. The burgers here were pretty good. For fast food. It was another necessary evil of living on the road for weeks at a time. He'd soon be back to eating fresh food again once he got home.

With nothing better to do until his burger arrived, he perused the other patrons. Three men, all wearing Hi-Vis filled a table near the counter. He recognized one of the truckies and tipped his head in greeting as Big Henry met his gaze. The other two must be from over east. They didn't look new to the circuit, but he didn't recognize them either.

Two women sat at the table between himself and the three men. The older of the two had stunning red hair. Even though she did have it tucked all the way up into a baseball cap that had the Overlander logo on the front, enough was peeking out the bottom to notice the color. And when she turned to gaze around the room, he saw jade-green eyes that went nicely with the hair. Pity about the caftan; he couldn't really tell what kind of body she was hiding underneath. The blonde was much younger. Pretty, if you liked that kind of thing, but she was wearing Hi-Vis too, which confused him a little. They looked like an odd couple. But then again, it took all kinds of people to make the world go around. Mother and daughter perhaps?

Jack's gaze slid to the next table, and he studied the two young blokes stuffing burgers in their mouths. Tourists, definitely. Probably on their way to Carnarvon or Coral Bay for some snorkeling, judging by their board shorts and thongs. Another table held four men and one woman, all farm hands by the looks of them—dirty and rough—having a meal and drink on their way back to the station.

He spent the next few minutes people-watching, making judgements about all the patrons and how they lived their lives. It was interesting, trying to see if he could figure out who a person was just by their clothes and what they were eating, by their mannerisms and speech. It was a hobby of his, and he was getting pretty good at pegging people.

His introspection took him back to the table next to him, where the two women had their heads close together in a heated discussion. Were they together perhaps? A cougar with her much younger girlfriend?

All of a sudden, the blonde stood and sashayed over to Big Henry's table. He couldn't hear what she was saying over the hubbub of all the other customers, but her body language was pretty clear. She was trying to charm a lift from them.

He'd seen it before.

Jack lowered his brow in a frown. Big Henry had a reputation for being handsy. He hoped the young blonde knew what she was getting into. And the other two truckies? Well, they were unknown entities. They could be perfectly legit, but by the way the one on the left was eyeballing the young chick, he'd hazard a guess he'd be asking for some form of payment before he let the ladies out of his cab.

Why would these two women need a lift? The idea was intriguing. But none of his business.

Martha's large bosom suddenly blocked his view as she placed his burger, fries, and a chocolate milk on the table in front of him. "Bon appétit," she said in a bad French accent. His mouth watered as the smell of bacon and cheese and pickle wafted up his nose. "I've got another good'un for you," Martha said with a lazy smile.

Jack listened politely, smiling though his enormous bite of meat and bun.

By the time Martha left his table, the two women had gone, and Big Henry and his mates were finishing up their meals.

He wondered vaguely if the girl had got what she wanted.

Twenty minutes later, he came out of the men's toilets feeling a little more human. The shower wasn't the best, but Martha kept it relatively clean—to entice the truckers to pay to use it no doubt. Now that night had fallen properly, the air had cooled. He stopped and tipped his head back. The stars were looking especially magnificent tonight. He couldn't wait to get home, sit out on the rear deck, and spend some time with those celestial bodies. Get lost in their depths for hours. That's what he most loved to do.

No time to ponder life and the universe now, however, he still had a job to do. He walked toward his truck.

"Hey, mister."

Jack turned to see a figure emerge from the shadows of the

ablution block. It was the young blonde from the restaurant. Another shape materialized beside her. Slightly shorter but holding her head high. Classy, even when she was wearing a caftan and a baseball cap.

"Yeah?" What did these two want?

"You own that truck?" The blonde gestured toward his rig.

He didn't answer.

She stepped closer, coming into the light cast from the overhead spotlight. She was gorgeous, he could see that now. But the bruise developing on the side of her face was an ominous feature.

"We're looking for a ride. Where're you headed?" She batted her eyelids, like she had with Big Henry. That wouldn't work on him.

He didn't need to tell her anything. And he certainly didn't need to give them a lift. There was something odd going on here. Something he couldn't put his finger on. Was that more bruises the blonde girl was trying to hide beneath the high collar of her work shirt?

"What happened to the other truckers?" he asked casually.

Her eyes widening slightly was the only giveaway that he'd surprised her.

"That bastard tried to feel me up when I climbed into his truck." The older woman stepped into the light, right beside Blondie.

"Yeah, he did," the young one sighed. "I had to kick him in the balls to make him back off," she added.

Ah ha, so the stories about Big Henry were true.

"I don't normally take—"

"We can pay you," the older woman said suddenly.

Well, now hold on a minute. That would be breaking the unwritten law. Hitchhikers didn't pay. And truckies didn't ask for money. It was an act of kindness. A rule of the road. They shouldn't be asking for *favors* either, but some of the blokes were bored and horny, with too much time on their hands and no respect for women.

"I don't want your money," he drawled. But he knew it was no use; he'd already made his decision. "Where you gals headed?"

"If you're heading north, as far as you'll take us," the blonde parried back.

"I'm due in Exmouth by lunchtime tomorrow."

"That'd be perfect." The girl smiled at him, and he was nearly bowled over. She belonged on some catwalk in Milan, not dressed in dirty mining clothes in the middle of the bloody desert. *It takes all kinds,* he reminded himself.

"Jump in."

"Thank you," the redhead said. She'd seemed happy to let Blondie do all the talking, but he'd bet a pot of lobsters that she was the brains behind whatever scheme they had cooking.

"All good," he replied. "I need to fill her up, then we'll get on the road." So much for his planned sleep. He'd be all right to keep going, though; he'd done it before. These two could help keep him awake. And he'd buy a couple of Red Bulls when he paid for the diesel.

"You can chuck your bags in my bunk, if you like." Jack pointed through the curtains and the redhead poked her head into the gap.

"He's got a bed back there," she said to the younger one in a tone that testified she'd never been in the cabin of a truck before.

"I know, most truckies sleep in their cabs," Blondie replied. An old hand at taking lifts, it seemed.

Redhead followed Blondie's lead and threw her large duffel bag into his bunk. But she kept the smaller, black backpack nestled at her feet. Something precious in there, he surmised, but didn't comment. Not his business.

# CHAPTER NINE

Within ten minutes, the driver had his truck refueled and was grinding through the gears to get up to speed on the highway. Kait peered through the windscreen, not sure at all where this was going. She checked her backpack was still securely sitting at her feet for what might've been the hundredth time. Kait felt terribly exposed carrying around that much cash. She was beginning to wish she'd damn well left it where it was. It was causing more problems than it was solving.

Deanna had come up with this harebrained plan, and with no other bright ideas, Kait had agreed to it. She tugged her baseball cap down lower over her brow. It was a foolish attempt to try and camouflage her hair. It seemed to work for the celebrities, but somehow, Kait doubted it was working for her.

Deanna didn't think she needed to disguise herself. She justified it by saying the husband was looking for Kait, but no one knew about Deanna. That may no longer be true. What if that biker guy had phoned in before he approached them? What if they'd been spotted at the parking lot to Nature's Window by someone else? Another tourist. Or worse, what if someone had seen the whole thing when they tipped the man over the edge and was reporting them to the police right now?

Kait put her hand over her mouth to hold in the low moan that was clawing its way up her throat. It was better not to think about it. Not think about that man's crumpled body, looking like a broken toy at the bottom of the gorge. One thing was for sure; Dario hadn't fallen for her lie about going to see her sister if he already had his thugs on her tail a mere three days after she'd vanished. Monika's face flashed in front of her eyes. Perhaps it was a good thing, at least Monika wouldn't have to bear the brunt of Dario's wrath.

How had he found her? She'd been ultra-careful about only using cash to pay for everything, and her old iPhone was still turned off. Could it have been a mere coincidence? She doubted it. Dario didn't have enough men at his command to be scouring every inch of Western Australia. Was it her new truck? Had Dario somehow figured out her different mode of transport already? It was a good idea of Deanna's to get rid of the vehicle, for many reasons. Not a small one being that the police might be looking for it. And them. But also to put Dario off their trail.

"I'm Jack Wolfe," the man said, holding out his hand to Deanna, who was sitting in the middle seat, breaking Kait's train of thought. Deanna had offered to sit in the small dolly seat—that's what the driver had called it—between the two main bucket seats. They could swap later on, because it didn't look nearly as comfy as hers.

"I'm Deanna," she said, shaking his hand quickly. "And this is Kait." Jack leaned forward to peer around Deanna, but thankfully, didn't try and take her hand. He should really keep both hands on the wheel. He seemed a tad too blasé for her liking. This truck was huge. It felt like they were rushing along too fast, twenty feet off the ground, as if they were on some carnival ride. Or a giant Russian missile. Kait clung to the edge of the seat as she watched the nighttime desert race by.

Kait hadn't had a really good chance to check this Jack person out. She'd noticed him back in the diner but had dismissed him as she'd been too preoccupied with Deanna and her attempt to cajole those other truckies. Kait clenched her fist; she still wanted to smack that one who'd slipped his hand audaciously between her thighs as she'd stepped into the cabin. Then, when they'd approached Jack outside later, the weak overhead lights had cast all sorts of odd shadows over his features. By the lights of the dashboard, she could see he had a friendly face, with dimples in each cheek, at least three days' growth, and longish hair that he kept pushing back from his brow. It suited him, gave him a bohemian sort of vibe, a little out of character with the rest of the truckies they'd met so far, who were all balding, with a beer gut, an attitude, and covered in tattoos. While she'd noticed the odd tattoo poking out from the sleeve of Jack's shirt, that's where the similarities ended. Jack looked fit and healthy, as if he lived right. Which was also odd if he actually spent all his days driving a truck. He looked at ease in his casual blue jeans and black T-shirt, and Susan would've definitely approved. She might've even called him McDreamy. She'd loved Grey's Anatomy so much.

"Why you gals hitching?" The question was asked lightly enough, the man made it sound like he was asking it merely to pass the time. But she wasn't fooled. This guy was smart. Even if he was good-looking.

Deanna had sold Kait's dual cab to an old miner staying in the accommodation block out the back of the Overlander after she overheard him telling a mate that he needed a reliable vehicle to get him out to his gold prospecting lease, as his old one had carked it just the other day. He was over the moon with his purchase. And why wouldn't he be. Deanna had asked a measly two thousand dollars for the car. She said she needed to sound legit, otherwise, she would've sold it for a few hundred, just to get rid of it. Hopefully, the vehicle would be trundling down some long-forgotten road out in the desert soon, well away from prying eyes. A good way to make the car disappear without actually setting it on fire, which had been Deanna's first plan.

"Our car carked it," Deanna said, without missing a beat.

Kait had to stop herself from snorting at Deanna's use of the greasy, old miner's term.

"We might buy a new one when we get to Exmouth," Deanna went on helpfully. "We're sort of on a working holiday, like."

Kait gave an involuntary wince. Deanna was slipping back into old habits.

"We both want to see a bit of this big, brown land of ours. But we're doing it on the cheap, you know. Drifting wherever the wind takes us, like a pair of gypsies." Deanna was prattling, and Kait wished she wouldn't keep embellishing things. They were in enough deep shit as it was.

Kait's head was all in a jumble. She'd killed a man this morning. Not that he hadn't deserved it. And not that she'd meant to kill him. It was his own fault, really. If he'd stopped attacking Deanna when she'd screamed at him, maybe she wouldn't have pushed him. It'd been an accident. Self-defense.

But would the police believe that?

"I see," Jack replied. He had very expressive eyebrows. And right at this moment, they were creeping up his forehead, as if he didn't quite believe the words coming out of her mouth. Smart man. Which might be a problem for them. They needed to ditch him as soon as they got to this Exmouth. "You know it's heading into the wet season up north?"

"Yeah, so?" Deanna replied laconically.

Wet season? What the hell did that mean?

"So, you know they get cyclones up there? And the roads can sometimes get cut. You might not be able to drive anywhere in a month or so."

"Yeah, yeah, we know all that." Deanna waved a casual hand. Which put Kait's mind at ease, a little. But she still needed to find out more about this wet season, and what it entailed.

"Do you mind if we turn on the radio?" Deanna asked. "I'd like to hear some tunes."

Jack nodded. "Go for it. It's digital, so you should pick something up."

Good idea. Kait threw Deanna a grateful sideways look. They might catch a news broadcast at the same time. Find out if they were wanted criminals across the state.

Deanna seemed to be extraordinarily good at this. She was treating it almost like it was a game. But it was the furthest thing from a game you could get—more like a nightmare.

Deanna leaned forward and fiddled with the knob, trying to find a decent station. As she did so, Kait caught a glimpse of the bruises still forming on Deanna's neck. Oh, Lord, that poor girl. Kait suppressed a shudder at the memory of the tattooed man squeezing Deanna's neck until she could no longer breathe. They'd tried to hide the marks by making sure Deanna's Hi-Vis shirt was buttoned all the way to the top and the collar up. The mark on Deanna's face was less pronounced, but they still needed to buy some makeup to cover it at their next stop—wherever that might be. She was pretty sure Jack had noticed the bruises, even though he made no comment.

"Do you live in Exmouth?" Kait asked over the top of Deanna's head. It couldn't hurt to keep him engaged in conversation. At least that'd keep him away from other, more dangerous topics.

"No. But I am on my way home. I live a lot farther north, near Broome."

"Oh, Broome." At last, a place she'd heard of. Dario had taken her there years ago, said it would be romantic and restful. Which it had been, up to a point. "That's where they have the staircase to the moon, is that right?" Dario had planned their trip at the wrong time of the year to see that particular phenomenon, but Kait wished she'd been able to watch the full moon rise over the tidal flats, like it was described in the brochure. It sounded amazing.

"Yes, that's right." Something about the way he said it had her antenna buzzing.

"But what? You think it's overrated?"

"No, not at all." He hesitated. "I think it's become highly overrun with tourists, though."

Ah ha. He lived in a tourist town, yet he didn't appreciate the tourists.

"And Broome will be absolutely mobbed this month. The strawberry moon will draw them in by their thousands."

"Strawberry moon?" Kait rolled the words around on her tongue. It made her think of cocktails and chocolate. Hinted at fairies and cotton candy and all kinds of special things. She *would* like to see that.

"Yeah, there's supposed to be a pink super moon rising on the twentieth, I think. But it won't be a proper staircase to the moon, because you need extremely low tides for that, and they don't happen during the wet season. It'll still be pretty spectacular, however." Jack dragged a hand through his hair to push it back from his face. The unkempt look never normally appealed to Kait. Long hair on most men just didn't suit. On Jack, however...

Not that she should be noticing anything like that. She was a criminal on the run. From her violent husband at the very least, and now possibly from the police as well. But even in the sickly blue-green glow cast by the truck's dashboard lights, Kait liked the way Jack's square jaw jutted ever so slightly forward and the way his brow furrowed as he concentrated on the road ahead.

The twentieth was around two weeks from now, Kait calculated. Would Dario think to look for her in Broome?

"But I live in a little place on the other side of Broome, so I don't have to deal with the tourists," Jack continued.

"What little place?" Deanna asked, sitting back in her seat suddenly. A country and western song that Kait didn't recognize—probably because she'd never listened to country and western in her life—crooned from the speakers in the dashboard. Was this the best Deanna could do?

"What?" Jack raised a confused eyebrow.

"Where do you live? I heard you say you don't live in Broome." Deanna jiggled a little to get comfier in her seat.

Jack hesitated for a split second. "It's a small settlement called Cloudwater Bay. Not big enough to be called a town. Just a few beach shacks, really. It's pretty isolated. We don't even have a general store."

Kait's ears pricked up at the mention of the word *isolated*.

"Sounds cool," Deanna gushed. "What do you do out there?"

"Most folks who live out there like the solitude. Getting away from the rat race."

Deanna nodded encouragingly.

"People like to fish. There're heaps of barramundi up there. Anywhere a creek or river meets the ocean is a good spot, really. We've got Angel Creek nearby. Gotta watch out for the crocs, though."

"Do you mean crocodiles?" Kait squeaked, unable to help herself.

"Yeah, lots of big'uns around. But they won't hurt you as long as you know what you're doing."

"What about you, do you like to fish?" Deanna asked, frowning at Kait, and shaking her head.

"A little," Jack replied. "But the main reason I'm heading home right now is to help with the cleanup."

"What, like a rubbish collection?"

"Yes, but much bigger. Every six months a group of us get together to gather up all the ghost nets. We're all volunteers," Jack added.

Deanna already seemed to be more than half mesmerized by Jack, but when he mentioned ghost nets, Kait decided that's when she actually started fawning over him.

"Ghost nets? What are they? That sounds spooky. Tell me, tell me," Deanna squeaked.

Kait had to admit, it piqued her interest too, and she watched Jack with fascination.

"They are scary, but not for the reasons you think." Jack's voice took on a serious tone. This was clearly something he was passionate about. "A ghost net is a fishing net that's been lost or abandoned at sea by unethical fishermen. Often by people fishing illegally in our waters." Jack's frown deepened. "Because of the way the currents work in the Indian Ocean and the Timor Sea, nets from all over get washed onto our shores."

"So they pollute the water and the beaches. Fill them up with plastic," Deanna said helpfully.

"Yes, that's part of the problem. But not the worst bit. The nets still catch all kinds of marine animals, especially turtles and seals, who are then left to die a slow death of starvation or drowning. They are the real ghosts of the ghost nets."

"That's horrible," Kait said, staring at Jack. "Why isn't our government doing something about it? Send all these illegal fishing boats back to their own countries." Outrage was burning a hole in her chest, replacing the fear that'd been a heavy weight in her chest. It felt good to have something else to think about.

Jack made a cynical noise at the back of his throat.

"Believe me, they're trying. But these fishermen are determined. And often desperate. They have starving families to feed. So we do what we can by removing as much of the vile stuff as we can find from the beaches and close inland shores. We're part of a group led by indigenous rangers."

"Wow, that's amazing." Deanna was now making goo-goo eyes at Jack. Kait had to stop the girl before she did something stupid, like throw herself into his lap while he was driving. Kait wouldn't put it past her.

"That's a great thing to do. Very civil-minded of you." Kait touched the brim of her hat. She wanted to take the ridiculous cap off, it was getting itchy, but she dare not.

"I'd like to help," Deanna declared.

"I think we should talk about that first." Kait gave Deanna the hairy-eyeball to stop her making rash decisions before they'd had a chance to come up with a plan.

"Oh, right," Deanna said, growing subdued.

They all lapsed into a silence as they each considered ghost nets.

The music on the radio faded, and an announcer came on with the midnight news. Wow, was it midnight already? Kait should be feeling tired after the day they'd had. But she was more wired than anything else.

"The body of a man has been found in Z-Bend Gorge. Police aren't treating his death as suspicious but would like to talk to anyone who was in the vicinity of Nature's Window early this morning."

Kait stopped breathing. Her world seemed to spin. She didn't hear the rest of the announcer's words.

Then Deanna said, as casual as you like, "Oh, that poor man. Do you think he jumped?"

"What?" Jack shot her a look. "Sorry, I wasn't listening."

"Never mind."

Kait could hardly believe their luck. Had they really escaped with their crime that easily?

# CHAPTER TEN

"I think you should stay in Exmouth," Kait said. "I think it's time we parted ways."

"Well, I don't." Deanna crossed her arms and glared at Kait. The older woman had no right to say that to her, after all they'd been through together. They were standing at the side of an enormous warehouse, the corrugated iron walls radiating heat back at them, while Jack unloaded his truck by the rear dock. "We're in this together now, whether you like it or not. We're partners in crime. We both had a hand in that man's death. We're joined in a common need now."

Deanna was beginning to feel that she and Kait had become close, like Kait was a sister from another mother. Friends. Obviously, this wasn't the way Kait saw things, however. And it made her mad. And a little bit pitiful.

"I didn't want to drag you into this in the first place." Kait's eyes were red rimmed. Probably from lack of sleep— they'd driven through the night, Jack stopping near dawn so he could grab a few hours' kip, as he called it, while Deanna and Kait had tried to sleep in the two front seats, with limited success. Deanna suspected Kait's red eyes were also a result of worry. Kait was a definite stress head. Maybe she should teach her some meditation techniques. Either that or tell her to take a chill pill, because she was seriously freaking Deanna out.

"You didn't *drag* me into anything." Deanna softened her tone, hoping to appeal to Kait's logical side. "I practically forced you to take me with you." Deanna was determined to win this argument. Kait needed her. She'd be lost without her. Kait wasn't very worldly wise. Actually, she was pretty clueless when it came to living on the road. Deanna had experience traveling up and down this big state of theirs. And for some strange reason, she also felt…protective of the older woman.

It was an odd feeling, and one she couldn't rightly pin down. She didn't really want to dig into the psycho-babble of her feelings and how her parents dying while she was still so young had a bullshit effect on the rest of her life. She was sure that buried deep inside was probably an answer to the reason why she had an overwhelming need to look after Kait the way she wished someone had looked out for her, but right now was not the time to delve into those issues. Preferably never, if Deanna had her way. But definitely not right now.

She decided to force the issue. "You have no idea what you're going to do next, do you?"

When Kait didn't answer immediately, Deanna pressed harder. "Come on, Kait, tell me your plan. Where will you go so that your husband can't find you?"

Kait stared belligerently back at her, tugging the brim of her hastily bought cap down over her eyes. "That's not your concern."

Deanna had an ace up her sleeve, but she was loath to use it. If she told Kait that she had to take her with her, or she'd go to the police, Deanna knew Kait would agree. But all that hard-won trust would be lost. And trust was a big issue for Kait; Deanna had worked that much out. Having a domineering brute of a husband who would rather see her dead than leave his side might have something to do with that. But Kait also seemed to have a problem trusting her own judgement. Like she second-guessed every decision she ever made. Which was another reason she needed Deanna nearby.

"It is my concern," Deanna countered. "I'm worried about you. Wouldn't you worry about me if it were the other way around and we parted company?" She wanted to use the words *isn't that what friends do?* but she was afraid it would come out all whiney and needy.

"Of course, I would," Kait replied without hesitation.

"Well, isn't it better if we stick together? Who else can we rely on? I want to stay with you. I need to stay with you, Kait." Deanna touched Kait's arm. "Do you hear me?"

"Yes, I hear you." Kait sighed and slumped against the wall. Then immediately stood up again. "Wow, that's bloody hot."

Deanna suppressed a giggle. "Exmouth is hot. But you'll have to get used to it. It's only going to get hotter, the farther north we go." A surge of relief filled her. Kait wasn't going to send her away. Not today, at least. That was one hurdle down. Now to get Kait to agree to her next plan.

"We should get Jack to take us too Broome."

"What? No!" Kait shook her head emphatically. "That's not an option. We've already been with him too long. We need to find our own way from here."

"But Jack is our best bet," Deanna argued. "At least we know we can trust him not to molest us." That stopped Kait in her tracks. After that trucker had felt her up, Kait had suddenly developed a greater distrust of men. Or perhaps it'd been before that, but Deanna hadn't noticed. Actually, it was definitely before that, because when Deanna thought about it, Kait had a snake of a husband who sent other men to do his dirty work. Kait probably hadn't trusted men in a very long time. Again, another trust issue with Kait. Whatever; she was going to use the fact that Jack seemed to be one of the more trustworthy of the male species out there. And better looking too. Hell, even she was attracted to him, which was practically unheard of if you took his age into account.

"We need to get as far away from Perth as we can, and he's going in the right direction." It was true. Deanna had been mulling this over for most of the morning as they rolled down the road toward Exmouth.

"I thought we were going to buy a car here," Kait said, fanning her face. Deanna could sympathize. It was getting hotter by the second just standing here in the alleyway in the blazing midday sun.

"The less we show our face around town, the better," Deanna countered. It was a spur-of-the-moment comment, but the more she thought about it, the more logical it sounded. If the police were looking for them—which was a big *if*, as the cops were completely clueless when it came to that guy in the gorge—then they needed to stay out of sight. "It might take us precious hours, or even days, to track down a car suitable for our needs. And then we don't even know where we're going. But we could be back on the road tomorrow, with Jack doing all the driving."

"It's hot," Kait said, pulling up the hem of her caftan and waving it around her legs. "Can we go and find some shade?"

"Not until we make a decision." Deanna nearly stamped her foot. Kait was too easily distracted by petty physical hardships. She should try working on a mine site for a few days, that'd harden her up. "Besides, did you hear what Jack said about those ghost nets? I have to see them, Kait. I have to help him with the cleanup. Something about those nets floating aimlessly in the ocean…" Even as she said the words, she got tingles up her spine. She was meant to help; she just knew it.

"Fine." Kait waved agitatedly at a fly buzzing around her face. "Let's go to Broome. I'm sure I'll regret it, but..."

"That's great." Deanna couldn't help it, she actually hugged Kait. "You won't regret it. I know it's the right decision." And she did. Perhaps she had a tiny bit of clairvoyance in her. But she often got tingles when she was on to a good thing, as if some sixth sense were leading her in the right direction. Although her tingles had been wrong about Tamika, she remembered darkly. But now that she thought about it, maybe there hadn't actually been tingles when she first met Tamika. She'd been so overwhelmed by the stark beauty of the other woman that she'd forgotten to listen to her body.

"One thing you've failed to mention, is how you're going to convince Jack to take us with him," Kait said as Deanna released her.

"He won't be a problem." Deanna waved away Kait's concern. They'd manage to convince him somehow. Jack was a softie at heart, despite his hardened, truckie demeanor. Deanna had already worked out that much.

They'd said their goodbyes at the truck, as Jack jumped out to go and talk to the warehouse foreman, and he wasn't expecting to see them again. But during the trip up to Exmouth, Jack had mentioned he was looking forward to a better sleep tonight, in a proper bed, and that he'd continue his journey tomorrow. So, she knew he'd be staying in town tonight. Then she'd noticed a pen he'd left in the console of the truck, bearing the name of a hotel on the outskirts of town.

So Deanna was pretty sure she knew where to find him. It was so much fun playing amateur sleuth.

"We need to get our disguises worked out. That baseball cap isn't working. You need to dye your hair a less obvious color, and perhaps cut it as well."

"Cut my hair?" Kait took a step back, as if Deanna had actually slapped her. Deanna continued as if she hadn't seen the shocked look on the other woman's face.

"And you need to find something else besides that ridiculous caftan. You look like a bloody bird of paradise. It makes you more obvious, not less."

Kait looked down at her dress. "You might be right."

The black backpack with all the money was slung across Kait's shoulder, and she had a death grip on the strap. She was going to attract even more unwanted attention if she kept acting all suspicious like this. They needed to do something more practical with that money, too. She hoped Kait didn't think that she was sticking to her like glue just because of the money, because that just wasn't true. Perhaps it was time to reveal a little of the truth about her own financial circumstances. At least that'd put one of Kait's many trust issues to bed, if she didn't think Deanna was trying to steal all her money.

\* \* \*

Deanna scanned the room. "There he is. I told you he'd be here," she crowed.

"Poor man," Kait mumbled. "He has no idea what's about to hit him."

"Come on." Deanna towed Kait behind her as she made her way toward Jack's table. They simultaneously pulled out a chair, one on each side, and sat down uninvited. He looked up from his meal, then pursed his lips and stared at them, not speaking.

"Hi, Jack. Remember us?" Deanna decided to go with the flirty angle.

He continued to glare at them, still not saying a word. He was playing hardball, then.

"Guess what? We're staying at this hotel, as well. Isn't that a coincidence? We saw you from across the room, and Kait said we should buy you dinner. You know, as a thank you for the lift, lik—" Deanna stopped herself just in time. That little word kept trying to pop out. It was a harder habit than she thought to break.

"Right." Jack went back to eating his meal. Some sort of Caesar salad, if she wasn't mistaken. Salad? A truckie eating salad? She filed that away for further investigation later. He didn't ask them to join him, but Deanna ignored his blatant go-away vibes and leaned her elbows on the table. Kait followed her lead, but she gave Deanna a sideways look that spoke of growing panic. She of little faith. They were committed to this scheme, and she wasn't going down without a fight. She'd conquered much more inflexible men than Jack Wolfe before.

With an uneasy flick of her wrist, Kait took off her baseball cap and shook out her new hairstyle.

"What happened to your hair?" Jack seemed genuinely shocked, and Deanna was pleased they'd finally got a reaction out of him.

Deanna quite liked Kait's new color. Raven, the box had said. And it was exactly that. Like shiny black ink, Kait's hair did indeed remind Deanna of a raven's feathers. She hadn't been able to convince Kait to chop it off. Kait wasn't having a bar of the cute little pixie cut that Deanna thought would look great on her. But the color did the job, for now. It certainly gave Kait a different look. More sophisticated. But also, slightly more wild and mysterious. They'd done it over the bathroom sink in the hotel room this afternoon.

"Oh, this?" Kait plucked at a strand of hair. "I dye my hair different colors all the time. The red was a dye job, too." Kait was doing a great job of lying through her ass. She applauded the older woman; Deanna couldn't have done better herself. Maybe some of her style was finally starting to rub off on Kait.

Jack didn't comment about Kait's change of apparel, but his eyes raked up and down her frame a few times. Maybe he liked what he saw. Kait was a good-looking woman. And around the same age as Jack, if she wasn't mistaken. She'd changed into some of the more conservative clothes they'd bought back in Geraldton. A nice pair of dark-blue capris and a T-shirt with blue and white flowers all over. Much more sedate; now she'd blend in with the rest of the crowd.

Deanna had changed as well, but her change wasn't as drastic. She figured Kait was the one with the ex-husband looking for her. Her hair was still her signature blonde, but it was now tied up in a tight knot at the nape of her neck. Just that simple arrangement changed the look of Deanna's features. It showed off her oval face to its best advantage. Made her look older, perhaps even a little wiser. But it also made the bruises from that brute stand out, and so she'd applied a few dabs of concealer to her face to hide them. And she was now sporting a pair of cargo shorts and a simple black tee, with a jazzy scarf borrowed from Kait to hide the other bruises on her neck, which were a lot darker and more stubborn than the one on her face. Biker Boy hadn't been gentle when he'd tried to strangle her. Gone was the Hi-Vis uniform. Because, as Kait had pointed out, the whole point of Hi-Vis clothing was to make you more visible. *Duh.* Deanna had thought she was hiding behind the manly clothing, but perhaps Kait was right.

They'd also got busy in town. Kait had found a Commonwealth Bank and opened an account, depositing twenty thousand dollars in it, much to the teller's surprise. It wasn't ideal; they required ID and Kait only had her normal driver's license so she had to open it in her own name. As soon as they stopped somewhere for longer than a day, Deanna would organize some fake papers for Kait. It wasn't hard, you just had to find someone willing to help. But they needed to stop carting around this ridiculous amount of cash with them. If Kait got mugged... It didn't bear thinking of. Deanna desperately hoped that you needed some sort of police clearance to find out details about people's bank details. She didn't really know, but surely Dario's reach didn't stretch quite as far as searching confidential bank records for new accounts. Unless he had corrupt friends in high places, but they couldn't cover every scenario, and if Dario did discover Kait's new bank account, at least they weren't staying in Exmouth long.

Kait had a further ten thousand just shoved in her purse, in an envelope, like it was a really fat shopping list or something equally useless. They'd decided to put the rest of the money in a storage unit.

Kait had argued and argued with Deanna, but finally she'd given in, because she had nothing better. They took the smallest unit they could hire, three meters square, and Deanna used her charm to get the guy at the counter to waive the need for ID, giving him a false name and address with a wink and a smile that held all sorts of promises she had no plan of following through with. All they needed then was their own padlock, and they had a secure spot to leave the money until they could think of something better. The black backpack had looked sad and lonely, tucked into one corner of the three-by-three room.

It was less than ideal, and it meant they'd have to come back to Exmouth at some stage to retrieve it. But at least if Dario found Kait, he wouldn't automatically get his money back.

Jack narrowed his eyes at both of them. Uh oh, was he getting suspicious? They couldn't have that.

"So, whaddya think? Will you let us pay for your dinner?" Deanna asked brightly, waving to a passing waiter, who ignored her.

"Depends," he said in his laconic tone. "What do you want in return?"

"We already told you," Deanna replied. "To thank you for bringing us this far."

"Cut the crap." He stopped eating and laid down his fork.

Shit, this was going south, fast. Jack was on to them. Kait shot her a look. Then she held up her hand as Deanna opened her mouth to say something.

"Look, Jack." Kait put her elbows back on the table and leaned in real close. "You're right, we do want something from you. I know we said we were looking forward to exploring Exmouth, and we couldn't wait to get out and do some snorkeling in Turquoise Bay. But the truth is, you really got Deanna all worked up when you started talking about those ghost nets. She wants to see them for herself." Kait tilted her head toward Deanna, who snapped her mouth shut and quickly made puppy dog eyes at Jack. "She wants to help you save the bloody ocean, or some such crap. She hasn't stopped talking about it all day." She gave Jack a conspiratorial glance. "And you and I both know how she can talk."

He nodded back. Like he understood what she was saying.

Holy shit, Kait was doing it. And here she was thinking that Kait was *her* prodigy.

"You want to help me collect ghost nets, huh?" Jack fixed her with his blue eyes. Considering her. She'd never noticed how pale they were before. Almost a light gray, now she really looked. A steely sort of light gray.

"Yes. Yes, I do." At least this part was no act. She really wanted to see those ghost nets for herself. Wanted to save a poor turtle, rescue the stranded sea life. Never before had she thought much about the environment; she'd been too busy looking after herself to worry about other creatures. But the way Jack told of those poor turtles dying of starvation, caught in a net without any hope of escape, had touched something deep inside her.

"Would you let me help?" she pleaded.

"We can always do with more volunteers," he replied. "Do you have any deep-water diving skills?"

"What? No. Do I need to know how to dive?" Her heart sank as he stared at her.

"Not necessarily. We're always in need of people who can get out in the water, but we also have some volunteers who work the beach and shallows."

Deanna covered her heart with her hand. "Oh, thank God. I thought you were going to tell me I couldn't come for a second?"

"What about you?" He turned that appraising gaze to Kait.

"What?" Kait looked startled for a second. "Oh, yes. I want to help clean up ghost nets, too."

Deanna wished Kait sounded a little more convincing.

Jack went back to eating his salad. "So you want to come to Cloudwater? And I'm guessing that you also want a ride in my truck?" he said through a mouthful but staring at Kait at the same time.

"Yes, please. That, too," Kait said.

Was Kait blushing? Why was she blushing? Was it because Jack had fixed her with his steely gaze? Weighing up her request? Or weighing up her? It was hard to tell.

"I'll be leaving before sparrow's fart tomorrow morning. It's a thirteen to fourteen hour trip. You girls up for that?"

"Of course we are," Kait answered in a heartbeat.

Deanna let out a gush of breath. "Oh, thank you, Jack." So much had been riding on Jack taking them with him that she suddenly felt faint with relief. Or was that hunger? She was so famished she could even eat Jack's salad. She waved the waitress over, and this time the woman in the short skirt and low-cut top saw her and waved back.

"Where are you guys thinking of staying when you get to Cloudwater Bay? There're no hotels out there. Nothing but sand, the ocean, and a few shanties. And it's a fair way from Broome, so unless you get a car…" Jack surmised with a hint of a wry smile touching the corner of his lips.

Oh. He had them on that one. They hadn't thought that far ahead.

# CHAPTER ELEVEN

Jack knew he was being taken for a ride. He knew it down to the marrow of his bones, but he couldn't help himself. Those women had got under his skin, without him even knowing it. And now they were manipulating him and he was letting them do it. One thing was for certain: he wasn't letting them stay at his place. Jack swore softly under his breath.

"What did you say?" Deanna asked brightly from beside him.

He glanced across at the young woman sitting in the middle, and then at Kait over in the passenger seat. He almost did a double take when he saw her black hair. He should be used to it by now, but the black was just so... different from the warm red color when he'd first met her. He'd half fallen in love with her just because of that color. That bullshit story about her trying on different hair dyes all the time was exactly that. Bullshit. She was the type of woman who only went to the most expensive hairdresser, who'd only touch up her color with highlights, or whatever they were called. She was most definitely not a dye-job-in-the-hotel-sink type of woman. Why hadn't he called her out on it? Probably because she'd been looking at him with those trusting, green eyes. If he was to be completely honest with himself, it was Kait, more than Deanna, who was getting under his skin. She was intriguing. A woman with an aura around her that he couldn't help but be drawn to. Vulnerable. Although she was hiding that vulnerability beneath a thick veneer of…well, he hated to use the word again, but bullshit.

"Nothing," he replied, returning his gaze back to the road. They'd been driving for less than an hour and had a long, long way to go. He hadn't been joking when he said he'd leave at sparrow's fart; they wouldn't reach home till nearly sundown as it was. It was still dark when the women had climbed bleary-eyed, into his cab. They'd watched the sun rise over the desert stretching out to their right in companionable silence, the radio playing a country song softly in the background. Then he'd told Deanna to climb in the back and find the paper bag of pastries he'd nabbed from the roadhouse as he filled the truck with gas this morning. Nothing like a roadhouse pastry to get you going in the morning. But now there were crumbs scattered all over the floor of his cab. He didn't want to look like some anal asshole and ask them to clean up, but he liked his truck to be just so. And having these two women tagging along was getting in the way of his ordered life. Deanna had even found his stack of neatly folded T-shirts in the back of the cab.

"They're all black," she said holding one up.

"Yeah, so?" he'd drawled in reply, while silently cursing the woman and her meddling ways. What was wrong with him wanting things to be easy? Wearing black every day was easy; he didn't have to even think about what T-shirt he was going to put on in the morning. And it didn't show the sweat or the dirt. Easy was good. At least it was on the road. When he got home, he was a bit more relaxed. But he'd still had to choke off the words *stop messing with my stuff*, because he knew he'd sound like some kind of neat freak. He really hoped she'd folded it and put it back exactly where she'd found it, however.

"So, Jack, tell us more about you," Deanna said, and he snapped back to the present. Kait glanced at him from the other side of the truck with a spark of interest in her eyes.

Shit, he should've kept quiet. Now he'd awoken the beast, and she was going to hound him all the way to Broome.

"There's not a lot to tell," he replied, gruffly, hoping to put her off.

"Don't say that," Deanna trilled. "I'm sure there're heaps of skeletons in your closet. Like, how long have you been driving trucks?" She looked at him expectantly.

He was the one who should be asking the questions. Such as, where was the black backpack Kait had kept glued to her side on the whole trip up to Exmouth? And how had these two unlikely women become friends in the first place? They were obviously close, but there were times when Kait acted all aloof and cool to Deanna, and there were times when Deanna would look at Kait as if she'd caught her off guard, saying something that took her completely by surprise. And then there were the bruises Deanna was trying hard to disguise. He'd caught a glimpse of what looked to be fingerprints beneath that ridiculous scarf. Was Deanna a victim of domestic violence? Was that what this pair was running from?

He caved, and instead of answering a question with a question, he said with a sigh, "Around eight years. I bought my first truck from a mate who wanted to get out of the business and built it up from there. This baby is relatively new." He patted the steering wheel lovingly. He'd fallen in love with this Kenworth truck because they were tough and reliable, and he'd saved up so he could afford to upgrade after only three years on the road. The truck was a few years old when he bought it, but to him, it felt brand new.

"Eight years, is that a long time?" Deanna furrowed her

brow. "It seems like a long time. But then…" She speared him with her bright blue gaze. "How old are you?" she asked suddenly.

"Deanna," Kait said sharply.

"What?" Deanna sounded exactly like a chastised teenager and Jack hid a smirk

"It's not polite to ask people their ages."

"That's a load of dog poo. Just because you don't want to tell anyone *your* age," she quipped.

Kait scowled at the younger woman but said no more. Not for the first time, Jack wondered how old Kait actually was. He'd say she was late thirties if he was asked. But she could be older than that, just well preserved. Her skin had that peaches and cream complexion that often made it hard to pinpoint a woman's age. She'd certainly led an indoor life, that much was for sure. No freckles or sun damage on her soft skin.

"I don't care," Jack answered. "I'm forty-two. And no, driving for eight years isn't a long time. I know blokes who've been driving all their lives."

"Well, I don't care either," Kait said suddenly. "I'm forty-four." She sat up straighter and looked him directly in the eye.

Two years older than him, there you go.

Deanna swiveled her head between the two of them, squinting at Jack as if she was unsure what was going on between these two bewildering older people. As if deciding on a course of action, Deanna's face cleared. "Good, I'm glad we got that sorted. Now back to truck driving." She leaned forward, elbows on knees, as if settling in for a good story. "Why did you become a truck driver?"

Jack considered that question for a few moments. Sometimes it was just better to go with the truth, like ripping off a Band-Aid. Because by the looks of this young woman, she wasn't going to let it rest until she had the truth. "Because I needed something mindless to do after my previous job."

"Which was?" It was Kait this time, encouraging him to go on.

"I was an agent for a company involved in child recovery," he said evenly. There was a second of stunned silence inside the cab, the only sounds those of the tires humming on the road and Keith Urban belting out a song about falling.

"You mean you were some kind of mercenary?" Kait was staring at him intently, her newly black hair gleaming in the morning sunlight streaming through the window.

"Some people call it that." He kept his eyes on the road but could feel that familiar anger building in his gut. He'd been anything but a mercenary. He believed what his small agency was doing was vital work. Reuniting children with their rightful parents when the government could only sit and watch, their hands tied by red tape and paperwork, had been satisfying work. Until the day everything had gone wrong.

"A mercenary?" Deanna repeated the word slowly. "Like you used real guns and stuff, and went on missions? But don't you have to have military training for that?"

"It certainly helps," he drawled as nonchalantly as he could manage, pushing the rage back down into the box where he kept it safe and secure. "I was in the Australian Army for twelve years before I joined the recovery program."

"Well, I'll be," Kait exclaimed. "Scratch the surface and you're an interesting man after all." Her green eyes fixed on him, and he suddenly wondered what she was thinking behind that new black fringe of hers.

Jack wasn't sure if that was meant as a compliment, so he left it alone.

"So, that means you've traveled to other countries?" Deanna asked, animation making her face look even younger, more vulnerable. When he nodded in the affirmative, she said, "I want to travel one day. Outside Australia, I mean." Her eyes took on a dreamy look. "Tell me what it's like. Where did you go? Which was your favorite?"

Jack didn't know which question to answer first. Maybe it was time to run an experiment. He'd been avoiding this topic for the past eight years. What would happen if he spoke about it now?

"I've spent a lot of time in Asian countries. While I was in the army, I was deployed to East Timor. Spent nearly two years working there, helping get their police force up and running again after they gained their independence from Indonesia. Then while I was an agent, I worked out of Sydney, but we extracted kids from places like Peru, North Africa, and even the Middle East." A shudder went through him as he said the last name, an image of a child's pleading face through the window of a speeding car impaling his mind. This was why he didn't like to talk about it. Too many unwanted memories. Nope, this experiment was a failure. Time to lock all those memories away again for at least another eight years.

"Oh, wow," Deanna sighed, seeming not to notice his grimace.

Kait merely rolled her eyes behind the young woman's back, making it clear that she wasn't as enamored with travel. Perhaps it meant she'd done some of her own globetrotting. Time to divert the attention away from him. They could answer some of his questions for a change.

"How about you?" It was directed at both women, but he fixed his gaze on Kait as he spoke. "You said you're traveling around Australia." Deanna had likened them to gypsies, drifting from one place to the next. But surely, they had more of a plan than that? It was time to test their story. Put some pressure on the two of them and see if they'd stick to their spiel. Find out what they were really up to. "Any plans after this? I mean, I know you want to come to Cloudwater and help with the ghost nets. But what will you do after that?"

Kait's face took on a look of slight panic, and she froze, much like a startled rabbit. But she jumped in just as Deanna opened her mouth. "We might go back to Exmouth afterward. We never really got to see the area. When this opportunity to join you came up, we thought we'd grab it."

"Go back, huh?" That was unusual. Once a person started working their way around the top end, they generally only went in one direction.

"Oh, the news is on." Deanna waved her hand to shush them both.

Why was she so fascinated by the news? Nothing much changed out here. It was the same old drivel, just repackaged in a different week, or month. Like this guy who'd fallen to his death in a Kalbarri gorge. The announcer was still going on about it, asking for any witnesses. The poor guy most likely jumped. There were lots of reasons men decided they no longer wanted to stay in this world. A failed business. A failed marriage. Hell, he'd been close a time or two. That dark abyss often looked attractive, especially when you were at your lowest ebb. Especially in the weeks after he'd left the Child Protection Agency. It was one of the reasons he'd started up his own truck driving business. No one to tell him what to do. No one relying on him. No responsibilities, aside from delivering the next load on time. A quiet life and no one around to rock the boat. Even so, he'd often wondered if the world would really be any worse off if he'd left it? Probably not. They should leave the man in peace.

Both women seemed to be fixated on the newsreader's voice.

A strange thought suddenly struck him. Were they listening out for something specific on the news feed? He sorted through the various stories as they came to air. A fatal car crash on the highway between Perth and Yanchep, two backpackers in a minivan killed. It happened all the time, tourists who weren't used to the roads and the conditions. Some local politician accused of cheating on his wife, being hounded out of his position on the bench. Eggs had been thrown at his office headquarters window, and he'd received death threats. Hah, that was nothing new either. A toddler who'd gone missing from a farm in the Wheatbelt had been found, safe and well. *At last, a good news story*. The guy who'd thrown himself into the gorge. That was about it. The newsreader went on to tell them to expect more hot weather over the coming week. Really, dude? It was the middle of bloody summer. Hot, hot, hot was all they got, especially up here. Hotter and wetter, due to the oncoming wet season.

Which story, if any, were the women most interested in? Was one of them perhaps the mistreated wife of the politician who was being hounded? Kait might fit that bill. Perhaps she was running away from all the media attention. But then, how did Deanna fit into the picture? She was young enough to be Kait's daughter, but they'd made it a point to tell him that wasn't the case. Why would they lie about that?

And what had been in the missing backpack? What about the bruises on Deanna's neck? Were they on the run from the law? Some kind of modern-day Thelma and Louise?

He glanced over at the two women, who were now bickering over the last pastry. Nah, these two weren't acting like wanted criminals. In fact, they were the exact opposite. More like Laverne and Shirley. Jack smiled to himself and looked out over the Cloudwater plain stretching into the Great Sandy Desert. Red earth, covered with stunted olive-colored shrubs for as far as the eye could see. Beautiful.

He couldn't wait to get home.

# CHAPTER TWELVE

Unease sat between Kait's shoulder blades like a big, fat unwanted toad. She had so many things she was worried about she almost didn't know which one to put at the top of the list.

The money was probably uppermost in her worry inventory. They'd left it back in Exmouth, in a stupid storage locker, where anyone could have access to it if they knew where to look. That was probably causing Kait the most discomfort, and it was the reason she'd blurted out that she wanted to go back to Exmouth. She wouldn't rest easy until that money was safely in a bank, out of Dario's reach. But it would've looked too suspicious for her to deposit a million dollars into her newly opened bank account. As it was, the bank teller had glanced at her in alarm when she'd handed over the twenty thousand in cash. But at least if Dario found out about this account, then she wouldn't be losing all the money.

It'd been Deanna's idea to leave it in the storage unit, and perhaps that was the real cause of her discomfort. Because a small slither of suspicion had entered her mind when she'd caught Deanna glancing back not once, but twice, at the locker as they left the facility. That's when it dawned on her that she might need to watch Deanna, make sure she didn't take off one day without her. Kait was sure she trusted Deanna. But when it came to that much money, could she really trust anyone?

Kait glanced back into the small sleeping compartment behind the seats. Deanna was fast asleep, her fist curled beneath her chin, her eyelashes resting soft on her cheeks. The bruise on her face was faint, covered by makeup, but Kait knew it was there, could still picture the man's hand as it raked across her cheekbone. She looked young and innocent, and for a moment Kait felt a spike of maternal warmth surge through her. Of course she could trust Deanna.

Kait didn't have many female friends. Susan had been her closest. And toward the end of Susan's illness, Kait was her only true friend. All the rest had distanced themselves, not able to deal with the encroaching, inevitable death. Too caught up in their own inconsequential lives to give her or Susan more than a passing thought. Even though Deanna was so much younger than Kait, and they were so different in almost every way, Kait felt a connection with her. Would she go so far as to list Deanna as a friend? Maybe.

Kait touched her newly black hair. Her reflection still shocked her every time she caught a glimpse of herself. It'd been Deanna's idea to dye her hair and cut in the fringe. And she'd been correct; her hair was like a red flag out there, waving around for anyone who was looking to see it.

Kait was still haunted by the image of that man's arms flailing as he tipped over the edge of the cliff. And of his broken body lying at the bottom of the gorge. Deanna seemed completely unfazed by their act of violence, however. Every time Kait brought it up, she said the man was a pig, and he deserved everything he got. But by capsizing the man sent to bring her home into the gorge, Kait knew they'd killed him, no matter how Deanna tried to spin the story.

Even though the snapshot of the dead man rolled in a never-ending reel in her head, making her shake with fear at the thought of what might become of them because they'd taken a life, Kait felt something else strange growing inside of her. An emotion she couldn't put her finger on. She wasn't even sure if it was an emotion. It was more like a potential for something. Something like...empowerment. She was capable of killing. If someone got in her way, she knew her abilities. It meant she didn't need to be controlled by anyone anymore. Certainly not by her husband. The idea was a new one, all bright and shiny. She knew she couldn't really resort to murder again—the mere idea was almost too appalling to even think about. But just the possibility that she *could* do it, if she were provoked beyond the point of no return, was enough for now.

Kait was sure Dario wouldn't leave it at that. When he found out what'd happened to his bounty hunter—and he probably already knew—he'd send someone else after her. He might even come after her himself, if he was angry enough.

She needed to know what was going on back in Perth. Had Dario reported her missing? Or was he keeping her defection a secret, hoping to drag her back by the hair and pretend nothing had happened? That was the more likely scenario, because if Dario was one thing it was narcissistic. He wouldn't want any of his associates to know that he'd lost control of his own wife.

If he *had* reported her missing to the police, wouldn't they put out an announcement on the news? She didn't know enough about these sorts of things.

Would Dario dob her into the cops when he found out about the dead guy? Because if the cops were looking for her, that was less likely to make it onto the news. They might not want to alert her to the fact they were after her. But she'd seen and heard many news articles over the years where the police stated they were looking to speak to such-and-such as a *person of interest,* or *a possible witness in a crime.* Nothing like that had been mentioned on the radio. But maybe it'd only be reported on the Perth news? Would it even make it as far north as Exmouth? She had no idea, and the constant worry about so many scenarios was driving her crazy.

With an irritated flick of her wrist, she pushed a chunk of hair behind her ear.

"You should go back to red. The black…it's okay, but it's too severe." Jack's comment took her by surprise, jolting her out of her musings.

Distraction, yes, that'd help. And Jack had certainly uttered some surprising facts about his life earlier, enough to distract her for a while.

"Oh, okay. Thanks for the advice," she replied, unsuccessful at hiding the sarcasm. She was on the run from an overly controlling husband. One thing was for sure; she wasn't going to put up with it anymore. Starting from now, she made a decision that no man was ever going to tell her what to do ever again.

"Sorry." Jack held up a placating hand. "I didn't mean that as a criticism. You'd look good, no matter what color your hair was."

"Oh." What did she say to that? Shame heated her face. She probably shouldn't compare Jack to her husband; they were nothing alike; apart from being of the male persuasion. "Thank you," she added.

The road hummed beneath the wheels as they barreled down the blacktop. It was almost peaceful, in a strange kind of way. Kait was sure the never-ending red dirt stretching away on either side would get boring after a while, but to her eyes, it was both desolate and somehow beautiful at the same time.

"Tell me about your home," she said, suddenly interested.

"What's it like up there? I mean, the little I remember about Broome is tropical breezes and swaying palm trees. But we didn't travel far from the resort. I have a feeling that's not the true Broome."

Jack snorted. "No. You got that one right. You might've seen the tourist side of the town, but you probably barely scratched the surface." He took his eyes off the road long enough to flick her a glance. "People often get Broome confused with, say, Darwin. Broome is subtropical. It has definite wet and dry seasons. It's a lot dryer, and the vegetation is mainly scrubby tea tree thickets and dune grasslands rolling over the red sand."

"Oh, right," Kait replied meditatively. "And what about Cloudwater Bay? What's that like?"

"The township is pretty basic. It's all dirt tracks out there, with around a hundred and fifty people living in fifty or sixty dwellings."

"Oh wow, that's…smaller than I thought."

"Hmm," Jack hummed thoughtfully. "It's been called all sorts of things, by all sorts of people. Barren and inhospitable. Stark but bewitching. An oasis in a sea of humanity gone mad." He laughed at this one. "I guess it all depends on your point of view and why you're there in the first place."

Kait wanted to ask Jack why he lived there, but something stopped the words on her tongue. He seemed to be in a chatty mood, and she didn't want him to clam up because she asked the wrong question.

"It sounds…interesting. Is there a reason the settlement is there? I mean, why not just live on the outskirts of Broome?"

"If you lived in Broome for a while, you might understand the answer to that question," he replied with a dark frown. "But I guess Cloudwater first started as a sort of fishing village. Full of huts and lean-tos built by weekend fishermen, as a place to get away. And even now, you can still get some good fishing in, if you know where to go." Jack cocked his head to the side and pursed his lips. "I guess the other reason is there's a year-round water source. Cloudwater Bay sits above the same underground aquifer that feeds Broome. It's one of the reasons Broome is so green amongst all this red dirt. The water is drinkable—just—and people use it to grow veggies in their gardens."

Jack was making it sound almost quaint. Kait was drawn to the idea of a little fishing village tucked away on the Kimberley coast. Away from the rest of humanity. Away from prying eyes.

"There're lots of Aboriginal middens scattered everywhere along the coastline around Cloudwater. Which shows it was once a popular place for nomadic groups to camp out during the dry months. Sometimes I like to imagine what the coast would've been like back then, thousands of years ago. Practically untouched, abounding with as many fish and other ocean creatures as they could eat. What would've it been like to live through that? To be completely reliant on the land?"

Jack seemed to have drifted off on a tangent. And not that Kait wasn't interested in the history of the indigenous people of the Kimberley, she was just more fixated on her own problems.

"Is there any possibility we could stay at Cloudwater Bay? I know you said there were no hotels, but what about someone with an extra room? A house for rent? Something like that?"

"I have a friend. She owns one of the larger houses in the community. Sometimes, she lets out a room, if there is a need. Her name is Raine. I can take you out and let you meet her, if you like."

"Oh, yes, please. We'd like that very much."

"I guess you'll figure this out for yourself, but I'll warn you now that Raine is a little…different. Actually, most people out in the Cloudwater settlement are different. We're all looking for a place to escape, get off the grid for a while."

That sounded exactly like what she needed.

"Is that what this Raine is doing?"

"Yes. And no. Raine inherited her house from her grandfather, old Roland, who lived out there for more years than anyone can remember. The house is huge, Roland built most of it by hand, by himself. Now he's gone, Raine rattles around in that big house by herself a lot of the time. Which is why she rents out her rooms. For the company."

"Do you get lots of people passing through Cloudwater, then?"

"More than you'd think. People come for all sorts of reasons. Some come to help with the ghost nets. You know, lots of environmentalists and hippy types. But not many stay. They all move on, eventually."

"Are you an environmentalist?"

"Hell no!" He laughed, and the sound sent goose bumps up her arms. "Not even close. But I hate seeing what those bloody nets do to the wildlife. I hate the injustice of it all. Those poor animals trapped and dying. And I don't like all that bloody plastic pollution that washes up on the beaches, either. It's my small contribution to the coastal community."

It sounded like Jack *was* a bit of an environmentalist, but he wasn't going to admit to it, and Kait decided there was no reason to label him if he didn't want to be labelled.

A sign appeared on the roadside verge, warning of roadworks up ahead. Jack applied the brakes gently and reached for the stick shift to change down a gear. The truck's engine growled as he shifted through the gears, sounding like a lion on the prowl. Kait watched Jack's sure hands, one on the gearshift, the other on the wheel, as he directed the enormous vehicle with smooth competence. She glimpsed a tattoo on his inner arm, just below his elbow. It was a series of numbers. A date perhaps. Something of significance to only him. Her gaze flicked up his arm, enjoying the way the cuff of his T-shirt hugged his rather firm biceps, to see the hint of black lines from another tattoo peeking out from beneath the hem of the sleeve on the inside of his arm. It looked to be an Australian Flag. He'd said he'd been in the army for a while, so it wasn't surprising for him to have tattoos. Plenty of men had them these days. Thankfully, he hadn't chosen to go for the full sleeve of tattoos, like some of the younger guys. Kait often wondered what those arms full of ink would look like in fifty years' time. But the sight of these particular ones on Jack's arm did something strange to her stomach. Almost as if she liked them. As if they added an aura of danger to this seemingly innocuous man sitting beside her.

She wondered if there was any more ink on his body. In places that most people never got to see. The idea had her suddenly feeling hot and bothered, and she glanced away from his capable hands to stare out the window until the disloyal feelings subsided.

A comfortable silence fell between them, and Kait suddenly felt like she'd known Jack for a lot longer than she actually had.

Her mind wandered from topic to topic, rehashing the things she'd learned about Jack today. She hadn't forgotten about that pink moon—strawberry moon Jack had called it. If they were still in the area in two weeks' time, she was going to make it a priority to see that phenomenon.

Settling back into her seat, she let the passing scenery lull her into an almost dreamlike state. It was going to be a long drive, but she had the idea that this Cloudwater Bay might be worth the trip.

An image of Deanna's house back in Geraldton, the one her parents had built, flittered into her mind. She wanted to live in something like that house. Built with love and purpose. Built by hand and designed by someone who knew about the flow of life and how a house should fit into the environment. It could be just her and the ocean and a glass of cold chardonnay out on the deck. Would that ever be possible? Not until she could get Dario out of her life completely, that much was for sure.

# CHAPTER THIRTEEN

The road to Cloudwater Bay could barely be called a road. Deanna watched Jack guide his B-Double—she loved saying the name; it had a certain ring to it—with expertise that spoke of a long familiarity with the sandy track. Deanna was almost bouncing in her seat with anticipation, she could hardly wait to see the little township. She had a good feeling about this place. As soon as Jack had said the name, she'd had tingles all over her body. A good sign indeed.

Jack crested the rise of a gradual sand dune and there was the township scattered on the open expanse below, the ocean stretching from one horizon to the other in the background. The sun reflecting off the sand nearly blinded her, making it difficult to see the details. From here, the smattering of buildings looked washed out, bleached of all color by the relentless sun. A tiny speck of humanity amongst this vast, wasted land.

"I warned you." Jack gave a mirthless laugh.

He'd misunderstood her staring for dismay. Which it wasn't; she was enthralled.

"It's great. Bigger than I thought," Deanna gushed.

"Yeah, you can see almost the whole town from up here, but once you get down amongst it, you can only see two or three houses at a time, as they're hidden in dips and hollows between the dunes."

Kait said nothing, merely stared through the high windshield, then tucked her newly dark hair into a bun and put on her hat. She was in what Deanna had nicknamed *ostrich mode*. Where she seemed to shut off from the world and pretend life wasn't really happening. It was one way to deal with your problems, Deanna surmised, but it usually led to more problems in the end if you ignored things for too long. Deanna decided that Kait was too stuck in her old expectations, she needed to leave her stuffy, pretentious ideals behind and grab life by the balls and shake it up a little.

The track wound down the hill and Jack shifted down through the gears, so the truck was almost crawling. They came to the first house—shack, really—hunkered down in a hollow, just as Jack had described. Made of fibro sheeting and a tin roof, it was shaded by a large, gangly eucalyptus tree. Deanna saw at least four or five motorcycle bodies in the front yard.

"That's Mac's place," Jack offered helpfully. "He likes to do up Harley Davidson bikes."

*No shit.* Deanna didn't say it out loud though.

As they got closer to the beach, the houses—shacks—got bigger, some with neat yards out the front, but most with scraggly bushes and dead grass where a garden should be. The road meandered amongst the houses, not seeming to go in any particular direction, but after passing about twenty houses, somewhere around the middle of the small community, Jack drew the truck to a halt beside a large, rambling construction. It was the first double-story house Deanna had seen, and she studied it with interest.

"This is Raine's place," Jack said, engaging the truck's brakes as they all turned to stare at the monstrosity.

"It's...intriguing." Kait touched the brim of her hat self-consciously. "You think she'll have room for us?"

"Let's go and ask." Jack opened his door and jumped down.

Deanna tumbled out the other side and was immediately hit by the heat. Jaysus, it was hot here. Was that a turret she could see peeking out the top of the building? This place reminded her of the Addams Family house. It was obvious parts had been added onto the main structure at a later date. It looked like a tree sprouting new branches—or in this case, rooms—as it grew. Never in a million years would Deanna have guessed she'd find something like this in the middle of bloody nowhere.

Jack led them up the impressive front steps, at least ten stairs sweeping up to a wide, shady veranda. Deanna followed Jack eagerly, but Kait dragged her heels, bringing up the rear.

He knocked loudly, and they all stood on the front door mat, waiting.

"Jack, you're back. Good to see you." A tall woman with long, gray hair swept up in a classy chignon hugged Jack in a warm embrace. Dressed in flowing cotton pants and a breezy lightweight top that showed off tanned shoulders, she stood back and seemed to notice the two women for the first time.

"Who do we have here?" A look passed between Jack and Raine that Deanna didn't much care for. It was almost like she was asking him what he'd brought to her now, more flotsam and jetsam washed up on the beach of life.

Deanna frowned, ready to dislike this woman. She hated to be looked down on. Hated people who thought they were better than her. But when Raine turned her gray-eyed gaze on Deanna, she felt something else altogether. A sense of warmth and acceptance. As Raine inspected her and Kait, one eyebrow winged up in a half-amused smile, Deanna didn't feel judged. She felt...recognized. As if Raine could see through all her bullshit to the true Deanna. And that wasn't all. She got tingles, all up and down her spine, even between her legs. Now that was new.

*What the...*? This woman must be fifty if she was a day. Deanna wasn't attracted to cougars. She preferred women or, at a stretch, men her own age. Mostly.

Deanna glanced sideways at Kait, trying to judge her reaction to this interesting woman.

Kait shuffled her feet, glancing first at Jack and then at Raine.

"These two are looking for a place to stay," Jack said.

"Are they now?"

"Have you got room?" he asked, keeping his own level stare on her.

"Maybe. Tell me a little about yourselves. You can start." Raine pointed at Kait.

Deanna took the chance to study their potential new landlord while she talked to Kait. Perhaps Raine wasn't as old as Deanna had first thought. The lines around her eyes were practically nonexistent, her cheeks smooth and full, and eyes bright and clear. Maybe the gray hair was a premature thing, a trick to keep people guessing.

Then it was Deanna's turn. "What about you? What's your story?" Raine speared her with her assessing gaze.

Deanna's mind went blank suddenly. *WTF*? Was this woman a sorceress or something? "Ah...I'm the same as Kait." Shit, she should've listened harder to what Kait was saying. They were supposed to be traveling together. They should've worked out their story better. Fooling Jack with their half-assed story was easy, but this woman was a whole new kettle of fish. "We're on a bit of a journey. Around Australia. As well as a journey to find ourselves. We've both just left bad relationships. And we need a bit of time out."

Was that inspirational or what? Deanna mentally high-fived herself.

"I can see that." Raine reached out and gently touched Deanna's neck, tracing the bruises beneath the scarf with a soft finger. "And so here you are," she added. The woman was beyond perceptive. But Deanna had never met a person she couldn't charm. At least until Tamika.

"Yes," Deanna answered quickly. "Here we are."

After a few seconds of silence, Raine stated, "I'm vegan. And everyone who lives under my roof has to abide by my preferences."

Of course she was. And of course they did. Deanna flicked a glance at Jack. He was smirking. He clearly knew Raine's rules. Deanna sadly waved away any thoughts of juicy steaks and burgers, dripping with cheese and bacon. She loved her meat and was definitely a carnivore. But she was also open to trying anything. Veganism might be nice for a while. Actually, the more she thought about it, the more she liked the idea.

"That's not a problem for me," Deanna answered.

Kait glowered at Jack as if this was all his fault.

"Grab your bags and come on in, then." Raine stepped back inside, but left the door open for them.

Deanna leaped down the stairs and scrambled back up into the truck before handing both their bags down to Kait, who'd followed, dragging her feet. Didn't she realize that this was a brand new adventure? A chance to live a new life for a few days?

Jack ambled around the front, heading for the driver's side.

"Aren't you coming in?" It was more than surprise Deanna heard in Kait's tone. There was a smidgen of fear as well, as if she needed his now familiar presence to help her get through the next awkward hours, settling into Raine's house.

"Nope. You gals will be fine," he said, springing easily up into the cab. "Don't worry, Raine grows on you. She's not as scary as she looks. And she can point you in the right direction when you're ready to come and visit me."

"Thanks for the lift, Jack," Deanna called. "And thanks for all your help, too." It felt a little lackadaisical, merely waving him away after all he'd done for them. Even if he didn't realize it, he'd possibly saved their asses the night he'd picked them up at the Overlander, and they owed him. But Deanna wasn't one to dwell, so she gave the final wave and picked up her bag. She'd decided a while ago that her life was a collection of chapters, verses, and scenes. This felt like a new scene starting in the chapter of her and Kait, together.

"Have fun." He waved a hand out the window as the big truck pulled away in a cloud of dust. Kait's frown followed him all the way down the road.

The house was cool inside, at least compared to outside, and Deanna let out an expansive sigh. Kait followed her in.

"You can take your hat off now, if you like." Raine's comment was directed at Kait, but it still caught Deanna by surprise, and she looked up, following the sound of her voice. A set of wooden stairs led up to the second floor. Raine was standing at the top of the landing, watching them with her steely gaze. Kait looked up also, tilting her head back, to see past the brim of her cap.

"You don't have to worry, your secrets are safe with me," Raine added, almost as an afterthought.

*Uh oh.* Deanna shot Kait a look. Had she really seen through their façade that easily?

"I'll leave it on, for now," Kait replied. Not antagonistic, but firm. A statement, that she wasn't easily bullied into submission, if that's what Raine was aiming for. But somehow Deanna didn't think Raine was a bully. This was more likely a test of some sort.

"That's fine with me," Raine replied breezily. Almost too casually. Deanna wondered if Kait had passed the test.

"Come on up." She beckoned them up the stairs.

Raine showed them to two adjacent rooms at the end of the landing. Deanna peeked into one and nearly gasped out loud. It was huge. Bigger than most bedrooms.

"Bags this one," Deanna called, not even waiting to see the other one. The room had a high ceiling with a fan circling lazily high above the polished wooden floorboards. Really old, but classy. The color palette was all crimson and gold, it made a bold statement. It reminded her of those old-fashioned houses from the colonial era, like in the game of Cluedo, where Professor Plum murdered the victim in the library with the candlestick. There was a four-poster-bed for Christ's sake and an old enamel washbasin on top of an antique sideboard. Large windows looked out onto the backyard, where a huge, rambling garden meandered around the base of the house. Draped with heavy, ruby velvet curtains that reached the floor, the windows also gave an expansive view out to the red dunes rolling away in swathes to the horizon. Deanna could see the exact borderline between Raine's garden and the natural open plains, where lush jade turned to brown and tan.

"This place is bloody gorgeous," Deanna said, wandering out into the hallway to inspect Kait's room.

"I'm glad you like it," Raine replied with a dry smile. "My father built it, but I've added to it over the years. Done the place up, tinkered with it here and there."

"You've done a wonderful job," Kait echoed Deanna's comment. Kait seemed genuinely impressed, which didn't happen very often. She must really like the place.

Kait's room was done up in duck-egg blue and tan, softer and calming. Very Kait. It was almost like the rooms had chosen them, rather than the other way around.

"Jack said you'd let us stay here for free. Is that right?" Deanna asked. No point in beating around the bush. She didn't mind paying, but it was better to know from the outset.

"That's correct, I don't want money from you," Raine replied, her gray gaze roving up and down Deanna's figure. "I might ask for payment in other ways, however."

Deanna frowned and Kait seemed to stand up taller, almost bristling. What sort of payment did this woman mean?

Raine actually laughed at them. "You should see your faces. What on earth did you think I meant by that?"

"I don't know, what do you mean?" Kait replied woodenly.

"I mean, like a bit of cleaning, or assistance with the cooking. I'd also like some help in my garden, it's a big project to keep this going all by myself. Most of my fresh food comes from there, so it's important to me."

Oh. Deanna relaxed her shoulders. Was that all? "I'll help," she offered. "I haven't done a lot of gardening, but I've always wanted to learn."

"Great. I love a willing student." Raine studied Deanna for a second, before they came to rest on Kait, a question in her raised eyebrow.

Refusing to rise to the bait, Kait said, "Do you mind if I take half an hour to unwind? It's been a long ride and I'm exhausted."

Raine's gaze softened. "Of course, both of you take your time. I'll be down in the kitchen when you're ready."

# CHAPTER FOURTEEN

A knock on his door drew Jack away from his musings. He got up from the kitchen table and trundled on bare feet down the hallway.

Kait was standing on his front porch when he opened the door.

"Morning," he said, keeping his tone even, subtly dragging his gaze over from her soft curves. She was wearing cream capris, a tank top, and flip-flops, her black hair drawn back into a low ponytail, and she looked refreshed and cool, as if she'd just stepped out of the shower. The subtle waft of soap told him he was probably right. But he got the feeling she wasn't a woman who appreciated men gawking at her. Unlike Deanna who flouted her sexuality, Kait kept hers under a tight rein.

"This is your house?"

Why did Kait sound so surprised? "Yes," he answered, priding himself on not sounding too piqued. Why would she think this wasn't his house?

"This place is just full of surprises," she said cryptically, her gaze shooting out to the dusty street and then back to his veranda. "I hope this is okay," she added hurriedly. "You did say to come over once we were settled."

"Of course. Come in." He gestured for to her to precede him through the door. "I've just brewed a fresh pot of coffee. Would you like one?"

She swept past him, bringing the heat of the morning with her. It was building up to be another scorcher, without a cloud in the sky. "Are you kidding? I'd kill for a coffee. That stuff Raine drinks in the morning is the farthest thing from coffee I've ever tasted."

Jack laughed. Raine was nothing if not unconventional. "Did she try and convert you to her dandelion coffee?" Jack led her down the darkened hallway and into his large kitchen.

"Is that what it was?" Kait grimaced. "I had to chuck it in the garden when she wasn't looking."

Jack nodded and chuckled. "I hope Raine didn't see you do that. She *hates* to waste anything."

"I'm beginning to learn that already." Kait raised her eyebrows. "And I've only been in her house less than twenty-four hours."

He pulled out a chair at the kitchen table for her, and after a second's hesitation, she took it, making sure she didn't touch him as she sat down. A woman who liked to keep her distance. He wondered if it was just from him, or from all men?

"What, no black shirt today?" Kait asked, quirking her mouth up at the corner ever so slightly.

"I don't always wear black." He smoothed down the light-blue button-up shirt sporting the Billabong logo. "It's just easier when I'm out on the road for days on end." A trick he'd learned from his army days. If you kept everything the same, it left time to think about more important things.

"Sorry. I'm not judging you," she said, her gaze never leaving his face. And he knew she really wasn't. "I'm just curious, that's all."

"Where's Deanna?" Jack asked, attempting to change the topic, reaching for the coffee beans and taking his grinder from the cupboard.

"She said she'll pop over later." Kait hesitated and Jack wondered what she wasn't saying. "Raine is cooking up a batch of her supposedly famous zucchini relish this morning and Deanna wanted to stay and watch."

"Ah, ha," Was that a hint of jealousy he detected in Kait's tone? "Raine's relish is amazing," he added. "You didn't want to stay and learn the recipe?"

"No, I needed to get out of there for a while. Raine is very…intense."

"That's one word for it." He turned the handle on his grinder, drawing in the smell of fresh coffee beans. "She's lived here for a long time, longer than almost anybody else. She grew up here, before she went off to boarding school, then came back as soon as she could. This is a harsh landscape, and it tends to shape the people who decide to stay. But Raine is a good person, she just has certain quirks, that's all."

"Yeah, I get that. Those quirks might take a little getting used to," Kait answered, watching him pack the coffee into his espresso machine.

It was old, he'd bought it secondhand from a café that was closing down, and he'd carted it around with him wherever he went. It was temperamental and needy, and took up half his countertop, but it made the best coffee in the world.

"Raine sure likes to throw around words like, *fate* and *karma* and *yoga*." Kait shuddered at the last one. "Deanna agreed to do yoga with her before dawn this morning, while I chose to sleep in." She shuddered again and rolled her eyes. Jack wasn't surprised; he hadn't picked Kait as an early morning person. More of a late-night socialite.

Jack threw his head back and laughed at the ceiling,

recalling Raine trying to convince him to take up yoga when he first moved here. And she'd never really accepted no as an answer. She still hinted that it'd help him find his inner peace almost every time he saw her.

"Actually, this whole place is...interesting," Kait continued. "Raine told us that some of the men who live in Cloudwater are bastards and to steer clear of them. And some of the women are freaks and to stay away from them too." Kait glanced up at him, tilting her head to the side. "Except for you, of course. She said you were one of the good guys."

"That's nice to hear." Jack barked out another laugh.

"But on the whole, Raine said that most people in this community are just trying to get on with their lives. They're good people, some who fell on hard times. So, I think *interesting* is a fair summation of the citizens of Cloudwater," Kait added.

"I tend to agree with you." He turned the nozzle, and the drone of the coffee machine filled the air.

Kait lifted her nose. "Oh, God, that smells amazing." He couldn't help but admire her cheekbones and the long stretch of her neck. "Can I have a double shot? Please." He had to laugh at the near desperation in her tone. "And I drink it black," she added.

"Sure." Whatever the lady wanted was fine by him.

"It's lovely and cool in here. Do you have air-conditioning?" she asked.

Jack scoffed. "Not likely. It's just the way the house has been designed. I have high roofs, which helps direct the hot air up and out. See there?" He pointed to a dark corner high up near the ceiling. "There are ten outlets like that one, to funnel hot air outside. And I've got two solar chimneys on the roof, which also help draw the hot air away."

"Nice. I've heard of houses that are intended to be solar passive, is that the right term?"

"Got it in one," he replied, surprised at her knowledge. This lady had a broad intelligence and a sharp wit to go with it. "There are other design features, such as the house is also built on just the right angle to catch the afternoon sea breeze when it comes in. So, I can open those high windows up there"—again, he pointed to the rafters—"and the sea breeze acts as my air conditioner."

He felt an absurd stirring of pride. He'd studied lots of books and websites to discover how to keep his house passively cool and was happy that it worked, especially in a renowned hot spot like north Western Australia. There was a lot more involved in designing this type of house, like insulation, thermal mass, the surface colors you chose, a large overhanging roofline and lots of shaded areas, but he wasn't sure she wanted to hear all that.

"Bring your coffee and we'll sit out in the garden," he said, handing her a mug.

She buried her nose in the steam and breathed in deeply. "Heaven," she said.

He waited until she joined him on the other side of the kitchen, then he led her out the back door and down three stairs into his garden.

"Oh, wow." Kait tilted her head back to stare at the two ghost gums, their white bark glowing in the morning sun. One of his first tasks when he'd devised this garden had been to plant a tree at each corner of his house. They were still young yet, but they were already providing much needed shade to the rear of his house. One more way to keep his house cool.

A large wooden deck, covered by a pergola, stretched out from the back steps, with a comfortable wicker outdoor setting of four chairs and a table set in the middle. He dragged a chair out for Kait and took the seat opposite. The rest of his garden was designed with drought-hardy plants fringing the edge of the deck, with only a small patch of grass that helped the space look green and lush.

"I imagine not too many other houses in Cloudwater are as sustainable or as beautiful as this one," Kait said, twisting her head to take in the spectacle.

"This is my pet project. I've spent all my spare time over the past five or so years creating this place, and I don't mind pouring every last cent into it either. But most people out here don't have the time or the money to do what I've done," he consented.

"How do people survive out here?" She took a sip and stretched her legs out beneath the table. "I mean, what do they do for a living?"

"Everyone's different." Jack shrugged. It was almost impossible to encapsulate Cloudwater into one amorphous idea. "A fair few are on welfare." It was a common fact of life up here. Jobs were often hard to come by, and some people made a living out of not working. They preferred a certain type of freedom that working nine to five just didn't allow. A lot of people survived on the breadline, and poverty was only a hair's breadth away for some. "Some like to fish, sometimes they can make a decent wage from their haul, by selling their fish to the locals. Some are self-sufficient, like Raine. Some have jobs, like me, and only come here when they can. To them this place is a sanctuary. Some are retired and live on their pension. A lot of them like to drink hard and there are even a few illegal gambling clubs out here. I'm not going to lie, it's a rough sort of place. But on the whole, people are still people, no matter where you go. We're a community, albeit an odd bunch, and most people who live here are okay. At least in my book."

Kait stared at him, discerning green eyes lasered in on his face, a slight frown marring her forehead. "That's a pretty succinct round up of this place. I already know you fall into the minority of working-for-a-living category, but what drew you here in the first place? If you don't mind me asking?"

The face of the little boy being driven off in the car, flashed across his mind, but he shook it away.

"It was an accident, really. I was up here to look at a secondhand truck." He thought back to that time. He'd left the protection agency and had been drifting for many months, living off his savings, when he'd met a trucker in a diner out near Kalgoorlie. Talking to the guy had been his lightbulb moment, when he decided he wanted to start his own business. "It was about eight years ago, and I was just starting up my business and couldn't afford a new truck. The directions the guy gave me to his property outside Broome were pretty vague, and I got lost, and ended up down here instead. I was amazed, I never really knew places like this existed."

"Me either," Kait agreed.

"I got out of my car and just walked around and that's when I ran into Raine. She said she was on her way to the local bar for a drink and would I like to join her."

"There's a bar out here?" The look of surprise on Kait's face was comical.

"Kind of. It's more of the locals getting together and setting up a few beers on a bench so they can have a chinwag and pretend it's a bar."

"Oh right. That sounds…interesting."

Kait had no idea. She was in for more than one surprise if she stayed here for any length of time. This place was more than just rough around the edges. It had its own story to tell.

"Anyway, Raine sort of took me under her wing, and after I told her about my dream to build a sustainable house, she told me she might know of a block of land up for sale."

"She seems to do that a lot," Kait said, almost under her breath.

"Yes," he agreed, but he didn't see that as a bad thing. He wondered why Kait had a chip on her shoulder about it? Or was that she was just that wary about everyone? Perhaps it was hard for her to understand why anyone would want to be nice. Give something for nothing.

He drew in a sharp breath. Time to change the subject. "Have you had a chance to check out the beach yet?"

Kait pursed her lips and shook her head. "Nope, we've been sequestered up at Raine's since you dropped us off yesterday."

"Finish your coffee and I'll take you down," he offered.

She took one last, large gulp and smacked her lips. "Best coffee this side of the border," she exclaimed. "You just saved my life. I can never start the day without at least one cup of heart-starter, a double shot of the best dark brew I can get my hands on." Kait spread her arms wide and tilted her head to the ceiling. "And now, I'm ready for anything."

It was a tiny insight into Kait's previous life, and he suddenly glimpsed her sitting in some chic little café overlooking the beach, sipping her coffee and laughing at something her stylishly dressed friend had said. If his hunch was correct, it was a long way to come from the ritzy coastal suburbs of Perth to hitchhiking all the way up the north coast. Cloudwater Bay attracted all types, from all walks of life. Kait didn't seem to hold with fate, or karma; she'd screwed her nose up when Raine had used those words. But something had brought her to Cloudwater. And he'd love to know what.

"Have you got a hat?" he asked, collecting both their mugs.

She pulled the Overlander cap out of her back pocket and waved it at him.

"Wait here." He ducked back inside, deposited the mugs in the sink and grabbed his own hat from the row of pegs near the back door. "Follow me." He led Kait across his compact lawn to a gate in the side fence, partially hidden by a spray of bougainvillea just starting to bloom, cascading its hot-pink flowers down the wooden slats. "Watch for the thorns," he warned, holding one of the trailing fronds away, so she wouldn't get snagged. Bougainvillea bushes were almost as good at keeping trespassers out of a property as a guard dog, you just needed time to let it grow. They emerged out the gate and into a dusty side alley where there was a large warehouse-sized shed, the main roller door sitting open to reveal his truck. He'd spent the morning shining the chrome on the main cab and it now sparkled in the sunlight.

"Ah, ha. I wondered where your truck had disappeared to." Kait scanned the large B-Double parked in the shed to keep it out of the elements. It also kept it locked up and hidden away from prying eyes, so no one could cause mischief. He'd already had his truck spray-painted with tags and obscenities by some young hooligans while he'd been parked up behind a warehouse in Perth a few months ago, and he wasn't about to encourage that out here. He ran a hand over the metal roo bar as they passed in front of the truck. She was his baby.

He led Kait out onto the sandy track that passed as a road out here. It was hot out in the direct sun, not a breath of wind stirring the dead grass by the side of the road.

"Why did you build so far from the beach?" Kait asked, tugging her hair away from her neck and flapping it like a fan. "And how do you buy a block of land out here, anyway?"

"Raine's family own most of this land. Now she's the custodian of this country. She only sells it to people she thinks are worthy."

"Really?" Kait looked taken aback. "She owns all of this?"

"Yes. Her father bought the land way back. In the early days, some people squatted here illegally. Her father sold a package of land whenever they needed money. Some of the houses here have been handed down through a generation or two. The community grew slowly over time. But Raine's father wasn't as choosey about who lived here as she is. Which is where some of the...less desirables came from." Perhaps Kait now understood a little more about Raine and why she wanted to stay here.

"So, she's rich, then?" Kait stopped walking to stare at him. What was that he just saw flicker through Kait's eyes? It wasn't greed or scorn. Commiseration? Why would she think Raine needed her sympathy?

"I wouldn't say that," Jack countered. "Land isn't worth much out here. And like I said, she only sells if she wants to. But, yes, she uses the money to live."

"Obviously, she liked you. Because she sold you a block." Kait began walking again, her gaze returning to the sandy road. He couldn't help but admire her svelte legs, stalking along in a set of flip-flops that somehow made her seem unaffected, like a young girl out to buy ice cream on a hot summer's day.

"Yes, I showed her the vision I had for my passive solar house, and she liked it."

He was quietly proud that Raine had agreed to sell to him. It was a rare occurrence these days, according to old Jim, who lived in the shanty closest to the beach. Jim had been here the longest, or so he told everyone. Jack had chosen this block to build on because it was two dunes back from the beach, far enough away so he didn't get sandblasted to oblivion every time the southerly blew up—which was frequently—but close enough to still get the benefits of the cooling breeze. The only houses with ocean views in Cloudwater had been built fifty years ago, when no one realized how much damage they were doing by building on the first dune to be closer to the beach. Now, people knew it only encouraged beach erosion.

The road emerged from between a hollow in the last line of dunes and the beach opened in front of them. A cooling breeze tickled the sand, bringing a welcome relief from the suffocating heat of the township.

"Oh, wow." Kait stopped to stare, her head swiveling from one side to the other. "When you said the beach, I never expected…" She trailed off, her words lost in the long, never-ending sweep of white sand and blue ocean. It was a gorgeous day, the swell was small, the sun not yet too high, and not a cloud to be seen. "Now I see why it's called Cloudwater Bay. And I also see why you live here," she breathed.

He knew what she meant; it got him every time. The slow curve of sand disappearing into the Cloudwater blue haze of the sky. Nothing in front of them but water as far as the eye could see. Pure. Simple. Nature at her uncomplicated best. This was as close to heaven as he was ever going to get.

# CHATPER FIFTEEN

Kait wanted to dive into that Cloudwater blue. She walked toward the ocean, as if drawn on a string. "Look, Susan, it's gorgeous," she whispered. Susan agreed wholeheartedly, and lifting her arms to the sky as if in prayer, she urged Kait forward.

Kait was almost at the edge of the waves and was kicking off her flip-flops to paddle her feet in the water, when a voice behind her stopped her in her tracks.

"You probably don't want to swim there."

"Why not?" She turned to face Jack, and was hit by a jolt of...what? Lust? Surely not. Just because Jack looked all windswept and interesting, his sleeves rolled up to reveal tanned biceps and his legs—also tanned—long and lean beneath his shorts. She backed away from him as if he might bite. Those little kernels of attraction she'd felt for him on their trip north in his truck had easily been ignored, stored away in a safe place for contemplation later. But then, sitting in his garden this morning, drinking his delicious coffee, his appeal had gone up another ten notches. That sublime coffee. That gorgeous house. His effortless, intelligent banter which set her at ease. Those dimples lighting up his cheeks. And right now, with just the two of them on the beach, no one else for miles around, and him dressed like some sexy—albeit mature—surfer dude, looking at her with casual amusement in his blue-gray eyes was doing strange things to her heartstrings.

"Crocodiles."

What had he said? Her mind refused to fire on all cylinders. Had he really just said crocodiles? "Oh, shit." She leaped away from the waves, back toward him. Jack was the lesser of two evils in this particular case. Standing beside him, she turned to survey the enticing surf, small wavelets breaking harmlessly on the waterline. "What a terrible waste of all that glorious water," she lamented.

"Yeah, I know. There are also box jellyfish in the wet season, and they aren't real nice either. We don't see too many crocs around here. One shows up every now and then. Tries to steal a fisherman's haul, that sort of thing. But it's enough to keep all of us locals out of the water."

"I bet," Kait sighed mournfully. "But I'm sure I swam at the beach in Broome," she continued. "Isn't that the same ocean?" Why was it so different there? This water was ten times as enticing as Cable Beach had been. She really, really wanted to dip a toe in. Susan was still encouraging her from the background and Kait flicked her an annoyed glance.

"Yes, they have lifesavers patrolling the waters up in Broome, looking for crocs and sharks." He hesitated for a second, then said, "You can go in here, if you like. It's early in the wet season, the box jellyfish are still mostly out at sea. Chances are, you'll be safe."

Kait took another step away from the water. "No thanks, I'll pass."

She tipped her head to the sky. Jack had mentioned the wet season, but she still hadn't had any time to Google what that meant. Back in the truck, he'd talked about cyclones and roads getting cut. But there didn't seem to be a cloud in the sky. Where was all this rain if this was supposed to be the wet? Of course she'd heard of cyclones creating havoc and damage up north on the news, but they were only vague reports that she never really listened to. Down in Perth, they were rarely bothered by cyclones. Sometimes they got the tail end of the strong winds or a smattering of rain, but that was the extent of it. Did they need to be worried about cyclones out here in Cloudwater Bay?

Jack began to amble down the beach. He'd also removed his thongs and his bare feet made neat prints in the sand just above the tide line. She fell into step beside him. Not a soul was visible in either direction. Kait squinted into the sea spray smudging each end of the disappearing beach. If she hadn't known the little community of Cloudwater was tucked in behind this very dune, she might think they were the only people in the world.

"It's quite isolated here, isn't it?"

"Yep. And that's the way we like it. Most of us truly enjoy our own company." Jack answered with a wry tilt to his mouth, one dimple showing.

"Hmm." Not for the first time, Kait wondered about Jack's love life. She'd already checked his left hand for a ring, but it was bare, not even a telltale dent or tan line to say that he'd once worn one. Why was a good-looking man in his prime living alone all the way out here? Unless he wasn't alone. Perhaps he had a girlfriend tucked away in the township somewhere. Surely, he had someone he cared for, a woman who loved him? Otherwise, it was a tragic waste of all that beautiful man-flesh.

Before she could censor her mouth, she asked, "So, you're not married then?" She tried to keep her question light, but the way he gave her a quick sideways glance, she knew she hadn't managed.

They walked for so long in silence Kait thought he wasn't

going to answer. And why would he? She'd strayed into his private business and perhaps he didn't want her to know.

A seagull cried high above, swept away into the sky by the air currents. "I was married, a long time ago. She couldn't hack all the time I spent away with the army. Sent me a Dear John letter while I was deployed in East Timor. Luckily, we weren't married long enough to have kids, so in the end it was all fairly painless."

Kait didn't think any type of divorce could be painless. And the slight tightening of the lines around Jack's mouth called him out as a liar.

"Oh. I'm sorry."

"No need to be sorry, it's ancient history. And I'm better off without her in my world." He let his gaze rest on the incoming wavelets. "I like my life just the way it is. Simple. Uncomplicated. No one else to worry about."

She could definitely see the appeal of an uncomplicated life, one where you didn't have to answer to anyone apart from yourself. Except...what about love? Didn't everyone need love in their lives? Even though her love life was a shambles, she felt a little sad for Jack that he chose to live without.

But then again, perhaps he was the one who had it right. Look where love had led her. To a life of misery and dominance. Now she was free from Dario, there was no way she was ever hurrying back into romance. No way.

"Deanna mentioned you both left bad relationships recently," Jack said. His voice was smooth, belying the hit his comment gave to her solar plexus.

Shit. She guessed she deserved that. She'd opened the door by asking him about his personal life. Now what was she supposed to say? Silently, she cursed Deanna. The younger woman had been flustered by Raine's penetrating questions when she'd dropped that seemingly innocuous gem of information on the front veranda yesterday.

"Ah…yes, that's right." Kait didn't want Jack—or anybody, for that matter—to know she'd fled an abusive relationship. Didn't want anyone getting hints about her true identity. Because Dario was after her, and the only way to escape his clutches was to disappear into the top end of Australia. Blend in and keep her head low until Dario stopped looking for her. Or she came up with a better plan. She'd only told Deanna out of pure necessity. No one else could know the truth of her previous life. Well, Deanna and Monika. Because Monika was blood. And one day Kait hoped she could be reunited with her sister, could renew their relationship, become best friends again. Which reminded her, she needed to speak to Monika again soon. But she was wandering away from the real situation. What to tell Jack?

"My husband and I were having…problems, I guess." There she'd admitted she'd been married. It suddenly made her feel dirty and diminished somehow. How would Jack view her now? Just one more statistic on marriage failure list. But he was also a divorce statistic. So perhaps he didn't view her as quite so much of a failure as she did herself.

She didn't want to talk to Jack about her problems with Dario. She didn't want him to know how diminished and helpless he'd made her feel. The way Dario had degraded her very soul. She was broken, but she didn't want him to know that. Cloudwater was a chance to start a new life. To create a new Kait. And what better time to try out a new persona than now.

A source of deflection, that's what she needed. She should tell him something close to honesty. Close but not exact.

"But the main reason I'm on this journey of discovery is because I lost my best friend not long ago. She died of cancer, and her death made me second-guess my life. I left my husband and my old life behind to try and find something new."

His smile lost the dimples, and instead, emitted waves of commiseration.

"I'm sorry for your loss." He reached out and touched her shoulder. A simple touch, the barest of contact, but her stomach suddenly clenched. Her words had been meant to deflect his interest away from who her husband was and why she'd left him. But instead, she'd uttered the simple truth. A slice of grief clawed at her guts, so raw she had to hold in a sob.

"The loss of a good friend is often harder than the loss of a family member," he murmured, and she suddenly wondered if he was speaking from personal experience. "Not least of all because we choose our friends, choose who we let into our lives."

God, it was as if he were speaking to her very soul. Deanna knew the bare bones of Kait's grief, knew that she'd recently lost her best friend. But Kait had downplayed the loss at the time, not wanting to fall into a bought of hysterical crying in front of the young woman.

And she didn't want to do any hysterical crying in front of Jack either.

"That's so true," she said on a half sob. Shit, here came the tears regardless. "I miss Susan so much. She was my rock. She was so brave, and she made me want to be brave." Another tear fell, and Jack rested his hand lightly on her shoulder. They continued to walk in silence, him lending her his steadying presence. He didn't pull her into an embrace, and she didn't want him to.

After a while, she lifted her head and stared out to sea, the gentle waves acting as a balm to her wounded spirit. Jack's hand anchored her to the here and now, so she wasn't carried away on a wave of tears and emotion.

"I remember her best when I'm at the beach. She loved the

water and the sand."

"Then you should come here often," he replied. "As often as you need to, so you can spend time with her."

Kait gave him a teary glance. Who was this man? Some sort of spiritual guru? She half expected him to have transformed into a little monk in an orange robe. But he was still just Jack, walking along beside her. Handsome Jack. Sexy Jack.

"But you know as soon as you tell Raine your story she'll start spouting her guff about karma and how she believes that's why you belong in Cloudwater." He gave her a lopsided wink, and she raised a watery smile in return.

Jack dropped his hand, and Kait drew in a deep breath.

Well, that'd been unexpected.

She never thought she'd be telling Jack about her dead friend, and she never thought it'd be so cathartic.

The wind had picked up as they'd walked down the beach and now it tugged at her cap, threatening to tear it off and tumble it into the water. The congenial silence stretched out between them. Then, as if they were two birds on the wing— the kind that changes direction without seeming to have any sort of communication—they swung around and headed back the way they'd come.

Jack drew in a breath. "I'm meeting with two of the indigenous rangers tomorrow. You're welcome to join me and find out more about the cleanup if you like."

Kait considered him for a second. "If it gets me out of doing yoga with Raine, then I'm in."

"Good, I'll come and collect you at around nine thirty tomorrow. Deanna's welcome as well."

"Great. Thank you." That was good, something to take her mind off her problems.

When Deanna had talked about joining Jack to help him find the ghost nets, Kait had agreed to join them on the surface, but hadn't really thought she'd actually do it. It'd just been a conversation, another way to persuade Jack to take them to Cloudwater Bay. But now she was here and had seen how beautiful this coastline was, something stirred inside her. If she could do something solid and tangible to help, then why wouldn't she?

# CHAPTER SIXTEEN

Deanna drew a deep breath into her lungs. Held it there for three seconds. Then she gently expelled the air through her mouth. This deep breathing thing was kind of trippy. But she had to admit she was feeling calmer already. Cracking one eye open, she glanced sideways at Raine, who was sitting cross-legged on the mat beside her. This was the second morning she'd agreed to do yoga with Raine.

"Concentrate," Raine warned her gently.

Snapping her eyes closed, Deanna lifted her chin and continued to breathe deeply. How the hell did that woman know she had her eyes open? Deanna suspected she was clairvoyant.

The sun's early-morning rays played over Deanna's face and she tilted her head to catch the warmth. Raine insisted on starting at six am every morning, whether the sun was up or not. Because it was summer, and the days were long, the golden orb had already bobbed over the horizon. The sound of birds drifted past, brought by the gentle morning breeze. Raine's idea of yoga in the garden this morning had been a good one. They'd set up mats side by side in the cool air, and Raine had talked her through the sun salutation warmup, gliding through the movements with practiced ease. Deanna almost felt like she *could* be worshiping the sun and let herself flow through the poses, just as Raine directed.

"Ten minutes mediation this morning. Are you joining me?" Raine's melodious voice had washed over her. That was the one thing Raine didn't insist on Deanna completing if she didn't want to. Yesterday, Deanna had decided against partaking. But today she thought she'd give it a try.

"Yes, I will."

"Good," Raine purred. "Close your eyes and empty your mind."

The rules were simple: sit cross-legged on your mat and concentrate on your breathing. Nothing else. She could do this. Raine had said it was good for a person's soul. Meditation every day helped to clear the mind. Clear the chakras. Made you ready to receive what the day had to give.

Deanna's nose itched. What should she do? Raine had said no moving. No thinking. Nothing.

The itch got worse.

As slowly as she could, Deanna lifted her hand and scratched her nose quietly.

Good. Now she could go back to thinking about nothing.

But a million thoughts crowded her mind. Like how long were she and Kait really going to stay in this oasis? Like finding the right moment to tell Kait about her own financial windfall—so the other woman could let go any fears she might have that Deanna meant to up and steal her money. Like the way... Nope. She pushed the thoughts away and concentrated again.

Her legs felt restless, like they wanted to unfurl and stretch out.

This shouldn't be so hard.

Not daring to crack her eyes open this time, she bit her lip and thought about getting up. Nope. She could do this. She could sit still for ten minutes. She was a grown woman for fuck's sake.

Without her consent, her mind wandered again, this time to the woman sitting beside her.

Raine was an interesting character, and Deanna felt herself being drawn into her personality, almost against her will, like the moon orbiting the earth.

Yesterday, Deanna had helped Raine in the garden. They'd picked a basket full of zucchinis, so big and green and fresh, Deanna had never seen anything like them before. You certainly didn't get vegetables like this in the supermarkets. She could hardly believe all this produce came from one small square of earth. Deanna hadn't been kidding when she said she wanted to learn to garden. And so, she'd reached in and cut off the zucchinis one by one. Digging her fingers into the earth and pulling out some weeds when Raine showed her which ones didn't belong. It was kind of soothing, having your hands covered in dirt. The earth was a dark red, almost black, in the raised garden beds. When Deanna pointed out it was different to the ochre-colored plains behind them, and the white sand crowding in from the beach, Raine smiled as if she'd said something intelligent.

"I add lots of organic matter," Raine had said. "Blood and bone and all the scraps from my kitchen. Otherwise, nothing would grow in this soil. Apart from the native plants, which are well adapted to practically no nutrients and low rainfall."

"Cool" was all Deanna could find to say.

Then she followed Raine into her large, rambling kitchen, with copper pots hanging from a rack in the ceiling and bunches of dried herbs everywhere. It reminded Deanna a little of a witch's kitchen.

They added capsicum and tomatoes, also grown in Raine's garden, then spices, sugar, and water before cooking it up in one giant pot. The smell filled the whole house. Tangy and slightly sweet. Deanna watched Raine's nimble hands chopping and dicing, weaving the knife around like a dancer on a stage. Raine had long fingers. Fine-boned, but also strong and tanned, probably from all the time she spent in her garden. Raine was like a balm over Deanna's raging river of emotions and hormones. The calm to Deanna's stormy ocean. Raine was the complete opposite to Tamika. Wise. Nothing seemed to ruffle her. Which made Deanna raise her eyebrows in contemplation. She'd like to see Raine lose her refined mask. Wondered what she would find underneath.

Deanna knew she was in trouble. She was crushing big time on Raine. And she was completely helpless to stop herself from falling.

After the relish had simmered all morning, they'd put it into sterilized jars, keeping one out to eat that day. It was such a domestic scene. Deanna almost laughed and told Raine she thought she must be dreaming. But ever the optimist, and always open-minded, Deanne decided to soak it all in. She could store this memory away with the other secret memories, to open and explore when times got bad again. Because they always did.

Afterward, they had a lunch of crusty bread topped with piles of the pickles. It was the most delicious thing Deanna had ever tasted. It might've been better with some tangy cheese, but Deanna was happy to embrace Raine's veganism for the moment. Kait had joined them, babbling on and on about how beautiful the beach was. And how it was never-ending. And how amazing Jack's house was. Not that Raine's wasn't amazing as well, Kait had amended quickly. Kait still seemed hooked up on Jack, as if he were somehow a lifeline. To what, Deanna wasn't sure. A lifeline to her old life, perhaps.

This morning, after yoga was finished, she and Kait were going for a drive out along the beach with Jack. Deanna could hardly contain her excitement. She'd asked if Raine wanted to come with them, but Raine had shaken her head no, with a grimace of distaste. Clearly something to do with either Jack or the ghost nets weren't to Raine's liking. But Deanna decided not to ask what. They were going to meet with some indigenous rangers and talk about collecting the ghost nets. She might even get to see one of these famous nets. Wouldn't that be—

Raine's soft voice cut through Deanna's thoughts, and she gave a guilty little jump. "Time's up," Raine said. "You can open your eyes now."

Would Raine know that Deanna had failed at the meditation?

Raine put her hands together as if in prayer, bowed her head, and said reverently, "Namaste."

"Namaste," Deanna repeated, not understanding the word, but getting the gist that it was Raine's version of conveying her gratitude. Gratitude to whom, Deanna wasn't so sure. To the world in general? To the sun? Perhaps even herself? She would figure it out. She always did. Tamika had said she had street smarts. Deanna didn't know about that, but she did know she was good at figuring people out, working out their secret wants and motivations.

"Time for breakfast," Raine said cheerily, standing and stretching her arms above her head.

Deanna took a second to admire the older woman's figure. Dressed in figure-hugging yoga pants and a small crop top, it was clear to Deanna that Raine had not an ounce of fat on her body. Slim and willowy, she seemed to have kept her youth. Perhaps all this yoga stuff was good for you after all. Raine released her hair from where she'd pulled it back into a bun to keep it out of her face this morning. Long, silvery strands fell over her shoulders and down her back. Without thinking, Deanna reached out and took a lock of hair between her fingers.

"It's so soft," she murmured.

Raine considered her with cool, gray eyes. "I'm glad you think so," she finally said. Raine reached up and trapped Deanna's hand in hers, tipping it over she kissed each one of her fingertips. "You're so sweet," she continued, a small frown marring her smooth forehead. "What am I going to do with you?"

Deanna's head was reeling from the feel of Raine's lips on her skin and she couldn't fully digest the meaning of her words. Sweet? She'd never been called sweet before. What did it mean? Did it mean Raine liked her? Because she desperately wanted the other woman's esteem. Or did it mean she thought she was young and gullible? Perhaps too young for such a worldly wise woman as herself. Well, Deanna was going to prove her wrong.

"Come on. I bartered a bag of my tomatoes for some mushrooms from Kelly and Roger yesterday. They grow them in a dark shed, in boxes of manure. We can fry them up and have them on toast with some of my homemade baked beans? How does that sound?"

"Delicious," Deanna said, meaning it. One thing was for sure; she certainly wasn't going hungry eating vegan food.

Kait arrived downstairs just as breakfast was being served. The wonderful smell of frying mushrooms must've drawn her out of her room. Hair in a tangle and still in her pajamas, it was obvious Kait had just got up. No early morning yoga for her. Deanna was sure she could change her friend's mind; she just needed to work on her a little more.

"Just in time," Raine sang gaily as Kait joined them at the large, rustic kitchen table. "Need to keep your strength up if you're going to spend the day with Jack." Raine pushed the plate of mushrooms toward Kait and watched her expectantly.

"Thank you," Kait said graciously, sitting ramrod straight

in her chair and dragging her fingers through her hair in an attempt to tame it. "This looks amazing." Kait leaned in and drew in the aroma of the freshly cooked mushrooms.

From Deanna's perspective, it seemed that Raine was trying extra hard to bring Kait out of her shell. Ever since they'd arrived at Cloudwater Bay, Kait had reverted to the woman Deanna had met at the roadhouse that first day. The false façade had sprung back up. The slightly ditsy, slightly aloof woman, and she was once more an unreadable book. Especially when they were around Raine, as if she didn't completely trust the woman. Which was sad, because Deanna knew that Raine might very well be the best person in their lives right now. Apart from Jack, of course. But she understood that Kait found it hard to trust, and so she decided to give her friend a little more time to adjust.

Not able to wait any longer, while the other two women went through this polite dance with each other, Deanna pounced on the food, piling her plate high with toast and mushrooms, adding baked beans on the side. Then she began to shovel the food into her mouth.

"I love that you appreciate my cooking so much," Raine said with the tinkling laugh.

"Yes," Kait joined in. "I've never seen anyone appreciate their food quite so much."

Deanna didn't care that they were poking fun at her. She had broad shoulders; she could take it. When you worked on the mines, surrounded by egotistical, misogynistic men, you had to learn to eat fast and take what you wanted before it all disappeared.

"Why do we need to keep our strength up?" Deanna asked through a mouthful of food.

"Because Jack has a habit of losing track of the time. Especially when he's talking conservation with the rangers. He might keep you out there till sunset, and he'll forget you haven't eaten lunch."

"I don't mind," Deanna said eagerly. "I can't wait to get out there and be of help."

Kait, always more circumspect, said, "In that case, I'm definitely coming back for seconds."

Deanna nearly rolled her eyes. Kait always ate like a sparrow compared to her. Sitting at the table, using a knife and fork as if she was some sort of queen, and complaining about Deanna's table manners. From the little Kait had told her about her life with her husband, Kait had been rich, pampered, and sheltered. Except for having to put up with an abusive husband, Kait seemed to have led a cushy life. She needed to learn that you should eat what you could when you could, because it wasn't always going to be there when you wanted it. Deanna had learned that the hard way. Even though she'd inherited her parents' money, her adolescence hadn't always been smooth. Without a proper father or mother figure to guide her, she'd sometimes fallen in with the wrong crowd, and she'd often found herself on the wrong side of the law. Her grandmother hadn't been happy when Deanna announced she had a job working at the mine in Kalgoorlie, but she also said that if anyone could do it, Deanna could. She had an inner strength not many others possessed, as her grandmother had often told her.

"I want to thank you again for your hospitality," Kait said to Raine, laying down her knife and fork. "And I also want you to know, I don't intend to shirk my duties. I wasn't around much yesterday, and I apologize for that. So, please let me know what I can do to pay my way while we stay at your house."

"Not a problem," Raine replied. "Everyone takes their own time to adjust to this place." She waved a hand in the air dismissively.

"Even so, I want to pull my weight."

"Fair enough." Raine narrowed her eyes and pursed her lips, thinking. Deanna wasn't fooled; Raine would have figured out exactly what she wanted from Kait long ago. "The front veranda needs sweeping, and the tables and chairs need a clean. The best and worst thing about living this close to the ocean is the sea breeze. But that same breeze always carries half the beach in with it." Raine helped herself to the pot of baked beans, piling nearly as many on her plate as Deanna had. Hah, at least Raine had a hearty appetite.

"That sounds easy enough," Kait replied, looking almost relieved.

"And if you could brush away some of the cobwebs around the eaves, too. You know, generally tidy the place up."

"Sure thing." Kait smiled, but the small, tight lines remained around her mouth. "I'll get on to that straight after breakfast."

\* \* \*

Exactly an hour and a half later, Kait's voice drifted up the stairs. "Jack's here." She'd been sitting out front, waiting for him for the past ten minutes on her sparkling clean veranda.

Deanna bounded down the stairs from her bedroom, expecting to see the B-Double truck parked outside. She stopped at the top of the front steps, taken aback by the sleek, black Toyota ute that sat on the sand waiting for them.

"Where's your truck?" But she regretted the words as soon as they were out of her mouth. Of course, they wouldn't be driving his huge truck up and down the beach. Now she just looked stupid.

"This one is much more fun," Jack said, ducking his head and peering at her through the passenger window, making her feel immediately better. Jack wouldn't hold it against her if she acted like a dimwit; he wasn't the judgmental type. Kait had already snagged shotgun, which left Deanna to jump in the rear seat.

"You're right, this car will be much more fun," Deanna gushed. Hooning down the sand in a big four-wheel drive was definitely her idea of a good time. But Jack drove sedately through the sandy streets, so Deanna wound down her window and enjoyed the view instead.

"How's it working out with Raine?" Jack asked, directing the question to both of them.

"Really good," Deanna replied enthusiastically. "She's great. Thanks for suggesting her place."

"I'm glad you're getting along," Jack replied cryptically, raising an eyebrow in Kait's direction. Kait didn't reply, merely raised her eyebrow in return, transmitting some sort of secret message. She wished Kait liked Raine a little more. But maybe with time…

Deanna sighed and watched as the rustic shanties and beach shacks slipped by on either side of the car. Raine's house was definitely one of the nicest in this township. Most of them looked run-down, and unkempt.

It was time Deanna got out and about. Met some of the locals, listened to some of their gossip, and found out what was what in this little town. She hadn't forgotten that she was going to help Kait construct a new life away from her dominating husband. And the first and most critical part of that was to change her identity. Which meant building a fake life, using fake paperwork. Someone in this little hamlet would be able to help her; this place was full of dodgy characters, most of them trying to avoid the law in one way or another. They couldn't have chosen a more perfect place if they'd tried to hide away from humanity for a few weeks. At least, Deanna hoped it was only a few weeks, even with her growing attraction toward Raine, Deanna didn't want to be stuck in this isolated little bloody place for too long.

The vehicle turned away from the town, down a sandy

path edged with limestone rocks, and suddenly they were on the beach. Jack skillfully maneuvered the car through the soft sand until they were on the edge where the waves met the beach. Then he pushed the accelerator, and they were suddenly flying down the shore, so fast they left the seagulls behind. Deanna hung out of her open window, whooping with delight.

"This is more like it," she yelled at Jack, letting the wind whip her hair into a frenzy.

He grinned at her from the front seat and even Kait extended her hand out the front window to feel the breeze blow between her fingers.

They must've driven like this for at least twenty minutes, until Jack slowed, but the beach still stretched out before them. Miles and miles of sand. Ahead of them, another four-wheel drive was stopped up near where the dunes rolled away in hillocks above the beach. Two figures stood up as they approached and Deanna strained to see what the couple had been staring at.

Jack pulled up next to the white four-wheel drive and hopped out and went to stare at whatever it was in the dune.

Deanna scrambled out after him, almost slipping over in the soft sand, then stood at Jack's elbow.

They were all looking at a mess of blue twine piled high in a hollow of the dunes.

"Waru. Maya." Jack nodded at the two strangers—presumably the indigenous rangers. They nodded sagely back. Deanna noted there was no effusive greeting. No handshakes, no fist-bumping. Just a quiet acknowledgment. One ranger was male; Deanna had no idea how old he was—could be anywhere between forty to sixty—with a sparse gray beard and dark, sparkling eyes. She decided he must be Waru. The other was a younger woman, short and a little stout, her black hair pulled back into a ponytail. She must be

Maya. They both wore a dark-green shirt emblazoned with an insignia of some kind. Kait finally arrived at Deanna's elbow and all three stared at the plastic tangle at their feet.

"This is Kait." Jack motioned his hand in her direction. "And Deanna. They're keen to lend us a hand this year."

"Morning," the woman replied quietly. Waru merely let his dark gaze drift over them speculatively. Not much for small talk it seemed.

"Is this a ghost net?" Deanna asked, unable to hold her tongue any longer.

"Yes," Jack replied with a laugh. "You finally get your first look at a ghost net."

"What are they going to do with it?" she asked, still in awe.

"They'll record any dead sea creatures they find, then haul it into the tray and take it to the dump. Get it off the beach and away, where it can't do any more damage."

"How did it get here?" Deanna dropped to her knees to get closer. She could see a myriad of shells and coral caught in the mesh.

"Washed up by the last king tide," Waru spoke for the first time. "Big waves carry it in and leave it on the beach. But it can still trap animals. Still be a problem for the beach. Lots of plastic. So we take it away."

"Oh, look." Deanna pointed to a pile of bleached bones. "Something died in there."

"That's a turtle," Jack said sadly. "Like I told you before, they get trapped and drown. See his shell, it's farther in under that pile of seaweed." He hunkered down and pointed into the dark recesses of the netting.

Deanna covered her mouth. "Oh, no, the poor thing. Look, Kait."

Kait got down on her knees next to Deanna and removed her cap, squinting her eyes against the bright sunshine, and peered into the tangled mess where her finger was pointing.

"That is sad," Kait agreed. "Especially when some of our turtle species are endangered."

Deanna looked for more signs of drowned sea creatures. There were a couple of large fish skeletons, some white fisherman's buoys, broken pieces of coral, and as she looked closer, short segments of rope twined through the blue netting. This particular ghost net must've been washed up on the beach for at least a couple of months to have nothing but skeletons left behind. Deanna imagined the poor turtle struggling for hours, or perhaps even days, to get free. Jack had said the animals usually drowned. What a terrible waste of life. These poor animals didn't deserve this sort of death.

Kait stood, perhaps not wanting to look at all this death any longer. But Deanna was determined to imprint every little soul in her mind. She needed to get out there, out in the ocean where it was all happening to try and stop this. It was too late by the time the nets were washed up on the beach. Yes, the rangers were doing a good thing by removing the rubbish from the otherwise pristine strip of sand, but more needed to be done.

"I'd love to hear more about what you do," Kait said. "Jack has already told me some of it."

Maya was the one to speak up, Waru watching her with unreadable eyes.

"Parts of this coastland are owned by indigenous groups and organizations.," she started. "That's why us rangers are so important. We live and work on country. Most of us grew up in this area."

Deanna got to her feet so she could listen better to what Maya was saying.

"We also monitor the dugong and sea turtle populations in this area. Make sure they stay healthy and strong."

"Indigenous groups are still allowed to hunt the dugong, as long as they do it using traditional methods," Jack chimed in.

"Really?" Kait sounded as surprised as Deanna felt. She'd always thought dugongs were protected.

"Yes," Maya picked up the conversation again. "We only kill what we need. One dugong can feed many families. We don't waste anything."

She didn't say it, but she didn't have to. Even Deanna knew how wasteful Western society was.

"I want to go out in the boats with you," Deanna said, turning to Jack. "I know I said I can't dive but I want you to teach me," she demanded.

"I don't..." He looked like he was about to argue. But then maybe something in her pleading face made him change his mind. "Sure, I'll see what I can do."

"You'll need to make it soon," Waru said quietly.

Jack's eyes turned sharp, but his tone was nonchalant, to match Waru's. "Why's that?"

"Big storm on the way."

"Really? There's nothing forecast."

Waru shrugged one shoulder and smiled, showing two missing front teeth. Then he tapped his nose. "Local knowledge always better. I feel it in my bones. Who you believe? Some white fella sitting in some office somewhere? Or my bones?"

"His bones never been wrong before," Maya added.

Jack whistled and looked at the sky. "So you're saying the first cyclone of the season is on the way?"

"Yep," Waru replied in his succinct manner.

Deanna had never lived through a proper cyclone. It was rare that a cyclone ever came as far south as Geraldton. She'd seen on the news how much havoc they could wreak. Cool. Something new for her to experience.

The look Kait threw in her direction, however, told a completely different story. She was scared. There was no need to be scared. Didn't Kait realize that Cloudwater Bay had withstood many cyclones over the years? This would be just one more.

"How long do you think?"

"Four or five days." Waru was already turning away. "Give us a hand to get this on the truck?"

"Sure." All three of them scrambled to help the rangers drag the net out of the sand. It was so much heavier than Deanna had expected.

# CHAPTER SEVENTEEN

Kait stared nervously at the rolling waves disappearing beneath the boat and clung to the metal railing around the rear. She'd made a mistake; she should never have let Deanna talk her into this.

It'd been three days since they'd met the rangers on the beach. Three days since she made the blasé decision to go out in Jack's boat. After seeing all the dead things caught in the ghost net, and seeing the Deanna's distraught reaction, she knew she had to go. Jack had taken her and Deanna out in his boat yesterday on a trial run and taught them the basics of how to snorkel and showed them how to wriggle their way into the skin-tight wetsuits he'd borrowed from someone in the Cloudwater community. The tropical water was warm enough, the suits were more to stop jellyfish stings.

But that wasn't good enough for Deanna, she'd demanded that Jack show her how to scuba dive, and he'd just laughed, saying scuba tank diving was way beyond her capabilities, and way beyond his capabilities for teaching her and did she realize she needed to do an accredited scuba diving course to get a diving ticket before he let her off the boat anyway?

Kait had been fine yesterday. Put on a brave face and hopped in the water, following all of Jack's advice. She'd been so proud of herself. This was the first thing she'd done where she was truly outside her comfort zone. The first time she was testing her resolve to do more with her life, to become more, not merely sit in the bleachers, but to become a full-time player.

Apart from leaving her husband and stealing his money. Oh, and the dead man at the bottom of the gorge, of course.

Susan had also been proud, clapping from her seat at the back of the boat as she watched Kait duck beneath the waves. Susan was predictably missing today, however. Keeping her own council as to the sanity of this project.

Clouds gathered on the horizon. Looking fluffy and nonthreatening. Jack assured the two women, it was indeed the beginning of the buildup to a cyclone. Waru had been right with his prediction as today, the bureau of meteorology had issued a warning of a deep low forming off the northern coast.

Jack had said they either go out today, or they'd have to wait a week—perhaps more—before they could venture out again. And even then, the water would be murky and full of sand and debris after the storm.

Three other small boats had joined Jack on this mission today. The Indigenous rangers—teaming up with two more members from their clan—a second bunch of locals, and four guys up from Broome, who'd brought their own fast, flashy boat. They'd launched the boats right off the beach. Kait had never seen anything like it before, and she and Deanna watched in awe as they made it seem so easy. Just as Jack made it seem so easy. Was there anything that man wasn't good at?

Kait hadn't even realized Jack owned a boat. Until he turned up pulling it on a trailer behind his ute yesterday to take them out for their snorkel lesson. Supposedly, he kept it in Roger's shed because he didn't have room in his own; his truck and his ute took up all the space. It was bigger than she expected. Made of steel with a double hull, it looked old, and when Kait gave it a worried glance, Jack said not to worry, this boat would never sink.

Deanna bounced on her toes eagerly next to Kait, her loose hair whipping about her face in the breeze. Sometimes she wished the girl didn't have quite so much energy. But one glance at Deanna's broad smile made Kait's lips twitch as well. This was an adventure, after all.

Jack was driving, sitting in a small seat beneath the large shade canopy and using a steering wheel to guide the boat. His tanned hands sat easy on the wheel, and he looked as at home in the boat as he had driving the enormous semitrailer. Kait had lost sight of the other vessels, as they'd all fanned out in a large arc, heading straight out to sea.

It was this fact that was scaring Kait most of all. The big, unfathomable deep blue surrounded them on all sides. She could no longer see the beach and it made her heart beat faster with the knowledge. Yesterday, they'd only gone about half a kilometer out, where the beach remained a white strip of sand, still within reach, and the water was a crystal clear aqua blue. Now, it was indigo blue, almost black, and foreboding. The water here must be really deep. So deep she'd never hope to touch the bottom.

"I think I see something." One of the two other men accompanying them on Jack's boat—they'd been quickly introduced as Ryan and Pete—raised his hand and pointed to something.

At first glance, the dark, amorphous shape could've been a shadow, or perhaps a patch of seaweed. But on closer inspection, Kait could see the terrible tangle of rope and netting drifting below the surface. It seemed to go on forever. Two foam buoys floated on top of the water, attached to the large mass beneath, possibly the reason the man had spotted the net in the first place.

"That's huge," she murmured. At least four times the size of the net she'd helped the indigenous rangers pile onto their ute the other day.

"Yeah, it's bigger than normal," Ryan agreed.

Jack brought the boat to a halt close to the floating aggregation and dropped the anchor, while the other two men bustled about getting ready. Then they took turns to sit on the backboard that hovered a few inches above the water, and one by one, dropped into the ocean. It was the women's turn next. Deanna followed the men's example and dangled her legs in the water.

"Wait, Deanna," Kait almost screeched. "How does this work?" She asked Jack, turning toward him and putting off the inevitable for a few more seconds, wanting to make sure she knew exactly what was expected of her.

"It's pretty self-explanatory. Everyone encircles the net and drags it toward the boat. I'll take the lead, and walk it up on deck first, while the rest of you gather it up and bring it to me. It'll be heavier than you expect, so don't try and force it. Slow and steady, that's how we'll get it in."

Kait nodded, and Deanna asked, "Can I go now?"

"Sure. Just be careful you don't get tangled in the net yourself," Jack warned.

With a squeak of excitement, Deanna launched herself into the water. Kait was slower to walk down the two steps and dangle her flippered feet in the small, lapping waves. She watched Deanna's blonde head dip below the water and then resurface a few feet away, blowing air and water from her snorkel.

Where was Susan when she needed her?

Jack stood on the step behind her, decked out in scuba gear —he'd already attained his diving ticket years ago. Like he'd said to Deanna yesterday, not all the nets would be floating on the surface and easy to reach. Some would be snagged on the ocean floor, caught on rocky outcrops or reefs, or in large drifts of seaweed. Jack, Ryan and Pete were all wearing scuba gear and would do any deep diving that might be required. Most of the people on the other boats were also scuba divers, but Kait had been heartened to see Waru and Maya wore a simple snorkel set as well.

"Are you okay?" Jack touched her fleetingly on the shoulder, blue-gray eyes compassionate. Did he know how nervous she was? "You don't have to—"

"Don't." She held up a hand in his face. "Don't you dare give me an excuse. I'm going in." She'd set this challenge for herself, and she was going through with it, dammit.

Taking a deep lung full of air, she launched herself into the water. There was a moment of shock as the cool liquid seeped into her wetsuit; then she popped to the surface like a cork.

But this felt different to yesterday.

Something was wrong.

It was hard to breathe, and her chest constricted painfully.

She took the snorkel out of her mouth and dragged in great gulps of air. But that didn't seem to help, and she began to claw at the water. The boat. She needed to get back on the boat.

Suddenly, Jack was beside her, his wet hair glistening in the sunshine. "Lie on your back, and breathe out long and slow," he said. "You're hyperventilating, you need to slow your breathing down. It's okay I've got you." His arm went under her shoulders as she did what she was told, staring up at the bright blue sky above, trying not to think of what was below her. She slowed her breathing, resorting to an old trick she learnt from Susan. In through the nose, out through the mouth. It was a sure way to get your body back under control, Susan had told her before.

"It's just so...deep," she gasped, wanting to explain her

feelings. The fear of the unknown. The big blue. And boy was it big. Her mind was also going to other places she didn't want. "And...what about...sharks?" She asked turning her face toward him, unable to hide the panic that must be showing in her eyes.

"You're wearing a shark shield, that's the big bracelet I put around your ankle. We're all wearing one. I'm not going to lie, there are sharks out here, but we're taking precautions, I've never known anyone to be attacked by a shark while hauling in ghost nets."

His soothing voice and supportive arm had a calming effect. She trusted him. Which was an interesting discovery. He was all masculine, all male, but without that stupid bluster and arrogance a lot of men had. She believed him when he said she would be okay.

All of a sudden, Kait felt a tingle right in the middle of her chest—the touch of her best friend's hand. Susan was telling her she was going to be fine. Part of Kait wanted to do this for her friend. Susan would never get a chance to dive into the great blue ocean. She could do this one thing for her.

"I'm okay now," Kait said. "You can let me go." It took an effort of will not to think about what might be circling beneath her. But she put the snorkel in her mouth and moved her rubbery arms until she was sort of swimming toward the ghost net.

"You have to come see this," Deanna called, waving her arms enthusiastically from the other side of the net. "I just rescued a fish. It was caught, and I set it free."

With the idea of freeing more sea creatures keeping her afloat, she set off in Deanna's direction.

Half an hour later, Kait grabbed the back of the boat. "I did it," she said, taking Jack's hand as he helped haul her up the steps.

"Yes, you did." Jack's eyes shone with delight. "You're a

brave woman, Kait. You need to give yourself more credit," he said softly in her ear, the words meant for her alone. Her chest expanded, and she felt as if she was floating on air. She'd conquered her fear of the water, and it felt amazing. What would she be capable of next? Bungee jumping? Skydiving? The world was her oyster. For the next few minutes at least, until she came back down to earth.

Ryan and Pete clambered onto the boat, and Jack pulled up the anchor and got the boat moving again, talking into his CB radio to find out the other boats' locations. Kait joined Deanna kneeling on the large, open deck at the rear of the boat as she picked through the frothy piles of mysterious ghost net. Water still drained from the heap, making the wooden deck slippery. The net had a strange story to tell. There were many, many fish corpses in all states of decay; the net was very good at doing what it was designed for. But there were also bits of driftwood, a plastic toothbrush, a child's toy, and the list went on.

Deanna began to pull things out of the netting, making a pile of odds and ends on the deck next to her. Mostly, it was the bones from the dead fish, sometimes it was the bones of a larger sea animal, long gone.

"When I told Raine we were coming out here with Jack, she said that while the ghost nets are a terrible thing, sometimes beauty can be found even in the worst places," Deanna said quietly.

"What did she mean by that?" Kait asked.

"I'm not really sure. But she said people had been known to make all sorts of things from the remains of the nets. Like artwork and sculptures and stuff. As a way of raising people's awareness about the travesty that is happening up here." Deanna carefully placed a bone on top of her collection, and fixed her blue gaze on Kait. "I reckon I could do that. Make art from this waste."

It took a few seconds for Kait to digest Deanna's words. Quashing her immediate reaction, which was to scoff out loud, she thought about Deanna's suggestion.

"Why not?" she replied. "Both your parents were incredibly artistic. I bet you've inherited their ability."

"Do you think so?" Deanna's eyes shone with the possibility.

"Yes, you should go for it. What are you thinking? Where would you start?"

Deanna picked up a handful of the fragile fishbones and laid them in the palm of her hand. "These remind me of blades of grass. And the fish scales remind me of flower petals. I don't really know." Deanna shrugged. "But I could make a picture from these bones."

"Great idea." Kait could almost see what Deanna was talking about. If it made the girl happy, then what was the harm in it?

Kait stood and leaned against the railing, bending her knees to keep her balance as the boat puttered across the ocean, looking for the next piece of pollution. She could hardly believe she was here. It was all a little dreamlike. She could almost forget about Dario and his thugs. Almost forget that she killed a man in an effort to keep her freedom. But she couldn't allow herself to forget. Because that would be dangerous.

Cloudwater Bay was just a small reprieve, a place to regroup and find her feet again. Decide what she was going to do. Perhaps not with the rest of her life, but at least the next few months.

She also needed to get in touch with Monika again. Her sister would be wondering what was going on. It was almost a week since she'd last spoken to her. She may also have some news. Had Dario tried to contact her? And if he had, what story had he concocted to cover Kait's disappearance?

There was no cell phone reception in the community of Cloudwater. But Jack had said he, along with some others, owned a satellite phone, in case of emergency. Should she ask Jack if she could borrow his sat phone? It was taking a risk. He might ask who she was calling. And she knew little about how sat phones worked. Would her sister's number be stored in the phone afterward? Or could she erase it? The only other alternative was to get someone to drive her into Broome, where she could get some reception.

And then there was all that money sitting in a storage locker in Exmouth. She'd have to go back and retrieve it at some stage. She was fooling herself that she was safe here. She'd let the sun and the sand and the isolation lull her into a false sense of security, but she couldn't let that go on forever.

Glancing down to where Deanna sat at her feet, she studied the top of the woman's head. What would Deanna do when Kait decided to move on? She seemed to be forming a strong attachment to both Raine and Cloudwater Bay. Would she demand to come with Kait, or would her growing connections keep her here? Deanna and Kait were on two different paths in life. Deanna was young, had her whole life ahead of her. She had the potential to find a job, find a partner, settle down, even have kids if that was what she wanted. Kait had no room left in her life for any of that. Theirs was a strange friendship; they had nothing in common —except for the secret of a murdered man at the bottom of the gorge. But Kait couldn't ignore this ever-changing friendship. For whatever reason, she liked the bubbly, flighty, sometimes overzealous, but always optimistic woman. Sometimes she felt her maternal instinct take over, and she just wanted to take Deanna under her wing and tell her everything would be okay. And then at other times, it was Deanna who seemed to be the wise one. But most of the time it was an equal, balanced relationship. Give and take from both sides.

She didn't want to leave Deanna behind, but she could see no other option. Her life would be one of a fugitive, and Deanna didn't deserve that.

# CHAPTER EIGHTEEN

Jack sat at his kitchen table and listened to the wind build to a crescendo, rattling the rafters and shaking the windows. Even with the cyclone shutters up, the house was being buffeted by the fierce wind. Jack had spent most of yesterday preparing for the coming storm. Making sure his outdoor furniture was all stacked in the shed and there was nothing loose lying around the garden that could blow away. He'd checked the generator was topped up with diesel and the shed that housed his truck was battened down. He'd filled his bathtub and plastic containers with water, and inventoried his tinned food store to make sure it'd last him through at least the next few weeks. If the roads got cut, it might be a long time before they could restock. Then he'd double-checked his CB radio was working fine. Most people who lived in Cloudwater had one installed in their house. Phone reception out here was so sketchy, they were the only reliable way to stay in contact with each other. And if the cell tower was damaged in this storm, it might be the only source of contact they'd have with the outside world at all.

He got up, coffee cup in hand, and went to peer through the small window in his front door. It was getting crazy out there. The wind howled like a keening child; the sound almost deafening. Swirling sand and debris, small sticks, litter, a fisherman's buoy, all formed a maelstrom of noise and wreckage that barreled down the sandy road in front of his house. The sound was almost deafening and made his ears throb as the drumbeats of wind attacked his house. They were predicting a category four cyclone. A big one. The first ones of the season often were.

He looked down at his bare feet and then back out the window.

Shit.

He had to go and see if they were all right.

Practically jogging to his bedroom, he pulled on socks and work boots, then grabbed a jacket from behind the door. It was nuts to go out in this weather, but he knew he wouldn't rest easy until he checked on Raine and her two guests.

Raine's house had withstood numerous cyclones over the years. So had all the houses in Cloudwater Bay and pulled through. If they didn't survive, the people either left the bay or rebuilt, stronger and better. These little shanties might seem flimsy, but they were built into the side of the sand dunes purposely, affording them shelter from the strongest gusts. The rooflines were low, and aerodynamic. It was one of the reasons there were no double-story houses in the bay. Except Raine's.

So far, nothing seemed to touch her house.

But Jack was worried. He knew Raine would be okay, she always was. But he couldn't rid himself of the nagging voice telling him to go check on them. He'd suggested the two women stay with Raine, and he'd never forgive himself if something happened to them.

If he was completely truthful with himself, it was Kait he most wanted to check on.

She'd done a great job out on his boat the other day. By the end of the day, they'd pulled in four ghost nets, a stack of abandoned lobster traps, and other rubbish left to lie on the ocean floor. He'd watched Kait conquer her demons. A lot of people freaked out when they first stepped into the deep blue. And a lot of people never made it back in a second time. With his help, she'd overcome that terrible cloying fear. Made a conscious decision to do this thing that scared her so much. And by day's end, she'd been like a happy schoolgirl, without a care in the world. It was a great thing to see.

Deanna had done a great job, too; she'd jumped into the water as if she were an old hand. Helping Ryan and Pete drag corners of the net toward the boat, while chattering gaily about how beautiful it was way out in the ocean. For some reason, however, Kait's battle with her fears had left him feeling as if another subtle connection had been made between them. As if each moment he spent with her, they became a little closer.

Leaving Jack conflicted about his feelings for Kait. About his feelings full stop.

Ever since he'd left the Child Protection Agency, his goals had become very simple. Lead a quiet life, away from the bulk of humanity. Away from their greed and unscrupulous behavior. Away from his old life of violence and aggression and tyrannical people who thought they could control everything. And away from love. He didn't need love. He was content with his lot. And falling in love, having another person to care for, and be responsible for, made things too complicated. Too hard.

That was why he'd chosen to drive trucks and live in this little backwater. He was finally satisfied with where he was and who he was becoming. But Kait had put all his hard-won equanimity at risk. And he wasn't sure how to handle it. All he knew was that he wasn't prepared to give it up. If it came down to a choice between Kait and serenity, he knew which one he would choose. Kait had made it quite clear she wasn't staying. She'd be moving on soon, and perhaps it was that, more than anything, which allowed his interest to grow. Just because he wasn't looking for a long-term relationship, didn't mean he couldn't be attracted to a woman. Especially a woman who'd made it clear she was moving on. Did that make him shallow? Looking for a quick fling and nothing more? Because he definitely wasn't looking for anything more.

Opening his front door, he nearly lost his grip as the wind tried to tear it out of his hands with breathtaking force. He had to pull with all his might just to get it to close.

It was dangerous to be out here. The strength of the storm was like a feral dog howling and snarling, trying to knock him over. But he stuck as close to the road verges as he could, and finally came to the narrow alleyway which would take him through the back streets straight to Raine's place. He battled the wind, almost having to bend double at the waist when an extra-strong gust threatened to bowl him over. Keeping an eye open for any large pieces of flying debris, he sheltered his face behind his elbow as best he could, to keep the suffocating sand and grit out of his mouth. Rain pelted him from all angles, spitting and hissing. It was just past midday, but the murky air made it feel more like dusk.

He finally rounded the corner and spotted Raine's house. The cyclone shutters were up in all the windows. That was good. Not bothering to knock on the front door—they'd never hear him anyway—he let himself in through the side gate and went around to the back garden.

Banging his fist against the wooden door, he shouted, "It's Jack, I've come to make sure you're okay." He was about to knock again when it rattled, and Kait's pale face appeared in the gap.

She opened the door wider so he could slip inside. "What are you doing out in this weather?" she asked. "It's like

Armageddon out there."

He didn't disagree, but he was also overwhelmingly happy to see her face. "How are you gals coping?" Removing his wet jacket, he hung it on the coat stand near the back door.

"I'm not sure," Kait replied, leading him down the short hallway to the kitchen. The large room was lit by two kerosene lamps and looked almost warm and inviting compared to the weather outside. Deanna was sitting at the table, a mug of tea between hands.

"Oh, Jack, it's you." Deanna leapt up and embraced him enthusiastically. "It's great to see you." It seemed even Deanna's normal fearlessness had been dampened somewhat by the ferocity of the storm, as she clung to him a little longer than necessary.

Kait picked up her mug of tea and turned to lean her hip against the table. "To be perfectly honest, I'm a little scared. This is my first proper cyclone." She fixed him with her jade-green eyes, worry carved into the lines around her mouth. "Is this normal? I mean, I know cyclones are scary, but this is worse than being on a carnival ride. It just goes on and on and on."

"This is a particularly strong one," Jack admitted. "That's why I popped over to make sure you're safe."

Deanna let him go and re-taken her seat. "Kait has been very worried, so thank you for coming. But this is just another adventure, really. Isn't it?" She shot him a brilliant smile.

"Where's Raine?" Jack asked.

"She's outside, trying to get the generator working," Kait replied. "The lights stopped working a little while ago, which is why we lit the lamps. It was getting dark in here. But she thought she'd go and have a look. Hoping it was something easy to fix, so she could get it going again."

"Crazy woman," Jack muttered under his breath.

"I wanted to go with her," Deanna pouted. "But she said I'd be more hindrance than help."

"Yes, and when you wouldn't listen, she threatened to stab you with the screwdriver if you didn't stay inside," Kait said, raising an eyebrow in Deanna's direction. "I told you to stop bugging her," she added with a slightly patronizing smile.

"I did warn you Raine wasn't a woman to be trifled with," Jack said, trying to hide his smile. Raine hadn't survived out here for this long without having a core of steel. Not many people saw it, but Raine always got what she wanted in the end. And she would've only been trying to protect Deanna, whose lack of experience, both in fixing a generator and dealing with the weather conditions, would've been a hindrance, not a help.

"Yes," Kait added thoughtfully, ignoring Deanna's pout. "That woman is growing on me, slowly but surely."

Jack was glad to hear it.

"I'll go out and see if she needs a hand."

"Watch out she doesn't stab you with the screwdriver," Deanna muttered bitterly.

Jack grabbed his jacket and went back out into the storm.

Five minutes later, he and Raine blew into the kitchen, both of them shaking the rain, from their hair.

"I can't fix it," Raine announced. "Not in this weather, anyway."

Yeah, and Jack suspected, not without a new alternator, either. Which would have to come from a hardware shop in Broome, and that could've been on the moon as far as they were concerned at the moment.

"Why don't you all come down to my house?" Jack suggested. He'd rather have all three women safe in his house with him, then he could rest easy tonight. "My generator is still running, and my solar storage batteries are full. You know my place is built to withstand this sort of thing." Raine should know; she'd been the one to approve selling land him in the first place. And that approval was based on the plans for a sustainable, cyclone-proof house. He didn't want to rub it in, but modern building techniques, along with better building materials, his concrete foundations, double brick walls, and low-profile steel roof, all made his place practically bomb proof. "I've got plenty of room." He had three spare bedrooms, plus a study. And he could always sleep on the couch if need be. Some people might ask why he needed so much space when there was only him. He could never really answer that question. Hope, perhaps? Who knew?

Raine shot him a look, and he turned his steady gaze pointedly to the other two women, then back to her.

Raine perceived his unspoken message loud and clear. She screwed up her nose, but he knew she wasn't going to argue. Raine would've survived without the generator. But there was something about this storm that had Jack on edge, and he could feel that same unease running through Raine, as well.

"Right, ladies. Grab your jackets, you're coming to stay at my house tonight. You won't need anything else. I've got plenty of food, drinks, books to read if you get bored."

"What? Really?" Deanna bounced out of her chair. "Great."

Kait was slower to react, placing her mug carefully on the table. But she didn't argue, getting to her feet instead, and saying simply, "I don't have a jacket."

Raine organized wet weather gear for the two women, and they were all piling out the back door within minutes. Was he imagining it? Or had the wind picked up since he'd arrived?

He took the lead, telling Kait and Deanna to follow single file and stay close, while Raine took up the rear. But his words were whipped away and he wasn't even sure if they heard him. A large shrub rolled past him down the sandy path, uprooted by the sheer force of the wind and he had to step out of the way. At least there weren't many tall trees in this scrubby hinterland. All the coastal native plants had long ago been beaten down by the Cloudwater sea gales. The only large trees around were those Raine's grandfather had planted along the entrance road to the township, the odd tree in someone's front garden, and those surrounding his backyard. But those weren't big enough to become a problem yet. And when they were, he'd make sure they were well-pruned and maintained.

Someone grabbed the back of his jacket—he thought it might be Kait—as if afraid to lose him in the howling storm.

It took him longer to get home than it had to get to Raine's house, and by the time they all hurried through his front door, they were panting for breath and soaked through.

"Did you see that sheet of iron fly past us?" Deanna asked, shaking out her wet jacket, not caring about the puddles she was making on his pristine floorboards. "It could've cut one of our heads off if it hit us," she crowed with delight. The girl had a strange sense of humor.

Jack gathered up their jackets and led them through to his kitchen. "Make yourself at home," he gestured to the table. "I'll get the coffee machine going."

"I brought my dandelion coffee." Raine offered him a small tin. She must've grabbed it right before she left. She never drank anything else. "Anybody else want one?" she asked expectantly.

"I wouldn't mind one of Jack's coffees," Deanna replied, ignoring the frown Raine gave her. "It's been ages since I had a *real* coffee." Jack almost laughed at the wistfulness in her voice.

He already knew what Kait's answer would be. He remembered she liked it strong—a double shot—and black.

"Wow, cool house," Deanna said, releasing her blonde hair from its braid and letting it drip all over the table as she took a seat.

"I'll give you a tour, once we've had coffee," Jack offered.

Raine busied herself, topping up the kettle with water and getting out four mugs. She was a regular visitor to his house and knew her way around, and he was happy to leave her to her own devices.

Once he'd turned on the coffee machine to warm up, he went in search of towels for them all, as they looked a little like drowned cats.

"How long will the cyclone last?" Deanna asked as he put a towel in front of her.

"The worst of it will happen tonight. By tomorrow, there will still be strong winds and rain, but the destructive part should be over," Raine answer for him.

"Who wants a game of Monopoly?" Deanna appeared in the doorway, carrying the board game. She'd certainly taken his offer to explore as much as she wanted to heart. "We can play on the living room rug." She gestured behind her, back down the hallway.

"Normally, I prefer Scrabble," Raine said. "But this seems like a Monopoly kind of moment. Why not?" She uncurled her legs gracefully from where she had them tucked up beneath her at the table. "Come on, Jack, I bet there's a secret real estate mogul hiding somewhere inside that broad chest of yours."

They played and drank coffee and listened to the wind howl outside for hours. Eventually, he sent the women to bed, each of them choosing a spare room to sleep in. Jack too, went to lie down, but sleep was elusive.

At one stage during the night, there was a loud thump, as if something had hit the outside wall of his bedroom. Jack got up and examined the wall carefully. It didn't look like there was any internal damage, and no water was leaking in. No point in him going out in this weather to see what it was. It'd have to wait till morning.

Around two o'clock in the morning, he finally got up to prowl around the house, checking all the shutters were still in place and there were no leaks. The storm still raged and howled like a wild animal outside, but inside, it felt safe and secure.

Lastly, he padded down the hallway to get a glass of water from the kitchen. A dark shape huddled at the kitchen table almost made him leap out of his skin.

"Kait, is that you?" he asked.

"Sorry, I couldn't sleep. I didn't want to wake anyone, so I left the lights off." Her voice was thin, almost insubstantial in the night.

"Well, I don't have any such qualms." He flicked on the light above the stove, but left the main lights off, lending a cosy atmosphere to the kitchen. "Shall I make us a hot chocolate? It'll have to be powdered milk. I hope that's okay?"

"Sounds lovely," she replied, shielding her eyes from the sudden light. Dressed in a thin cotton T-shirt, and shorts, Kait looked younger and somehow more vulnerable in the soft light. Her eyes appeared slightly red rimmed, and he wondered if she'd been crying, but decided not to ask. He was discovering that Kait was a fiercely private woman, and she would tell him if she wanted to, in her own time.

Nattering on about not much at all, Jack puttered around his familiar kitchen, hoping to put her at ease. He set a steaming mug of hot chocolate in front of her, then cupped his own between his hands, taking a seat opposite. The air wasn't cold; in fact it was decidedly steamy in the house with all the windows locked up tight, and no air getting in. But the hot chocolate was comforting, nonetheless. Kait's gaze flickered across his naked chest, so quickly he almost missed it. He was wearing pajama bottoms, but he rarely slept with a

T-shirt on; it was too hot. He hadn't even thought to put one on when he'd got out of bed. Did she like what she saw?

"Is it the storm that's upsetting you?" he asked, catching her gaze for the first time.

"Yes. No. Sort of," she admitted. "I guess I'm suddenly feeling the effects of being cooped up. Trapped, if you like." She played with her mug, staring at the table. "It's bringing up a lot of…unfinished business. I spent a long time feeling trapped. By my husband. By my life. I swore I wouldn't let it happen again."

Shit. He hadn't expected that.

"This cyclone will be over before you know it," he soothed. "I'll tell you as soon as it's safe to go outside."

"I know. But try telling that to the part of my animal brain that doesn't want to hear it."

Was she shaking? Jack suddenly wanted to punch that deplorable husband of hers. He'd really done a number on her. He wondered if he dared ask more. Would she tell him, or push him away like she always did? He reached over and covered her hands with one of his.

"I'm here, if you ever need to talk about it."

"Thank you. But you don't want to know." She lifted her chin and gave him a wobbly smile, jade-green eyes ensnaring him.

"Are you in some kind of danger?" He was taking a stab in the dark. But all the strange things she and Deanna had said, the way they'd acted, as if they were running away from something, all pointed in that direction. "I can help, if you are."

"Thank you. But no, you can't," she replied with a sad droop to the corners of her mouth.

"Don't forget I'm ex-army." He didn't like to brag, but she needed to know what he was capable of. "As well as six years in protective security and child recovery. I can do things other men wouldn't dream of doing. I have weapons training. Know how to stay under the radar and away from police detection. Good investigative skills. Strategy, extraction and protection, are all words I don't take lightly." He winced as a memory of the boy being whisked away in the car hit him hard. Perhaps he had been good at those things once. But all it took was one loss to make him doubt himself every day from then on. But even if he tried to forget his time in the military, forget all the violence and heedless aggression, it was all still there, bottled up and waiting if he ever needed to tap into it again.

"Wow." Kait's wide eyes met his. "That sounds very impressive."

He hadn't wanted to big-note himself. They'd already touched on this topic in his truck on the way up here. His first thought had been to make Kait feel safer, but the more he thought about it, the truer his words became. Something big and dark and growly rose up in him every time he thought of Kait in danger. And he knew he would revisit all those old skills in a heartbeat if it meant keeping her safe.

"What I'm trying to say, is that if you are in danger, perhaps I can be of some assistance." He squeezed her hand to emphasize this point. She looked down at their linked hands and then back at him, her eyes taking on a speculative look. But it was gone as quickly as it arrived.

"No. You can't help. I can't tell you. My problem shouldn't be your problem."

Ah ha. At least he knew there was a problem now.

"Why not? Are you in trouble with the police?" It was an instinctive question, but the way Kait's nostrils flared gave him the answer he needed, even though she shook her head emphatically.

"No. No. Definitely not. Please don't ask any more," she pleaded.

He kept this knowledge to himself, but decided he wasn't going to let this go. Kait might be a hard nut to crack, but if he turned his attention to Deanna, she might give him what he sought. Deanna was smart, but she was also young and inexperienced. He wasn't above exploiting her youthful gullibility if it got him what he wanted.

And that was to help Kait. To safeguard her if possible. From this unnamed, unspoken, devil on her tail. Why did he feel so protective of this woman? Only God knew. But this compulsion couldn't be ignored. He'd been told once, by his boss at the child recovery agency, that he had an overly protective personality, and he needed to take care that he didn't become too personally involved. Jack had shrugged off the comment at the time, not believing in all that psychobabble bullshit. But perhaps there was a grain of truth to it. When you looked at his chosen professions, it might well be true. Especially to Jalil. Which was why it hurt so bad when the little boy had died.

"Good hot chocolate," Kait said, holding up her mug between them, and subtly releasing her hands from his in the process.

"Thank you." He'd let her change the topic, for now. But this was not over.

"Why don't we take it into the living room?" he suggested. It was more comfortable than sitting at the kitchen table. Who knew, Kait may even be able to snuggle up on the couch and snooze a little. Jack wouldn't sleep. But that was okay, he could get some shut-eye when this was over.

The Monopoly board was still set out where they'd left it upon retiring to bed. Deanna was winning, her messy piles of money scattered in a semicircle on the rug. Raine had been coming a close second, leaving him and Kait as the poor destitute cousins, with hardly any houses on the board and even less money.

They took an end of the couch each, slurping noisily on their hot chocolate.

"I probably don't have any right to pry, but..." Kait started pensively.

Uh oh. His hands tightened around his mug.

"What exactly are the skills you're talking about? I mean, you come across as quite mild-mannered and civilized," she added with a demure smile. She watched him over the rim of her mug, and he wondered what her point was. "Deanna called you a mercenary, but I don't think that's completely correct."

He wasn't sure he liked the way she was studying him. As if he was being assessed. Would she find him lacking? Or would he come up with five gold stars? He merely raised an eyebrow. If she got to keep her secrets, then so did he.

"I think you're more like an overprotective father figure," she went on. "You know, the kind who lectures their kids to be home by curfew but will drive out at two am to pick them up from the nightclub if they call. Let's call you a warmhearted grizzly bear."

He couldn't help the laughter that erupted from his throat. He wasn't sure if he was deeply offended or feeling slightly smug by her observation.

"I remember you saying you worked in East Timor. And then later in Asia and the Middle East. But you always seem to return to Australia."

"That's because Australia is my home," he said simply.

"Would you ever consider moving back to one of those places? For good, I mean?"

He was about to retort that of course he wouldn't, but something in her question stopped him.

"Why? Are you thinking of leaving Australia?"

"Maybe." She kept her eyes on her hot chocolate and wouldn't look at him.

# CHAPTER NINETEEN

Kait woke slowly, stretching luxuriously, but didn't open her eyes. Funny, but the last thought she'd had before she fell asleep was that she would never be able to sleep through this cyclone. But it seemed she had. Wait. What was that soft thing cushioning her head? She cracked open an eye.

Oh, shit.

Jack was staring down at her, an amused glint in his eye, as she lay with her head in his lap. She'd never sat up so quick in her life, a red flush seeping up her neck.

Jesus, he was still shirtless, and she'd just got an eyeful of all that glorious, muscular tanned skin.

"Oh, God. I'm so sorry. I never meant to…" What? Fall asleep while this gorgeous man cradled her head? While he watched her sleep? No, that'd certainly not been on her agenda. How had it even happened anyway? The last thing she remembered was sitting at the opposite end of the couch sipping hot chocolate and talking about travel. Specifically, about places where a person could get off the beaten track, perhaps disappear for a while. Jack had never asked why she was so interested but she noticed the speculative look in his eye. Jack wasn't dumb. Far from it. He just had the manners not to push the point. Now she regretted mentioning the fact she was interested in leaving the country. She didn't need him to be any more suspicious than he already was.

"No need to get all worked up about it. I didn't mind," he said, a twinkle in his eye.

She groaned inwardly. He might not have minded, but now she was feeling decidedly awkward. And to make matters worse, he seemed to be enjoying her embarrassment.

"What time is it?" she asked, as a way to distract them both.

Jack checked his watch. Did men even wear watches anymore? It was kind of sexy, that big sporty-looking watch nestled on his tanned wrist. "Just after seven," he replied.

Wow it was morning already. They'd made it through the night.

"It sounds like the cyclone might be easing off. I'm going to chuck on a shirt and pop outside and take a look."

Great idea about putting on a shirt. Kait cocked her head to the side and listened. He was right, the screaming wind had lessened. "Oh, sure," Kait stammered a reply. "Do you mind if I fire up your coffee machine while you're outside?"

"If you can figure out how to work it, go right ahead," he agreed. "I'll probably need a strong one when I come back in." He got off the couch and stretched expansively, and Kait felt another pang of guilt. He was probably all cramped up from being stuck in one position for the last four hours. A quick surge of something else also ran through her veins. Was that lust?

"By the way, you're cute when you're sleeping," he said with a wry lift to the corner of his mouth.

Holy crap. Kait shot off the couch and scuttled down the hallway. That was the last thing she needed to hear. As if she wasn't mortified enough already. Did he really have to rub it in?

She paused until she heard the front door open and then

close a few moments later before she bent her head over the coffee machine. She'd watched Jack make coffee twice now; it shouldn't be that hard to figure out.

Digging the bag of ground coffee out of the cupboard, she flicked on the switch and waited for the machine to warm up. Jack's generator must still be working fine, as all the lights and appliances were on.

Staring at the wall, she pursed her lips. Why was she so flustered by the mere fact that she'd slept in Jack's lap?

*Because you like him*, Susan said.

"No, I don't," Kait replied to the kitchen.

*Yes, you do*, Susan taunted back. *Because he's everything that Dario isn't.*

Well, that at least was true. But she couldn't afford to like any man. Not now. Not ever.

The espresso machine hissed, and Kait turned to pack the ground coffee into the receptacle.

Less than five minutes later, she was doubly glad she'd awoken when she had, as Raine appeared in the doorway. Her discomfort would've been ten times worse if Raine or Deanna had caught her.

"Morning. How did you sleep?" Raine asked.

"Better than I expected," Kait answered cryptically. "How about you?"

"Good. But I'm worried about my house. I want to get up there as soon as I can to check on it."

"Jack's just gone outside. He should be back any moment with a report."

"Good." Raine filled the kettle and turned it on, dropping some of her disgusting powdered tea in the bottom of a mug.

Deanna toddled through the doorway and took a seat at the table, her blonde hair all mussed up, her T-shirt slightly askew. "Morning," Deanna said with a yawn. Her gaze slid to Raine, then quickly away. It was a small moment of awkwardness, but it was enough to make Kait wonder.

"How did you sleep?" Kait asked, watching both women with interest.

"Oh, ah…really well, actually," Deanna stuttered. "Is that a coffee I smell?" she added quickly. "Sorry, Raine, but I'd kill for one of Jack's coffees."

"It's your choice what you put in your body," Raine replied easily.

Raine was a good-looking woman, with her long, slim limbs and stunning gray hair. She wouldn't be surprised if Deanna was attracted to her. But Kait wanted to tell Deanna to be careful. Raine was a wise, strong woman, who knew exactly what she wanted. And Deanna seemed so…gullible. No, that wasn't the word. It wasn't vulnerable either. Deanna had a childlike quality about her, and Kait would hate to see anyone take advantage of her.

Deanna was her friend, and if she started a relationship with Raine, then Kait would support her, because that's what friends did. But she just hoped Deanna knew what she was doing.

The front door banged shut, and Jack strode into the room.

"How's it looking out there?" Raine leaned forward to pierce him with her gray eyes.

"Pretty ugly," Jack admitted. "There's a lot of debris lying around. But it could've been much worse. All the houses seem to be intact, at least in this street anyway. A corner of Old George's roof down the end of the row has peeled back, but that's the most damage I can see for now."

"Good," Raine said thoughtfully. "We'll need to organize everyone and get a clean-up crew out soon."

"What? You mean people from Cloudwater do it? Won't the authorities come and fix it for you?" Deanna asked, eyes wide. But when Jack and Raine stared at her incredulously, she coughed in sudden understanding, then said, "Oh, no, of course not."

"Give it until lunchtime. The wind is still pretty fierce," Jack said.

"If you say so," Raine agreed grudgingly.

"We can finish our game of Monopoly," Deanna said with a squeak of triumph.

"Do we have to?" Kait complained. "We already know who's going to win."

"Don't be such a spoilsport." Deanna accepted her mug of coffee from Kait with a brilliant smile. "Thank you." She breathed in the aroma from the steam with a sigh of delight.

They enjoyed a leisurely breakfast of toast and homemade jam and copious cups of coffee, then Raine asked Jack if he minded if she used his shower.

"Go right ahead," he replied in his good-natured tone. "Just don't make it a long one. The hot water tank isn't huge and all four of us need to shower."

The hot water tank might not be huge, but at least Jack had all the mod cons. Apart from a television, that was. He didn't believe in those. Which irked Kait a little, as she'd like to know what was going on in the nightly news; if there'd been any further mention of the man found dead in the gorge. Not for the first time, Kait wondered why he needed such a large house. It worked out well for her, Deanna, and Raine that he had three spare bedrooms, but what did he do with all that space normally?

Kait confirmed her theory about Deanna and Raine when she walked past the spare bedroom allotted to Deanna, and saw the bed was still made. Deanna never made her bed first thing in the morning, which meant she hadn't slept there. Kait tried to ignore the vague feeling of disquiet the idea gave her.

With Raine in the shower and Jack fussing around in his kitchen, Kait found Deanna sitting on the rug in the living room, staring morosely at the Monopoly game. She plonked herself down on the couch. "What's up?" she asked Deanna gently. Surely, the girl wasn't moping because no one wanted to finish the game with her.

"I was just thinking, how much I like it here. Even with the cyclone and everything, this place is just so different." Deanna turned an earnest blue gaze up to Kait. "I'm not sure I want to leave."

"Me either," Kait admitted, leaning in and talking in a low voice. "But you know I can't stay here forever. Actually, I probably need to move on sooner, rather than later."

It was the first time she and Deanna had had a chance to talk in days. Kait wanted to know what Deanna was thinking. They'd been drifting along day to day, without discussing what might happen in the future. But Kait couldn't be that complacent. She needed to take charge of her life; otherwise, Dario was sure to find her.

"This was only supposed to be a stopgap measure. A place to drop off the radar for a few days."

"Yeah, I know," Deanna replied. "And don't think I've forgotten about my promise to you. I've been talking to people. I might have found someone who can help us. Help you, specifically."

"Help me, how?" Kait was lost.

"With your new ID, duh." Deanna goggled at her as if she were the most stupid moron on earth, and how could she have forgotten such an important thing. Whereas, in reality, Kait had never taken her claim seriously.

Sometimes, this girl seemed to be terribly wise beyond her years, and at other times, she acted so young and…annoying.

"Do you mean to tell me that you can actually do this? You're not just kidding?"

"No, I said I'd do it, didn't I?" Deanna spoke slowly, as if Kait was somehow being intentionally obtuse. "You've just gotta know the right people to ask. And I think Old George can help us."

"How did you even...?" Kait couldn't finish her question. How had Deanna found all this out? It seemed that while Kait had been spending time with Jack, concentrating on learning to snorkel, and worrying about the oncoming cyclone, Deanna had been busily introducing herself to everyone in the small township, and not just hanging out with Raine all day, as she'd assumed.

"What about a passport," she asked eagerly.

"That might be a bit trickier." Deanna tapped her finger to her lips. "You'll need someone with special skills for that. George ain't that clever."

Who was this girl? How did she know all this stuff? But a brand-new identity *was* possible. Something inside of Kait glowed with anticipation. If she could leave the country, she might be able to find a safehaven, after all.

"We might have to go to Broome if you want a passport. George could know someone there." Deanna's blue eyes were suddenly as sharp as a razor blade. "Why are you so keen for a passport? Are you thinking of traveling?"

"Not necessarily," Kait lied. "It's a great form of ID, it trumps all others. If you have a passport, you often don't need all that other stuff, like a bill from your electricity supplier, or even a driver's license to prove who you are."

"Yeah, I get that." But the reservation didn't leave Deanna's face.

Silence fell around them like a shroud. An unbidden thought entered Kait's head. Deanna wouldn't mention anything about their true purpose in Cloudwater Bay, would she? If Deanna and Raine were getting close, would she confide in the other woman? Tell her all the dirty secrets? A hot flush rushed through Kait at the thought.

A sudden urge to know the intricacies of the Deanna's

relationship with their host made her say, "I know this is none of my business, but did you and Raine...?" She was suddenly lost for words. She was crossing a boundary here; she should trust Deanna, not let suspicion eat away at the foundations of their friendship. Especially after all that Deanna was doing for her. She was about to take the question back, when Deanna spoke.

"If you meant to ask did we sleep in the same bed? Yes we did," Deanna said, looking her straight in the eye. "But if the question is did we have sex? Then the answer is no," she stated matter-of-factly. "I was scared, okay. The cyclone was scary. Raine said I could come into her bed if I wanted to."

"Fair enough." Kait raised her hands in supplication. "I'm not going to stand in judgement."

"Well, I hope not. Because if you did, I'd then have to ask if you and Jack slept together?" she added, as if butter wouldn't melt in her mouth.

Kait reared back on the couch. "I would never... He would never—"

"Shower's free," Raine sang out from the hallway. "Who's next?" She poked her head through the door, wet hair swinging against her shoulders. "Oh, sorry. Not interrupting anything, am I?"

"Nah." Deanna stood and stretched like a cat. "I'll go next," she said, slanting a wink back over her shoulder at Kait before heading through the door.

Ooh, that girl had a way of getting under her skin. Thank God she hadn't actually seen Kait asleep in the Jack's lap.

* * *

"Holy fuck." Jack didn't swear much, so when he did, Kait knew he really meant it. And she felt exactly the same way. "I'm so sorry, Raine." He slung his arm around her shoulders. "We'll get it fixed don't worry."

Raine could do nothing but stand and stare at her house,

sagging against Jack for support.

At least half of the top floor of Raine's house was missing. The roof had peeled back, exposing the bare walls. Furniture was jumbled around as if a giant had been using it as a doll's house and swept an angry hand through the lot. Some of the furniture even lay in the garden below. Shattered wooden beams sagged into the gaping hole now left in the wake of the cyclone.

It hadn't escaped Kait that the bedroom she'd been allotted was now a jumbled pile of timber and metal. What if she'd been asleep in there at the time? She shuddered and clutched at Deanna, who was also staring, her mouth slightly agape. Was it fate trying to tell her something?

"Looks like you were right, Jack." Raine finally pushed herself upright. "That storm was too big for my old house to handle."

"You know you're welcome to stay at my place as long as you need. And both of you as well," he added in a hurry, nodding toward Kait and Deanna.

"I think you might regret saying that," Raine replied with the grimace. "This is going to take a while to fix."

The wind was still blowing hard, whipping up whitecaps on the ocean and threatening to tear the hat from Kait's head, but it was no longer howling like a banshee and throwing large pieces of debris around like they were bits of Lego. Other residents were out wandering the streets, checking on the damage, poking at piles of rubbish and blinking like owls suddenly released into the daylight.

"We'll help," Deanna offered. "Of course, we'll help. We won't let you face this alone." She took Raine's other hand and squeezed it emphatically, then glanced at Kait with a frown.

Belatedly, Kait added, "Yes, you can count on us." But inwardly, she was shaking her head. They couldn't possibly stick around for the months it was going to take to repair this house. A week or so perhaps, but no longer.

"I'll go and make sure it's safe to go inside," Jack declared, already striding toward the front door.

"Yeah, well, macho man, it's my house and I'm going in with you," Raine countered, striding after him.

That left her and Deanna standing in the road, wondering what to do next. This reminded her of some sort of frontier town, like they'd just descended into the Wild West two hundred years ago.

"I guess we'd better go with them," Kait finally said.

Raine had already unlocked the front door and was helping Jack to pull two large branches down the steps and off the veranda so they could get inside.

"Don't go upstairs until I've checked it out," Jack warned.

The ground floor wasn't in too bad condition, considering. On the right-hand side of the stairs, the formal dining room seemed relatively untouched, protected by the still-intact roofline. The large mahogany dining table and chairs were covered with a layer of leaves and grit, but otherwise, looked to be in good condition. But to the left of the stairs, where the lounge was situated, was a different story

Rain had poured in through the open ceiling above, saturating the beautiful wooden floors, the gorgeous Persian rugs, and the eclectic furniture. Raine moved about the room, tutting loudly as she picked up a cushion and moved a chair.

"We need to get all this outside where it can dry," Raine said, practicality winning out over sentiment. "I won't know what I can salvage until it's all dry."

Jack returned and announced that the stairs were still structurally sound, although he advised against going upstairs without a sturdy pair of shoes on their feet and gloves on their hands.

"There'll be all sorts of nasty things waiting to spike you

up there. Nails sticking out at all angles, large splinters of wood, and other debris carried in by the wind."

Kait looked down at her flip-flops and agreed they were decidedly unsuitable for the task upstairs.

"That's okay, we can start moving the downstairs furniture out," Deanna replied, doggedly grabbing hold of one of the large armchairs and scraping it across the floor.

"Wait. I'll help you." Kait jumped in before Raine could shout at Deanna. "Let's take it out into the back garden, there's more room," she suggested.

Raine had wandered down the hallway and turned into the kitchen. Kait and Deanna followed, struggling with the armchair between them. A quick glance into the kitchen, told them it was untouched by the storm. Which probably meant the downstairs bathroom and laundry would be okay too. Small mercies, Kait supposed. The back door was locked, and they had to wait for Raine to open it.

"Oh, no." Deanna covered her mouth as they went outside. "Your beautiful garden, it's ruined." Tears actually formed in the young woman's eyes. "All those wonderful veggies."

But Raine's face hardened as she took in the scene. "I know, it happens every time we have a storm. There's not a lot I can do to protect the garden. But don't worry, I have seedlings in the laundry ready to plant out. It won't take long to start again."

Kait admired the resilience of the woman. If it'd been her garden, she probably would've dropped to her knees and howled like a baby. But she was city born and bred, soft compared to these country people who took hardship in their stride.

Kait was becoming more enamored with this small community every day. Which was such as shame, as she had to leave. And soon.

# CHAPTER TWENTY

Deanna would never admit this to Raine, not in a million years, but living in Jack's house was easier somehow than living at Raine's place. It was clean and modern, with the world's best coffee making machine. Not that Raine's house wasn't clean—well it had been up until the storm. But there was always something to do at Raine's house. Here at Jack's place, the air of expectation didn't sit so tightly around her shoulders. She could take half an hour to browse the books in his bookshelves, or to sit in the sunshine in his lovely garden. Protected by the large trees and sturdy fences, his garden hadn't been nearly as badly affected as Raine's. The only thing Jack's house was missing was a television. Jack said he never watched it, he preferred the radio, or just the simple silence. Which was all good and well for Jack, but Deanna wouldn't have minded watching a little Netflix now and then. Sometimes the simple life wasn't always all it was cracked up to be; not if you had to forgo a simple pleasure like watching a few episodes of *Stranger Things*.

Not that they weren't spending every waking hour up at Raine's house anyway, getting it ready for the repairs. Dressed in gumboots, gloves, long pants, and long sleeves— Deanna had reverted to her Hi-Vis workwear—they'd toiled for days to remove all the debris from the upstairs section, as well as pull out all the damaged furniture and set it in the back garden to dry. There was now a huge pile of rubbish next to the road out the front, full of everything they'd removed from Raine's house. It was the same up and down the street, as everyone dug in and got on with the cleanup. Once the purge was complete, Jack had offered his truck to collect all the garbage and drive it up to the makeshift dump in the dunes behind the settlement.

It was heartening to see everyone come together, neighbors helping neighbors, putting aside any of their differences to help others in need. Surprisingly, most of the houses had survived unscathed, even the seemingly old and decrepit ones that looked like they'd tumble down at the first hint of a storm had blithely brushed the cyclone away and laughed in the face of it all. Jack explained that even though these houses were old, they were built to withstand just such a storm. It was the new, modern, cheaply built houses in towns such as Broome and Karratha that would suffer the most from this huge wind. People would wail and complain bitterly, and there would be a special commission into the building standards in cyclone prone areas. But it wouldn't stop the cowboys building on the cheap or cutting corners just to finish a project on time.

Deanna stretched her arms above her head. Every single one of her muscles ached from the tireless work over the past three days. But it was a good ache; she wasn't afraid of hard physical labour. She'd collapsed on the couch as soon as they came back through the front door this afternoon, however, too tired to move a step farther. Jack and Kait had gone to wash up so they could start preparing dinner, and Raine would be another half an hour yet, as she was still madly planting out seedlings; she had wanted to keep going while there was still some evening light left.

Deanna had no time to make a start on her ghost-net artwork, but she'd been mulling over ideas in her head the whole time she was helping to clean Raine's house. And now she had a pretty good idea of what she wanted to do and how she was going to create her first work of art.

A clang from the kitchen let her know that Kait was already in there, probably putting away the dishes from this morning to clear a space so she could start dinner. Deanna should go and help. Wearily, she got to her feet and plodded through to the kitchen.

"What can I do?" she asked.

"You look as tired as I feel," Kait replied. "We're having a veggie curry. Could you chop those sweet potatoes into cubes? And here"—Kait bent to retrieve half a pumpkin from the bottom draw in the refrigerator—"this one, too, please."

Every meal was vegan, so that Raine could eat with them. Deanna respected Raine's wishes and didn't mind vegetables —especially the way Raine prepared them, which was always delicious—but she couldn't quite rid herself of the urge to chow down on a big, juicy burger. God, what she wouldn't do for one of those right now.

Jack walked in, wearing a clean T-shirt and jeans. "Sorry, I had to have a quick shower. I couldn't face the kitchen covered in all that grime."

"I know what you mean," Kait replied emphatically. "After a long day, you feel like a new person when you step out of that shower."

That was the other thing Deanna liked about Jack's house, the reliable hot water and wonderfully huge bathroom. Luxury. Deanna pulled herself up short. Was she turning into a snob? Perhaps all this time spent around Kait had softened her. She'd never cared about little luxuries before. Working on a mine site, you had to cope with basic facilities. Deanna dug around in her psyche for a few moments as she chopped the pumpkin on autopilot. When had she started to appreciate the finer things in life? Was it after she met Kait, or had the change started to take place before that?

She and Kait hadn't had time to discuss future plans. Every day from dusk till dawn had been spent helping to get this little community back in order. She also hadn't found the time to set Kait's mind at ease about the million dollars back in the storage shed. Well, that wasn't completely true. She'd been about to reveal that she too had nearly a million dollars in the bank on the morning after the cyclone, but then Kait had accused her of sleeping with Raine and it made her suddenly, unfathomably disagreeable. Because what she and Raine meant to each other was still very unclear and it put Deanna on edge so that she'd snapped at Kait, turning the tables on her instead.

She was determined to speak to Kait today. If only she could get rid of Jack for a second.

"While I've got you both here," Jack said, leaning his hip against the countertop. "I wanted to remind you that the strawberry moon will be happening in a few days, on the twentieth. Do you still fancy seeing it?" He turned blue-gray eyes toward Kait. "Because I can run you into Broome, if you do."

Deanna had completely forgotten about the upcoming phenomena.

But it seemed Kait may have remembered. "Really? I'd sort of given up on seeing it. But we can't ask you to do that. Not with all this cleanup going on. And won't they be cleaning up in Broome too? Will the event even go ahead?"

Deanna didn't think Kait noticed the way Jack's gaze softened whenever it landed on her. But Deanna did.

"I have to go into town anyway. I've double-checked, the main highway is open and usable," he replied. "Our one and only cell phone tower was knocked out in the storm. I'm going in to find out what they're doing about fixing it. They're notoriously slow at getting to the remote outposts, but if you make a lot of noise, sometimes they get their butts into gear. It'll also give us a chance to check out the rest of the cyclone damage. Like you said, Broome will also be cleaning up. But they have a lot more official manpower at their disposal. From what I hear things aren't too bad there, considering." He strolled over and picked up a knife, then began chopping a zucchini to add to the pile the vegetables Deanna had already sliced. "And the Moon Festival will definitely be going ahead. The council have invested lots of money already on the event, and will be relying on the incoming tourists to help replenish their coffers. It'd take more than an annoying old cyclone to stop that."

"Oh, good. But are you sure? I don't want to put you out." But the way Kait's face took on a hopeful smile, told a different story.

"Yes, I'm sure. We can even stay the night. The Town Beach Markets will be on. We can buy some food and go and sit on the beach and watch. It'll be busy, mind you."

"Just let us know when you're leaving, and we'll be there with bells on. Right?" Kait swung around to look at Deanna.

"Yeah, wouldn't miss it for the world."

"We'll leave early on Friday then, say around seven. That'll give me time to get everything done in town before the moon show." Deanna groaned inwardly. So many early mornings. She'd kill for a lie-in now and then.

"Is Raine coming with us?" Deanna queried.

"I doubt she'll leave her house right now, but you can ask." Jack gave an imprecise shrug. "She's seen this type of thing plenty of times before," he added.

"Yeah, but not a pink moon, I bet." Deanna liked the idea of the pink moon. It reminded her of cupcakes and birthdays and all things good and wholesome.

Deanna went back to chopping her pumpkin, while Kait excused herself to go and have a shower, leaving her and Jack alone in the kitchen. He turned to fetch a few jars of Raine's homemade curry paste out of the fridge and lined them up on the countertop. She then started on the green peppers to add to the mix.

She could use this opportunity of a trip to Broome to look into passports for both her and Kait. They wouldn't come cheap, but then, Kait had plenty of money. They just needed to access it. She considered asking Jack if he knew anyone who might have the skills she was looking for, but she quickly dismissed the idea. There was no point in getting Jack involved in their clandestine activities. From what Deanna could tell, Jack was pretty much a straight-down-the-line kind of guy, he probably wouldn't have a clue where to start. And he might ask too many questions about why they needed new papers. Might get a bit huffy about it all. Could possibly even throw them out of this house if he got too uptight, which wouldn't do.

A few days before the cyclone hit, on the morning before Jack had taken them out in his boat to practice snorkeling, Deanna had uncovered Old George. She'd asked a few of the right questions from some of the guys standing around smoking, pretending to mend a boat down on the beach, and got the right answers, eventually.

At first, they'd looked her up and down, pegging her for some stupid bimbo, who didn't know her own ass from her elbow. But she bummed a smoke and yarned with them, slotting easily into their macho bullshit conversation until they relaxed enough to tell her what she needed to know. Tamika used to call her a chameleon. Deanna had never liked the word; she was just good at sussing people out, knowing what they wanted and how to act accordingly to get what she wanted.

It'd taken even less convincing to get Old George on side. He understood she was serious right from the get go. She hadn't even needed to sit in his lap to get him to agree. He was just happy to stare his fill, and she was happy to let him look. Probably didn't get too many beautiful, young women around Cloudwater Bay. Poor old guy was lonely, and Deanna didn't have a problem chatting. Her time was free, and she had the patience. George told her he was good for forging birth certificates, educational certificates, utility bills with fake addresses, and even drivers licenses.

Kait didn't know it yet, but Deanna was going to reinvent herself as well. It never hurt to have more than one identity. And if she was going to stick with Kait, then she'd need to do so incognito. She'd even picked out their new names. Kait might not like hers but it was too bad, Deanna had to come up with them on the spur of the moment. Kait's new name was Bernadette Baldwin. Bland, unexceptional, and average. All things Kait needed to learn to be. Deanna's new name was Summer Spanks. She giggled as she thought of it. Deanna had always liked alliteration and had always wished to be called Summer. It was such a light and happy name. Summery. Unlike Deanna, which she thought sounded heavy and dark. And the Spanks part, well that was just a bit of fun.

She would go back and visit Old George in the next few days. Hopefully, he wasn't too busy with repairs to his house to finish the job for her. She'd paid the man a deposit from her own cash reserve. But she'd need the rest of the money—another two thousand—from Kait. And they'd need a couple of good quality digital photos too, for the driver's licenses. Deanna had already made up a new address in Broome for them both.

"Will we only stay the one night?" she asked Jack, her voice breaking the steady sound of chopping.

"What? Yeah, probably. Unless you have a reason to stay

longer?"

She did, but not a reason she could tell him. Could she perhaps stay on a few days, and hitch a ride back out to Cloudwater, later? The idea had merit, but she'd need to consider it from all angles before she decided. It was probably a good thing if Raine didn't accompany them in that case; she'd get too suspicious.

"I just thought it might be nice, that's all. We could play tourist. Do the camel riding thing on Cable Beach. What do you reckon?"

Jack merely grunted, and she remembered he didn't like tourists. Perhaps she should get Kait to ask Jack, she usually got a better response.

If she did manage to talk Jack and Kait into spending a few nights in Broome, she could organize a few other girly things for them to do. Like get a bikini wax. Maybe even see a hairdresser for a trim. All those sorts of mod cons. Even buy some supplies for the works of art she was planning.

Deanna's thoughts turned back to Raine. She was still sharing Raine's bed while they stayed at Jack's, but nothing more than kissing had happened yet. Raine was taking it slow, holding back Deanna's normal inclination to jump in first and think about the repercussions later. Which for once, Deanna didn't mind. There was something so grown up about keeping things unhurried, letting feelings develop naturally, like a deep, wide old river chugging along, floating in the currents and eddies, but not letting them derail her.

Kait reappeared through the kitchen door, hair still dripping. Deanna smiled at her friend. It seemed she might finally be relaxing a little. Almost as if she belonged here. This place was definitely good for her. Could Deanna possibly convince her to stay? Did Deanna even want to stay? Neither of those questions had answers. Yet.

"What do you say to spending two or three nights in

Broome?" Deanna asked before Kait even had time to pick up a saucepan. "That'd be fun, don't you think?"

"I guess that all depends on Jack," she replied, and Deanna sighed. Kait was always the pragmatist. Why couldn't she be a little spontaneous once in a while?

"Let me think about it," he equivocated.

Deanna could try appealing to his manly side. She suspected even straight-as-an-arrow Jack wouldn't be able to refuse her doe-eyed pleading. Hardly any man—make that *no* man—was fully immune to her wide-eyed, innocent blonde trick, when she turned the full power of her charm on them. Kait, however, would see right through it, and probably admonish her. She'd have to wait until she could get Jack alone again.

"Okay," she replied, hoping she sounded breezy and indifferent. "If the shower's free, I'll go and hop in. Promise to be quick," she added as Kait pursed her lips in Deanna's direction. Jeez. Just because she liked to avail herself of the wondrous flow of hot water at Jack's, and perhaps she'd stood in the shower just a tad too long the first few times, didn't mean she hadn't learnt her lesson.

Deanna stripped quickly and dropped her clothes in a heedless pile by the door. She turned on the taps and then stared carefully at herself in the mirror as she waited for the hot water to flow. Turning sideways, she studied her flat stomach and pert breasts, checking there was no sagging. Then she checked her face for any new wrinkles that might've sprung up overnight. Not that wrinkles were a bad thing, they certainly leant Raine an air of sophistication. But twenty-two was a little too young to be getting wrinkles, wasn't it? When she was sure everything was as it should be, she stepped into the shower.

A few moments later, just as Deanna was washing the shampoo from her hair, the bathroom door opened and closed again. Deanna twitched aside the shower curtain and peered around the large, tiled room, interested to see who might be brave enough to interrupt her shower.

It was Raine, and she merely raised one eyebrow as she undid the buttons on her trousers and slithered out of them, revealing slim, pale legs.

This was an interesting development. It looked like Raine might be ready to take things up a notch. Ballsy of her to do it in Jack's house, but she guessed the other two were too caught up in their own little dance in the kitchen to care what was happening at the other end of the house. And Raine was a woman who, once she made her mind up, always got what she wanted.

Deanna opened the shower curtain wide and beckoned her in. It looked like they might use up all the hot water after all.

# CHAPTER TWENTY-ONE

The town was mobbed. There were people everywhere, most of them tourists, while the locals fought their way in between the mass of sightseers for space on the footpath. Jack scrubbed at his chin and tried not to screw up his nose in dislike.

Kait seemed to be in agreement, staring at the crowds with growing dismay, withdrawing visibly from the passenger window as they made their way down the main street of Broome.

Deanna, on the other hand, was bouncing in her seat with delight. "Ooh, look at everyone. They're like a gaggle of galahs," she laughed. He couldn't help but agree with her. The brightly colored pink-and-gray birds that sat on the telegraph wires in their hundreds and squawked at the top of their lungs were an exact metaphor for all these milling people.

Deanna had chosen to take the back seat for their trip into town, happy to stare out the window and listen to Kait and Jack discuss the ramifications and intelligence of trying to tame this huge, brown, open land enough to run cattle or sheep on it.

The highway had been open and clear; the council workers

had obviously done their job, clearing any debris or fallen trees with an army of graders. But large bodies of water still pooled in the depressions along either side of the road, a reminder of the cyclone's passage.

As they'd got closer to Broome, the cyclone's impact became clearer, with piles of rubbish forming along the roadways as locals cleared up the damage—much as they'd done in Cloudwater. More puddles of water reflected the sun from the side of the road and around people's driveways. But they would be gone in the next few days, the heat of the tropical sun burning the water off in no time.

"Oh, look at that house." Deanna pointed to a two-story house with its roof torn off and dumped into the backyard pool. "Those poor people. That's much worse than Raine's house," she added thoughtfully.

"Yes," he replied, silently thinking that Raine was lucky indeed as they drove past another house that'd been partially destroyed by the monstrous winds. But the damage was minimal compared to some cyclones he'd seen come through over the years.

Main Street had fared better than the outlying suburbs, all the shopfronts seeming to have survived. Jack could imagine how the owners would've taken great care to sandbag and board up their shops, a ritual that would be familiar to those who lived up here for any length of time. And now they were open and welcoming in tourists as if nothing had happened. He could hardly believe it was this busy already; it was only ten in the morning. By tonight, this place would be absolutely overrun. There'd been no accommodation available either. Every hotel and cabin this side of Karratha was booked out. The amount of caravans and camper vans parked along the shore front was unseemly, with gray nomads spilling out and onto the street as far as the eye could see. Luckily, he had friends who owned a house in Broome. The couple were away for the month, gone east to visit the grandkids, but Lennie had been happy to let Jack and his friends stay for a few nights when he'd talked to him over the CB radio yesterday. It'd "keep the thieving bastards at bay," Lennie had said. Lennie was also keen for Jack to report back on the status of his house after the cyclone. His neighbors had used the spare key to get in and rolled down the cyclone shutters for him before the storm hit. They'd reported back that the place hadn't sustained any major damage but they'd only made a cursory examination. Jack promised he'd take a close look at the building and gardens when he got there.

Jack's black four-by-four was definitely easier to drive— and park—than his B-Double, but there were no parking spots to be found close to town anyway.

"I'll park down at Lennie's and we can walk in," he said. "This place is a circus."

Lennie's house was only four or five streets back from Town Beach where all the action happened. A five-minute walk, at best. It was hard to get a true beachfront house around Broome. Most people didn't realize it, but a lot of this coast was taken up by mangroves and mudflats, leaving very little sandy areas in between. Except for Cable Beach which stretched for over twenty-two kilometers, but it ran along the other side of the peninsula, away from the town centre.

Lennie had bought his block back in the seventies, knocked down the old shanty that perhaps had its origins in the pearling boat heyday, and built his house on the site. Now, thanks to tourism and a hundred-fold increase in Broome's population, Lennie's house was worth a small fortune.

Jack pulled into the driveway with a sigh of relief. Even though he drove a truck for a living and had to deal with traffic every day on the road, he was becoming more and more of a country bumpkin when it came to city driving. Living in Cloudwater Bay was doing that to him.

"I'll just get the key. Wait here," he instructed. Exiting the car, he headed down the side of the house, pushing through an overgrown section of tall palm fronds until he found the row of pot plants and lifted the third one along, checking carefully for spiders before retrieving the spare key. He cast a quick, appraising glance over the house, but everything seemed to be in order. The roof was still intact and the roller shutters were all down, protecting the inside of the house. The garden looked a little worse for wear, however.

Kait and Deanna were standing by the vehicle waiting for him when he returned, Deanna with an eager smile on her face, Kait with a more circumspect look as she studied the double-story house with interest. It was set back from the road, a large jungle-type front garden screening it from the road, crafted from dark-stained wood and lots of glass and open louvers to let the sea breeze flow through. He led them through a high wooden gate and into the rear yard. Like a lot of houses in this area, the house was built on stilts and the ground level became a covered, open-plan entertaining space, with a kidney-shaped pool within easy access to one side. It boasted a BBQ and pizza oven and lots of comfortable seating, arranged in cozy nooks for quiet conversations, and an extra-large wooden table that easily seated twelve or more people. Even with the tall fences surrounding the property, the garden had taken damage from the storm. A palm tree had succumbed to the winds and toppled over to land in the pool. The grassed area was littered with palm fronds and small branches, and the pool was a mess of debris and leaves and needed a good clean out. But Lennie had made sure to lock all the chairs and smaller items of furniture in a large storeroom near the stairs before he left, so the undercover area was relatively unscathed. A good sweep would tidy that up.

A staircase ascended from the middle of the lower level

and led them up to the living area on the first floor, which was encircled by a wide, airy veranda. Up here, more sleek wooden floors and simple, functional, but comfortable furniture were the main decor. Lots of white on the walls and in the kitchen gave the place a classy but uncomplicated feel.

Jack located the switches for the cyclone-proof shutters and all of them stopped to watch the iron screens roll up to reveal stately picture windows on three sides of the enormous room.

"Wow. This is nice," Kait said as sunshine flooded into the house.

"Yeah, it is," Jack agreed. "But the house is becoming a bit much for Lennie and his wife," he continued. "Their two adult children both moved away. One's in Sydney and other went to Brisbane."

"Oh, that's no good." Kait screwed up her nose in sympathy.

Jack knew Lennie was leaning toward selling the place one day in the not-too-distant future, so they could downsize and move closer to their kids and their families.

Perhaps Jack should consider putting a bid in to buy the house, it was beautiful, after all. And he could probably afford it. But the fleeting thought was gone before it ever really entered his head. His home was in Cloudwater Bay, he didn't need another house, not in Broome anyway.

"Bags the biggest bedroom," Deanna said, bouncing up the last stair and barging past them.

"You can have the one on the left, down the hallway," Jack called out to her. "This place has five bedrooms," Jack explained to Kait, because Deanna had already disappeared. "But I don't like to invade Lennie's personal space by taking over the main bedroom suit."

"I completely agree," Kait said, taking a few steps toward the large kitchen and trailing her fingertips over the cool, marble countertop. "It's a shame we're only staying one night," Kait continued, almost to herself.

"We can stay longer, if you like," Jack found himself saying before he could stop the words tumbling from his mouth. "We're in no rush to get back." Which was true, but he hadn't really wanted to spend more than one night here; there was still a lot to do back in the Bay, especially with Christmas looming next week. He had nothing booked in work wise until after New Year's. But then he'd be back on the road for nearly the whole month of January. He needed to make the most of the time he had left in the bay. It seemed he'd suddenly become eager to please this woman, however.

"Really? Again, I don't want to put you out, you're already doing us a great favor. But..." Her face lit up in a smile, and his pulse increased ever so slightly. "It would be nice."

"Let's stay then." He waved a hand around the living room. "Lennie won't mind. We can stay the whole weekend if you like."

"Did I just hear you say we're staying?" Deanna skipped down the hallway and landed a kiss on Jack's cheek as she went past. "That's great." She stopped and looked around the kitchen. "Nice place, by the way. You have some cashed-up friends, Jack."

Jack merely smiled. Deanna was a little whirlwind with a cheeky smile and a warm personality. She was harmless, and he liked her. At least he knew where he stood with Deanna. With Kait...not so much.

"Let me show you to your room." Jack picked up Kait's overnight bag and led her down the hallway. "I'm just going to clean up a little downstairs, then we'll head into town and find somewhere to have lunch," he called over his shoulder, catching Deanna opening the refrigerator door and peering inside. That girl was always hungry. And seemed to have no boundaries. He wanted to at least scoop most of the leaves and debris out of the pool, so he could get the pump going again and hopefully have a clean pool to swim in later. The rest of the garden could wait till tomorrow.

"Can we have a burger?" Deanna called after him.

"Sure, why not?" Funny, but Jack had been thinking along the same lines. Not that Raine's vegan food tasted bad. And a plant-based diet was also good for his waistline. But a juicy burger and some hand-cut fries, washed down with a famous ginger beer from Matso's Brewery, would go down nicely.

An hour later, the three of them walked into town and managed to snaffle one of the last remaining outside tables at the brewery beneath the large shade cloth, with a view across the dusty road straight out to the bay. It was still early for lunch, but the place was packed. Matso's seemed to have sustained little damage after the big storm, its sturdy tin roof and hardwood veranda built to withstand these climatic disasters. The palm trees out the front of Matso's looked a little sad and sorry for themselves, most of their leaves stripped by the vicious winds, and some of the large trees that normally shaded the beer garden were now offering a lot less shade, due to lost limbs and damaged leaf canopy. But the hard-working owners and staff had clearly got the place back into ship-shape condition in record time. The water in the bay wasn't its usual sparkling blue this morning, however, still murky and full of silt from the wave-churning storm.

"I've never tasted one of these," Kait admitted, smacking her lips after a large sip of ginger beer. "It's very refreshing." She traced a droplet of condensation down the outside of her cold glass with a fingertip.

"Yeah, but watch out, it's got quite a kick," Deanna said with a wink. "A couple of these and you'll be on your backside quicker than you can say Jack Rabbit."

Kait merely raised an eyebrow and took another swig.

Jack had opted for a beer; it'd go better with his burger. He wondered why Kait seemed not to have the practical knowledge of such simple pleasures as a Matso's ginger beer. She'd admitted coming to Broome with her husband before, but it seemed they'd only done the most basic of touristy things, preferring to stay at their luxury resort and sip cocktails by the pool. Shame, really. She'd missed out on so much. Jack would like to help her experience some of these things. There was often pleasure to be found in the small, unpretentious things in life. Money didn't always buy you happiness. It certainly hadn't with Kait, if he were any judge.

"This place has a license to print money," Deanna observed, swiveling to take in the crowded beer garden. There were even more people inside, but it was jam-packed and humid in there, where as out here, they at least they got a slight breeze.

"Yeah. But good on them, I say." Jack took a last gulp of his beer, then wondered how he'd drunk it so quickly. He glanced across at Kait, who seemed to be absorbed by the view out past the road to the gray ocean, her glass resting lightly against her lips as she studied the panorama. Today, she seemed more relaxed. Certainly less stressed than when he'd first picked the two women up as hitchhikers. Cloudwater Bay had been good for her. Wearing a pair of white capris and the blue top with butterflies, dark hair pulled back into a loose bun at the nape of her neck, she looked almost at home here. He'd got used to her black hair and blunt fringe. He was surprised to discover that it suited her. Not as alluring as the red had been, but it highlighted her fine facial features better. Tracing the line of her profile down her straight nose to the small pout of her lips, which turned up ever so slightly at the corners, he considered her. What would she taste like? If he kissed her?

Bottle-green eyes turned toward him, and he was suddenly caught staring, like a fox in a trap.

"What are your plans for this afternoon?" Deanna asked, breaking the delicate impasse between himself and Kait.

"Yes, Jack, what are the plans?" Kait mimicked Deanna, narrowing her eyes ever so slightly.

"Ah, I need to go and visit the telco company, see if I can rustle up a timeline on how long before they fix our cell tower. And I've got a list of items Raine needs to help her fix her house. With Christmas only a few days away, I've got orders from a few blokes to get them a ham on the bone, and I may as well stock up on a few food items for myself while I'm at it. But apart from that, I'm easy. Have you ladies got anything in mind?"

"You mean apart from the pink moon tonight?" Deanna queried a tad sarcastically. "I've been here a few times before, so I'm not really into all that touristy stuff, like riding the camels on Cable Beach or seeing the horizontal falls. But Kait might be." She turned to stare at her friend. "There are all kinds of things to do here. I hear the sunset boat cruise is good. Or a tour to learn all about the pearling industry." She tipped her head in Kait's direction and watched her with interest.

"Well, like I said to Jack before, I don't want to put him out." She turned to look at Jack thoughtfully, tapping her chin with her index finger. "I'm happy just to potter around town and soak it all in. I do like the sound of finding out more about the pearling industry, though. I mean, what woman isn't keen on a pearl or two." She smiled, her whole face lighting up, and Jack was struck by her simple happiness.

"Why don't the two of you book in for a tour this afternoon," Deanna gushed. "I have a friend up here who I haven't seen for ages. I might look them up while I have the chance. I can meet up with you guys later."

That was interesting. Deanna hadn't mentioned anything about a friend before. She was full of surprises. Before Jack could quiz her further, however, their food arrived, a waitress bustling around with three plates balanced precariously along her arm.

By the time they'd got their orders straight and Jack had asked the waitress for another beer, both women were waxing lyrical about the size—and taste—of their delicious burgers.

An hour later, Jack and Kait were strolling down Hamersley Street, dodging the hordes of tourists. Deanna had left them at the front gate of Matso's, skipping off in the opposite direction, waving at them from over her shoulder.

They ambled companionably together, Kait peering into each storefront, but refusing to go in, saying she was happy just to browse and soak in the atmosphere.

They were almost at the end of Roebuck Bay, where the main street terminated, when Kait stopped, a contemplative expression on her face.

"I've always wanted a tattoo," she said absently.

"What?" She'd caught him by surprise, and he looked up at the sign above the shop. Pearl Coast Tattoos.

She laughed, and said, "Don't look so shocked."

Jack held his hands up in surrender. "If you want a tattoo, more power to you." He had nothing against tattoos. They were a common accessory nowadays; most Gen Z women sported some kind of skin art. He was almost surprised to learn that Kait didn't have one already. He had a couple himself. One meant more to him than the others. The date inked into his forearm. Jalil's birthday was a reminder of how he'd failed the boy back in Iran. The others were a nod to his army service—in the ANZAC image on his shoulder and the Australian flag on his chest.

"What were you thinking?" The idea had him intrigued. What kind of image would a woman like Kait want permanently inked into her skin? He very much doubted she was the angel wings-across-the-lower-back tramp stamp kind of girl. Nor the tacky rose tattoo above the ankle either. He cocked his head and waited for her answer.

"The moon. It's a symbol of renewal and clarity. I was reading up on it in one of your books the other day," she added, a touch embarrassed.

"Nice," he said with a nod. "Do you want to go in now? Because I'm happy to wait if you do." Jack glanced quickly in through the window. The place looked empty. They'd probably welcome a walk-in.

"Um." She bit her lip and stared up at the sign. "What about the pearling tour?"

"Plenty of time to do that tomorrow." He stared at her intently. If she was serious about this, then he didn't want to give her any reason to back out. He really wanted to know where this moon tattoo was going on her body. But she already seemed uncomfortable about the whole thing, and he didn't want to scare her off completely. "Do you want me to come in with you?" he asked gently, not wanting to push, but also letting her know he was there to support her, if she needed it.

"What? Oh, no." She was still biting her lip, and he waited to see which way she would go. Her gaze flitted up the street and then back to the tattoo shop. He could see some of the inner turmoil going on behind her eyes. The good-girl image, warring with the rebel who was screaming to emerge.

"Yes. I'm going to do it." She stood a little straighter.

The rebel had won. Good on her. It took courage to break a mold, even if it was self-imposed.

"If you're sure you don't want me to come in with you, I might go talk to the phone provider," he said.

She shook her head at his offer to accompany her and put her hand on the door handle.

"I'll pop back in half an hour, or so, and see how you're

going."

"Okay." She waved him away absently, a light of determination in her eyes.

He waited until she'd disappeared into the shop interior before he turned to walk back down the street, heading toward the office he needed a few streets away. It was the main reason he'd come into town, after all. The company would most likely already know about the broken tower, but a squeaky wheel usually got more action. He might even go back tomorrow to rock the boat some more, just to make sure they'd got the message. But his mind was occupied by the idea of Kait getting a tattoo. She was one compelling woman, and everything she did took her higher in his estimation. Jack wasn't sure if this was a good thing, or not.

Still considering the dark-haired woman, he suddenly realized that he didn't even know her last name. Or Deanna's for that matter. Wasn't that odd? He was sharing his house with two women who he only knew by their first names. It hadn't seemed intentional, back when they'd first hopped into his truck and introduced themselves, but now he thought about it, he did wonder why the subject had never come up. There was so much he didn't know about Kait. Or Deanna. And he was reminded of that mysterious black backpack Kait had been carrying when they first met. What'd been in that backpack? He'd love to know.

# CHATPER TWENTY-TWO

Kait couldn't stop smiling. Even the burning pain of the tattoo couldn't wipe the smile off her face. She'd done it. She'd actually walked through that door and got herself a tattoo. The girl behind the desk with the dark eyeliner and so much ink Kait had stopped counting the individual tats, had been more than helpful. Once she knew what Kait wanted and her reason behind her choice, Shandy had hand-drawn the perfect design.

Kait brought her hand up to her chest, covering the small, white bandage over her heart beneath her shirt. She and Jack were walking back down the main street, headed for their accommodation, but she felt like she was walking on air.

Jack must've caught her movement because he asked, "Does it hurt?"

"A little," she replied. "But it's not as bad as I thought it was going to be. And it was worth every second of pain," she added with a grin.

"I'm glad," Jack said, his astute gaze fixed on her. "It seems like you're happy with your choice."

"Yes." She hesitated for a second, then said, "This tattoo was for me, but it was also for my friend, Susan."

*Thank you,* Susan whispered in her ear. *I love you, too.*

"Ah," Jack replied sagely, the light of comprehension entering his arresting blue eyes. "I can't wait to see it," he added, raising one eyebrow in question.

"When we get home," she promised. "I want to show you and Deanna together. She'd never forgive me if you were the first one to see it."

"Fair enough."

They walked in companionable silence, dodging the ever-increasing tourists crowding the street, Kait lost in her contemplation of what she'd just achieved.

All of a sudden, a shop door opened ahead, and two police officers stepped out onto the pavement. A man and a woman, both dressed in the distinctive uniform of sky-blue shirt and dark pants. Turning to face them, one of the officers caught sight of her and Jack and pointed straight at them. Kait stopped dead in her tracks, heart thudding like a jackhammer.

Oh, shit!

They'd found her. She was on the wanted criminal list after all. And they were coming to get her.

Her first instinct was to turn and run. But she couldn't move. Her feet were glued to the pavement.

Oblivious to her distress, Jack continued walking toward the officers.

"Hiya, Pete." Jack extended his hand to the male officer, and they greeted each other warmly. "How're things with you? Looks like you'll have your hands full tonight with this crowd." The female officer hung back, watching the people part around them like a river flowing past.

It took a few seconds for Kait to digest the fact that Jack knew this man and he was merely saying hello.

But the last thing she needed was for Jack to decide to introduce her to a couple of law enforcement officers.

Quick. She needed to get out of here.

Without looking, she ducked into the nearest doorway, which led into a large art gallery. She moved to the back of the room, away from the window, almost on autopilot, weaving between the customers surveying the aboriginal art hanging on the walls.

But there was nowhere to hide.

Was there a back door out of this place?

An elegantly dressed woman hovered at the rear of the room, near a counter with a discreetly placed cash register.

"Do you have a bathroom I could use?" Kait asked, not having to fake the urgency in her voice. "I'm busting."

"We don't normally let our customers use our facilities." The woman eyed her coldly. "There are public toilets in the park at the end of the street."

"I won't make it down there" Kait screwed up her face as if in pain. "Please," she pleaded.

"Oh, for God's sake," the woman murmured. "Through that door and to the right," she added, a twist of distaste curving her painted red lips.

Kait hurried through the rear door with the exit sign above it with a sigh of relief. Not stopping at the door that said toilet, she followed the hallway as it led her past a small storage room and then out into a back alley.

Safe.

She let out a gust of air, stopping and just breathing as the heat of the Kimberley washed over her. Had she overreacted? Perhaps the cops weren't looking for her at all, and she'd just made herself look like an idiot.

And now she had to come up with a story to fool Jack.

It took her ten minutes and a few wrong turns to make it back to the house. By then, her heart rate had returned to normal and she'd almost recovered her equilibrium.

No one was home when she let herself in using the spare key Jack had shown them. She sat down at the kitchen countertop and stared out the window, not really seeing the verdant jungle garden beneath.

This scare had proved one thing. She'd been stupid and neglectful. Had been living in a fantasy world where Dario and the dead body at the bottom of the gorge no longer existed. But that one glimpse of the police uniform had brought it all crashing back. When they'd first arrived at Cloudwater Bay, she'd promised herself she'd move on after the pink moon. It was time to start living her fugitive life once more, and not forget who, or what, she was running from. It'd been foolish to walk down the main street as if she owned it. Anyone could've recognized her. Not necessarily just the police. Dario's thugs could be anywhere.

The clatter of shoes on the wooden steps alerted her to someone arriving. Kait assumed it'd be Jack, wondering where she'd got to, and she scrambled for a believable story about her sudden disappearance. But it was Deanna's blonde head that emerged from the stairwell.

"Hello," she sang out, her gaze narrowing when it landed on Kait sitting alone at the counter. "Wow, it's hot out there. I'm pooped. Where's Jack?" she asked, reaching for a glass, then filling it with cold water from the fridge.

"I, ah…lost him back in the main street. I'm sure he'll be home soon."

"Good, because we need to talk." Deanna pulled a stool up close to Kait and looked her straight in the eye, not bothering with any of the normal preamble. "I wasn't visiting a friend today. That was just a cover story for Jack."

"Okay," Kait said slowly. Sometimes she found it hard to keep up with Deanna's lightning-fast changes in topic.

"I was actually tracking down a guy who can help us get new passports. And I found him. He's gonna do it for us." Deanna sat back with a triumphant smile on her face.

"Oh, wow." This was a good thing. At least one of them

hadn't lost sight of their end game. She was a little ashamed Deanna had done this alone. Kait should've been the one instigating it. Should at least have helped Deanna with her task. Then something about Deanna's words niggled at the back of her brain. "That's great. But what do you mean by *us*?"

"I need a new ID as well." Deanna paused for a second and the gleam of something mischievous entered her eyes. "By the way, I made up new names for each of us. Sorry I didn't ask you first, but I was put on the spot and had to come up with something quick. Your new name is Bernadette Baldwin, and I'm Summer Spanks."

Kait sat back on her stool. "You what?" Bernadette Baldwin. What kind of name was that? It was boring and bland. She would much rather have had some input into her new persona. Why couldn't she be something like Rita Hayworth, or Dona Drake. A little on the obvious side, but surely Deanna would get the gist. She was just about to open her mouth to argue when Deanna held up a hand to forestall her. "We don't have time for this discussion right now. The important thing is that they're gonna cost us fifteen grand each. So, we need to go back to Exmouth and get your money. I'll pay you back for mine, I promise."

"Wait." Kait shook her head. "Fifteen thousand each? That's thirty thousand dollars." She was shocked.

"That's the price you have to pay when you're on the lam," Deanna reminded her. "Do you want a new passport, or not?"

"Yes, I do," Kait conceded. "But…"

"No buts," Deanna held up her hand again, and it made Kait wonder who was the older and wiser of the two of them at this particular moment in time, because it certainly seemed like Deanna had taken charge. "We need them, which means we need to get your money back, and we've got a week to do it."

"Right." Kait scrubbed a hand through her hair. "But—"

"Hello. Kait, are you home?" Jack's voice drifted up the stairs, bringing their conversation to a halt.

Shit. She stood up, then immediately took her seat again. It wouldn't do to show her agitation.

"Hi, Jack," she called out. "Yes, I'm home. And so is Deanna."

Jack's dark hair and bright blue eyes came into view as he ascended the stairs two at a time.

"Oh, good. I was worried… You just disappeared." A frown creased his brow as he stopped right in front of her.

"Yeah, I saw this amazing piece of aboriginal art in this gallery, and I just had to go and look at it." Kait knew her voice sounded higher than it should. She took a deep breath. "But when I came out, you were gone." She widened her eyes slightly, like she'd seen Deanna do, in an attempt at guilelessness.

But Jack's frown merely deepened. "I ran into Pete, the chief of police in Broome, and his partner, and stopped to talk to them. When I turned around, you were gone."

"Really? I didn't see you stop, sorry. I was too engrossed by the painting."

Jack continued to stare at her, and she pushed down the sudden urge to swallow hard under his scrutiny. It was important he didn't think she'd run away because she was avoiding two cops.

"By the way, what's your last name?" Jack leaned in close and stared at her contemplatively.

She glared back at him, but he didn't back down, just lifted one eyebrow and lowered his chin slightly. "I just figured out that you never told me when we first met. And, well, you know my surname, so…" He let the sentiment drift off, but she knew he wasn't going to drop it.

But she wasn't going to let him rattle her. Not now, not when he was already suspicious. "Baldwin," she said slowly and succinctly, raising an answering eyebrow. "Why does it matter?"

He looked slightly taken aback, as if he'd half expected her to refuse to answer.

"And my last name is Spanks," Deanna sang out from the other side of the counter. "You know, like…" She half turned and slapped her own buttocks in a semi-seductive dance. "Just in case you were wondering," she added as Jack frowned at her.

"Right," Jack finally found his tongue after frowning hard at Deanna's dancing style. "No, you're right, it doesn't really matter." He turned toward Kait. "It's just that you know mine, and I thought…" He trailed off lamely, the probing look finally gone from his eyes, replaced with a hint of embarrassment.

"Never mind, everyone knows everyone's last name now, and I'm starving," Deanna interceded flippantly. "Are we going to eat here before we go and watch the moonrise?" She cast Kait a fleeting glance of understanding when Jack wasn't looking, and Kait nodded in gratitude.

Thank God Deanna had given her a false name today, or she might well have blurted out her real name instead. And then they'd be in all sorts of trouble.

"We could order in," Jack replied doubtfully. "I don't think there's a lot of food in the fridge."

"Sounds great. I think I saw some menus in one of the drawers." Deanna tripped lightly around the island countertop and pulled open a drawer, coming up with a fistful of flyers. "What do you feel like? Chinese? Pizza? Ooh, how about fish and chips? Looks like the shop is just around the corner."

"I could go some fish and chips," Kait replied.

"I'm easy," Jack added. He was still standing way too close for Kait's liking, that narrowed gaze zeroed in on her. "But before we order, Kait has something to show us."

"I do?" she squeaked, nearly falling off her stool.

"Yes. Your tattoo. Remember?"

"You got a tattoo?" Deanna's feet nearly lifted off the floor in her eagerness to run back around the island bench. "Let me see. Let me see." She clapped her hands excitedly, hovering beside Jack, both of them waiting.

"Oh, yes." Kait couldn't understand why she was suddenly reluctant to show these people—her friends—her new body decoration.

Tugging down the neckline of her T-shirt, she revealed the white bandage. Kait carefully pulled down one corner until the tattoo was exposed.

Deanna drew in a breath and leaned in closer.

At first glance it was a small picture of the full moon, inked above her left breast. But on closer inspection, you could see the moon's surface was made up of tiny, intertwined pink everlasting flowers.

Susan's favorite.

As well as being a pink moon in honor of the spectacle tonight.

"Oh, it's gorgeous," Deanna said, and Kait knew she really meant it.

"It's great," Jack echoed her sentiments. "It suits you," he added, catching her eye.

"Now I just have to see the pink moon," Kait laughed. "Then, it'll be a great reminder of my time in Broome." Her gaze slid to Jack without conscious thought. A reminder of Jack too, but she'd never articulate that thought. She watched him sidle around the countertop and pick up a menu.

"Let's phone the order in," Jack said. "Then I can walk down and collect it, if you like?"

"That'd be perfect," Deanna answered.

"Thank you," Kait acknowledged.

Good. That'd give Kait time to make a phone call. It was past time that she talked to Monika again and it'd been weighing on her mind. She needed to do it now before she got sidetracked again by the super moon this evening. She gave Jack her order and then excused herself, grabbing her burner phone from her room and taking it downstairs. This was a conversation that needed to be held in private. She kept her burner phone charged, but only turned it on once a day. But there were never any calls, which was good. It hopefully meant that Monika had kept her end of the bargain and deleted this number from her phone after their last chat.

Kait dialed and waited. Her sister answered after the second ring. "Kait, is that you?"

"Yes, Mon, it's me."

"Oh, thank God. I've been so worried about you." The distress in Monika's voice was palpable, and Kait knew in a moment of sharp-edged guilt that she'd been the cause of her sister's worry. "Where are you? Are you okay? It's been two weeks since I heard from you. I didn't know if you were dead or alive. I was going out of my mind."

"I'm fine," Kait replied in a soothing voice. "But I'm not going to tell you where I am. I think it's safer that way." While she placated Monika, she tried to count days in her head. Had it really been that long since she'd last spoken to her sister? Since she'd escaped Dario's clutches? The days had morphed into weeks without her realizing. That was part of the danger of Cloudwater Bay.

There was silence for a few seconds. "Agreed," Monika finally replied. "But I have to tell you, Dario has been in touch, and he's not a happy man." There was a quaver in Monika's voice that Kait had never heard before. Was her sister afraid? Of Dario?

"Tell me everything," she demanded.

"It was like you predicted. He phoned the day after you left him. He couldn't even wait twenty-four hours before he tried to track you down." Monika made a disgusted sound at the back of her throat. "I think I convinced him the first time he called that you were staying with me, but you were very upset about Susan and didn't want to talk to him. He was clearly unhappy with that, but he couldn't very well force me to put you on. So, he left it. Until the following day. When he rang me again."

"Mmm hmm," Kait encouraged, while inside her chest caved in slightly at the thought Dario might try to hurt Monika.

"This time it was harder to put him off. Eventually, I just hung up on him, telling him that he needed to give you some space."

"And then?" Kait asked, guessing what was to come next, but dreading it anyway.

"Yeah, you were right, he is an asshole. The next day some big guy dressed in a suit turned up at my door, demanding to see you, like some mafia strongman."

Kait's gut tightened. "Oh, God, Mon, I'm so sorry."

"Not to worry. Luckily, my next-door neighbor chose that second to come home. He's a big, burly dude, works out a lot at the gym—pity he's got a girlfriend—anyway, he asked if I needed any help and I think he scared the thug enough so he left and I haven't been bothered since." Monika lived on the third floor in an uptown apartment. She hated to garden and was a typical Libra who liked her luxuries. Which might well have saved her from more scrutiny from Dario's security.

"And you haven't heard from him since?" Kait was a little surprised Dario had left it at that. But now she thought about it, that was the same day she'd accidentally caused that man's death. Which meant Dario had already been on her trail by then. Should she tell Monika about the dead man? It'd just end up worrying her more, and so Kait decided against it.

"Nope. But… I have seen the same ruffian across the street from my place a few times. He's never approached me, but he's keeping an eye on me. I think they've figured out that you're not here. But now they're watching me just in case you turn up. So, whatever you do, don't come here, sis."

"Oh, I won't," Kait agreed. "But there are some contingency plans I think we should put into place. I've been thinking," she said carefully, "and this is what I want you to do."

Kait walked slow laps around the concrete edge of the pool, skirting the fallen palm tree as she talked and made plans with her sister. Perhaps they also needed to set up some kind of secret communication, where Kait could let her sister know that she was still alive and well at regular intervals. She hated that Monika had been left in the dark for so long. The lack of reception out at Cloudwater was partly to blame, but Kait knew she should've been more diligent about contacting her sister.

She waved at Jack as he departed through the side gate to collect their dinner, and she was still talking earnestly when he returned ten minutes later, arms laden with parcels of butcher's paper, the smell divine. By that time, she was feeling slightly more buoyant about Monika's inclusion in this little game of cat and mouse, and she rang off, promising to call more often.

Following the smell of deep-fried potatoes, she climbed the steps, her stomach rumbling.

# CHAPTER TWENTY-THREE

They found a spot on a grassy knoll to sit, squeezing in beside a family spread out on a large blanket and an old couple sitting in camp chairs sipping a glass of wine each. *Wine would've been a nice idea,* Jack decided idly, licking a stray grain of salt from his bottom lip. It'd top off this gorgeous evening nicely. The fish and chips had been delicious, crisp batter and deep-fried chips heavy on the salt and vinegar. He'd eaten so much he'd been tempted to loosen his belt a notch or two.

Deanna plonked down on the grass on one side of him, while Kait curled her legs beneath her and sat neatly on the other. The parkland area at the edge of Roebuck Bay was lit by streetlights from the road behind, but the beachfront and ocean remained dark and indeterminate. It was still half an hour until the moon was due to rise, but the place was packing out fast. This was the perfect night for it. The ocean was as calm as a millpond, the air balmy and buzzing with night insects, and the delicious aroma of deep-fried food and onions filled the air.

"I'm glad we had takeout at home," Kait observed, looking over her shoulder to the queues of people lining up at the food carts. In the dim light, he could only make out the contours of her face, not the minute details. When she turned toward the streetlights, he caught the flash of her green eyes as her features were cast into stark relief. Then everything softened as she looked toward the ocean once more.

"Yes, that was a good idea of yours, Deanna." Jack smiled warmly at her.

It was funny, but Kait seemed more relaxed now—especially after her phone call—while Deanna seemed more uptight for some reason. He wondered what had gone on between the two women before he'd come up the stairs.

And he also wondered about Kait's little disappearing act in town earlier this afternoon. She was lying about looking at the artwork; of that much, he was sure. She'd definitely seen the two police officers come out of the shop. And she'd also seen him go up and shake Pete's hand. Something had freaked her out and caused her to take off like a startled rabbit. And it was obvious to him now Kait had an aversion to the law. But why? During their heart-to-heart while the cyclone was ravaging the bay, Jack had asked Kait if she were in trouble with the law. And she'd pointedly denied it. But she'd been lying. Deep down, he'd known she was lying back then, but today it'd been confirmed beyond doubt. He was pretty sure it had something to do with her ex-husband. But she was such a closed book when it came to her past and her troubles, she didn't want to confide in anyone. He let out a frustrated breath. If she didn't want to talk about it, then he'd just have to respect that. Although he'd like to know if he was harboring a fugitive from the law. He was sure he was being overly dramatic, so he dropped the thought.

"Where is the moon going to come up?" Deanna asked, and he sat up a little straighter so he could see over the heads of the people sitting in front.

"Over there." He pointed straight out to sea.

"Cool." Deanna seemed to think for a second before she

asked, "Why do they call it a strawberry moon?"

"Yeah, why?" Kait echoed, leaning forward to join their conversation.

"Well, believe it or not, I can answer that one." He wasn't going to admit that he'd looked it up after the two women had expressed their interest that day driving from Exmouth back to Cloudwater. "This is the last full moon of the year, and in the northern hemisphere it's called a cold moon. But down here in the south it's called a strawberry moon, often relating to when they pick strawberries in summer. But really, this is what's called a super moon phenomenon, when the moon's orbit brings it closer to the earth."

"Cool," Deanna said again. "But is it really going to be pink? Because, if it's not, I'll be disappointed."

"So will I," Kait agreed from beside his left shoulder.

Certainly, with a brand-new tattoo of a pink moon on her chest, he could sympathize with her.

"I think you might need to get ready for disappointment, then," he warned. "I believe it will be normal moon color tonight, perhaps with a slight orange tinge, if anything." Jack was slightly distracted by the feel of Kait's shoulder pressed against his as she leaned in to listen.

"Oh, bum." Deanna pouted.

"It'll still be great," Kait chimed in. "This is the first, and possibly only time, I'll ever get to see a super moon rising over Broome. You should embrace the experience, Deanna."

The younger woman gave Kait an amused glance. "That sounds like my line," she laughed. "Maybe I'm rubbing off on you."

"Yes, I think you are."

Kait left her shoulder resting against his, and Jack dared not move. He was enjoying the sensation too much. Her body radiated a soft warmth, and he caught a whiff of her shampoo as her long hair curled enticingly around her neck in the breeze. He suddenly didn't want to lose this connection. Wanted to know more about her.

"Do you have any more fun facts about the pink moon?" Kait asked softly, her breath tickling his ear.

"Well, as a matter of fact..." He gave a broad grin. "I know that one day on the moon is approximately twenty-seven earth days."

"No way." Deanna stared at him with her big, blue eyes, looking more childlike in that moment than he'd ever seen her.

"I also know that because the gravitational pull is less on the moon, you can jump six times higher."

Kait gave a low laugh. "I'd like to see that."

He was enjoying being the center of female attention. Enjoying their undivided conversation.

"Hands up who wants to fly to the moon?" Deanna asked. "I mean trips into space are already becoming a tourist attraction, it's only a matter of time before we can all go to the moon."

"Yeah, if you've got squillions of dollars," Jack said gloomily.

"Even if I had billions of dollars, I don't think I'd go," Kait mused softly. "I think it's better to keep some things a mystery."

"I'd go in a heartbeat," Deanna replied, and Jack didn't doubt she would.

"I'm not sure," Jack mused. "I think I'm leaning toward Kait's way of thinking. I mean, we humans like to explore the last frontier and all that, but I think you're right. If we do that, then the mystery is destroyed, and it becomes just another thing we've conquered."

He turned to Kait, and they spent the next five minutes discussing the magical and spiritual connections humans had with the moon.

When he glanced around, Deanna was gone.

"She'll be fine," Kait replied, catching his look of confusion. "Deanna is a special kind of person; things always turn out right for her. She's probably found the most perfect spot to watch the moon rise ever, and some young hot guy—or girl—is feeding her champagne and caviar at the same time."

Jack let out a bark of laughter. Kait had just encompassed Deanna so succinctly. But not in a mean-spirited way, more like a woman who understands the heart of another woman and doesn't begrudge them their fortune.

They continued talking, solving the world's problems, moving from the phases of the moon to how global warming was causing the sea level to rise all over the world. Kait was of the opinion that Perth needed to do something soon to navigate the coming big tides, or the rich coastal suburbs would all have the ocean lapping at their doors within the next ten to twenty years. Jack wasn't so pessimistic, but he did acknowledge that global warming was a big problem and not enough was being done about it. Jack took pleasure in Kait's sharp mind and intelligence, although a lot of her opinions seemed to be based not so much on real-life-experience, but more in things she'd read about. At one stage, she mentioned that her friend, Susan, was passionate about native flora, after decades working for the Kings Park Botanical Gardens, and grew many rare or endangered native species in her own special garden. Kait wasn't sure what would happen to Susan's garden, now that it was just her husband maintaining it. Her face lost a little of its animation and Jack was sad. He'd been savoring getting inside Kait's head just a little.

"Oh look," Kait exclaimed, and Jack suddenly realized that the conversation around them had died down to hushed whispers. Other people were also pointing out to sea.

The tip of a glowing orb was rising out of the mirror-like ocean, casting its reflection on the water as it rose. They sat transfixed as the moon inched its way above the surface.

"It's huge," Kait breathed. "And so pretty." Almost as if without thought, she reached down and took his hand, entwining her fingers with his.

He couldn't help himself. Slowly, his gaze swung away from the rising moon to watch her face. She was as fascinated by the lunar event as he was with contemplating the curve of her cheekbones, the dip below her nose, the slight purse to her lips.

"What are you looking at?" she asked, without turning around. "You need to watch the moon. Look, it really is a light pink. Or is it just my imagination?"

But he wouldn't look.

Then she turned toward him and leaned in, her breath warm against his mouth. He stared into her eyes and did what his body commanded. He kissed her.

Her lips were warm, but hesitant. She didn't pull away, however, bringing her hand up to rest on his chest instead.

While everyone around them watched the moon rise over the water, Jack kissed Kait, and she kissed him back. He didn't push or demand but let her do the driving. She explored his mouth with her tongue, then tentatively tilted her head and sucked on his bottom lip, as if tasting something delicious. Finally, she broke the kiss, leaning her forehead against his, her breathing a little too fast, her hand still over his heart.

"We're supposed to be watching the moon," she whispered.

"I know. Sorry." But he wasn't sorry. And he hoped she wasn't either.

They kissed again, and this time she was less tentative, more sure of herself. When they finally broke apart, Kait snuggled against his shoulder, and they turned to watch the wonderful event happening over the ocean. The moon had finally broken free from the tethers of the surface of the water, and was floating in all her pearlescent glory in the inky sky.

"I've never seen anything like it. It's so big. Like I could reach out and touch it." She reached a finger forward as if she really could cross the miles and place her finger on the surface. They stayed like that—his arm around her shoulder, her head resting against him—for a long time, even after other people began to pack up their things and leave. It felt good, like he was a grown-up.

In the aftermath of the kiss, all sorts of questions began scrambling for answers in his head. Should he have initiated the kiss? Did she enjoy it as much as he had? She was clearly escaping from an abusive relationship, was she even ready to move on? He had no idea how she was feeling or what she was thinking. Or even what she'd gone through because she wouldn't tell him. Was he an asshole, taking advantage of a woman who was vulnerable and hurting and breakable? Probably.

But she *had* kissed him back.

It was too early to dissect all the ramifications. Perhaps he should just enjoy the feeling of bliss instead and let it be. For now.

# CHAPTER TWENTY-FOUR

Kait sipped her coffee and stared out over the balcony. This coffee was nearly as good as the one Jack's machine made back in Cloudwater. The morning was hot and sultry already. Kait had slept like a baby last night. Which was strange, considering. Considering she'd kissed a man who wasn't her husband.

It'd caught her unawares, that first, fleeting touch of lips, when really there was nothing surprising about the kiss itself. It'd been brewing for days. The attraction between her and Jack was so strong she was amazed it wasn't visible to the naked eye.

"Morning." Jack came to stand beside her and stare out over the rooftops toward the ocean, which was just visible through a gap in the trees. He stood close, but not touching her. He was wearing his sweatpants but no top, like he did every morning. But this morning, Kait was more acutely aware of his fine, naked, male torso right there within touching distance.

"Morning," she replied, feeling not at all awkward. Jack had a way of making her feel comfortable. Like she could be her true self around him. Even if he was distracting with all those muscles and bare skin right up in her face.

"How are you…after last night?"

"I'm good." She turned and touched him lightly on the arm. "I mean that. There's not an ounce of remorse in me today." When he finally met her gaze, she dropped her hand, satisfied he understood. Actually, she was more than fine; she felt lighter, less nervous about her future, be that near or far. Susan had yet to comment on her kiss with Jack, but she wasn't worried about what her friend would think. She would've been the first one to tell Kait to go for it. Anything to wash Dario from her soul.

The slight awkwardness from yesterday when Jack had asked about her last name had disappeared with the new dawn. But Kait knew that keeping secrets wasn't good for their friendship…or whatever this was. Jack had also dropped the subject of her obvious avoidance of the police, for now. It'd only be a matter of time before he asked more questions, however. She sighed and wished things were different. But for now, she was happy to bask in this new day and the memory of a kiss with a wonderful man. She could leave her other problems at the door for today at least.

"You?" she queried.

"If you're good, then so am I," he replied, blue eyes crinkling around the edges. It was one of the most attractive things about Jack. The smile lines around his eyes, they were like a direct line to his thoughts. When he was happy, it showed. Like right now.

They stood for many moments, merely contemplating the view. It was effortless being with Jack. A tiny part of her mourned the fact she hadn't found a man like Jack earlier. Wondered why it was her fate to marry Dario. But that road took her nowhere, so she banished the thought.

"So, what are the plans for today?" Deanna padded on bare feet out onto the balcony, hair tousled and pajamas askew.

"I'm still keen to do the pearl tour this morning, if Jack's up for it," Kait suggested.

"Sure. I've been meaning to do that tour for years now, and this is as good an opportunity as any. Did you want to join us?" Jack asked. They both looked at Deanna, and Kait tried to push down the ridiculous little voice that was begging Deanna to say no. A chance to spend more time alone with Jack was so tempting.

Deanna considered them through sleepy eyes. "Nah. I've got plenty to keep me busy around here. I might go get a bikini wax. It's getting pretty wild down there, if you know what I mean." Deanna made a gruesome face and Jack flinched slightly. "Maybe we could meet up for lunch somewhere later, though."

"Sounds good. What about at the Dragonfly Café?" Jack suggested, recovering his composure quickly. "I have a friend who works there, she might slip us a free beer or two."

Deanna merely nodded, then seemed to notice they were both holding mugs. "Ooh, that smells good." She brought her nose close to Kait's mug to drag in the aroma of coffee.

"I'll make you one if you like," Jack suggested.

"Thank you, that'd be lovely." Deanna beamed at him. As soon as Jack disappeared inside, she turned to Kait, her eyes losing their sleepy glaze.

"While we've got a few seconds alone, I need you to think about something," Deanna said, moving in closer and turning Kait around so their backs were to the open door. "I've looked into buses to Exmouth. There's one leaving at eight tomorrow morning."

"Okay," Kait replied faintly.

"That's the best way to get to Exmouth, don't you agree? It's either that or steal a car. I'm pretty sure we won't be able to cajole Jack into driving us this time. Unless you can come up with another plan?"

Kait shook her head faintly. She hadn't exactly forgotten her conversation with Deanna yesterday about the passports, but you could say it wasn't top of her mind either.

"It'll take us around three days to get there and back, the bus trip is nearly seventeen hours, one way."

"Wow. Surely it didn't take us that long when we drove with Jack?"

"No, I think it's more like twelve hours to drive. It's longer on the bus." But Deanna wasn't to be easily sidetracked. "We need to come up with some story to get Jack off our backs. Tell him we want to stay a few more days in Broome, and we'll find our own way back to Cloudwater when we're ready. We should be back for Christmas, at least."

Kait wasn't sure she wanted to get Jack off her back, so to speak. She was enjoying spending time with him. But she knew that time was limited.

Deanna's blue gaze bored into her, a worried frown hovering on her brow. The younger woman was right. They needed those new passports. And they needed the money to be able to do that. Once she had a new identity, Kait could open a bank account and deposit the rest of the money. Then she, and possibly Deanna—although she still needed to talk to her about her exact reasons—could leave the country. Go somewhere Dario would never find her.

"Okay. Can you book the tickets this morning, then?"

"Will do." The lines disappeared from Deanna's forehead. "The bus gets us into Exmouth just after midnight. We can grab the bag and get back on the next bus to Broome. Easy peasy."

"Here you go." Kait whirled around in time to see Jack returning to the deck with a steaming mug of coffee, which he handed to Deanna.

She took a sip and made a purring noise. "Mm, just the way I like it. You are a man after my own heart, Jack Wolfe."

She stood on tiptoe and kissed him on the cheek, and Kait felt a faint stab of jealousy. Even though she shouldn't be jealous. Deanna was clearly enamored with Raine, and Jack...well, she was pretty sure he could see right through Deanna.

"We'll leave in an hour, if that's okay with you," Jack said, smiling, but stepping back out of Deanna's reach, much to the joy of Kait's green-eyed monster. "I want to have a go at cleaning up some more of the garden this morning," he said, gaze drifting down over the balcony to the debris still blanketing the lawn below.

"We'll both give you a hand, won't we?" Deanna sang out unexpectedly. Kait berated herself that she was so surprised at Deanna's offer and nodded in agreement. Deanna could be a hard worker when required. That flighty, slightly lazy persona she projected was just that: a false facade she used to fool people. Kait needed to remember there was a sharp wit and a will of iron beneath that blonde bimbo act.

An hour or so later, Kait and Jack were striding toward the tourist bureau, where the tours were to depart. Kait had opted to wear the floppy hat and large sunglasses she'd bought in Geraldton. Jack had raised an eyebrow at her outfit but said nothing. Hopefully with this disguise, along with her black hair, she'd be less recognizable. Her near run-in with Pete the police officer yesterday had made her more cautious. Perhaps she shouldn't even be doing this tour. She'd be doubly sure not to make a spectacle of herself this time, that was all.

There was a queue at the information center and Kait hung back while Jack went to buy their tickets. He was back sooner than she expected, grabbing her by the hand and leading her around the corner where another crowd of people were gathering.

"The woman said we got the last two tickets, it's extra busy today," Jack said. But she was barely listening, concentrating on her hand in his. The warm connection seemed to go directly to her heart, which was beating irregularly, as if trying to keep up with her fluctuating emotions.

They stood at the back of the crowd and waited for the tour to start. A slim, young woman dressed in a black skirt and navy T-shirt called out to everyone, telling them she was their guide for the one-and-a-half-hour walking tour to show them the history of the pearling industry in Broome.

Kait listened as the exuberant woman led the way to the old wooden luggers, a short walk into the Chinatown section. She learned about the hardships of the life of a pearl diver, how many of them died from the bends, which was such a tragic tale. About the darker side of the industry in the early days, of the slavery and murder of the aboriginal men who were forced to dive for the precious pearls for their white captors. It was sad and a little humbling to hear. Then they walked along the edge of Roebuck Bay, the hot sun beating down on them mercilessly, learning about how the industry had first been established. Kait saw the park where they'd sat last night watching the moon rise and remembered how Jack had kissed her.

All the while, Jack held her hand.

Eventually, he had to let her go, when they were led inside the history museum to look at the diving equipment and other historical paraphernalia, when the crush to get through the door pulled them apart. She turned to see him smile ruefully over her shoulder.

But after they finished tasting a slice of pearl meat—the muscle from the oyster that produced the pearls—he retook her hand as they filed out the door at the end of the tour.

"Where to next?" he asked, his bass voice hitting her deep in the gut.

"Somewhere cool," she suggested. "This heat is getting to me a little." Somehow, the tropical heat seemed more intense here in the middle of the town. At least back at Cloudwater Bay, there'd been the open expanse of beach, allowing the breeze to wash through the dunes and keep the heat in check.

"We could go back to the house for a swim," he suggested. Jack had made sure the pool was clean and sparkling again as his first task yesterday when they'd arrived.

Kait considered the idea for a few moments and decided she liked it. Cool water against her skin would be nice to wash the heat from her bones. "Yes, okay."

"Then we can go and meet Deanna for lunch afterward. If she's not still loafing around the house, that is."

"It's a plan," Kait agreed. They strolled down the wide streets toward Lennie's house, keeping to the shade of the street trees when they could.

Deanna wasn't at home when they arrived, and Kait slipped upstairs to pull on her bathers. A dark-blue, no-nonsense one-piece suit that she'd worn underneath the wetsuit while they'd been pulling in ghost nets. Back then, she hadn't been bothered by Jack seeing her in her swimsuit, because they'd been doing a job, achieving something important, occupied by valuable duties. But this was a bit of frivolous entertainment. And suddenly she felt self-conscious as she walked down the stairs.

Jack was already in the pool, dark hair slicked back from his face, blue gaze following her as she came across the wooden decking and opened the gate of the glass safety fence. She hesitated by the edge, but the aqua water looked so inviting. After surviving her baptism of fire jumping into the ocean the other day, this pool was a piece of cake. Throwing caution to the wind, she dived in at the deep end, surfacing halfway up the length of the pool and turned back to laugh at Jack.

"Oh, this is heaven," she cried. "Why didn't we just start with the pool this morning, instead of getting all hot and bothered?"

"Because everything is sweeter after you've earned it," he replied, stroking slowly through the water toward her.

She supposed it was true.

He swam up beside her, slipping an arm around her waist, holding her suspended. "Did anyone tell you, you look spectacular in a swimsuit," he said, voice low and husky.

She almost laughed, but the sound died in her throat when she saw the hunger in Jack's eyes. He meant it.

His other hand came out of the water, and he brushed his thumb across her mouth. Heat pooled between her legs.

He kissed her. Gently easing her lips open, letting the warmth of his tongue mix with the cold drops of water. She let herself drift, half floating, half supported by Jack's strong arms. Dappled sunlight played over her face, streaming in through the trees surrounding the garden's edge.

Jack pulled her in tighter, one hand supporting her head. She could feel his erection, hard and demanding between them, pushing into her belly. His kiss became more insistent, and she responded, deepening their connection, his lips consuming hers.

A sudden image of Dario standing over her, gloating, as she lay on the bed waiting for him to do his thing engulfed her. Concentrating on the way Jack's mouth was so tender on hers, she tried to push the picture away. But suddenly Jack's hand on her waist felt like it was too hot, too close. Too controlling. She needed air. She needed to breathe. She stiffened in his embrace.

He let her go, sensing her sudden change of heart.

"What's the matter?" he asked, tugging her over to the shallow end of the pool. She dragged herself up the steps and sat one down from the top, her legs still encased in cool water. Jack sat next to her.

"I'm sorry," she said. "I was enjoying that. I enjoyed

kissing you last night too."

"But?" he asked softly.

"But…I don't know." She hadn't really thought about what she was doing with Jack. Like she'd said, kissing him had been nice. And somewhere at the back of her mind, she thought she'd decided that if she could kiss another man—kiss Jack—then she could do more with him too. Her body responded to him just like it should.

It seemed, however, her psyche had different ideas.

"I thought…" Jack didn't seem to know how to finish his sentence.

"I thought so too," she replied, looking him in the eye. Then she shook her head.

She'd thought she was ready to take the next step with Jack. But clearly, she wasn't.

"I'm sorry."

"You have no need to apologize. I should be the one to say sorry. You've obviously been through something traumatic, and I would never dream of pushing you." He picked up her hand and held it between the two of his. "I mean that."

Something loosened slightly in her chest. A featherlight touch of an emotion she hadn't felt in a very long time. A hint of joy. Of infatuation.

Suddenly, she wanted to tell Jack everything. How Dario had never truly seen her as her own person. She was his possession, to be used as he wished. There for his pleasure and to make his life seem perfect. How he'd imposed his own version of sexual subjugation on her to make her feel small and dirty, not fit for anyone else's consumption. She'd already insinuated in a conversation with Jack that Dario had been a controlling asshole. But she'd steered the talk away from why, and more importantly *who* her husband was.

"I think I hate my husband," she whispered. "I hate him for what he's done to me. What he's still doing to me."

Jack draped an arm around her shoulder. "I said this before, but if you need to talk about it, I'm here."

"I'm not sure talking about it will change anything. He'll still be an asshole, and I'll still be..." What? Broken? Irreparable? Afraid of letting anyone else in?

"No, but it might shake some of those bottled-up emotions loose," he replied gently.

*You should talk to him,* Susan said out of the blue, and Kait almost jumped out of her skin; it'd been a while since Susan had been present.

She thought about it for a while.

"He used sex to control me. Almost daily. Susan used to tell me it was a form of rape, and I should report him. Although perhaps it wasn't really rape, but more like the duty of marriage in its most basic form. A man enjoying himself, while the woman lies back and thinks of England."

Jack's hand tightened on her shoulder, she could feel the tension pulsing through his arm, but he kept a tight-lipped silence, letting her unravel her sordid story in her own time.

"For the first few years, I told myself it'd get better, that I'd learn to like it, eventually. But I never did. I just came to resent him. Then eventually, to hate him."

"Hate is a very strong word." Jack's thumb traced small, soothing circles on her bare shoulder. "But in this case, I think it may be warranted," he growled. "This man sounds like a complete douche bag. And for the record, I believe in total consent from a woman. Susan was right. What he did to you was rape." His frank words shocked her. "Why didn't you...?" Jack stopped, midsentence.

Kait knew he'd been going to ask why she hadn't left him years ago. It was the same question she'd asked herself over and over. But it was complicated. Marriage usually was. Especially marriage where a man manipulated his wife to make her feel small and unworthy, so that she didn't think she had a choice. And Jack seemed to understand. She wasn't sure about the word rape, however. She could never quite bring herself to admit that Dario had gone that far.

"That's why I'm on this journey. To get as far away from him as I can. I never want to see him again. All I want is a divorce, so I can be free of him. But he doesn't see it that way. He wants me to come home, so things can go back to the way they were."

"You could stay in Cloudwater Bay," he said softly. "You could be safe there. You can stay at my place for as long as you like." Jack's piercing blue eyes ensnared her, his hand hot and heavy on her skin.

Kait shook her head. "Thank you, Jack." Her heart expanded at his sincere offer. He meant every word he said, she could tell by the glint in his dark eyes. Jack would never understand what Dario was capable of, however. "But he's a very rich man. He doesn't take no for an answer. It's not that easy. He will try and find me."

"Is that why you were wearing that stupid floppy hat today? Was it some kind of disguise?"

She nodded unhappily. "At the moment, the only way to stay out of his hands, is to keep moving. Not settle down anywhere."

"That's no kind of life," Jack objected.

"No, it's not," she agreed. "But I am going to find a way." She tried to sound bright and upbeat. "Deanna knows about my husband, and she's helping me get through it."

"That's good. I'm glad you have her, at least." She could see the unasked questions in his eyes about Deanna and their unusual relationship. But in true Jack style, he didn't push, understanding that she'd tell him in her own good time. If, or even when, she was ready. "I still think I could help you, if only you'd let me. Like I said, I know things. I could keep this asshole away from you. Arrange for...an unfortunate accident."

"Thank you." She smiled at him then, profound and heartfelt. He was a good man.

At that thought, misery settled heavily on Kait's shoulders. All Jack wanted to do was help her. But she couldn't tell him the total truth. About the money. And about Dario's henchmen who were out hunting for her. Or about the man at the bottom of the gorge.

And now she was going to have to tell him another lie. She'd have to convince him to go back to Cloudwater and leave her and Deanna in town to have fun. The words stuck like feral claws in her throat, and she couldn't force them out.

Her eyes snagged the ANZAC rising sun tattoo on his shoulder nearest to her. Without thought, her finger came up to trace the lines of the black ink. It reminded her of his time spent in the army, doing his best to protect and serve. This was a mark to show his respect to the men who gave their lives for their country. A sign of the kind of man he was. A reputable man. She suddenly wondered why this man was still single. It was true, she'd often asked herself this question in passing, but today the thought intruded into her mind with deep urgency. He would make a great husband. Be a great father to a horde of children. He'd already told her about his failed marriage, but that'd been over fifteen years ago. Why had he not found someone else since then?

"You'd make a good dad, you know," she blurted, her gaze still fixed on his tattoo.

"What? Where did that come from?" His confusion at her out-of-the-blue comment was probably warranted.

She shrugged. "I was just wondering why you never remarried. Why you never had kids. It's just a shame," she added lamely.

He studied her with serious blue eyes.

"There's an easy answer to that," he finally replied. Out of her peripheral vision she saw his gaze drift out over the pool, eyes unfocussed. "I never remarried because in the end, I was married to the army. It was my whole life for quite a while. I was deployed overseas, and I never found anyone who held my interest for long enough." He turned back to look at her. "I was happy being single, and kids were never on my radar."

Kait sensed his explanation held the truth. But she could also feel there was more to it than that. He was holding back for some reason. That might've been accurate while he was deployed, but he'd been a civilian for over ten years now. He would've been in his early thirties when he left; a man in the prime of his life. So what was stopping him from moving on now?

"If that's the easy answer, what's the hard answer, then?" She lifted her gaze from his shoulder and looked into his face, just in time to see a spasm of pain cross his features. She must've hit a nerve, and she suddenly regretted asking such a personal question. It was none of her business.

"I guess you just shared some of your story, so maybe I owe you a little of mine in return."

She opened her mouth to disagree; she hadn't told him about Dario just to get him to open up. But he held up a hand. Then he turned his arm over, baring the tattoo of a date inked into his skin.

"This is to remind me of my biggest failure."

"Oh, I don't…" She didn't know what to say to that, taken by surprise as he plowed on.

"It's the birth date of a little boy called Jalil. He was six years old. He was killed in an extraction gone wrong while we were in Iran. The father had abducted him from the mother and flown him from Australia to Iran while she was in the middle of a court hearing to gain custody."

She couldn't help herself, she curled her fingers over his

where they sat splayed out on the concrete between them, lending him her sympathy. This wasn't what she'd expected to hear at all.

"We were supposed to grab him from the car as his father pulled into the driveway of his home," Jack continued. "But he spotted one of our guys at the last second and got spooked. Instead of turning into the drive, he took off down the street like a bat out of hell, trying to escape with his boy. A truck came around the corner at the end of the street and hit them head on. We saw the car go up in a ball of flame. There was nothing we could do for the boy or his father. I got out of the child protection game after that. Started my truck driving venture instead."

"Oh, Jack." There were no words. It suddenly became clear why he was hiding out in an isolated backwater. No wonder he'd put aside the idea of having children. He'd seen firsthand how love could make you do horrible things. Spiteful things. How a child could be ripped from this world in a single moment of madness. But to blame himself? That was just wrong. "I'm sorry for the boy, and his mother, and the family. And you," she added. "But I can't see how that was your fault."

"I was in charge of the mission. I should've predicted the father was a fanatic. I think he drove that car into the truck on purpose. Just so we didn't get the boy. I should've cordoned off the street, picked a better spot to spring our trap."

Kait could understand all the reasons why Jack would second-guess himself. He was that type of man, one who bore the weight of his own actions on his shoulders. It would do no good for her to tell him he wasn't to blame. It sounded like he was already mired deep into that black hole of culpability. But she said it anyway.

"I'm sure better people than I have already told you this a multitude of times, but that boy's death was not your fault.

The burden rests solely on his father who stole him—went against Australian law—and then decided to drive away, putting the boy in incredible danger." She moved her hand to rest it on his knee, his bare skin still beaded with droplets of cool water.

Jack made a noise somewhere between a grunt and a dismissal. "You're right. You're not the first person to say that."

"Maybe you should start listening."

"Maybe I will, one day," he replied.

They sat side by side, staring at the azure water, the sun beating down on their shoulders. Life threw you all kinds of curveballs. Everyone had their flaws, their faults, their secrets. And everyone dealt with their problems differently. Who was Kait to tell Jack how to live his life? Or how much guilt he should carry around on those broad shoulders of his. This insight he'd given her into his past was an intriguing interlude. It showed that Jack certainly wasn't perfect. But neither was she. They were both coping the best way they knew how.

Two flawed human beings trying to find their way through this world.

She was suddenly tired of all these heavy thoughts weighing her down. They had a whole afternoon ahead of them. Perhaps they could even go on a sunset camel ride this evening. One last hurrah as the happy-and-carefree-Kait with Jack by her side, before she had to get on that bus and become Kait-the-runaway once more.

"Come swim with me. It's a shame to waste such a beautiful day." She dove into the water, feeling Jack close behind her as she stroked underwater to the other end. It was true. She might not be ready to make love with Jack just yet, but she could still enjoy his company, even if it was for just one more day.

# CHAPTER TWENTY-FIVE

Jack shoved the gearstick into overdrive with a grunt. Then he slammed his palm against the steering wheel. He was driving his black four-wheel drive way too fast, but for the moment he didn't give a shit. Dammit. Why was he so angry? Those two women were adults. What they got up to was none of his concern.

But he was angry. Seething with an urge to hit something.

Because Kait had lied to him.

So had Deanna, but that often came with the territory when dealing with Deanna. She liked to stretch the truth to suit herself.

But Kait. He thought he could trust Kait. After their kisses. After they'd bared their souls to each other in the pool. How wrong could he be?

Last night had been special too. After their swim, Jack had spent a few hours collecting the items Raine had requested for her house, and then he'd taken up Kait on her suggestion they try the sunset camel ride on Cable Beach—he'd been more than happy to oblige. Deanna had tagged along with them, but that was okay. The night was carefree, full of laughter and lighthearted banter. The sunset had been magnificent, lighting the sky on fire with vibrant red, orange, and yellow as the sun dropped below the ocean horizon. There was nothing better than a northern WA sunset. Camels weren't his favorite animal, but having to sit astride as they lumbered ungainly along wasn't too high a price to pay to spend time with Kait.

It wasn't until they were sitting down to a glass of beer and a Thai takeaway back at the house that they'd sprung the news on him.

"So, Jack," Kait had begun. "We've been talking." She shot Deanna a quick smile. "And we'd like to stay a few more days in Broome. There are so many things to see and do. But we know you're itching to get back to Cloudwater. So we'd like to propose that you go home tomorrow as planned, and we stay on a few more days..." Kait trailed off and Deanna took a swig of beer and watched him carefully over the rim of her glass. "As long as that's okay with you and Lennie, of course," Kait added.

He was sure Lennie wouldn't mind. But that wasn't the point. What was going on here? The back of his neck began to itch. "How are you going to get back to Cloudwater?" he asked calmly.

"Oh, don't you worry about us. We're old hands at this hitchhiking thing." Deanna gave him a wink and a smile. Which was true, he couldn't argue with that.

"We'll be back before Christmas," Kait promised. "We're really looking forward to spending Christmas Day with you and Raine and the rest of the Cloudwater Bay crowd." Kait wouldn't meet his eye as she said this. "But this way we can get some Christmas shopping done, too."

He didn't want to leave them here on their own, but it seemed like he was being railroaded into agreeing.

He was about to open his mouth to present more arguments as to why they possibly shouldn't stay here on their own, when Deanna had gushed, "Thanks, Jack, you're a star." Then she turned to Kait and said, "I made us an appointment at the hairdresser tomorrow morning. I can't wait to get these split ends tidied up."

"Oh, yeah," Kait said. "Me, too." But her response seemed stilted somehow.

"And then I think we should book a dinner cruise out on the bay. And I've got a friend in town who's keen to show us this really cool rock pool you can swim in, out at Gantheaume Point." Deanna sat back in her chair and practically glowed with enthusiasm.

"Hmm," Jack replied distractedly. He'd heard there were great rock pools out at that point, but still…

"What time will you be off tomorrow, Jack?" Deanna asked, tilting her head to the side with a coy smile, giving him no room to argue.

"Well, I guess I'll leave early. No point in hanging around. Like you said, I've got plenty to do back in the bay. I'll grab the rest of the food from the supermarket on my way out." He needed to remember that this trip into town wasn't all about him. There were people relying on him back in Cloudwater.

Their night had ended soon after, Kait excused herself, saying she was tired and headed off to bed, giving him no chance to talk to her alone. He'd considered knocking on her door and stood there deliberating for many moments before deciding against it. If Kait wanted to play games by staying in Broome without him, then that was her business.

This morning, he'd thrown his bag in the car and waved goodbye as he'd reversed out of the driveway, pretending to be heading toward the main supermarket in the middle of town. But something about the whole thing didn't sit right. So instead, he'd waited around the corner and followed them when they left Lennie's house half an hour later. He might blame himself for Jalil's death, but that didn't mean he wasn't still good at covertly following a target while staying out of sight.

The first hint that they weren't heading to the hairdresser was when they emerged carrying their bags. They headed straight for the bus station, a ten-minute walk from the house, and boarded a bus headed for Exmouth as he watched from down the street.

Part of him desperately wanted to follow that bus. To make sure they were okay. The other part, the angry and wounded part over the fact Kait had lied to him, was telling him they were big enough and old enough to look after themselves. He'd jumped back into his four-wheel drive and taken off in the opposite direction, not looking back even once. He probably forgot half the supplies people had asked him to collect in his muddled state of mind, but he hardly cared as he stomped out of the supermarket laden down with food.

Now he was half an hour down the road, but the anger hadn't subsided one bit. Indeed. Rather, it was building. Jack rarely got angry, but when he did, it was like a pit of boiling lava in his stomach. He hated people who lied. Who betrayed him.

He'd been warring back and forth that it was none of his business for the last half an hour.

Why were they going to Exmouth? They must have their reasons for sneaking off without telling him. He thought he might know the answer. It had something to do with the black backpack that Kait had been carrying. Because she definitely didn't have it when she'd got back into his truck the morning after their stay in Exmouth. What was in that backpack? Either that, or it had something to do with Kait's ex-husband. Actually, there was no ex about it. She said they were separated, but not divorced. So she was still technically married to him.

He slowed the car. Perhaps he should turn around. If it was

something to do with the husband, they might need his help. They might be in danger. Could the ex have found her, then instead of telling him, she'd snuck off to keep him from danger?

He smacked the steering wheel with his palm a few more times. Goddamnit.

Nope, he wasn't going to follow them. He'd had enough of this bullshit.

He was heading back to Cloudwater to have Christmas with Raine and Old George and Ella and Toby. Like he always did. And if Kait and Deanna returned, they'd be welcome to join the party. But afterward, he was going to ask them to leave. Enough was enough. He needed his old life back. He'd chosen to live at Cloudwater for a reason. It was the place where he could enjoy nature at its best, not have to deal with the baggage of human relationships, as well as forget about past trauma. He'd almost been sucked in by the feeling of Kait in his arms, by the possibilities she offered. But this little interlude with Kait had only proven one thing. He couldn't be trusted to figure out when he was being played by somebody. It was just sheer chance he discovered Kait's duplicity before it was too late.

Jack had several delivery jobs lined up straight after New Year. He needed to keep paying the bills. But more than that, he needed the solitude of driving his truck alone down the road, with no one to tell him what to do, and no one waiting for him to come home. No responsibilities. Nothing to tie him down. Just him, the road, and his truck.

Pushing the gas pedal to the floor, Jack headed for home.

# CHAPTER TWENTY-SIX

Deanna shifted in her seat, trying to get comfortable. Buses were fun for the first hour. But then the novelty of riding in a big tin can speeding down the bitumen wore off, and now she was just restless and bored. And they still had a long way to go.

At least she had the window seat, Kait had the aisle. Deanna had curled her legs up under her and was leaning her elbow on the windowsill, contemplating the country outside. Sparse, red and dry, rolling on Cloudwaterly.

They'd had to hustle to make it to the bus stop in time after they'd seen Jack off this morning. He wasn't too happy about leaving them. Deanna had to step in and add her two bobs worth last night before Jack had been convinced by their little story. Deanna could see that Kait was faltering at the last hurdle and needed a little push in the right direction. She just wasn't very good at lying. But that was okay, because Deanna was good enough for the both of them. She'd made up some shit story that she'd booked them on a sunset boat tour tonight, and then her friend was taking them to a cool rock pool the following day, so Jack had nothing to worry about. As long as Lennie would be okay with them staying on a little longer, then everything would be great.

Jack had finally acquiesced to their wishes, saying he needed to get back to Cloudwater Bay and couldn't really afford another two days in Broome. But his gaze lingered on Kait for many long moments before he drove off down the street.

Deanna glanced over at her friend who was staring down the aisle and out the front window. They really should've thought to bring a book or something to keep them occupied. Instead, Deanna studied Kait's face, which looked a little drawn. Now that she thought about it, Kait's had that expression on her face ever since Jack had left this morning. Deanna wasn't blind; she could see how Kait and Jack looked at each other. It wasn't with the same intensity that she felt whenever she looked at Raine, but there was definitely heat there.

With nothing else to do, Deanna decided to poke the bear.

"You and Jack are cute together."

"What?" Kait's head swiveled so quick Deanna thought it might give her whiplash. "We're not...together."

Deanna hid her smug smile. It was exactly the response she was expecting. Kait was so predictable.

"Yeah, I know. But I could feel the vibes. You like him. And he likes you."

Kait brushed her fringe out of her eyes, in what was fast becoming a new telltale sign of irritation. "Well, whatever *vibes* you're feeling, they're not correct," Kait huffed.

"Whatever." Deanna went back to staring out the window. It was just a simple observation. If Kait didn't want to admit to her feelings, that was her business.

After a few minutes, Kait tapped her on the shoulder and said, "I'm sorry. I shouldn't have snapped at you."

"No problem." Deanna was used to a lot worse. And Kait was just being human, no need to apologize for that.

"It's just that... You're right. There is a connection between me and Jack. And for so many reasons I can't follow up on that. Top of the list being, that we're leaving as soon as we get those passports. But even if I was free to pursue a relationship with him, I don't think I'm ready."

"It's too soon to fall in love again after leaving your husband, I get that."

"No, it's more than that." Kait pursed her lips and looked out the window, perhaps hoping the red earth flashing past would give her inspiration. "Physically I'm ready to discover if there is anything else to lovemaking other than an unsatisfactory five minutes of ignoring the act as far as possible. But mentally...my mind won't let me move on. Won't let me forget. I don't ever want to be dominated by another man again. I'm not sure I'm ready to let any man into my life. And I'm certainly not going to hand over control ever again."

"And neither you should," Deanna said, sitting up straighter in her chair.

"I'm not sure love even exists," Kait added softly.

Indignation rose inside Deanna. Poor Kait; she so badly wanted her to shake off the shackles of being married to that pig. To learn to be a normal human being again. Which included learning to find passion and affection.

"Seems to me that love is a giving thing," Deanna started hesitantly, not sure where her thoughts were leading her. "You both have to give a part of yourself. But with you and your husband, all he was doing was taking. Taking what he wanted. Maybe you have nothing left to give at the moment."

"Maybe." Kait seemed to consider Deanna's words, a heavy frown marring her forehead. "It's certainly one way of looking at it."

"Just my observation. I could be wrong. But Jack seems to be a very giving person."

"Yes, he is," Kait agreed.

They lapsed into silence, each one lost in their own thoughts.

Deanna was having mixed feelings about leaving Cloudwater Bay. She wanted the excitement and the adventure of traveling with Kait. The idea of seeing foreign countries and new cultures had fired up the passion inside of her. And of course, Kait still needed her protection, not that she would ever admit it. She felt like she owed it to Kait, to show her how life could be so good, but to also keep her safe from harm. Because there were a lot of wolves out there ready to rip her throat out. Deanna liked Kait, despite the way she was sometimes patronizing and aloof. She had a kind heart and a quirky sense of humor when she let it show.

But Deanna would miss Cloudwater. Miss the simplistic lifestyle. There were so many things she could still achieve in Cloudwater. Like helping Raine to complete the repairs on her house. Learning more about being self-sufficient and working in the garden with Raine. Then there was her artwork she planned to make from the remains out of the ghost nets. She wanted to help raise awareness of the terrible toll those nets took on the ocean creatures, as well as the long-lasting plastic pollution problem they caused. It would be a passion project, one she was sure could possibly become something big. If only she stayed.

And then there was Raine. Their fledgling relationship was just that, a new beginning. But what a beginning it was. Deanna wanted to explore the possibilities of what Raine had to offer.

But if Kait was determined to move on, then Deanna would follow. Perhaps she could come back one day. She was pretty sure Cloudwater wasn't going anywhere in a hurry.

"I hope the money is still there," Kait said. But Deanna could tell she was only half joking.

"Of course it'll still be there. No one knows what was in

that bag. No one would suspect we'd hide a million in a storage unit." Deanna lowered her voice, making sure the old codger sitting behind them didn't overhear. What was Kait thinking? Putting all these doubts in Deanna's mind.

"I think Jack might suspect something," Kait replied quietly.

Deanna frowned as she thought about that. "He never said anything."

"No. But I know he noticed the backpack was missing when we got into his truck that morning."

"Pshaw." Deanna waved a hand. "He's not that smart."

"I'm not so sure."

Silently, Deanna agreed. But even if Jack had suspected something fishy about the backpack, he would never have guessed in a million years what was inside. Jack was no threat to them; of that much, she was sure.

"Oh, by the way. I will pay you the money back. I just need to make a phone call to get my finance guy to transfer some cash, that's all."

"You have a finance guy?" Kait narrowed her eyes, and Deanna wanted to slap a hand over her own mouth. She hadn't meant to let that slip. But then again, she'd been meaning to tell Kait about her fiscal situation soon. Mainly so that Kait didn't think she was following her around just because of the money. Perhaps now was the time.

"Yeah. I have a financial guy who handles my trust account. My parents left me a fair bit of money. I don't tend to have much use for it, so I leave it in his hands. He invests it for me."

"How much money we talking?" Kait had gone perfectly still.

"Almost as much as you have stashed in that black backpack."

"Oh." Kait's mouth made an O of surprise. "Oh," she said

again, and Deanna could practically hear the cogs turning inside Kait's head. Did that change things for Kait? It didn't make the slightest difference to Deanna, but she could see a light of contemplation entering Kait's eyes.

"I'll make the phone call when we reach Exmouth," Deanna added sheepishly.

"No problem," Kait replied. But there was something about the way she was looking at Deanna. Like she didn't quite believe the words coming out of her mouth.

"I only told you, so you didn't think I was going to try and sponge off you," Deanna blurted out.

Kait's face turned red. "I would never think—"

"Don't bullshit a bullshitter," Deanna said, not unkindly.

"I wasn't... I wouldn't," Kait stuttered.

"It's okay, Kait. I know it's a shock. But I just wanted you to know that I can pay my own way when we go overseas together."

Kait clicked her mouth shut, green eyes going wide. It took a few seconds for Kait to regroup. But to her credit, all she said was, "That's good to know."

At least she didn't argue or try and talk Deanna out of coming with her. Perhaps she was warming to the idea of the two women traveling together. They'd make a great team. Deanna could see it now, how much fun they could have sipping Singapore Slings in the Raffles Hotel, drift-snorkeling in the sparkling clear waters of the Maldives, or riding camels in the desert around the great Egyptian pyramids. Kait's husband wouldn't have a clue where they were, and if the police ever worked out that thug hadn't been alone when he fell into that gorge, they'd never track them down either.

Deanna went back to staring out the window, daydreaming about all the wonderful things they could do together.

\* \* \*

Seventeen hours was a bloody long time to sit on a bus. Even with the mandated stops every three hours so they could get off and stretch their legs, Deanna was just about ready to claw her way out the window by the time the lights of Exmouth came into view. It was just after midnight as the bus growled down through the gears and came to a slow stop in the deserted station with the hiss of air brakes.

"Oh, God, fresh air," Deanna said, as she stepped down off the bus. Exmouth's warm, humid air was a balm to her skin, her throat husky and raw from the freezing air-conditioning they'd had to endure all the way here. Standing on the sidewalk, she held her arms aloft to try and thaw the cold from her bones. She'd make damn sure she kept out a sweater to wear on the way home.

There was no actual bus depot in Exmouth. The bus had dropped them in a large parking lot. Deanna could see a public toilet block at one end, a set of shops at the other, and a large expense of green grass with scattered palm trees— probably the city center's main parkland area—across the road.

"I can't feel my bum," Kait complained, stepping down beside Deanna. "I'm not looking forward to the return trip."

"Me either. But I guess it beats walking all the way," Deanna quipped.

"Let's just get this over and done with." Kait put her hands in the small of her back and stretched out her shoulders.

There were only eight other people on the bus, and four of them waited to collect their small bags from the storage compartment beneath the bus, the other four must be continuing on to Perth, and had stayed in their seats on the bus. Deanna dropped her duffel with a groan on the sidewalk. "Not sure why we brought these," she groused. It wasn't like the bag was heavy, and it was easy enough to swing up over one shoulder, but Deanna didn't care to be lugging it through the dark streets of Exmouth.

"Just in case." Kait picked up her smaller overnight bag by the handles and began to walk in the direction of town. Did the older woman even know where she was going?

"Just in case of what?" Deanna grumbled, following after her. But she knew what Kait meant. Just in case they never got back to Broome. Just in case they got stuck in Exmouth. Plans could change in an instant.

"It's a fucking long walk, you know that, don't you? It's right on the other side of town."

"This was your idea," Kait shot back. "So we'd better get going, if we want to get back in time to catch the six am bus home."

Deanna stopped to consider her friend for a second. Did she even realize what she'd just said? What was Kait thinking calling Cloudwater Bay home? Deanna stumbled along behind Kait, tired, hungry, and just plain grumpy. But they needed to get this over and done; they had no other choice. All their other bus companions had disappeared. Most of them hopping into waiting cars—family members come to collect them. An empty chip packet blew down the deserted street, and a cat gave a plaintive meow from the dark shadow behind a dustbin. Deanna hurried to catch up to Kait.

It was a forty-five-minute walk to the storage sheds, Deanna dragging her feet all the way. Thank God the place had twenty-four-hour access. All you needed was the pin code to get through the gate. Deanna had already made sure that Kait was carrying the key to the padlock at least a dozen times on the bus already. A large spotlight lit up the main entrance, but the pathways between the rows and rows of metal sheds weren't as well illuminated, dark shadows casting odd angles, making things seem bigger and scarier than they actually were.

"This is spooky," Deanna admitted, a little chill skittering down her spine. They were creeping along like clandestine criminals; it was all quite dramatic. Deanna's testy mood disappeared. This was more like it. A little bit of fear to get the heart racing again.

They took two wrong turns before they finally found storage locker number sixty-seven. Kait fumbled for so long with the key in the padlock Deanna was tempted to snatch it away and do it herself. But finally, there was a click, and the door swung open with a squeak. It was completely black inside.

"Where's the bag? I can't see the bag." Kait's voice rose in pitch.

Deanna used the flashlight on her phone to light up the small square room, and they both drew in a sharp breath simultaneously. The black backpack was still there, sitting in the corner, all coy and innocent.

"Thank Christ," Kait said on a loud exhale. She jogged over and opened the top. Deanna watched as Kait peered into the bag, her black hair gleaming in the bright light. "It's all still here." Kait nodded, and she sat back on her haunches in relief.

"Good. Let's get out of here." A strange sensation slithered down Deanna's spine. Like she was being watched.

Kait swung the backpack over her shoulder and made a hasty retreat. They retraced their steps to the wrought iron front gate, but just before they stepped through, Kait put a hand on her shoulder, stopping her, and leaned out so she could check the dark street. What was she looking for? No person in their right mind was out of their bed at this ungodly hour of the morning. But Kait was just being cautious, and Deanna decided there was nothing wrong with that, especially considering what was in the backpack.

Their trek back to the bus stop followed the same path, but they kept to the shadows more often, stopping at each corner or intersection to make sure the road was deserted. Once, a set of headlights appeared in the distance, and by unspoken consent, they both stepped into a darkened shop doorway, flattening themselves against the glass door, until the car had passed.

Nothing was open at this time of night. There might be a twenty-four-hour gas station still open on the outskirts of town, but here, everything was closed and shuttered. The town wasn't even big enough to warrant a McDonalds or a KFC, let alone the twenty-four-hour variety.

"I'm hungry," Deanna grumbled as they trudged along a dusty street, almost able to taste the salt on the McDonald's chip she was so desperate to eat.

"So am I. I've got some muesli bars in my bag. We can have one when we get to the bus stop."

"Yuck." But Deanna kept her comment quiet enough that Kait didn't hear. It wasn't her fault that nothing was open in this deadbeat town at three am.

They were close to the station when voices suddenly echoed from around the next corner. They stopped and crept forward until they could peer around the edge of the building. Two drunk men sat in the gutter about a hundred meters away passing a bottle in a brown paper bag between them and arguing about someone called Marjorie, who it seemed had withdrawn her sexual favors from the taller man. The short man was offering his advice on how to get his wife back in his good books.

The men were directly between them and the bus stop.

"Bugger, we'll have to go around them." Kait stood and chewed her lip. They didn't want to take any chances of being seen. These men were probably harmless, but they couldn't afford to even stop and chat. If one of the men took a liking to the backpack…

"We can just double back and take the next street down,"

Deanna suggested. It'd take them an extra five minutes of walking and bring them out at the rear of the parking lot where the bus stopped, rather than the front, but that was okay.

They arrived without incident, and the parking lot was still deserted, unsurprisingly. There was a single bench beneath a concrete construction marking the spot where the bus would pull in, but apart from that, there was nowhere to sit.

"So, we just gonna wait here until the bus comes?"

"I think that's the best plan, don't you?"

"Why don't we wait in the park across the road." Deanna pointed toward a couple of pergolas she could see below the weak glow of a streetlight. "We'll be able to see when the bus arrives from there."

"Good idea."

They trudged across the road, and Kait chose to sit beneath the pergola farthest away from the streetlight. Hovering in the dim shadows, they would be almost invisible to anyone passing by, at least until the sun came up, and by then, they'd be getting on the bus. Deanna sank down onto the wooden bench on one side of the rickety table, and Kait took the opposite side, tucking the backpack well under the table, getting it out of sight as much as she could. Then she passed Deanna a muesli bar, which she took without delight but ate it anyway.

Deanna spent the next couple of hours wandering around the park, keeping an eye out for any strangers, or anything untoward, and trying not to sit down. If she was going to spend the next seventeen hours sitting, then she was going to make the most of her freedom now. Kait never moved from her spot by the pergola, standing guard over the backpack, a bit like a jealous mother hen guarding her eggs. Deanna thought she was making it more obvious that she had something to hide, with all her shuffling, and constantly looking over her shoulder. Kait would never make it as a big-league underworld figure; she just didn't have the poker face required for such subterfuge.

Around five am, a street sweeper swooshed slowly down the road. Deanna watched him with fascination. It was most interesting thing she'd seen in the last few hours. The bus from Perth arrived at five-thirty. It would wait half an hour so they could change drivers before it departed at six. Five people emerged from the bus as soon as it stopped, stretching and yawning, shuffling around the parking lot, looking like sloths who'd just been woken from a deep sleep. Deanna couldn't think of anything worse than enduring the whole trip from Perth right through to Broome. What a nightmare. Then more people began drifting into the area, dragging luggage behind them, all looking expectantly at the bus, but the door would remain firmly closed until the new driver came to open it up. The sky was just starting to lighten, the purple tinge on the horizon hinting that the sun was on its way.

"Shall we go over now?" Deanna asked, but Kait shook her head.

"I'd rather stay here where we can watch everyone for a while longer."

Deanna gave a huff of disappointment. She was tired of waiting around. This was taking things to extremes. All the people on the bus were going to see them soon enough anyway. Why were they continuing to lurk in the shadows? All she wanted was to get on that bus and out of this town. Back to the aptly named Cloudwater Bay. Back to the Cloudwater beach, the Cloudwater blue sky. Back to Raine and her morning yoga and her soft arms, and even her vegan cooking.

"I'm just going to use the toilet, then." Deanna began to walk off.

"Wait. I'll come with you." Kait stood and stretched. "You're right, it's getting close to departure time. We may as well both go."

"Great." Deanna brightened. Not that she was happy about getting back on the bus. But she certainly wasn't happy with all this standing around in a stupid park half the night either.

After they'd used the amenities, they drifted toward the small crowd who were gathering near the bus, ready to board. Kait hung back, leaning against a tree around halfway between the toilet block and the bus. At first, Deanna waited with her, dropping her bag on the ground and staring at the scattered group of people. Dawn was now creeping stealthy fingers across the land and as the dark fled behind the sun, Deanna began to make out people's features.

A young blond guy caught her eye. He was good-looking. Tall and broad-shouldered, with a hawklike nose and piercing blue eyes. Dressed in blue jeans, with a sports jacket over a black T-shirt. He dropped his bag next to the bus so it could be loaded and wandered away looking at his phone. She was drawn to the graceful way he walked, like a boxer, always on his toes. She drifted closer. She liked to people watch, and she studied a few of the other patrons. There was a baby-faced couple, perhaps still in their teens, with large backpacks and eager grins on their faces. An old man with a huge beer gut shuffled past, and she got a whiff of his BO and made a mental note to sit down the other end of the bus from him. Then blond guy glanced up and saw Deanna watching him, and smiled. Without thinking, she smiled back, and he began to make his way over to her.

Shit. She was supposed to be lying low, not attracting any attention. And yet, what was she doing? Exactly that. Now she'd have to remember to not say anything stupid and try and get rid of the guy as soon as she could.

"Hi," he said, flashing her a grin that was all white,

sparkling teeth. This one surely was built. Muscular, like he worked out in the gym. A lot. He lifted his arm to put his phone in his shirt pocket, and she noticed an expensive watch glinting on his wrist. That was weird. He wasn't dressed like a tourist. And he obviously had money, if he could afford a watch like that. What was he doing riding a bus to nowhere?

"You heading all the way to Broome?" he asked, in an easy, conversational manner.

Alarm bells began ringing in Deanna's head. She shifted gears. She didn't answer, merely cocked her head to the side, and gave him a girlish grin.

"That's where I'm going. I'm meeting a friend up there. Never been to Broome before, but I hear it's beautiful. Have you been?" he asked.

She shook her head and widened her eyes at him.

"You traveling alone?" He tried to make the question sound flirty, but she caught the hard glint in his eye, right before he turned to check on the bus driver's whereabouts. "I find it hard to believe a pretty girl like you would be alone."

"Yeah, nah," she said vaguely. "I'm going to meet my boyfriend."

She tossed her hair over her shoulder and gave a little giggle, at the same time managing to snag Kait's attention out of the corner of her eye, sending her a warning. This guy might be on to them. Deanna didn't know the exact details. Did he work directly for Dario? Or had Dario put out an all-stations alert to his underground relations to be on the lookout? Was he offering some kind of bounty? Oh, God. It'd never occurred to her there might be a bounty on her head. Did he have a photo of her and Kait? Had he already pinpointed her as one of the woman he was interested in? Or did he only have a general description, been told to be on the lookout for two women traveling together. Which made it all the more imperative he didn't see Kait. All she knew was he didn't fit in. And he had the eyes of a killer. All these thoughts skittered through her mind as she kept the smile plastered to her face, her chin set at a flirty angle.

Kait startled and stood up straighter at Deanna's look. But then slouched back against the tree trunk, reaching down to touch the bag in an unconscious move, eyes darting all around. Deanna nearly groaned out loud. She really needed to sit the woman down and teach her some basic 101 skills about keeping her emotions off her face.

"My boyfriend works at Tom Price. I haven't seen him for two weeks, and I can't wait," she continued the ruse, giving a girlish twirl, as if the excitement was too much for her.

"Oh, right." The guy seemed at a loss for words. She knew he probably didn't believe her, especially if he'd already pegged her as one of his targets. But he couldn't very well call her out in front of all these people. This was a game they were playing, and she was determined to win. She needed to keep him on edge, keep him guessing for as long as possible. If she kept up the ruse, and hope to hell he didn't have a recent photograph of her on that phone of his, perhaps he might even dismiss her as his intended mark. After all, how in the hell would Dario be completely sure they were in Exmouth? No one else knew they were in Exmouth, not even Jack. Maybe he had undercover spies riding the buses along this route on the off chance they'd spot Kait or Deanna, together or alone.

"What about you?" Now that she'd sussed him out, she needed to keep him busy until they got on the bus. She wasn't about to let him out of her sight. "Have you got a girlfriend? Or a boyfriend? Is that who you're meeting in Broome?"

"What? Oh, nah." He began to edge away from her, but she followed him. The bus driver started loading the bags. It'd be time to board soon.

Kait shuffled her feet, and Deanna noticed her sending a subtle lift of her eyebrow in Deanna's direction, asking what the plan was. Keeping her hands behind her back and out of sight of the blond man, she waved Kait away, pointing in the direction of the ablutions block. Hoping that Kait got the message, she continued to babble mindlessly at the man beside her, keeping his attention on her. And away from the woman standing under the tree, trying to juggle three bags. "That's a shame. It'd be nice to see Broome with a girlfriend, don't you think? What are you gonna do up there? I hear you can ride camels on the beach. That'd be exciting."

"Yeah." He ran a distracted hand through his blond locks.

She edged him toward the queue forming to get on the bus as she carried on talking. No longer able to see Kait—who she hoped was now walking briskly toward the toilets—she kept asking inane questions, fingers crossed behind her back, until it was their turn to board the bus.

"Oh, I just remembered. I need to go tinkle. I'll see you on the bus. Save me a seat." She waved gaily, pushing her way through the thinning crowd.

"There's a toilet on the bus," she heard him say in a confused tone as she disappeared. But she pretended not to hear him and kept her pace to a steady walk toward the women's toilets. Kait was nowhere in sight. Thank God.

# CHAPTER TWENTY-SEVEN

Kait stared at herself in the hazy mirror, worrying her bottom lip with her teeth. There were dark circles under her eyes. No wonder, she'd hardly slept on the bus, and they'd spent the rest of the night wandering the streets of Exmouth. Shifting from foot to foot, she checked the black backpack was still tucked beneath the countertop, along with her and Deanna's overnight bags. Had she understood Deanna correctly? Was this what she wanted her to do? Come and hide out in the toilets? If she stayed here much longer, she'd miss the bus.

She hesitated, staring at her reflection in the mirror. She'd removed her baseball cap when she'd entered the toilets, and her hair lay flat and plastered to her skull, just a few flyaway strands escaping. The woman who gazed back at her looked old and tired.

Making a decision, she bent down to gather at the bags. And was nearly bowled over when she stood up just as the door flew open.

"Thank God you're here. We can't get on that bus," Deanna whispered urgently, pulling Kait into a tiny cubicle, taking the bags with them. They hardly fit, and Kait had to squash alongside the stainless-steel toilet bowl. The floor was dirty, it didn't look like it'd been cleaned in weeks, and she was loath to put the bags down.

"Why not?" But Kait had a terrible feeling she already knew the answer.

"There's something cagey about that guy I was talking to."

"What? Do you think he recognized you?" Kait wanted to yell condemnation at Deanna. Why had the girl wandered over to the group in the first place? It was just inviting trouble. Why couldn't she have stayed under the tree with Kait? But now was no time for accusations.

"Maybe," Deanna admitted.

"How do you know? How did he find you? Find us?"

"I don't know. Maybe he had photos. A description. I don't know. I'm not sure he was even after us. But I got this feeling, you know?"

Kait huffed. Deanna and her *feelings*. But they couldn't afford to dismiss this one. And Kait had a sneaky feeling in her gut that this was indeed one of Dario's spies. "But I changed my appearance." Kait screwed up her mouth. Not only was her hair now as black as the ace of spades, her clothes all bought in Target, but she'd barely taken that stupid cap and large sunglasses off for the whole bus ride. If Dario had spies out looking for them, surely they'd be looking for a redhead dressed in expensive clothes?

"But I didn't," Deanna admitted with a groan.

Kait considered her friend for a second. Could Dario have discovered the two women were traveling together? And if he had, how would he have appropriated a photo of Deanna? Nothing was impossible, but she had no idea how he'd done it. If this man on the bus had noticed Deanna, then where did he think Kait was at?

"Do you think he spotted me?" Kait asked, still worrying at her bottom lip.

"I'm not sure. I'm hoping not. I'm hoping I kept him so preoccupied that he had no chance to look for you." Kait had seen Deanna talking to the man. She'd been in full flight, batting her eyelashes, tossing her hair, giggling flirtatiously. The poor guy wouldn't have stood a chance, and Kait relaxed slightly.

"What do we do now?" Kait asked, clenching the handle of her bag until her knuckles hurt. She was getting sick of all this running. All this subterfuge. All this half-perceived danger.

"Let's make sure the guy stays on the bus, first. Then we need a plan B," Deanna replied, opening the cubicle door a crack and peering out to make sure no one else had entered the bathroom. "You wait here. I'll go and check that he got on the bus. The driver won't wait too much longer. Even though we booked tickets, he won't hang around forever. He'll just think we're no-shows."

Kait wanted to go with her. She hated being left behind not knowing what was happening. But she knew it was better if she stayed to guard the bags and kept out of sight. Deanna slipped out of the door and Kait was left alone. A shaking began low in her guts. She couldn't let Dario find her. Not now she'd come so far. It was kind of funny, but Kait was beginning to realize she was more scared of being dragged back to Perth by Dario, into her life of servitude, than she was of the police arresting her for murder. Of course she didn't want to spend time in jail. But if she was given two options, that would be the lesser evil. How sad was that? She'd rather go to jail than spend one more second in her husband's company.

She shook her head, hoping to rid herself of these dangerous thoughts. Right now, she and Deanna had to come up with another way to get back to Broome, so they could pay for the passports and then keep moving. She needed to make sure Deanna was safe. The poor girl had already been dragged unwillingly into this mess, but Kait was determined to keep her out of any further repercussions as best she could. And if that meant abandoning Deanna along the way...then Kait hoped she was strong enough to do it.

Kait waited, the constant drip, drip, drip of the leaking tap into the basin the only sound. The fluorescent light bathed everything in a sickly glow, reflecting dully off the stainless-steel sinks. At last, she thought she heard the low rumble of an engine. Was that the bus pulling out? Twenty seconds later, Deanna barreled back into the bathroom.

"He stayed on the bus," she puffed. "But I could see him staring out the window, desperately wondering where I'd got to. He was also talking on his phone. He looked angry. We need to get out of here before he calls in the cavalry." As she spoke, she picked up her duffel bag and then bent down to reach for the black backpack. But Kait was faster, snatching the backpack almost from the other girl's grasp.

"I'll carry it," Kait said, averting her face as she picked up her own bag. Not that she didn't trust Deanna, because she did. Unconditionally. Especially after Deanna had given her the surprising news of her own financial independence. No, this was her burden to bear, that was all.

Deanna cast her a knowing look, and Kait swore silently under her breath. She did trust Deanna. She did. But this precious cargo was the ticket to Kait's freedom. She couldn't let it out of her sight.

They exited the toilets, and Kait tried not to look suspicious as they walked around to the rear of the brick building. The only person visible was a man standing near the doors to the local supermarket waiting for his dog to finish peeing on a sign post. But he never glanced up from checking his phone as the women disappeared around the back. Daybreak had taken over properly now, everything lit up in the soft glow of the residual sunrise. They needed to get off the streets before people started to rouse.

But what should they do? Wait and catch the next bus tomorrow? Perhaps they could fly. Now she had her money, they could afford anything. Yes, that was it. They'd fly back to Broome.

Deanna was powering ahead of her. They'd cut through the rear of the parking lot and were heading back up the street they'd come down earlier that morning. It looked different in the daylight. Friendlier. No dark shadows in which danger could be lurking.

"Wait up." Kait ran forward, the backpack bouncing on her shoulder, and grabbed Deanna's arm. "Wait. I've got an idea."

"What?" Deanna snapped, stopping dead in her tracks.

"We could fly to Broome. It'll be much quicker. We could be there by lunchtime."

"Yes, and we'll probably be nabbed before we can leave the airport. We need to get out of this town, Kait. Before it's crawling with Dario's thugs."

"But—"

"No buts," Deanna replied resolutely. "I got us into this mess, and I'm gonna get us out."

"Huh? What are you going to do?"

But Deanna was already forging head, motioning for Kait to keep up.

"Deanna. Tell me—" In her hurry to catch up, Kait wasn't looking where she was going and missed the step down into the gutter. Her ankle gave way beneath her, and she heard a snapping sound as she tumbled onto the road.

She yelped in pain and lay on the blacktop, cradling her foot.

"Stop. I've hurt my ankle," she cried out in despair.

Deanna was by her side in an instant. "Oh, God." Deanna helped her to sit up. "Let me take a look."

"I think it's broken," Kait sobbed. She'd never had a

broken bone before. But this pain was excruciating. It must be broken; it couldn't be anything else.

Deanna gently pulled Kait's injured leg out and probed around her ankle. "Does this hurt?" she asked, pushing on the bony protuberance.

Kait shook her head. Not really, which surprised her.

"What about this?" Deanna rotated her foot to the left, and Kait nearly jumped out of her skin as a sharp pain shot at her leg.

"Yes, yes." She pulled out of Deanna's grasp and wrapped her arms around her knee, nursing her injured leg like a child.

"Good news. It's not broken," Deanna announced.

"How do you know?" Kait sobbed. "You're not a doctor."

"No," Deanna agreed. "But I know a broken ankle when I see one. And yours ain't broken. It's most likely a bad sprain."

"Even if it's only a sprain, I don't think I can walk," Kait said, turning bleary eyes up to her friend. What did Deanna know? The amount of pain Kait was in right now, the damn thing had to be broken.

Deanna eyed her for a second, and Kait thought she detected a distinct lack of compassion in the other woman's gaze. It wasn't like she'd meant to fall and hurt her ankle. Far from it. And she wasn't being a drama queen, if that's what Deanna's sharp look was indicating. Her ankle really, really hurt, like nothing she'd ever felt before. A tear rolled down her cheek, then another followed. She dashed them away with one hand, but they were quickly replaced by more. What were they going to do now? If she had to go to hospital—she was sure her leg needed to be put into plaster—that'd make them even more of a target for Dario's thugs. Even now Deanna, was scanning the empty street with narrowed eyes, like she was formulating some kind of plan.

"This is no time to act like a baby," Deanna said, her tone surprisingly cool and calm.

"I'm not, I'm—" The rest of her words were swept away as Deanna lifted her bodily under her armpit, forcing her to her feet. "What the hell...?"

"Try and put some weight on it," Deanna demanded.

Kait mumbled a few choice curses, but eventually did as she was told, gingerly lowering her foot to the ground. Greatly surprised, she found that she could indeed bear some weight on her broken ankle. It was painful, but not impossible. Okay, maybe it wasn't broken. But everyone knew you couldn't run on a badly sprained ankle, so what did Deanna think she was achieving? She shot a disconcerted glance at Deanna from beneath the brim of her cap. She hobbled a few steps with Deanna's help, the bags making it harder to walk and lean on Deanna, also juggling the heavy luggage.

Deanna took Kait's overnight bag from her to ease her burden, then mumbled something that sounded like, "I told you so," but Kait pretended not to hear it. "Right, let's get you somewhere safe," Deanna added loudly.

"What do you mean?"

"There was an alley a little way back up the street," Deanna said, totally ignoring her question. "I saw a couple of dumpsters in there, you can hide behind those until I come back for you." She began to lead Kait back down the street, supporting her under one shoulder, but Kait wasn't about to have a bar of it.

"No, what do you mean, I can hide until you come back? You're not going anywhere without me. This is my money, and my plan, and I...we need to stick together." She'd been about to say that she wasn't going to be told what to do. Wasn't going to be ordered around by a woman half her age. It felt like Kait was losing control of this whole situation. Yes, she'd agreed to Deanna's harebrained plan to catch the bus to Exmouth to retrieve her money. And yes, she'd even consented to Deanna organizing to get them both passports from some dodgy underground counterfeiter. But everything had gone to shit all of a sudden, and Kait needed to put her foot down—figuratively speaking, of course. This wasn't the Deanna show; this was the Kait show, and Deanna was just tagging along. And Deanna needed to remember that. Anger bubbled behind her eyes, and she clenched her teeth.

Deanna dropped Kait's arm and stepped back, her eyes hardening, almost as if she could tell what Kait was thinking. "Look, Kait, now is not the time to play games. I'm not questioning your authority, I'm just trying to keep us alive."

Kait knew she was being ungrateful, but the ungracious words tumbled out of her mouth anyway. "Yeah, well, it was your stupid plan that got us into this mess in the first place. If you'd just been able to keep your mouth shut and thought something through for five seconds without acting first, maybe none of this would've happened." The words tasted like acid on her tongue, but she couldn't seem to stop the torrent from spewing out. "Life isn't all rainbows and unicorns, Deanna. This is some real shit. At least it's real to me. My life depended on getting back on that bus. But oh, no, you had to sidle up to some good-looking guy and bat your eyelashes at him. Now that option is gone, and we're well and truly fucked." She was panting now, her words getting louder and louder, an unexplained pain in her chest making her clutch at her throat. But for some reason, she didn't feel better after getting that off her chest, she felt worse. Small and diminished somehow. Her anger still surged, however, and she allowed it to carry her through as she squared her shoulders and stared at Deanna, not letting her see how much she already regretted her words.

Deanna's lips thinned, but that was the only sign she'd

heard any of Kait's nasty invective. "Are you quite finished?"

Kait said nothing more, even though it felt like there was steam coming out of her ears, and she was still panting slightly. Her ankle was beginning to throb as the two women glared at each other.

"This isn't my fault. Just think about it for a second. If I hadn't talked to that guy, we would've got on that bus none the wiser. And maybe Dario's thugs would be already following the bus, waiting to pounce on us at the next stop. Hmmm?" Deanna glared at Kait, who felt a sudden rush of doubt, and then guilt. Was the younger woman right? Had she stopped them walking headfirst into a trap? Deanna wasn't finished, however. "But I'm still going to fix our little problem. I'm going to find us a car, while you wait here." She enunciated each word carefully, as if expecting Kait to argue with her. When she didn't, she added, "We can finish this... discussion later." Deanna's cool words and frosty manner were like a wet blanket to Kait's steaming anger.

"You're going to find us a car?" Kait said, softening her stance slightly. "How? Where?"

"Leave that to me. I learned a few things while I was living on the streets of Geraldton. I can hot-wire a car like a pro."

Oh, God, Deanna was talking about hot-wiring a car again, just like she had after they'd sold Kait's four-by-four. Kait had only half-believed her boastful claims back then, but now, looking up into the young woman's composed blue eyes, Kait finally decided she might well be able to do it. With a shrug, Kait finally conceded defeat. She was in no shape to run, and if Deanna could procure them an escape vehicle, then that was what had to happen.

She hobbled back down the street toward the alley, noticing that her ankle wasn't really that bad. After the initial searing pain had worn off, the agony had tapered to a dull throb. As long as she didn't try to twist or turn on it, she could manage a slow, limping walk. Deanna followed at a distance, head swiveling in all directions, as if looking for danger. But the street was empty, the sun just now beginning to reflect off the shop windows as it rose over the horizon. Peering into the alley, she saw the row of dumpsters Deanna had mentioned. Hobbling past the first two, she found a gap between the second and third that was just about her size. The smell got worse the farther down the alley she went, and she was tempted to hold her nose. She noticed that Deanna stayed at the entrance to the small alley, not bothering to follow her in.

"This is disgusting," Kait complained and was suddenly struck by the irony of her situation. Oh, how far she'd fallen. From the lofty peaks of her mansion with the marble staircase to the ignominy of sitting in an alley in a pile of refuse.

Settling herself into the gap, she hugged the backpack with the money to her chest. "Is this what you were envisioning?" She called out, trying but failing to keep the spiteful tone out of her voice. "Me hiding in this shit hole, while you run off and save us." Kait peered around the edge of the dumpster.

Deanna didn't answer but her frown deepened. "I can still see your feet," she said, instead. "You need to bend your knees and tuck them right in," she directed.

With a sigh, Kait did as she was told, than was suddenly startled when Deanna loomed over her. She'd come down the alley after all.

"Give me the backpack," Deanna said.

Kait glared at Deanna. "No." She clutched the backpack tighter to her chest.

"What if someone spots you? You can't run on your sprained ankle."

"No," Kait declared again. "I'm not giving you my money," she ground out from between clenched teeth.

"You have to. You have to trust me, Kait." Deanna's voice

had lost its hard edge and was almost pleading now.

"And what if you get caught?" Kait countered.

"I won't." Deanna said it with such self-assurance. Kait suddenly wished she had half of Deanna's confidence.

"And what if..." Kait didn't finish her question. Even though she was thinking it, she couldn't bring herself to say it. *And what if you don't come back for me? What if you take my money and run?*

It was unfair of her to even think it, but she couldn't stop the traitorous notion. She glared up at Deanna as the other woman waited.

What should she do? Deanna was right, if it came to a chase, the younger woman stood more of a chance of getting away. But where would that leave Kait if they got separated? How would they find each other again? No. She'd rather take her chances of getting caught while holding the money, than giving it to Deanna.

"No." Kait shook her head again. "Not happening."

Deanna stood over her for two more arduous seconds, and then she turned and said, "I'll pull up and honk the horn. Be ready to jump in when I do." Then she was gone, leaving Kait alone in the dawning light.

Kait tucked her feet in tight and held her breath. If she leaned her head against the wall—dirty as it may be—it allowed her to see between the gap behind the dumpster out into the street. It was a limited view, but it was all she had, and it was better than staring at the dank wall across from her.

She waited. And waited. The street remained deserted, but it'd only be a matter of time before people started to emerge. The one silver lining was that today was Sunday, so most of the shops wouldn't open until much later, if at all.

The waiting was killing her. She was literally going to die right here behind this disgusting dumpster. Her mind was spinning with all the alternating scenarios. Why had she let this happen? Was Deanna really going to come back for her? After all the spiteful things Kait had said, she wouldn't blame the young woman if she didn't. If the shoe had been on the other foot, would Kait come back for Deanna?

*You fucked up, lady.*

"Shut up, Susan," Kait hissed to the empty alley. The last thing she needed was her dead friend judging her.

*You should have trusted Deanna. She is trustworthy.*

"Go away." Kait thumped the side of her head, willing the voice to leave her alone. She needed to think, and Susan's remonstrations weren't helping.

Had she fucked up? Should she really have let Deanna take the bag with all the money?

Kait suddenly knew that this was about much more than the money. It was about trust. And when it came down to it, she'd proven she didn't trust Deanna. Her chest tightened at the revelation.

But then again, why should she trust Deanna? Dario had taught her the hard way that trust was for fools. This was Kait's life. And she needed to be the person in charge of her own destiny. Deanna was a friend—good friend, she had to keep reminding herself—but if the worst happened, and Dario caught up with her, it'd be Kait returning to a life of hell, a life of servitude, not Deanna. If Dario caught her, Kait knew she wouldn't be able to stand it.

Kait remembered right after Susan had died and grief had overtaken her, she'd thought about jumping off the balcony into the crashing waves below. Of escaping from this life because it was an easy way out of the all-encompassing pain she was feeling. The fact that she didn't want to face the world without her best friend. But back then, she knew she would never have really gone through with it. And now... Her trip north had opened her eyes, proven to her that there were many ways in which to live a free and fulfilling life.

But if she had to go back to Dario... She knew she would choose death. One hundred percent. She *would* not, *could* not go back to her old life. Not now. Which meant that while she knew she needed to accept Deanna's help, ultimately the decisions as to where and how she was going to spend the rest of her life were up to her, and her alone.

Her mind was suddenly made up. It became crystal clear to her in that moment. As soon as they made it back to Broome and got their hands on those passports, she was hopping on the first plane out of there. She couldn't afford to stay in Australia one second longer. Not if it meant even the slightest possibility that Dario might track her down. She needed to be gone. From her old life, from Cloudwater Bay, even from her sister. A part of her had been holding a small hope close to her heart that she might be able to go to Sydney to visit Monika one last time. But now, she knew that was impossible. Dario would always be a threat to her happiness.

And she definitely had to stop thinking about Jack. There was no future there. Not with him. Apart from the fact that she didn't want his life put in mortal danger just because she was around, she couldn't lead him on, pretending there was a chance of happiness together, because, in the end, she would always have to move on. She couldn't do that to him.

The sound of a car engine in the street outside brought Kait back to the present. She leaned her head against the wall and peered out. Was it Deanna back with a getaway car? Kait bunched her muscles, ready to spring up and out of the alley. The car slowed out front of the entrance.

But no. Wait. It was a cop car. She could see the blue police insignia running down the side panel. The cruiser stopped directly in front of the alley. Were they checking out the alley? Kait curled into the tightest ball possible. Were they looking for her? Or was this just some random coincidence? Was this just an early morning patrol?

Seconds ticked by as she watched through her little spy hole, holding her breath.

Finally, the cruiser moved on, slowly pulling forward and the entrance was clear once more. Now what should she do? Should she stay here? Or move? Had she been compromised? She didn't think they'd spotted her, otherwise, they would've stormed the alley and arrested her. Wouldn't they? She just didn't know.

Before she could make up her mind, another shape slid into view at the entryway. It was a white four-wheel drive, and Kait held her breath. The car sounded its horn, three short staccato blasts. It was Deanna. Oh, thank God. Kait scrambled up, momentarily forgetting about her ankle until she almost fell back down in a heap. She managed to catch herself on the edge of the dumpster before she slung the backpack over her shoulder.

Deanna was motioning to her from the driver's seat. Kait hobbled in and Deanna was already moving before Kait had even shut the door.

"Cops," Kait puffed. "I saw a cop car go that way." She pointed down the street in the opposite direction. "I think they were looking for me...for us."

"I know," Deanna replied. "I saw them, and I waited till they pulled around the corner. We've gotta get out of this town."

Kait couldn't agree more.

# CHAPTER TWENTY-EIGHT

Deanna put her foot flat to the floor as soon as they hit the city limits. She was silently fuming, but up till now, she'd kept her wrath at bay. They had more important things to think about. But Deanna *was* going to confront Kait on her behavior. Oh, yes, she was. That woman needed a good kick up the backside. Or a good, all-night dirty sex session with some horny guy. Jack immediately sprang to mind. Perhaps that would loosen the stick that was shoved so far up her ass that Deanna was surprised Kait couldn't smell her own shit.

The woman was full of it. How dare she turn on Deanna like that? They were supposed to be friends. The things she'd said... Deanna tightened her fingers around the wheel and ground her teeth in an attempt not to turn and hiss at her supposed friend.

She kept her lips pressed together in a thin line in an effort to keep the words back. The wind whipped her hair into a frenzy through the open windows, but for once, Deanna didn't care. It'd be an unmanageable tangle of knots when she stopped, but she'd deal with it then.

"Perhaps you should slow down a little," Kait finally spoke. Her eyes had been glued to the side and rearview mirrors all the way out of Exmouth.

"What?" Deanna snapped.

"You'll get us pulled over for speeding."

"Oh. Right." She eased her foot off the gas pedal. She supposed Kait was correct. But that didn't mean the other woman was *always* right. She had no call getting all high and mighty with Deanna. When she'd first met Kait, she'd found her slightly pompous, gentrified air amusing. Kait's old-fashioned morals had almost been endearing. But now, those traits were grating on Deanna like fingernails down a blackboard. Like she'd said before, the woman needed to get that stick out of her ass, and fast, otherwise... Well, she wasn't rightly sure what might happen, but one thing was for sure: they couldn't keep going as friends if Kait was going to treat her like this.

"Find us the next turnoff. We need to get off the main highway," Deanna said. She hadn't had time to study a map, but there must be a secondary road somewhere that'd take them in the direction they needed to go and get them off the main route. Away from prying eyes. Deanna wondered if there'd been someone on the bus from Broome to Exmouth spying on them and they hadn't realized it.

For once, Kait did what was requested without arguing. After a few minutes, she said, "We have to get off the peninsula first. But once we turn onto the road toward Broome, there's another road around five kilometers farther on that will take us back toward the coast."

"That'll have to do," Deanna replied. The problem with trying to leave Exmouth was it was situated on a thin finger of land that jutted out to sea, and there was only one road in or out. It was a forty-five-minute drive to the Broome turnoff. "Keep your eyes peeled," she added.

But there was no need to caution Kait, her eyes widened in fear every time another car appeared on the horizon, and she stiffened in her seat, staring so hard Deanna thought laser beams might suddenly shoot from her eyes. Deanna kept flicking her gaze to her rearview mirror, watching for a car speeding up behind them, or worse still, blue and red flashing lights. But no one followed. There were only flat, red hills on either side of the car, rolling away into the distance, with the black strip of roadway unfolding in front.

They both let out a collective breath when Deanna finally slowed for the sign indicating the turnoff to Broome. Now they were driving directly into the rising sun, and Deanna had to pull the sunshade down as far as it would go and squint into the bright flare just to see where she was going. Thankfully, a few minutes later, Kait directed her onto a rough, one-lane road and she was no longer driving straight into the sun. At least it was blacktop, but it clearly hadn't had any work done in many years. That was fine by Deanna; the more out of the way, the less chance anyone might follow them. Or spot them. The one down-side of taking the scenic route was it was going to take them a lot longer to get back to Broome. And they needed to be back by tomorrow morning. That's when she'd organized to pick up the passports, and she wasn't going to miss that meeting, even if it meant driving all through the night. Which was probably a better plan anyway. They'd be less visible at night.

Kait seemed to relax once they were off the highway and she finally let go of the backpack, placing it on the floor at her feet and taking a look around the inside of the vehicle. "Where did you get this—" Kait wrinkled her nose. "—car?" She wound her window down as far as it would go, as if that might ease the smell.

Yeah, as if Kait really cared. Deanna mentally reprimanded herself for her unkind thought, drawing in a deep breath. It was time to get back onto a more even keel. Nothing would be solved if they kept snapping at each other all day long.

"It was parked up the back of some dingy old house a few

blocks over. The place looked pretty much unloved, so I took a punt that no one would miss this old banger. At least, not for a while." And it *was* an old banger. A rusted, white, Toyota short wheelbase, it looked like it'd been used and abused, full of sand and various old fishing equipment—it definitely smelled of dried fish—and she'd been more than a little surprised when it'd started first go. "I reckon some bloke uses it on the weekends to go out to his little fishing shack, or something. It's old, but it seems to run okay. And there were even two spare jerry cans full of gas in the back."

"I guess that's good, then," Kait replied, attempting to wipe a little of the built-up salty residue off the dashboard before giving up with a grimace.

For some reason, Kait's comment riled Deanna up. *Good.* Was that all she could say? She'd searched frantically for just the right car to steal. Trying not to draw attention to herself, a woman on her own, wandering the empty streets in the early morning hours carrying two bags. She'd been sweating bullets. But then, she'd noticed the front bumper bar of the four-by-four poking out from behind the battered house and she'd walked audaciously up the driveway, bold as brass. No one had challenged her. No one had even seen her. And she'd made a snap decision that this was the one. At least the older model cars were easier to hot-wire. The only downside was the air-conditioning no longer worked. They'd have to drive the entire way to Broome with the windows down and the wind slapping in their faces.

"Yes, it is fucking *good*. It's the perfect vehicle for us." Deanna sneered. "No one will look at an old banger like this twice. Especially not on this road out by the coastline. So you can just take that bloody snooty look off your face and be grateful for once."

Kait reared back in her seat and stared at Deanna. "No, I didn't mean it like that—" she began to protest, but Deanna cut her off.

"Yes, you did. You constantly talk down to me, as if I'm not good enough for you. As if I can't make a proper decision. As if you don't trust me." There, she'd said it. And she wasn't sorry. This was the crux of the whole problem. The crux of all their arguments.

To her great surprise, Kait lowered her gaze and looked slightly shamefaced. She removed the cap from her head and ran an agitated hand through her black hair, which was flat and lifeless after days of wearing the disguise. Deanna noticed the big, dark bags beneath Kait's eyes, and she suddenly registered how much of an ordeal this had been for the older woman. A little of the fire burning in Deanna's gut subsided. She'd forgotten how much of a sheltered life Kait must've lived before this. How this whole situation must be draining all her reserves. Deanna, on the other hand, found it exhilarating, even while admitting she was also scared out of her wits.

"You're right," Kait said softly.

"Pardon?" Deanna could hardly believe what she was hearing. "Can you repeat that, please?" Deanna hid the smile that threatened to take over her lips when Kait's mouth formed a tight little purse.

But Kait drew in a deep breath, as if fortifying herself. "You're right," she said, louder this time. "I don't trust you... I mean, I didn't trust you. But that's going to change. I was blaming you for my predicament, pretending I was some kind of unwilling participant. As if you were driving the bus, and I was just along for the ride. But that's not fair on you. And it's time I started taking responsibility for my own actions. For my own life. I made a decision while I was waiting in the alley for you to come back." Kait finally glanced up from where her gaze had been directed down at her lap. "I need to apologize, Deanna. None of this is your fault. I dragged you into this crazy mess, and I did nothing to help get us out. This is all on me. Even that man's death. He was after me, not you. Every single last fuckup is on me."

Deanna was a little shocked at the depth of Kait's guilt. Yes, she needed to own her actions, but she didn't need to shoulder all the blame. Actually, the more Deanna thought about it, the more a single thought crystalized in her brain.

"That's where you're wrong. None of this is your fault," she replied quietly. "If anyone is to blame, it's that bastard husband of yours. If he'd just let you divorce him, like any half-decent person, you could still be living your life back down in Perth. Not running halfway across the state, afraid for your life." Deanna drew a breath, as her emotions swelled in her chest. She was angry again. But not at Kait this time. She was angry *for* Kait. Kait shouldn't feel responsible for wanting her life back. For wanting what most women took for granted. Freedom. "Even the guy who fell to his death in the gorge, the blame for that goes on Dario as well," she went on. "He should never have sent that thug to drag you back like he owned you. Like you were his property, and he could do whatever he wanted. Break the law just to get you back."

When Deanna glanced across the cab, she saw Kait staring at her, both eyebrows raised in surprise. "This is all Dario's fault?" She didn't sound convinced.

"Yes, it damn well is," Deanna shouted.

"Maybe," Kait mused. "But I'm not sure that defense would stand up in a court of law. All those crimes we've committed in the name of freedom..." Kait gave a nonchalant shrug. "Theft of a million dollars, manslaughter—at the very least. Fleeing the scene of a crime. Not to mention grand theft auto, as well as concealing our identities, and fraud if we actually go ahead and use our counterfeit passports."

Deanna smiled ecstatically. "Yeah. We some baaaad bitches." Then she began to laugh.

Kait joined in and they both laughed so hard Deanna had to pull over, because she could hardly see the road anymore for the tears streaming down her face. It felt so good to laugh. Like she was all flushed clean again. It allowed room for other things, and she was suddenly flooded with emotion. A pure, simple emotion. Deanna reached over and dragged Kait into a hug. "I love you," she said, then pulled away and moved the car back onto the road.

There was silence in the cab for about five seconds, until Kait said, "I've never said this to another woman before, but I love you too."

Deanna winked at her from across the cab, and Kait gave a wobbly smile.

"I never even said it to Susan, and she was my very best friend. I was too scared. Too… I don't know. Too caught up in my own problems. But I did love Susan, and I wish I'd told her that now. I wish I'd been brave enough. I wish…"

"She knows," Deanna said simply as tears began to fall down Kait's cheeks. She let Kait cry, because it was good she acknowledged how much Susan had meant to her.

Deanna drove for another ten minutes, a little in awe at the surge of emotions they'd both just survived. Like surfing a huge wave and then landing safely on the beach. Kait was still sniffling, but her tears were easing off.

They came upon a crossroad, and Deanna slowed the car. "Which way?" The barest hint of a blue strip of ocean was visible over the red dunes. They were so close to the coast.

Kait scrubbed her face and consulted her phone. "Right," she directed.

"We're going to take turns driving," Deanna said as she swung the steering wheel. "We're going to drive all day and night to get to Broome by tomorrow."

"Yes, I agree." Kait turned her face to the window and let the warm wind dry the rest of her tears. A look of determination settled over her face. A hardness that hadn't been there before. Deanna hoped it meant Kait was finally stepping up and accepting who she was. Accepting what needed to be done if they were both to survive. Accepting that they were a team. Together they were stronger.

* * *

"I'm going to steal another car," Deanna announced as she hopped back into the passenger side of the car. It was two am, and they were parked up on the road verge just the other side of a sign announcing the township of Broome welcomed all visitors. She'd been desperate for a wee and had ducked out to stumble a few feet into the sparse woodland, hoping like hell the snakes were all in their holes at this time of night—morning—whatever the hell it was.

But at least they were here. They'd made it to Broome without incident, having driven for over twenty hours straight to get here, only stopping to relieve themselves and buy bottled water, snacks and gas at some out-of-the-way, bait-come-service station in the middle of nowhere. The shop was clearly there to service locals, and must not get a lot of customers, as Deanna had surprised the guy behind the counter, who'd been asleep in his chair with his mouth open, emitting loud snores when she plonked her purchases on the counter. He'd woken with a grunt and then proceeded to scratch his balls the whole time Deanna was paying for the items. Even though she doubted this little tin-pot shack had CCTV, she made sure to disguise herself by tucking her blonde hair up into a cap and donning an oversized Billabong T-shirt, both of which she'd found in the tray of the four-wheel drive and both of which smelled of fish. She made Kait do the same, much to her annoyance, but at least now they both looked like some kind of skanky locals who thought the best thing in life was a shack on the beach and a fishing rod in their hands. But she needn't have bothered trying to look like a local, because the guy never even met her eyes, and as soon as she walked out of the shop, he was repositioning himself for another snooze in his chair.

Kait groaned, but said, "Okay. Where from this time?" Kait was in the driver's seat; she'd done the last three-hour stretch of dirt road following the line of Eighty Mile Beach, which was probably no more than a service road to a large cattle station they'd passed a while back. But it'd got them to their destination. Dog tired, covered in dust from driving with the windows down, and desperate to get out and stretch their legs.

"The long-stay parking lot at the Broome airport." Deanna was delighted with the sheer brilliance of her idea. They would just drive their old banger into the lot, unload their bags and pay for a stay of two weeks, as if they were normal, everyday tourists. Then they'd find a likely car, break into it, hot-wire it, pay the fee and drive out like they owned it. If they chose the right car, hopefully no one would miss it for days, or possibly even weeks. "If we do it now, while it's still dark, we're less likely to be spotted. But there's likely to be cameras, so we should go incognito."

Kait merely groaned again. But Deanna grinned. She was taking to this espionage stuff like a duck to water. And her little plan would help fill in time until they were due to meet with her contact at eight am.

"I think I could sleep for three days straight," Kait complained, and Deanna knew how she felt.

"After we steal the car, perhaps we can catch a few hours' kip," Deanna conceded. Even a couple of hours' sleep would be welcome. Her eyes felt gritty and if she cared to look in a mirror, they'd probably be red rimmed as well.

"I wish we could go back to Lennie's place," Kait said, trying but failing to keep the plaintive tone out of her voice. Some of that hard-won fortitude Kait had gained after they'd left Exmouth seemed to be slipping in the face of her lack of sleep.

"We already agreed, we can't go back to Lennie's," Deanna replied with a resigned sigh. Silently, she agreed. That big, luxurious bed she'd slept in at Lennie's sure would be a welcome sight right now. "They might be watching," she said, as much to remind herself as Kait that they needed to lie low. Whoever the hell *they* might be, she thought caustically. Dario's spies, the cops, and who the fuck else knew might also be out looking for them. A sudden idea occurred to her. "Hey, would Dario put out a bounty on your head?" If he had, half the bloody state might be out searching for them. They might be in even more danger than they already suspected. And just because they'd managed to get to Broome without being seen, didn't mean they were safe yet.

"What?" Kait was surprised by her sudden switch in conversation. "I don't know. Maybe." She shrugged. "I wouldn't put it past him. He has a wide network of friends. It just depends on how much his pride will let him reveal to those friends. He may not want them to know that his precious wife is missing. That he can't control me."

"Hmm," Deanna mused. "I guess we need to be extra careful, that's all."

"I thought we were being careful." Kait turned her head to stare at Deanna, but because they were sitting in the dark, Kait's features were barely discernible.

"I have no idea if we're being careful enough, though," Deanna replied. And it was true. Neither of them had enough experience of this underworld life to know who they could trust, what they should do, or even where it was safe to go. All they could do was to stay out of sight as much as possible, keep moving, and hope like hell they stayed off Dario's radar.

Kait leaned down and turned the key to start the engine. "Let's get another car," she said wearily. "I just need this to be over."

Deanna couldn't agree more.

Half an hour later, Deanna's heart was pounding like a drum, but the feeling was exhilarating rather than scary. "We did it!" She crowed, raising one hand off the steering wheel to fist-pump the air.

"Yes, we did." But Kait didn't seem as enthralled by the whole idea of stealing a car as she was.

Their new ride was another four-by-four—they were a dime-a-dozen up here—but at least this one had air-conditioning, which was a real luxury after that last heap of shit. Everything had gone exactly according to plan. They'd driven into the long-stay car park, which was thankfully open twenty-four hours, dropped off the old car in a parking spot, sat and waited for twenty minutes, so it wasn't too obvious they were leaving straight away, and then stol the car right next to them. Easy peasy.

"Why don't we park it out the back of the caravan park," Kait said suddenly. "We could get a few hours' sleep, then perhaps we could slip in and use the park's amenities before we head off to meet this contact of yours."

"Wow, you're starting to think like a real miscreant," Deanna replied with glee. "Take that as a compliment," she added when Kait shot her a sharp look. "If we're going to get out of here, we need to think like two hardened criminals. So this is a good thing."

"I'm not so sure about that," Kait grumbled.

The Broome Vacation Park was out on the edge of town, and Deanna drove there as sedately as she could, even though the roads were all empty. The only thing moving at this time of the morning was the tabby cat that shot across the road right in front of her tires. It only took ten minutes to find the campground and Deanna parked the car on a flat bit of gravel under a peppermint tree at the end of a cul-de-sac behind the park. There was a small metal fence delineating the grassed area full of tents and camper vans, but they could easily climb over that and make their way to ablutions block when the time came. If they went right on dawn, hardly anyone would be up to see them slip over the fence.

She turned off the engine, and they sat in the dark, listening to the car tick as it cooled.

Before they both caught some z's there was one question Deanna needed to ask. "What's the plan after we pick up the passports?" Neither of them had talked about anything past getting to Broome, almost as if it were an unspoken rule that they needed to take one careful step at a time. But it seemed the next step in their plan was required sooner rather than later now.

"I'm going to Darwin," Kait stated. "They have an international airport there. I'm going to leave the country. I *need* to leave the country." Kait's face glowed a sickly green in the dashboard lights. "And I don't think it's safe to fly from Broome."

Broome also had an international airport, so tourists from all over the world could come and sample Australia's top end delights.

"It's probably not safe to fly from anywhere," Deanna said. But she'd been thinking along the same lines as Kait. If Dario had caught even a sniff that Kait was in the vicinity, he'd definitely be watching the airports carefully.

Kait merely shrugged.

"Darwin is a two-day drive, at least."

"I know. But we… I'm…getting good at driving." Kait replied, not quite meeting Deanna's gaze.

"Darwin it is, then," she said, brooking no argument. If Kait was leaving the country, then so was she.

"Are you sure? I mean—" Kait screwed up her face in consternation.

"Yes, I'm sure." Kait seemed to think that once she left Deanna's side, she'd magically become safe. But Deanna knew differently. Kait wouldn't be saving her from anything. She'd still need to continuously look over her shoulder. If Dario was half the oaf Kait made him out to be, he'd be only too happy to use Deanna to try and get to Kait. Perhaps use her as a hostage to bring Kait back to him. And maybe if that didn't work, he might even kill her out of spite.

It was more than that, however. Deanna wanted to go with Kait. They'd started this adventure together, and they needed to see where it led them. Kait would probably cope fine on her own, Deanna conceded. She wasn't completely useless, and thanks to Deanna's teachings, she was beginning to form a hard outer shell that'd see her past the con artists and villains in this world.

"What about the money?" It was a fair question. Even Kait wasn't dumb enough to think she could just walk onto an international flight with nearly a million dollars in cash.

"We're both going to open bank accounts when we get to Darwin using our new papers," Kait said decisively.

Yes, that made sense. With the new passports and the fake paperwork and driver's licenses Old George had worked up for them, they now had all the new ID they needed to create their brand-new lives.

"And deposit fifty thousand each," Kait added.

"Okay," Deanna replied. That was mighty decent of Kait and showed a lot of her newfound trust coming to the fore. It meant they'd have enough to travel on for a good while. But the nagging question must've been there in her eyes.

"But we can't put the whole million dollars into an account all at once, that will raise too many red flags. So, the rest I'm going to leave with someone in Darwin. He's an old boyfriend of my sister's, Monika. He's an accountant. That's how they met. And he knows how to set up trust funds and managed funds and wrangle numbers and bank accounts so they look…if not innocent, then less like dirty money."

This was an interesting twist. "Can you trust him?"

"I hope so. I trust my sister. And she said Tim is the best. He'd do anything for her, even now. They broke up ten years ago, but they still keep in touch." Kait lifted one eyebrow. "Anyway, weren't you the one who said I needed to become more trusting?"

"Yes, but only of the right people," Deanna countered, a little shocked at this turn of events. It sounded like Kait had been cooking something up without Deanna's knowledge. Which was fine by her, but she had the uncomfortable thought perhaps she was underestimating Kait yet again.

"Which reminds me, I need to call Monika this morning before we leave Broome to update her on our plan," Kait tapped her finger to her chin and seemed to become lost in thought.

There was one thing that Deanna wanted to do before she left Australian shores, however. She knew it was dangerous, but as far as she was concerned, the benefits outweighed the dangers. Deanna had always been driven by emotions. And as far as emotions went, love was a hundred-fold stronger than fear.

"If we're really doing this, I need to see Raine before we go. I can't just leave without any explanation." Deanna speared Kait with her best pathetic puppy-dog gaze. "And I bet you'd love to see Jack once more too."

Kait blinked at that comment, then turned her face to stare out the side window.

"Please, Kait. A few hours, then we'll be on our way. We're going to drive right past the turnoff to Cloudwater anyway. And tomorrow is Christmas Day. If we can't spend it with the ones we love, then we can at least offer them some sort of an explanation."

After an eternity, Kait nodded. "Okay."

"Really?" Deanna clapped her hands in glee.

"Yes, really. You're right, I want to see Jack one last time."

# CHAPTER TWENTY- NINE

Jack took another sip of his beer and stared at his garden, not really taking in any of his lush little oasis. The heat of the day was becoming unbearable, even beneath the shade of his covered pergola, and it was probably time to head inside. He had food prep to do for the big lunch they'd planned for tomorrow at Raine's place. He'd agreed to bring a glazed ham, of all things. Old George was bringing the cooked lobster and Raine was doing a vegan nut roast and plenty of salads. Ella and Toby from next door were bringing a pile of freshly caught fish from their boat, and Sally was catering to the sweet tooths with her melt-in-the-mouth shortbread and a homemade plum pudding. It would be a feast, by all accounts. But still, he sat and brooded. It was lunchtime on Christmas Eve, and he still hadn't heard from Kait. Or Deanna for that matter.

Kait had promised they'd be back before Christmas. Where had they got to? A part of him was concerned that her ex had somehow caught up to her. And he'd spent the past hour gnawing at that thought like a dog with a bone.

He slugged back a cold draft of beer to clear his mind. He shouldn't be worried; they were two grown women with lives of their own. They'd been traveling alone when he'd met them, and it seemed like they were keen to keep going once Christmas was over. Leaving him to get back to his life of driving trucks and enjoying the simplicity of Cloudwater Bay. All he'd ever wanted.

He was still angry with Kait for lying to him. However, that anger had dulled over the past few days until it was more of a gentle simmer. She and Deanna had hopped onto the bus to Exmouth. Why were they going to Exmouth? And why had they made such a secret of it? He'd asked himself the same old questions and was still no closer to the answer. When he'd arrived home the other day, he'd been determined to put Kait out of his mind. She was no good for him. Fickle and unreliable.

It was just…

He had to admit Kait had got under his skin. He had tried to tell himself that she was trouble and not to get involved, but her goddamned vulnerability kept tugging at his heartstrings. Apart from that, she was one of the most beautiful women he'd ever encountered. And his stupid heart suddenly wanted more. Would it be such a bad thing to want to share his life with another human being? With a woman who was bewitching, and complicated, with past baggage he couldn't even begin to guess at?

There was a knock at the side gate. Shit. He really didn't feel like talking to anyone today. It was probably Raine, or Ella, come to ask about something to do with tomorrow's lunch. Couldn't they just leave him alone? He knew he was wallowing, but surely, he was allowed one day of self-pity? The knock came again, more insistent this time. Jack heaved himself out of his comfy cane chair to answer the summons.

He unlocked the gate and was still trying to arrange his features into a semblance of a friendly smile when he drew back in surprise.

Kait bustled past him without waiting for him to invite her

in. Was she limping?

"Hi." He stood back and watched her warily. There was something different about her. A restless energy. He thought if he touched her, she might actually jump out of her skin.

"Hi," she said. But her gaze searched the garden as if looking for some kind of inspiration rather than meeting his eyes. "Look…" She glanced at him, then away, then back up at him.

This was getting weirder by the second.

"I can't explain why, but I've only got two hours," Kait said without preamble. "I told Deanna one hour, but Deanna being Deanna, she bargained me up to two."

What the fuck was Kait talking about?

She took a step closer to him, something determined in her green gaze. A small hand came up to rest on his chest, right above his heart. Her touch was a shock. He wasn't expecting it. But his body reacted without his conscious thought, a fire unfurling along his skin beneath where her hand lay.

"Back in Broome, I wasn't ready to take the next step. But now I am…and I want it to be with you." She was still making no sense.

"I'm not sure—"

She closed the gap and covered his mouth with hers, stopping his words with her tongue. All his uncharitable thoughts fled under the intensity of that kiss. Under the heat of her lips. Under the urgency of her body now pressed against him. She made it crystal clear what she wanted. She wanted him to take her to bed. And he wanted the same. God did he want that.

"Come inside," she bid him, taking his hand in hers. But as she turned, she nearly stumbled over the pavers in the grass, letting out a small cry of pain. Without thought, he scooped her up into his arms, holding her close to his chest.

"I twisted my ankle," she said, her words a hot breath in

his ear, her body so right in his arms.

He carried her up the steps and into the house, his beer forgotten on the table outside. Solemnly, he carried her to his bedroom, setting her down gently on the edge of his bed. They needed to talk about this. Him making love to her wasn't a given. She couldn't just turn up at his house and expect him to jump at her command. Even though it felt as if his skin were breaking open with his need for her, as if he was suddenly hotter than the sun with his desire. He needed to find out where she'd been. Why did she look so bedraggled? And why did she have a twisted ankle?

Getting down on his knees in front of Kait so he could look her in the eyes, he breathed deep, organizing his scattered thoughts. But before he could form any words, she tugged her T-shirt over her head. Then she was sitting there in only her white bra. Keeping her gaze trained on his, she reached behind her back and released the fastener, baring her breasts for him to consume. They were right there. Right in front of his face. As beautiful as he'd imagined. Kait pulled the tie from her hair, letting it tumble free over her shoulders. Black like a raven's feathers against her creamy skin.

She stood, shimmying her shorts and panties over her hips until they spooled on the floor. Now, she stood completely naked in front of him, while he kneeled on the ground, dumfounded.

Words became impossible. She was offering herself to him. And there wasn't a single part of him that could refuse her. He wrapped his arms around her waist and leaned his head against her stomach, breathing in the essence of her, feeling the soft roundness of her belly beneath his cheek.

* * *

He kissed her like he was pouring himself into her, and she accepted him like it was the last thing she'd ever do. And maybe it was. Because she didn't care what happened after this.

His mouth was hot and wet on parts of her she never thought would come alive again. Sex had never felt like this with Dario. She'd been afraid she wouldn't be able to go through with it. But then he'd looked at her. Laid his cheek against her belly and worshiped her. And she'd broken out of herself like an insect shedding its skin; reborn.

Jack stroked her body like he was playing a musical instrument. Every touch of his fingers, every caress of his palm set her alight, as if a thousand fireworks were under her skin. She wanted Jack to feel what she was feeling, but she was like a babe in the woods when it came to understanding male arousal. All she knew was the grunting release her husband finally granted when he pulled out and rolled over after the act was finished. She let instinct guide her, hoping her touch was as thrilling to him. All she had to go on was the way his eyes darkened with hunger, and the way he pressed his body close, groaning into her collarbone as she found his erection and began to stroke it.

When she finally begged him to give her release, he sheathed himself with a condom before gently slipping inside her, watching her eyes as he did so and she held her breath. It wasn't pain she felt, but wonder. And sheer deliverance. Freedom from her shackles as the waves of pleasure broke over her.

Afterward, they lay naked, entangled and sweating, the sheets discarded on the floor.

"Are you okay?" He stroked the tendrils of sweaty hair away from her face, as she rolled onto her back, breath still hitching in her chest.

"Yes," she sighed into his cupped hand. She tried to gather her thoughts.

A small beat at the back of her mind kept reminding her she was running out of time. Time was draining away like the tide ebbing down the shore and she could do nothing to stop it. And when it time ran out, she would need to go. Leave him. Probably forever. Leaving a part of herself with him.

But at least he'd be safe. She could live with herself if she knew he was safe.

"That was...enlightening."

"Really?"

"Yes."

She turned her head over to meet his gaze. Before, she would never have thought she'd have the courage to say these words to a man. But now was a time of courage, for breaking barriers. "I've never had an orgasm with a man before. Only by my own hand." The admission should make her cringe. Should make her want to crawl beneath the pile of sheets on the floor. But with Jack, it only made her feel more empowered.

"No!" He rolled up on his elbow to stare down at her, disbelief in his light-blue eyes.

"Mmm hmm." She smiled at him, watching the way his eyes crinkled up at the edges as he tried to make sense of what she'd just said.

She knew it was possible. To have an orgasm with a man. All the romance books said it was true. Susan had said it was true. And she'd thought perhaps she was broken in that department. Turned out she'd been wrong. Oh, so wrong. And what a delight it was to find out how wrong she was.

Outlining the ANZAC tattoo on his shoulder with her finger, she said, "So, thank you, I guess."

"Kait, I don't even know where to begin," he replied, voice filled with sorrow. But she hadn't meant to bring him pain. She'd meant to bring him joy, that he'd been the one to release her.

"No." She sat up. "Don't be sorry for me. Be happy."

He stared back at her for many long moments. Jack's

bedroom was bright, the midafternoon sun streaming in through the curtains they'd had no time to close in their haste to devour each other's body. They were lucky the window didn't face the front of the house, and instead, looked out onto the backyard. In the harsh light, she could see every line on his face, see the stark reality of the few gray hairs beginning to sprout at his temples, see right down to the very depth of his light-blue eyes. But she didn't want to shrink away from the reality of him. She wanted to embrace him. To love him.

Oh.

Did she love him?

Was this what love really felt like?

# CHAPTER THIRTY

Kait had showered and dressed with five minutes to spare. She'd dragged out her time with Jack as far as she possibly could, but Deanna would be here any moment. Her body was moving on autopilot, while her brain was still stuck in bed with Jack, reliving those glorious few hours. Two hours that would remain sacred in her heart forever.

They stood quietly in the kitchen as Jack made them both a mug of coffee. "One for the road," he'd called it. Kait had offered no explanation for her sudden appearance or her desperate need, and Jack hadn't asked for one, making her feel incredibly guilty and incredibly thankful all at the same time.

Wordlessly, Jack handed her a mug, and she drew in the familiar smell deep into her lungs. So good. Her last coffee with Jack. Their eyes met over the rims of their mugs, caught and held. She hadn't told him she was in love with him. Those words would serve no purpose now. She was leaving, and he was staying.

There was a knock at the front door and both of them startled like newborn deer. She laughed. Then immediately sobered. Deanna was here to collect her. Jack put down his mug and headed down the hallway, back strong and straight, while Kait dreamed of running her fingers over those broad shoulders one more time.

Late afternoon light filtered down the hallway as Jack opened the door. Kait squinted into the sudden sunshine, only able to make out a dark silhouette framed in the doorway. But the shape was much taller and bulkier than Deanna. It almost looked like—

"Where's my wife?" a voice echoed down the hallway. "I know she's in there."

Kait froze. The mug slipped from her lifeless fingers to smash on the floor below.

"Kait, run!" Jack shouted and dived at Dario, tackling him to the ground.

Oh, shit. Oh, Jesus. Oh, fuck!

He'd found her.

What should she do?

"Kait, run." This time, Jack's command was muffled by the sounds of grunts and thumps as the two men struggled on the front porch.

She couldn't leave Jack. Could she?

Then instinct kicked in.

Yes, she could. It was her Dario was after. Once he knew she was gone, he'd leave Jack alone. Come after her. Jack was doing this to protect her. She needed to honor his sacrifice.

She took off for the back door. If she could escape through the shed, she could run and hide in the sand dunes. He'd never find her there.

But she'd forgotten about her twisted ankle, which twinged sharply as she took three lumbering steps. Shit, her injury was going to hamper her.

Yanking open the back door, she looked up to see the hulking shape of a man standing on the rear steps. It was the same young man from the bus; she recognized his broad shoulder and blond hair immediately.

Before she even had time to scream, the good-looking thug grinned at her viciously. "You ain't going nowhere, lady." He put out a hand to grab her by the shirtsleeve, but he suddenly stumbled forward, knocking her sideways as he fell. Kait stared stupidly down at the man, now lying senseless at her feet.

"Quick, come with me," Deanna commanded, beckoning to Kait with one hand while brandishing a tire iron in the other. It took Kait's stunned brain a few seconds to catch up to the fact that Deanna had hit the guy over the head. There was blood on the tire iron. This insignificant detail suddenly made it all real. Dario was here for her. With at least one of his henchmen. And he wasn't going to let her go easily. "We don't have time to stand and gawk," Deanna said, roughly grabbing Kait by the arm and dragging her down the steps. "I don't know how hard I hit the guy. He might wake up any second." Deanna's eyes were wild, her breathing erratic and loud. Kait could still hear the sounds of a scuffle coming from the front door.

Then there was the unmistakable sound of a gunshot.

Kait turned to run back inside. "Jack," she screamed. But Deanna had an iron grip on her arm and continued to tow her down the steps and toward the rear gate.

"There could be more of these guys," she warned through gritted teeth. "We can't help Jack now." Deanna pulled her through the gate, then got behind her and pushed her past the big rig parked beneath the shade and out into the street. The light was dazzling, almost blinding after the cool dimness of Jack's house. Without glancing over her shoulder, Deanna steered them both to the left, away from the house and toward the dunes at the back of the settlement.

"I have to go back," Kait huffed.

"No." It was like Deanna was made of stone. Impervious and immovable. "Keep moving," she directed. "I'm not going to let that bastard get you now." She was probably right. Dario had at least two other bodyguards that she knew of. Where were they? Had he brought them with him? He barely went anywhere without at least one by his side.

A curious face peered out of the window as they passed the last hut on the street. Kait could hear voices raised in anxious query as people cautiously spilled into the street. The locals would all know what a gunshot sounded like. There was no mistaking the sound. And some were probably coming to see what all the commotion was about. Her ankle slowed her down, and Deanna made worried noises as she continued to harry Kait until they finally made it into the dunes. Racing between two hillocks, the street disappeared from sight.

"What if Jack is hurt?" Kait pleaded, slowing a little now they were out of view.

"We don't know what that shot was, or even if anyone got hit," Deanna said, puffing with exertion. "The bullet could've gone wild. Dario might've been trying to scare Jack. Or Jack could've grabbed Dario's gun and shot him instead. The possibilities are Cloudwater. We can't speculate yet. Once we know it's safe we'll go back." Deanna's words made sense. But all Kait wanted was to turn around and run back into the house. To see for herself that Jack was okay.

"C'mon, Kait," Deanna urged irritably. "I stopped the car up the street when I saw Dario—I recognized him from that photo you showed me—walking up to Jack's house, bold as brass and I knew I had to come and get you. If we can loop back through the dunes, maybe we can make it back to the car and escape."

"Okay," Kait agreed numbly. Her mind was refusing to fire on all cylinders; it felt as if she were trying to push her way through a thick layer of cotton wool.

"I don't think anyone is following us," Deanna whispered

a few moments later as they ducked and weaved through the sand dunes, keeping low as they ran. Kait hobbled but ignored the pain as much as she could. Suddenly, a puff of sand flew up in front of Kait. It took her a second to understand it was a bullet embedding in the dune.

"Holy fuck!" Deanna squealed. They ran harder, dodging between the tufts of coastal grass, the soft sand making it almost impossible to run, especially with her sore ankle. She knew she was slowing Deanna down. And now Deanna was getting shot at because of her.

"I think it's Dario," Deanna hissed at Kait's back as they hunkered down behind a large tussock to catch their breath. "I saw the top of his greasy head right before we ducked down."

"Which way did he go?" Kait whispered back. The bullet had magically swept away the mental fog. She was thinking clearly again at last.

"He went that way." Deanna pointed to the right, deeper into the dunes. Away from them, for now.

"We need to split up," she hissed.

"I'm not leaving you," Deanna declared.

"I can't keep running much longer," Kait said pragmatically. It was the truth, but not the main reason she wanted Deanna to leave her. "I need you to circle back and get help," she told her. "I'll hunker down in the dunes and lie low. It'll be easier to hide if it's just me. And if I have to, I'll keep him distracted until you get back with the cavalry."

"Keep him distracted?" Deanna said, unbelieving. "He's shooting at us, Kait. He means to kill you. You won't be distracting him, you'll be inviting him to come up and murder you."

"It's the only way." Kait leaned her forehead against her young friend's, catching her gaze within her own. Startled blue eyes locked with hers. "You're young and strong and fit.

Go back and get the car. Round up some of the locals. Hell, bring a whole posse if you can. Drive down the beach, where I can see you. I'll come running as soon as I spot you," Kait promised. "And until then, I'll lead him away."

"No." But this time it was more of a plea than an ultimatum. "Please, don't make me do this," she murmured.

"If he catches us, we'll both die. This way, you have a chance to bring me help." She stared into her young friend's eyes, willing her to go. To see the sense in Kait's plan.

There was a noise off to their right and they both froze, still as statues. Waiting. Listening.

"Come out, come out, wherever you are." It was Dario taunting her. Her heart squeezed tight, and she wanted to get up and run like a frightened gazelle. If only she could run, her bloody ankle was killing her. Screwing her eyes shut for a second, she drew in a deep breath.

"Now's your chance," she whispered to Deanna. By taunting her, Dario's huge ego had given them an edge. Because now they knew where he was. And how far away.

It was Deanna's best chance. Deanna gave her a quick, fierce hug and then nodded. "I'll be back for you." Then she scuttled sideways like a crab, keeping low to stay hidden behind the dune. And suddenly, she was gone.

Ten minutes later, Kait's lungs were on fire. They burned with every breath. How had she let herself get so unfit? Her thighs and calves also burned, running—or hobbling—in the sand taking a toll on her muscles. Was Dario suffering the same way? Of course he wasn't. He was invincible. Undefeatable.

Kait stumbled down the steep side of a dune, taking a quick look behind her. She caught a glimpse of a dark head bobbing along two dunes back, a little farther down the beach.

A sob escaped her lips. How was she ever going to outrun

him? She'd promised Deanna that it'd be easier to hide when she was alone, but so far, there hadn't been any places to hide. This beach stretched on for hundreds of kilometers, but she didn't have the strength to run all night.

What'd happened to Deanna? She should be back in the settlement by now. She'd promised to return with help by her side. And what about Jack? She closed her eyes and sent up a prayer to whoever might be listening.

The soft, shifting sand in the dunes felt as if it was trying to suck her in, clutching at her feet like hands reaching up from the depths. She kicked off her shoes. They only made it harder to run on this shifting surface. It'd be easier to run on the hard sand. She'd be more of a target, but maybe if she ran for a little while on the beach, then ducked back into the dunes if she saw him behind her, it might be okay. The open beach beckoned.

Then something caught her eye. A shape loomed in the growing twilight at the leading edge of the first dune. One of the piles of ghost nets that she and Jack had gathered last week with the rangers, waiting for the truck to come along and pick them up.

Kait stopped in front of the large mess of tangled ropes. Blue, white, and red ropes in a maze of twisted sand. The beach stretched away interminably before her. The ocean was calm tonight, petite waves breaking on the shore in a perfect summer evening.

Kait got down on her knees and lifted the edge of one of the nets. She slid underneath, feeling like one of those octopi she'd seen in the rock pools the other day, pushing and squeezing itself into an impossibly small crevice, hoping to hide. It smelled bad, of damp sand, rotten fibers, and decaying fish skeletons. Sand rained down on her and the weight of the ropes was suffocating.

But Kait lay as still as death, letting her breathing come to equilibrium, her heart rate slowing. Lying on the sand beneath the nets, she held up the edge, letting a sliver of light into her hiding place. She could see the beach, right down to the water's edge from her hidey hole as a crab moved furtively across her line of vision. She could stay here all night if need be.

A noise made her breath freeze in her throat.

A pair of shoes walked through her line of sight.

Dario.

He kept walking.

She lifted the net half an inch and followed his ankles as he continued down the beach.

He hadn't seen her.

She waited. And waited, for what seemed an eternity as the sun slowly sank over the ocean. Now what?

She could lay here all night, waiting till Deanna drove down the beach. But what if she didn't come? And what about Jack? Was he dead? Was that why Deanna wasn't coming for her? She needed to know.

Creeping as silent as a mouse, she slid out from beneath the nets on all fours and stared down the beach. Where was Dario? He was no longer in sight. Had he turned back into the dunes? It'd be dark soon. Then she'd have to stumble her way through the night to get home. Was darkness her friend? Or her foe?

Time to take a chance.

She stood up and turned toward Cloudwater.

*Watch out.* But Susan's warning came too late.

"Hello, Kait." The familiar voice came from behind the pile of ghost nets. She turned to see a gun pointed directly at her face.

# CHAPTER THIRTY-ONE

"I followed your footsteps, you stupid bimbo." Dario's sneer made his beard seem to come alive, as if there was a small furry animal living on his face. He was standing in front of her now, still pointing the gun directly at her. Why hadn't she thought of that? But it was too late now to admonish her own ignorance. He was right; she *was* a stupid bimbo. Deanna would have thought about erasing their footprints. But Deanna wasn't here.

Ever so slowly, she took a step backward. Then another, until she felt the netting rise beneath her heels. It was strange seeing Dario in the flesh again. It made her skin crawl to look at him. He still had those dark, penetrating eyes and arrogant manner. But was he shorter than she remembered? A little plumper around the jaw? There was something diminished about him. He was somehow…less than she remembered. Less daunting. Less determined. As if he'd lost some of that swagger he'd used to command. Or perhaps she'd transformed him in her own mind. He was wearing black dress pants, shiny black shoes, and an Armani white short-sleeved shirt tucked into his Italian leather belt. Looking the epitome of a rich, entitled businessman, it was glaringly obvious that Dario didn't fit in to these surroundings.

"I'm surprised you thought you could get away with it," Dario said, his voice deceptively quiet. "I never picked you for a thief. Imagine, my own wife stealing from me. I'm impressed." He nodded thoughtfully. "But also very, very pissed off." He took a menacing step toward her, but she had nowhere to go with the nets blocking her retreat.

Kait shrugged. The irony wasn't lost on her. Perhaps it took a scam artist to know one. She thought about her phone calls to Monika. And the moment of exultation when Monika had confirmed they could make the transfer when the time came. Soon, it might not be just a million dollars Dario was missing. Even if Kait didn't survive tonight, Monika had her orders in place. All it'd take was one push of a button. All thanks to those documents Kait had spontaneously grabbed from the safe. They'd contained a goldmine of information. Dario should've been more careful about where he kept his bank details.

Her thoughts were scattered in an instant when Dario struck at her like a viper, ripping her T-shirt from the neck half-way down, baring her white cotton bra. She gasped at the raw viciousness of his action, but he just smirked, waving the gun around like it was a toy, enjoying his power over her. Instinctively, she pulled the edges of the shirt together, but it was too late. He'd seen it. Her moon tattoo.

"What the fuck is that shit?" He moved in closer and she tried to back away, but fell on her butt into the netting. He wrenched the shirt completely in half, baring her stomach and chest, and said, "That's not staying. No wife of mine will have a slutty tattoo."

A small kernel of defiance rose up inside. That tattoo was in memory of Susan. He didn't get to take that away from her.

"No," she said, staring up at him.

Dario merely bared his teeth at her, then slowly brought the gun up to level it at her head. "What did you say?" he asked quietly.

"The tattoo stays," she said, gritting her teeth to stop them from chattering in fear.

"So, you decided to grow some balls while you've been away from me, huh?" Dario narrowed his eyes and licked his lips. "Well, I was gonna wait till I got you home to punish you, but perhaps your first lesson in obedience needs to begin here." Dario dropped to his knees and his heavy body covered hers before she could stop him. The ghost nets scratched at her bare legs as she struggled to push him off. No! He wasn't going to do this again. The feel of his hands on her skin made her feel physically ill. His body was thick and heavy against hers as he pinned her down.

"No!" she screamed. She scratched at his face, trying to gouge out his eyes. Then she reared up and bit into the muscle of his neck, sinking her teeth into the flesh and growling like a dog.

"Ow. You fucking little—"

Something hard and metallic smashed into her temple, pain sparking like lightning through her skull. Things went dark and hazy, her limbs flopping useless by her side. Vaguely, she could feel Dario fumbling with her shorts and panties, tugging them down her legs, but there was nothing she could do to stop him, as she floated on the edge of unconsciousness, her eyes fluttering open and closed, open and closed. He flipped her over then, the coarse nets scratching her face and stomach like a thousand tiny needles. She wanted to struggle, to tell him to stop, but her world was all topsy-turvy, her brain felt like it was made of gooey molasses and her body was as limp as a rag. He could do whatever he wanted.

Then he took her from behind, his cock like sandpaper against her thighs as he shoved himself inside her. A tiny groan escaped her throat. But that was all the objection she could muster.

"I'll show you who's boss around here," he grunted as he thrust into her. "And I want my fucking money back, you bitch." Each word was punctuated by another thrust of his cock into her tender flesh. He wanted to hurt her. Wanted to assert his dominance over her. But there was something worse than the physical pain he was inflicting. It was the mental impact, driving her ego back into that dark place once more inside her mind. Of making her subjugate herself to him. Taking away part of her humanity, her hard-won freedom.

Would she let him do that?

A voice grew louder in her head. Perhaps it was Susan's voice, or perhaps it was her own. But it demanded that she do something. Demanded that she hurt him back.

The grogginess was wearing off, the haziness leaving her in small increments. Dario continued to thrust; he was getting close to the end, she could tell by his disgusting guttural sounds.

Her hands opened and closed, still numb and unwieldy, like she had starfish at the ends of her arms rather than fingers. Forcing her arms to move, she pushed her hands deeper into the nets, fumbling through the knots of twine. Something. She needed something to fend him off. A stick or a rock. She wanted to fight.

Finally her fingers closed over something round and hard. A piece of bone if she had to guess. The end was sharp, and she nicked her thumb on it, as if the bone had become bleached and brittle under the unrelenting sun and snapped in two, producing a jagged edge. She grasped it tighter, even as Dario pounded her face into the pile of disgusting netting as he hammered his way to an orgasm.

Could she do this?

*Yes!* Susan shouted. *Yes, yes, yes!*

She had to time it just right. Dario thrust a few more times, his grunts getting louder and closer together. Kait had become an expert on Dario's sexual technique. An expert on the minutia of his body language as he got close to orgasm— so that she would know how long her torment was to last. Any second now, he would climax with a shudder that would shake his whole body, turning him weak and flaccid for some moments.

There it was, the final grunt of satisfaction, then Dario began to shudder and sag.

Kait struck out with all her force. Bringing the bone up and backward, aiming for his face, where she could do the most damage. Even though she couldn't see behind her, she felt the bone strike flesh, rip through the soft fabric of his skin. Then he was gone from her in a howl of rage and pain.

She scrambled to her feet and limped backward down the beach toward the shoreline, waving the bone in great arcs in front her to ward him off. She ignored the fact she was naked from the waist down. That was the least of her worries. The gun. Where was his gun? He was no longer holding it, so perhaps he'd unknowingly discarded it during the attack. Searching for a wound, some sign that she had done Dario damage, she watched him, cataloguing his face and upper body. She'd definitely connected with him.

With one hand covering his neck, Dario reached for her with the other, but she struck at him and was rewarded by a scream of rage as she sliced a thin line across the palm of his hand. The light was fading fast now the sun had sunk below the horizon. But she could still see the ominous rage in his eyes; he was almost incandescent with it.

And now she could see the blood. There was a lot of it, flowing from between his fingers, down his neck, soaking into his shirt. Dario seemed oblivious to the ruby liquid, but Kait became fascinated with it. The way it pulsed like a living river of red underneath his hand. The pressure of his palm not enough to stop his life force from ebbing away. Had she done more damage with her make-shift weapon than she first thought?

Dario staggered just a little before regaining his feet and continuing to stalk her down the beach. She backed away; the bone held like a talisman between them, watching Dario with wary shock as he continued to follow.

"Come here, bitch," he snarled. Then he stopped and looked down at his shirt, perhaps realizing for the first time how much blood was blemishing the crisp, white fabric. So much so, it was now running down his trousers that hung loosely from his hips, belt and zipper undone, exposing his flaccid cock. It trickled over his fancy shoes and onto the sand. "What the fuck have you done to me?" He lunged at her, but this time it was easy for her to sidestep out of his way as his movements became slow and ponderous.

A wavelet rolled up the beach and tickled her toes and she stepped farther into the shallow water, never taking her eyes from her husband's face. He followed, not seeming to care that his shoes were now waterlogged. Another few steps and she was up to her knees in the water. If she had to, she would dive in and swim to safety, even with all of Jack's dire warnings about the crocodiles ringing in her head. But another glance at Dario told her that perhaps she wouldn't need to. The tide was turning. In her favor.

Dario stumbled again, falling to his knees in the water. His eyes lost their menace, and she could see the moment his anger was replaced by fear. Then abject terror.

"Help me." He reached for her. But he was no longer trying to hurt her, he was pleading for assistance, as he finally realized his plight. But it was too late.

She backed away a few more steps and shook her head.

Dario's hand dropped away from his neck, and he fell face-first into the ocean, blood ballooning around him, turning the water pink.

Kait stared in wonder, waiting for him to get up, spluttering and shaking the droplets from his hair.

But he just lay there, face down, his body lifting with the rise and fall of the small waves.

Was it over? Was it really and truly over?

Approaching cautiously, she prodded him with the sharp bone. Nothing. He remained lifeless and unmoving. Kait glanced up the beach. She was completely alone. Deanna hadn't arrived like she'd promised. There was no one here to save her. Except herself. Thinking about it, perhaps that was for the best. If there was no one to witness her struggle, there was no one to refute her story. Dropping the bone in the water, she grabbed his arm and towed him farther out to sea, through the small waves until she was waist deep. She pushed his body out past her and watched as his dark form bobbed along the surface of the shadowy waves. The light was fading to indigo. Soon, Dario would blend in with the inky ocean. Camouflaged to the human eye. But the crocodiles and the sharks would know he was there. They would smell his blood.

Kait hurried out of the water as fast as her injured ankle would allow and gathered the rest of her clothes, putting them on as best she could, wrapping the torn T-shirt around her shoulders. The gun. Should she look for the gun? It was too dark to see anything now, she'd have to leave it. The police would find it. Hopefully, it'd verify her story. She just had to decide what story to tell.

She began the long trek back up the beach toward Cloudwater.

She should be filled with a sense of freedom. Instead, she felt numb.

A sudden burst of brilliant light bounced crazily across the beach as a car lurched onto the sand far away. It was followed by a second set of headlights, then a third.

The cavalry was coming. But they were too late, she'd already saved herself.

# CHAPTER THIRTY-TWO

Deanna hugged her knees to her chest and stared out over the rooftops to the calm ocean beyond, and the sun dipping low on the horizon. From her perch on the front step of Raine's veranda, she could survey the comings and goings of the Cloudwater settlement like a queen watching from her throne. Life had been pretty hectic over the past few days. This was the first chance she'd had to just sit and contemplate things. Christmas Day had been completely overshadowed by the police investigation into the shootings. Which bummed Deanna out. But it was New Year's Eve tomorrow night. A good time for new beginnings as well as strengthening old ties.

Raine was in the kitchen, cooking up a vegan feast for dinner. It was what she was good at. It helped settle her nerves, and Deanna caught snatches of the song Raine was singing though the open front door. The house still required major repairs, but Raine had been determined to return and live in it while the restoration continued around her. At least the kitchen had survived, along with a downstairs bedroom, so their basic living conditions were being met.

Deanna was waiting for Kait and Jack to return from the Broome police station. They were supposed to be joining them for dinner. It was their third trip into town in as many days. The cops always seemed to have more questions for them—Kait especially. But she came through each session with flying colors, even if she looked weary and drained afterward.

Jack was intent on being by her side through all the police interrogations. He still walked a little gingerly, the wound above his hip slow to heal. The bullet had grazed his lower abdomen and left an angry scar in its wake. The doctor had told Jack he was the luckiest man alive. If the gun had been angled slightly more to the right, he'd have a bullet embedded in his internal organs, and it was highly likely he wouldn't have survived. The hospital had released him on Christmas Day and Jack was determined that he was fine, carrying on like a man who'd hadn't just been shot. Probably as much for Kait's benefit as from his own pigheadedness. Kait was bearing a lot of guilt about the whole debacle with Dario. And Jack being wounded was top of her self-flagellation list.

Deanna had a different guilt trip laid out for herself regarding that night. The fact that she hadn't been able to get a vehicle down to rescue Kait sooner. If she'd only got there ten minutes earlier, she might have stopped him raping her. It was the fact that Dario had assaulted her that weighed heaviest on her mind. Not the fact that Kait had killed Dario. If she'd got there earlier, perhaps she would've helped Kait kill him.

Deanna had become lost in the sand dunes on the way back to the settlement. She'd run too far inland in a bid to escape Dario and his gun. It was a stupid rookie mistake, and Deanna had become increasingly desperate when she couldn't find the opening that heralded the road back to Jack's place. Finally, as darkness had begun to descend, she'd seen the twinkle of lights and stumbled into the back blocks of Cloudwater. Running through the sandy streets, she'd arrived breathless and desperate at Jack's house, only to find the place in uproar. Jack had been shot and was being tended to by Ella from next door—she didn't seem to think the wound was life-threatening, but there was blood everywhere, which really spooked Deanna. Groups of locals huddled in the streets, wanting to know what'd happened. Three men stood guard over Dario's thug, who was groggy and groaning that he needed to go to hospital. Deanna was only a little sorry she'd had to hit the handsome guy with the tire iron. The cops had been called, along with an ambulance, but they were still forty minutes away.

It took her many more precious minutes to convince Jack's next door neighbor Toby that the man who'd shot Jack was now hunting Kait through the dunes farther down the beach, and more again to finally urge him to gather a few of the locals, who jumped in their cars and hurtled down the sand. But by then, it'd all been too late.

The sound of footsteps on the wooden boards behind her alerted Deanna to Raine's presence. "How you going, chickadee?" Raine's arm draped around her shoulder as she sat next to her on the step. Raine was worried about Deanna's mental health, even though she never stated it outright. But she constantly checked in with Deanna, always following her progress around the house with her serene gaze. Deanna wished she could let Raine into her head for a few moments, to see how fine she really was. But she guessed she'd need to keep reassuring Raine until she began to believe the words.

"I'm good," she replied, leaning her head on Raine's shoulder. "Just checking out the ocean's mood and seeing what everyone is up to today." Much like Raine was checking up on her moods, but Deanna decided not to confront her tonight, she was feeling too tranquil. "I still can't believe how beautiful it is here," Deanna sighed.

"Yes. It's a good place to call home," Raine agreed. But there was also a subtle question in her observation. She was asking if Deanna would stay and call this place her home too.

"Hmm." Deanna's reply was determinedly noncommittal.

"I just got a text from Jack." Raine said, sitting up straight. "They'll be here in twenty minutes. They got held up at the cop station. Again."

Raine had seen right through her ruse. Because she *had* been sitting out here watching for Jack's black truck to appear around the bend. And perhaps Deanna could see the irony of her situation. She was just as worried about Kait, as Raine was about her. But maybe that was what good friends were for.

"Thanks. Do you need a hand inside?" She turned to study Raine's face. Her skin shone radiant in the evening light. Gray hair pulled back in a loose bun and tanned shoulders bare beneath her loose linen top. She was so exquisite it made Deanna's heart fit to burst every time she looked at her.

"No. You stay out here. I'm nearly finished." Raine secretly preferred to do everything herself, because then she knew everything was perfect. But sometimes things were just as much fun when they weren't perfect. Deanna was hoping to show Raine how fun imperfect things could be. She leaned in and let her lips rest lightly against Raine's, enjoying the buzz of desire at the touch of her mouth. Deanna relished discovering something new about Raine's body every night. The gentle curve of her collarbone. The way she ground her teeth to stop herself crying out when Deanna found the ticklish spot below her belly button. It was a revelation that Deanna never wanted to end.

"Thank you," Deanna said as Raine got to her feet and padded across the veranda to go inside.

Deanna went back to considering Kait and Jack's imminent arrival.

There would be no fleeing to Darwin like a pair of fugitives now. No flight overseas to start a new life. No Summer Spanks, for which she was most sad—she'd been looking forward to using that name. Traveling to new and distant lands was still on her agenda, it'd just moved down her priority list for a while. She could wait. And for now, she was free to stay in Cloudwater for as long as she pleased. There was a small kernel of disappointment resting behind her breastbone that her days on the run with Kait were over. But it was only small, and she was sure it'd soon be washed out of her system by her newfound deliverance. Space to explore a life in Cloudwater with Raine. The idea both excited Deanna and made her palms go sweaty. It was the thought of settling down that had her nerves on edge. And it was why she hadn't given Raine a firm answer yet. She was definitely staying until she knew Kait was one hundred percent okay. And one hundred percent cleared by the police. They were still sniffing around, looking for a way to pin Dario's death on her. But so far, they had nothing. And up until yesterday, they didn't even have a body.

Dario's corpse had washed up on the beach early in the morning. Or rather, what was left of his body after a rather large crocodile—up to four meters in length according to Waru, the old ranger—had finished snacking on him. Both legs were missing, along with his right arm and top of his torso—including his head. What remained had been mauled by razor-sharp teeth so badly it was hard to see it'd once been human. Or at least that's what Waru had recounted to Jack this morning when he'd called past. Waru and Maya had been the ones to find the body on their early morning patrol. The police had given up searching days ago. But everyone knew it was just a matter of time. As long as he hadn't been completely consumed by a large predator, of course. Waru had taken solemn delight in relaying the exact details of their find.

Waru also said something that'd made Deanna's skin rise up in goose bumps all over. He'd decreed that the dead man was a bad man, and he'd been killed by a bad spirit. Loosely translated as the Featherfoot, this bad spirit often took his vengeance out on people who had committed a crime. But the spirit left no footprints because he had feathers on his feet. The scary part about Waru's story was that on the morning after Kait's ordeal on the beach, no sign could be found of a struggle or anything else untoward. A high tide had washed away any signs at the water's edge, and up near the pile of ghost netting, where Kait said she'd hid, the sand had mysteriously been footprint free. As if a great wind had blown the sand clean. But the sky had been clear and calm that night with no wind.

Deanna was dying to know what the police had asked Kait today. But as long as Kait kept her nerve, the police would never know the full story and she and Deanna would never have to go to trial. Only Kait, Deanna, Jack, and Raine knew the full truth.

Deanna sat, pondering the sanity of lying to the police for many long minutes, until the sound of an engine snapped her out of her contemplation. Jack's black four-wheel drive pulled up in front of the house, and Deanna flew down the steps to greet them.

"How did you go?" she gasped before Kait even had the door completely open.

Kait grimaced, but said nothing, tucking a few strands of her revived red hair over her shoulder. Deanna had to admit, Kait looked better as a redhead. More striking. More mature, but in a good way. Not old-looking, but like she was comfortable in her own skin.

"Let's talk inside," Jack suggested, trying to hide the way he leaned a little to one side as he walked. He flicked a glance at the surrounding houses and Deanna suddenly understood. They needed to talk away from prying ears. The small community had wrapped themselves around Kait and Deanna since the shooting, vowing to protect them. Cloudwater people were good at keeping secrets, and plenty of people here were not friends of the coppers. But it always paid to keep your cards close to your chest, and so Deanna nodded and bounded up the stairs in front of the couple.

Deanna waited until they'd hugged Raine in greeting and taken a seat at the table before she could no longer hold in her questions.

"Well, what did they ask this time?" Raine gave Deanna a quelling look as she poured them all a glass of white wine, but she ignored it; instead fixing her gaze intently on Kait.

Kait raised her glass in gratitude to Raine as if she were in desperate need of the drink, then said, "Of course they wanted to know how I thought Dario's body had ended up in the water."

"And what did you tell them?" Deanna asked, shuffling forward to sit on the edge of her chair.

Kait sighed wearily. "The same thing I've told them all along. That I don't know what happened to Dario. I certainly don't know how he died. After you left to go get help, Dario hunted me through the sand dunes and finally caught me. He raped me at gunpoint, but I managed to get away to run and hide beneath the nets. I stayed there until I heard you coming with all the four-wheel drives down the beach, then I ran toward you, still scared for my life. I don't know where Dario went. He must've thought I'd returned to the dunes. I could hear him taunting me, telling me that I'd never get away from him somewhere farther down the beach."

It was a good story, and Deanna was proud of Kait for keeping it straight. At first, the police were highly suspicious of Kait's account. But after they dug a little deeper into

Dario's life and business dealings and found out what a douche bag he was, they'd softened their attitude. Then Dario's gun was found somewhere in the dunes, just lying there, as if he'd dropped it. Or flung it there. With only his fingerprints on it. For a while the police even believed Dario might've gone AWOL. Walked down the beach and gone missing. Or got one of his bodyguards to come and collect him. And they'd put out a nation-wide ABP on him. But the mutilated corpse turning up had put paid to that idea.

"I wish they'd stop hounding you and just give it a rest." Jack laid his hand on top of Kait's resting on the table. The gesture was both instinctive and protective all at the same time, and Deanna couldn't hold back her smile. Jack and Kait were so sweet together. She'd always known they'd make a good pair, and she was so glad Kait had decided to risk her heart again. Especially after Dario had done such a number on her.

"Hmm," Raine said, turning around from where she was stirring a pot on the stove. "The cops are just doing their due diligence. But unless they find any hard evidence to link Kait to Dario's death—which they will never find, then how he died will remain a mystery. To the rest of the world, at least," she clarified with a smirk.

"I still wonder if I should tell them the truth," Kait said through pursed lips. "I'm sure if they heard the whole story, they'd acquit me on grounds of self-defense. It happens all the time. The battered woman syndrome. I was fighting for my life. He had a gun to my head." She raised beseeching eyes to stare at Jack, perhaps hoping this time they'd agree with her.

"And more times than not, the battered woman is not acquitted," Jack replied softly, his hand still covering hers. "You can't take that chance. Plenty of juries still aren't sympathetic toward women who endure domestic violence."

320

Good on Jack. He knew what was best for Kait. She needed to stay strong, that was all. It'd been Kait's idea in the first place to stretch the truth. She'd begun the fabricated lie on the night Dario died. The police were there within the hour, interviewing people and cordoning off sections of Jack's house and the beach. The evidence backed up her claim. That Dario had arrived armed and with a bodyguard in tow intent to do harm. Jack had been shot trying to wrestle the gun from Dario when he answered the door. The thug Deanna had hit over the head around the back had been found tied up and looking a little worse for wear as three of Cloudwater's burliest fishermen kept him under citizen's arrest so the cops could take him into custody. Dario had chased her into the dunes while shooting at her, and then he'd raped her—the police took her into town that same night to conduct a sexual assault forensic test, which came back positive. Kait hadn't lied about any of those things.

Kait glanced at Jack, the look on her face showing she wasn't completely convinced.

"And then there's the money you stole from him," he added with a frown.

"But that was as much my money as it was—"

Jack held up a hand, and Kait snapped her mouth shut. "No juror is going to view you as completely innocent when they find out you have a million dollars in the bank."

"That's true." Deanna reinforced Jack's evaluation. They'd been over this a hundred times already; why did Kait keep questioning it? "And the cops might try and take that money away," she added. "If they deem it to be the proceeds of criminal activities. Which it definitely is."

"I know, I know," Kait demurred.

"Then if they found out about our fake passports, we'd be truly fucked. We'd go to jail for fraud for sure." Deanna wasn't really sure about any of that, but she didn't want to risk it.

"This way is better," Raine crooned, joining them at the table. "The asshole got what he deserved. And you were only doing what you needed to do to survive. End of story. But the police won't be so kind if they find out the whole truth."

Kait shot Deanna a look. It was so quick neither Jack nor Raine would've seen it. But Deanna knew what it meant. She and Kait still kept one secret safe between them. The dead man at the bottom of the gorge in Kalbarri. They hadn't fessed up to that either. The official line seemed to be that it was either an unfortunate accident, or perhaps suicide—he wasn't the first person to jump to their death from the lookout.

"You need to stop second-guessing yourself," Deanna said, parroting Raine's matter-of-fact tone. "Now can we eat? I'm starving."

There were murmurs of assent, and Deanna leapt up to help Raine serve the food. Raine placed a whole roasted cauliflower smothered in a spicy Thai sauce—Deanna's favorite—in the middle of the table, accompanied by a black rice and miso dish that was to die for. There were plenty of other vegetable side dishes too—spinach and green peas with sesame seeds, and tomatoes and roasted capsicums with Thai basil leaves, and more.

Deanna sat and began piling her plate with food. She could still murder a steak, but that'd have to wait for a special occasion, like if she visited Jack and Kait for dinner, or they went into town and ate in a restaurant. It was coming to the point that she almost didn't miss meat. Not anymore.

"This is fucking fantastic," Deanna said through a mouthful of spicy cauliflower. Kait rolled her eyes and pursed her lips. But Deanna just laughed. Kait thought she ate like a pig, with her mouth open and making too much noise. That was just the way Deanna showed her appreciation of the food. Deep down, she knew Kait didn't really mind. Because she was her friend, and friends endured anything and everything because they knew the true you, warts and all.

Friendship was a weird thing. It made you do things you'd never normally dream of doing. Twisted your moral compass. But it was worth it. Deanna had never been the most law-abiding, virtuous person, even before she met Kait. And now... She'd definitely become a stronger person mentally. Prepared to stand up for what she knew was right and bugger the consequences. Deanna had come close to the edge of breaking the law when she was a teenager—rebellious and full of youthful bravado—but then she'd rejoined society, mainly due to her grandmother's guidance. And while she'd never been a stickler for the rules, she'd lived a decent life after that. Until she met Kait. And broken numerous laws, both federal and state, which could entail lengthy jail sentences if anyone found out.

And she would happily do it again.

Because friends were essential to your wellbeing. Having strong female ties in her life made her a better person. All her life she'd heard all that rhetoric about how having a solid group of friends around you improved your self-esteem, gave you a shoulder to cry on, and helped you work through any emotional upheaval, blah, blah, blah. She'd disregarded those banalities as being boring and not for her. She'd believed she was strong enough on her own.

But she was discovering there was more to friendship than that. And the best part was that Deanna could return all those good things to Kait and Raine, and more. It was a surprising revelation, and she hadn't realized how much of a loner she'd actually been until she got caught up with Kait. Perhaps meeting Kait had been the best thing to happen in her life. Who knew? Only time would tell.

# CHATPER THIRTY-THREE

Jack placed their coffees on the table and lay down on the couch, motioning for Kait to lie next to him. He needed to feel her body next to his. Wanted to entwine his body with hers, feel her heartbeat next to his, stroke her hair and have her warm breath on his neck. She needed time to heal from Dario's shocking attack—he could hardly believe someone could commit such violence against a woman. It was beyond his scope of understanding. The mere idea of it had his hands itching to close around the repulsive man's neck and squeeze, and squeeze… But of course, Dario was already dead.

Kait had finally got her vengeance. He'd tried to hurt her, to damage her beyond redemption so that she was ruined for any other man by taking the one thing he believed was his right, but she had been the victor in the end.

The rape had devastated Kait. But it hadn't destroyed her as Dario had meant to do. Most other women would've been broken beyond repair by this brute of a man. Kait, however, was strong. Strong on the inside where it counted most.

When she'd haltingly told him what Dario had done to her, he'd tried to take her in his arms, to support her, commiserate with her. But she'd pushed him away, saying she didn't want his pity. Dario had been sexually abusing her for as long as she could remember; she just hadn't been able to put a label on it before. She wasn't saying that his attack hadn't affected her. But perhaps she was saying was that she'd become desensitized to that physical act. Had learned to switch off her feelings, tamp down her emotions, until he could no longer reach the very core of who she was, no matter how hard he pounded himself into her.

What she did want, was Jack's love. And that he could give.

Kait eased down alongside him until her head was cradled by his shoulder, her bare legs below her cut-off shorts draped over his, and her arm tucked around his waist. She was still overly careful of his wound, but it was healing nicely.

"Dinner was good," Kait said into his ear.

"Yes, Raine really went all out tonight," he agreed. Raine was as worried about them as any mother hen could get. Worried as much about Kait's mental stability as her physical wellbeing. But Jack had already decided that Kait would get through this.

She'd been a sight to see this afternoon, striding down the hallway of the police station away from the interview room, after they finally decided there was no point continuing to harangue her. Back ramrod straight, she stared those cops down, never giving them an inch. Looking like a warrior woman from ages past, with her red hair thrown back, green eyes flashing. Beautiful and defiant. Something had changed in Kait when Dario attacked her. She'd lost that slightly apologetic air she had, especially around men. As if she'd finally decided *she* was enough. She didn't need any man's permission to live the life she wanted. She knew she was fighting for her life when she talked to the cops. They were trying to trap her into giving something up, a small slip of the tongue was all it'd take, but she was winning the battle. The police had nothing to go on. They wanted to blame Kait for

Dario's death, but they had no hard evidence.

He lifted his head so he could see her face, but her eyes were glazed over, as if she were far away. "Watcha thinking," he queried softly.

"Hmm?" Her eyes refocussed on him. "Oh. Nothing really. I didn't tell Raine or Deanna because I didn't want to worry them even more, but the detective hounded me again today on how I thought Dario's gun ended up in the dunes."

Jack eased himself up onto his elbow, so he could watch her as she spoke and nodded for her to go on.

"And the good thing is, I'm not lying when I say that I really don't know how the gun got there. I told them I assumed he'd dropped it there for some reason unknown to me. And in reality, I looked for it after he raped me, but I couldn't find it." She gave a small shrug of confusion.

Kait had told Jack every single detail of what'd transpired in the dunes after he was released from the hospital. At the time, everything had happened so fast; she said the hours surrounding the shooting were a blur. Kait had returned to the settlement just before the police had arrived, but he hadn't had a chance to say anything more than to reassure her he wasn't going to die. It was probably a good thing they hadn't talked until the following night. Perhaps if he'd know the full story, he might not have been so convincing when the police took his statement at his hospital bedside. Afterward, all the other witnesses had corroborated Jack's story; his next-door neighbor Toby, had heard the shouting and had come to see what all the fuss was about. So he saw the moment Dario shot Jack as they both struggled for the gun. Toby said Dario had threatened him with that same gun as he ran down the front steps of Jack's house, so he'd put his hands in the air and let the guy go, more worried about getting to Jack to see if he was okay than stopping a crazy man from running away.

"It's an interesting conundrum," Jack conceded. The police

had cordoned off the area once Kait had explained what'd happened. But they couldn't do much in the dark, and so it wasn't until first light that the proper search had started. "Maybe we'll never know." He gave a slight shrug. If Kait said she had no idea how the gun ended up so far into the dunes, then he believed her. How it got there, they might remain a mystery forever. "Perhaps the good spirits were looking after you," he said. The other strange thing that no one, especially the cops, could explain away, is the footprints that should've marked out what'd happened that night were mysteriously non-existent. It wasn't as if someone had brushed them away with grass or leaves. No. It seemed the sand around the nets was completely untouched by any human. Apart from the scuttling steps of the crabs and a few seagull footprints, it was as if the whole thing had never happened. And the way Kait described how she'd stabbed Dario, there should've been at least some blood spatter, or evidence of violence. But again, nothing.

"That's what Waru believes," she replied, eyes narrowed with doubt.

"Maybe we should believe it too."

She pouted her beautiful lips, pondering the sanity of believing in spirits and wraiths.

He wanted to kiss her and he decided it was time to give into that urge. Gently, he dropped his lips to hers.

He wanted to tell her that he'd be there for her always. If she'd have him.

Perhaps it was time he started acting on his feelings. Letting her know just exactly how much she meant to him. Love. Could he tell her that he loved her? Because he was pretty sure he did. But...

"I'm not good with the L word," Jack said, brushing the fringe out of her eyes. She looked so much better with her red hair; it made her porcelain skin glow.

"I can tell," Kait said with a soft smile. "You can't even bring yourself to say the whole word."

"Yes, well," he huffed, disgruntled that she'd pegged him so succinctly.

"I don't think I'm so good with the *L* word either." She sat up, pulled off her T-shirt in one easy move, exposing her magnificent breasts, and his mouth went dry. For a second, he was so distracted he lost the thread of their conversation. "How about we both agree to give each other space? No pressure. Just enjoy each other's company and let things... settle."

"Agreed," he replied, relief flowing over him in waves. He was such a coward. He should be able to say he loved a woman and be done with it. But Kait was right. They'd been through a lot; she'd been through a lot. It was too soon to talk about forever. Too soon to talk about emotions when emotions were still running so high. Kait needed to heal. And he needed to learn to trust a woman again.

"But we've got the whole evening ahead of us. Why don't we...see where it takes us?" She took his hand and laid it so that his palm cupped her breast.

"Are you sure?" A few minutes ago, he'd been happy to wait forever for Kait to want him again. But it seemed he'd misjudged her. He needed to stop doing that.

"Like I said, let's see where this takes us. With you, Jack Wolfe, anything is possible." She snuggled deeper into his side, and he let his hand wander over her perfect body. Right now, he was deliriously happy. And that was the best he could ask for.

* * *

Kait sat with her toes buried in the sand, watching a seagull fly overhead into the Cloudwater blue sky. Biscotti-colored beach stretched out on either side for as far at the eye could see, and the sun reflected off the sparkling ocean, so bright it almost blinded her. Shading her eyes, she enjoyed the heat of the sunshine beating down on her shoulders. It was getting hot. Although still early morning, Kait could already read the signs and she knew it was going to be a scorcher. Almost time to head back to Cloudwater.

Jack had wanted to accompany her on her walk up the beach but she'd said she needed time on her own. Choosing the opposite direction to the one where the pile of ghost nets still hunkered at the edge of the dunes—a shiver went through her at the thought of all that blue netting, and she may never be able to look at an innocent pile of ghost nets in quite the same way again—she'd taken off her flip-flops and walked and walked until her legs began to ache with the effort. But it was a good ache, and she welcomed it. Taking a seat in the sand, she'd spent a long while contemplating the surrounding isolation. Contemplating everything that'd happened.

Kait had spent the whole of Christmas Day in the police station, and Jack had spent Christmas Eve and most of Christmas Day in the hospital. She wasn't sure if she'd ever want to celebrate Christmas again. But now, it was New Year's Eve, where new beginnings were created. If Kait wished it, she could become a brand-new person.

They had quite a picnic on the beach planned for tonight with Raine, Deanna, and Ella and Toby from next door.

Today was also a month to the day from Susan's funeral. The day that'd set her life into an out-of-control spiral. The day of her reckoning. The day she'd chosen freedom over subjugation.

She tilted her head back and squinted at the sky. "What do you reckon, Susan? Am I doing the right thing?"

There was an eternity of silence. Kait began to wonder if Susan was still with her. She hadn't heard anything from her friend since Dario's attack.

Finally, there came a heavenly breath of wind. *Yes. You are. You're finally taking care of you, Kait. It's all I ever wanted for you.*

Kait's throat constricted. "I wish I could hug you right now," she said softly.

*Me too.*

Her throat clamped tighter still. God, she missed her friend. If only Susan could be here now, then everything might be pretty much perfect. But Deanna kept telling her that life was never meant to be perfect. Sometimes it was even better when it was imperfect. And maybe she was right.

Things had definitely skewed sideways from her and Deanna's ill-thought-out plan of leaving the country and taking the money with them. If Dario hadn't tracked her down—it seemed the guy on the bus had been his spy after all, but how he connected the dots to Cloudwater Bay was still anyone's guess—then she and Deanna would be living a life on the run in Thailand, or some other country where they could disappear forever. But now that Dario was dead, she could live without fear. And a life in Cloudwater was one million percent better than one on the run.

Kait had meant to confront Dario with her master stroke once she and Deanna were safely out of the country. She'd even dreamed of how his face would crumple into ruin when she revealed what she'd done. That she'd embezzled all his cash, not just the one million dollars she'd stolen, but all of it, over forty million dollars of dirty money. With the help of her sister, she'd funneled it off to various charities around the world. And after letting all that sink in, just exactly how broke he was, then she would've challenged him to report her to the police in her most haughty voice. Challenged him to call her bluff. There would've been absolutely nothing he could've done about it. Because to report it to the police, he'd have to admit that the money came from dubious sources. Kait had dreamed of turning Dario into a destitute man. Had dreamed up all kinds of satisfying scenarios for his demise. Maybe the people he was laundering money for would come for him in the dead of night, to take out their retribution for him losing all that cash. Or perhaps he would've shot himself when it became obvious he was trapped in the lies of his own making. Instead, she'd killed him. And he'd never know how he'd already lost it all. He'd got his comeuppance she supposed, but it wasn't nearly as satisfying as if she could've watched him finally understand what it felt like to be completely powerless.

Now, a charity supporting survivors of breast cancer was the shocked recipients of an extravagant, anonymous donation. Another volunteer group that ran a no-kill cat shelter in Perth also received a donation so big they wouldn't need to fundraise for years. The remainder of Dario's money had been scattered around the globe in a bid to help people. Something Dario had never done. He'd been a selfish, greedy son-of-a-bitch. The million dollars she'd taken from his safe was still sitting in the backpack hidden in Jack's house. Half of that money was Deanna's. Kait had made a promise to her, and she would keep it. Deanna was refusing to take the money, said she had enough of her own. But she might change her mind later. Deanna wanted to concentrate on her ghost net art creations and had decided she could make some real money from them. But even though the two skeleton pictures Deanna had constructed were good—really good—Deanna had no gallery to display them in, no way of selling them to the public. Maybe she would use Kait's money to start her own gallery up here in the North somewhere. But then again, Deanna always had a way of landing on her feet, and Kait wouldn't be surprised if she made a big name for herself as an artist in her own right in the years to come, with no use for the half-million Kait was offering.

Kait had told Jack about the money, but in typical Jack

style, he'd said the less he knew the better. He'd said she clearly deserved that money, but he also didn't want a dime of it. Jack wasn't motivated by wealth. He was motivated by his morals, by having a simple but happy life. Exactly the type of man she needed.

Sometimes, when Kait had been alone over the past few days, she couldn't help feeling a dark shame. A voice echoing deep down inside, telling her she was a wicked person. Or, if not wicked, at least as culpable in this whole shit show as Dario had been.

She had Dario's blood on her hands. Even though he'd been far from innocent, it still rattled her that she'd been so calm and cool after killing him. It worried her that maybe because she'd spent so much time married to Dario that some of his disregard for human life had rubbed off on her, hardened her soul like a blister slowly turning into a callus.

Then there was the specter of the biker who'd fallen into the gorge. A second man's death she was responsible for, if perhaps inadvertently. There'd been absolutely no mention of the man at Kalbarri by the police when they'd been interrogating her. So, it seemed they hadn't connected her and Deanna to him. As far as she knew, his fall had been deemed an unfortunate accident.

Her dreams had been haunted by the ghosts of her misdemeanors over the past few weeks. But perhaps that was the price of freedom. If she had to deal with bad dreams at night, with hot flashes of guilt searing her body daily, then maybe that was her penance for finally being free.

In the past five days, Raine had reiterated over and over that none of what'd happened on Christmas Eve was her fault. It all led back to Dario, and his complete and utter lack of respect for women. Raine had talked a lot to both her and Deanna about how violence against women was an insidious thing, and even now, in these modern times, men still got away with crimes against women every day.

Kait began to slowly accept that perhaps she had been a battered woman, after all. She'd never truly believed she'd suffered from domestic violence, but talking it through with Raine and Deanna, she was starting to see that was why men got away with their cruelty. Because women like her couldn't see through the veil of subtle lies. Dario told her it was just his way of showing her how much he loved her. But love wasn't supposed to be one-sided. It wasn't supposed to be her doing all the giving, and it wasn't supposed to be him taking everything he wanted.

Jack had shown her a different path toward love. One with equal partners. It'd take her time to trust a man again. But if she was going to trust anyone, it'd be Jack.

Jack had asked if she was going to stay on in Cloudwater. Her answer had been to kiss him soundly. That was a question for later. Yes, she wanted to stay in Cloudwater. For now. Who knew what the future held? Jack was more than happy to have her live in his house. But a part of her still wanted her independence. Her freedom. Maybe she'd cajole Raine into letting her buy her own piece of Cloudwater Bay and build her own version of a house. Something like the house Deanna's parents had built back in Geraldton. Made from love and eclectic local materials. And of course, it'd be as eco-friendly and as self-sustaining as possible.

Or maybe she might travel. Discover new cultures, new countries, new people.

Her friendships had taught her so much. Susan's friendship had finally driven her to leave Dario. Deanna's friendship had taught her how to find her inner strength. And Jack's friendship had shown her what a good life might look like, to hope for a future that was bright instead of dark.

**Did you love reading Finding Kait?**
**Would you like to read a FREE and EXCLUSIVE Novella**
**from on of my other bestselling Dark Tides Series?**

# https://dl.bookfunnel.com/6tgezpymng

Or you can stay in touch via my website
www.suzannecass.com
Or
Facebook: www.facebook.com/suzannecassauthor/
Instagram: www.instagram.com/suzanne.cass/
Pintrest: www.pinterest.com.au/suzanne_cass/

# Also by Suzanne Cass
## NEW

**Dark Tides Series**
Mystery and Romance collide.
Into the Rain
Rain Washed
The Clearing Rain

**Stormcloud Station Series**
(A Stargazer Spinoff Series)
Small Town Romantic Suspense
Clear Skies
Starlit Skies
Crystal Skies
Dawn Skies
Tangled Skies
Outback Skies

**Stargazer Ranch Romance Series**
Small Town Romantic Suspense
Combustion: Prequel Novella
Wildfire
Firelight
Snowbound: A Christmas Novella
Snowfall
Cloudburst
Silverstorm

**Island Bound Series**
Mystery Romance (on an Island)
*Books can be read as stand-alone*
Bound by Truth
Bound by Silence
Bound by the Stars

**Colors of the Earth Series**

## Small Town Romantic Suspense
*Books can be read as stand-alone*
### Shadows in the Dust
### Shadows in Deep Blue
### Shadows of Red Earth

## Romantic Suspense
*Single Title*
### Island Redemption
### Glass Clouds
### Chasing Bullets

## Love in the Mountains Novella Series
## Small Town Short Romance
*Novellas can be read as stand-alone*
### Rain on a Tin Roof
### Lost and Found
### Rescue his Heart

## Please Leave a Review
The greatest gift you could ever give an author is to leave a review. You will be helping other people to discover this book and making a difference to me as an Independently Published Author. If you liked this book and want other people to read it to, please leave a review.

# About the Author

Suzanne Cass is an Australian author who writes rural romance and romantic suspense abounding with passion and danger.

Her debut novel, Island Redemption, won the Romance Writers of Australia Emerald Award in 2016. Suzanne was also a finalist in the 2019 Romance Writers of Australia RUBY award.

She had always had a fascination with the tough resilience of people who live in our amazing red-dirt outback country. When not writing about the characters that inhabit her head, Suzanne can be found roaming the Perth beaches with her border collie, or encouraging from the sidelines as her two sons play sport.

Visit her website www.suzannecass.com or subscribe to her newsletter via: www.suzannecass.com/contact

Or you can stay in touch via my website
**www.suzannecass.com**

Facebook: www.facebook.com/suzannecassauthor/
Instagram: www.instagram.com/suzanne.cass/
Pintrest: www.pinterest.com.au/suzanne_cass/